PRAISE FOR BIRDS ARE SINGING

"Sankawulo's last song is his richest, deepest, most fearless plumbing of the insistent themes he explored throughout his writing life. Cinematic in imagery and scene, sage didacticism is balanced with exquisite descriptions of Haindi's elemental beauty (fast disappearing), stunning Poro revelations, and characters ranging from the scheming, manipulative, cruel, violent, murderous, rapacious, to the generous, kindhearted, wise. No one—whether rural or urban—is spared Sankawulo's hawk-eyed gaze. Monrovia of the Tubman years teems with cutthroats, backstabbers, con artists, swindlers, and ruthless social climbers. Traditional moorings are threatened by urban anonymity. The natural beauty of Haindi and its environs is set against the stronghold of both empowering and corrosive traditions. This book is Sankawulo's magnum opus, his final compulsive effort to be heard and understood, his vision of a just, egalitarian, productive Liberian society, his thorough understanding of both our better natures and our very ugly, wicked ways, and his prayer for our redemption. It is simultaneously a cautionary tale, a chronicle of pre-coup memory, a last gasp of hope, and a fatalistic dirge."

—Stephanie Horton
Sea Breeze Journal of Contemporary Liberian Writings

Birds Are Singing…gives great insight into Liberian history, culture and politics. Like Sankawulo's previous novels, *The Rain and the Night*, and *Sundown at Dawn*, it confirms his brilliant role as a teacher, historian and preserver of culture. *Birds Are Singing* not only imparts to the reader his knowledge of Liberia's past, but it also lays out, in Korli's parable, the need to analyze past failures to rectify them and chart a successful future as individuals and as a nation."

—Althea Romeo-Mark
author of *If Only the Dust Would Settle: Selected Poems*

Wilton Sankawulo is a gifted writer who knows three worlds well: traditional Kpelle society deep in the West African forest, a deeply hybrid but continually evolving Liberia, and a cosmopolitan 21st century America that hungers to know ways of life whose destruction it helped to cause….*Birds Are Singing* is both a warmly human account of the rise and fall of a talented but naïve country boy into the highest ranks of power, and a parable of a sick nation. The history of Liberia through the reign of President William Vacanarat Shadrack Tubman is told in thinly disguised story form. Moreover, the rest of Liberia's story up to and including the tragic civil conflicts of the 1980s, 1990s and early 2000s is present in embryo. The reader who knows Liberia well—in fact any reader who knows the tragedy of failed states around the world—will understand this story. Read it, enjoy it, and reflect on it."

—John Gay
author of *Red Dust on the Green Leaves* and *The Brightening Shadow*

"*Birds Are Singing* holds a mirror up to Liberia and reveals a place where the best and brightest are cut down time and time again to the detriment of all. And we—Liberian people—must read it with that same urgency with which Sankawulo put it down as the ultimate deadline loomed before him. And then read it again…until we see our face(s), hear our voice(s) and those of our ancestors, settlers and indigenous alike, as they really are. Maybe then we'll break the curse we would all like to pretend does not exist."

—Sengbe Kona Khasu
Musician, Screenwriter and Director
Hunting in America and *We Want Election, No More Selection: A Documentary on the Liberian Election of 2005*

"*Birds Are Singing* is of exceptional importance because it is the first novel by a prominent Liberian writer to evince a clear consciousness of a modern, indigenous Liberian's uneasy stance and moral confusion as he remains organically attached to his culture and ancestral mores while at the same time is irresistibly attracted to Western civilization and a Western education."

—Robert H. Brown
author of *To Seek a Newer World*

WILTON SANKAWULO

Wilton Sankawulo was Liberia's most prominent writer and folklorist, and a leading expert on traditional culture. Born in 1937 in Haindi, Bong County, he was educated at Lutheran mission schools, Cuttington University College, Pacific Lutheran Theological Seminary, and the University of Iowa, where he earned his MFA in English. Sankawulo was a Professor of English and Literature at the University of Liberia, and taught creative writing classes and workshops at various colleges in the United States. As a civil servant, Wilton Sankawulo held several government positions in Liberia—most notably Chairman of the Council of State from 1995-96. He died in February 2009, shortly after delivering the manuscript for *Birds Are Singing*.

ALSO BY WILTON SANKAWULO

NOVELS

The Rain and the Night

Sundown at Dawn: A Liberian Odyssey

FOLKTALE COLLECTIONS

Why Nobody Knows When He Will Die

The Marriage of Wisdom

Great Tales of Liberia

BIRDS ARE SINGING

WILTON SANKAWULO

cottonTree
Press

BIRDS ARE SINGING
Copyright © 2010 by Wilton Sankawulo, Sr.

First Cotton Tree Press edition: July 2010
Second Edition: October 2017

Published by Cotton Tree Press
Washington DC
Monrovia, Liberia
www.ctpbooks.com

ISBN 978-0-9800774-5-2 (Paperback)
eISBN 978-0-9800774-6-9 (Digital)

Printed in the United States of America

Library of Congress Control Number 2017949615

Cover design by Les Solot
Interior design by writingnights.org

NOTE: Most of the Kpelle words, Liberian slang, and some unusual terms in this novel are defined in the context of the story upon first use. This edition and the digital version includes a brief glossary as well.

For Amelia, Mammy, Minnie, Patience, and Kia

A Note from the Publisher

Wilton Sankawulo spent a lifetime writing, teaching, serving his country, and dreaming of the day when Liberia would have its own publishing houses, and, eventually, a publishing industry. When I met him in 2008, he was ecstatic to learn that I had just established Cotton Tree Press with the aim of developing and publishing the literary and nonfiction works of Liberians and other African writers. Later, as the Guest of Honor at the launch of our first title, *Redemption Road*, Professor Sankawulo submitted the manuscript for *Birds Are Singing* to me, expressing faith that I would do it justice and make him proud.

Because Professor Sankawulo is no longer here to hold this book in his hands and elaborate on its themes with us, I have included, in the pages following the novel, a 2006 interview that he granted to Liberian writer and scholar Annaird Naxela. In this fascinating conversation the reader will hear Sankawulo's extensive views on Liberian literature, on our struggle with press freedoms, and on the tragedy of the Liberian conflicts and civil war. He also shares his ideas for development and change, invaluable advice and encouragement for aspiring writers, and his vision for the future of Liberia. Finally, he challenges us all to begin a new social order that will respond to the needs and aspirations of the people. I believe that the issues Sankawulo addresses in both the novel and the interview will and *must* lead to useful discussions and fruitful debates.

It is with great pride and joy that I now present Wilton Sankawulo's masterpiece to the world. As I do so, I would like to acknowledge Stephanie Horton, Managing Editor and Founder of *Sea Breeze Journal of Contemporary Liberian Writings*, for the crucial role she played in the creation of *Birds Are Singing*. Initially just a short story, it was Ms. Horton who encouraged, critiqued, and guided the author into creating the novel it is today. Wilton Sankawulo held her in the highest esteem, as do all of us in Liberia's small but growing literary circle.

Elma Shaw
Editor and Publisher
Cotton Tree Press

"Birds tell you when to wake up in the morning, when to go to and from the farm, when strangers are coming to you, when your faraway relative dies, and when danger is near."

—*Sumowor Gbamokorli*

"...ask not what your country can do for you; ask what you can do for your country."

—*John F. Kennedy*

CONTENTS

PART I

PROLOGUE

When the man he had known all his life as his father told him at midnight that, in fact, he wasn't his father, Sumowor Vakpeeh Gbamokorli had lain stunned on his sleeping mat by the fireside, staring at the black rafter ceiling until the last glow of embers died and roosters declared dawn. Old Man Nuulaa had shaken him by the shoulder until he awoke, yawned, shoved the bedclothes down to his waist, and looked at him with squinting eyes.

"Yes, Data?" he drawled and rubbed the sleep from his eyes, still yawning.

Bending over him, Nuulaa whispered, "I have something very important to tell you. Come with me." Unbolting the coarse wooden door quietly, Nuulaa stepped onto the porch, which was fenced with wattle to keep off goats and sheep.

Korli sobered, his heart beat faster, he inhaled the musty air deeply and expelled it slowly. Sitting up with an effort and wrapping his arms around his knees, he wondered what errand his demanding Old Man had contrived for him so late in the night. Man-to-man talk usually occurred in a *Kpaan* on the outskirts of town, or on a hunting or fishing excursion. The tidings his father had for him must be ominous since they couldn't wait for day to break. Korli hoped they weren't another invitation for him to join *Gborlorkpilii*, a society he despised. Obviously testing his resolve, Nuulaa repeatedly urged him to join the water society as they hunted, fished, or worked on the farm, but Korli always expressed only his contempt for it.

"Membership in the Poro and snake societies is enough for me, Data," he'd tell him. Elaborating the obvious, he'd explain that the Poro taught him how to subdue the jungle with its fiendish creatures to make a living, and that the snake society taught him how to protect himself against snakebite and the curatives to treat it were he bitten. He'd add, to Nuulaa's disgust, "Data, the other societies are mere diversions and a menace. Any man who values his life won't bother with them."

Nuulaa usually took his stubborn and almost impertinent reply in stride but not without a bit of warning:

"Since you're a full-fledged *kenamu*, it's true you don't need to join the minor societies," he'd start on an encouraging note. "However, our ancestors passed them to us for our protection. You enjoy their blessings and benefit from the fellowship and confidence of men when you join them. The spirit and *gbon* societies, for example, give you power over spirits and witches, respectively. The leopard society makes leopards harmless when you confront them, and the sheep society makes you brave. The water society is especially important, for wherever you go, you'll meet creeks and rivers. Once you become a member of it, you'll have power over all water creatures. Besides these benefits, there's nothing like the fellowship you enjoy as a member of these societies. Son, you can't go through life alone however wise, rich, or powerful you may be."

Korli always had ready rejoinders for the argument, but in deference to his Poro training, he'd let his father have the last word. You don't argue with your senior, especially your parent. He decided, however, to make a clean breast of his resentment of the despicable society should his father raise the subject tonight. He was tired of it; it was making him feel like an alien.

Wrapped in thick homespun bedclothes to ward off December's biting cold, they sat facing each other in rattan chairs on the porch. Except for the screeching of crickets, the flickering lights of fireflies, and the perpetual roaring of the Deyn River, the night was utterly dark and quiet. Not a trace of moon- or starlight showed in the sky, and the silence was profound.

"You're now a man, a seasoned *kenamu*, ready for weighty news," the Old Man murmured almost inaudibly in Korli's attentive ears to prepare him for the grim message. But this initial remark only increased Korli's agitation.

His heart had bubbled with joy and pride when his father called him a man at so young an age—he was only eighteen—and appealed to his confidence, but the unusual setting of the secret talk and the solemn tone of his voice dispersed the ecstasy. After a long pause, Nuulaa drew a deep sigh and, looking at Korli's dim profile, said:

"I forbid you to cry or grieve over what I'm about to tell you. Now that you'll soon face the world on your own, I must confront you with these sad tidings to spare you unexplained sickness, accident, or sudden death. Crocodile killed your father while your mother was pregnant with you, and your mother died while giving you birth. Felenkpeh and I took

you as our child after your parents' death, so I'm really your uncle."
Nuulaa paused, stared briefly at the grisly night, and quickly wrapped up
his message: "We're still your parents, however, and this house is still your
home. According to our custom, the rightful father of a child is its uncle,
anyway, and a woman is mother to every child. You have all our blessings,
Korli. May God and the ancestors protect, prosper, and grant you long
life." Then Nuulaa rushed into the house to avoid any questions Korli
might have, leaving him to wrestle alone with the perplexing revelation.

ভ ভ ভ

Nuulaa Gbunakpele Bharsi was a man of discipline and industry, virtues
he instilled in his three sons, two of whom had married at a young age
and left the home. Mothers were responsible for the upbringing of girls,
but Nuulaa always reminded his only daughter Moima, whenever she
neglected her duties, that discipline was as important for a woman as for
a man. He was proud of rearing his children according to the best of
Kpelle traditions. Except for Korli, who had a mind and plan of his
own—he wondered how he had come by such attitude—the boys
followed his footsteps. With time, he hoped Korli would grasp his vision
as his brothers had done.

Nuulaa had been born premature and beset with every conceivable
childhood illness. His mother, the fifth wife of his father, Bhalasia, had
three children but only he and one of two sisters had survived. Bhalasia,
whose hands were full with the many responsibilities of his large family—
he fathered more than fifty children—did not care for his mother and her
children as he should have done, undoubtedly because she was the
youngest of his wives. Nobody expected Nuulaa to live, for sickness
crushed him constantly during most of his childhood days. His mother
went virtually naked by pawning her clothes to pay legions of *Zoes* to teach
her which herbs to use to treat him. At the age of five, Nuulaa still rode
his mother's back to and from the farm because he was too weak to walk.
Then one day he had insisted on walking to the farm on his own feet. It
was a slow and tedious journey, but as of that day, he could walk as freely
as his peers and even do petty chores on the farm. People said that his
sudden and unexpected recovery was a miracle. Having studied the herbs
his mother used to treat him, Nuulaa treated sick children as a child. As a
grown man, he could join broken bones, cure insanity, and drive spirits
and witches from people—powers, he said, his ancestors had given him
in dreams. His fame spread throughout Fuama Chiefdom, much to
everybody's surprise, for he was never a Zoe apprentice, nor was any

member of his family ever a Zoe. When the Chief Poro Zoe of Fuama Chiefdom died, the Land—the tribe and all its leaders, past and present—appointed him as his successor. Under his leadership, Poro initiations flourished and the Land was secure and fruitful.

℘   ℘   ℘

Originally cattle breeders, shepherds, and goat herders, the Kpelle had fled with their animals to the fertile rainforest in the west away from the eastern world where drought had killed every plant, and great winds had built enormous sand domes all over the land. They fought many hostile tribesmen *en route* to the forest region, losing hundreds of warriors and half their animals. They finally settled in Fuama, an evergreen forest replete with flora and fauna.

Fuama Chiefdom became a bone of contention when they began exploiting its fallow farmlands, herds of animals, and swarms of fishes. The Bassa from the east and the Gola from the south conquered it in succession, enslaved half the people and looted their possessions, but the people repossessed the land after many battles. The last wave of invaders comprised the wealthy Gbandi Chief Zolu Doma of Tahama Chiefdom near the Guinean border. He had fled with a large entourage from a raging war Guinean tribesman had waged on Gbandi- and Lomaland. Chief Doma had more than a hundred wives, thousands of cattle, countless warriors, man- and maidservants, and numerous bags of iron money. He could have conquered Fuama Chiefdom by force had he wished, for he came from a long line of brave warriors, such as Seimavile Halingi who offered himself as a living sacrifice to save his people from Wono giants in what is now Wubomai. But the old Chief discovered that love was the most potent weapon of conquest. He shared his cattle, money, and virgins with the Land and appealed to them for a sitting place. When Chief Kpakila Dwalu died, the Land made him his successor. They turned Fuama Chiefdom over to him with white kola and permitted him to settle wherever he liked. In a generation, Kpelle culture absorbed Chief Doma and his people; their origin no longer mattered to the people. Although his rule was brief, it made a lasting impact on the Land. The son who succeeded him was not as generous or gifted in leadership as his father had been. The only advantage he brought to the chieftaincy was his father's name and reputation, but he had a firm grip on the Land because the name "Doma" meant something in Fuama in those early days. The people endured him until a new president took the Chair in Liberia and decreed that tribal people elect their Chiefs. It wasn't customary with the people to contest leadership, but they did it, if only to put their own flesh and blood on the Stool again. Who else could be their candidate but the Chief of the Poro Zoes of Fuama Chiefdom?

To ensure victory, Zoe Nuulaa decided to sacrifice his most beloved son to the river goddess as other candidates were doing. Only Korli qualified for the supreme sacrifice. He was ambitious like his father, handsome, strong, reserved, and uncorrupted by the recklessness of youth such as chasing wild women, drinking strong drinks excessively, or devoting too much time to festivals. He enjoyed the love and respect of his family and was the pride of the Land. Everybody believed that he was destined for greatness.

Informing Felenkpeh about his decision was a duty Nuulaa preferred not to perform if he had a choice in the matter. Tradition required that both parents of a sacrificial victim give their consent before the victim was killed, or the sacrifice would not yield the desired result. Delivering the deadly blow to Felenkpeh was no problem, of course. Had he not dealt out death sentences to many a violator of Poro laws? But Zoe Nuulaa did not want to risk having Felenkpeh break down under the weight of the blow and consequently expose the secret. It'd mean her execution with Korli and a defamation of the family's name for all time. He consulted the Council of Poro Zoes on the matter. They recommended that three representatives of the Council of Sande Zoes deliver the blow. After giving the matter some thought, he refused to involve other people in what he perceived as a personal affair. Who would vote for a leader that could not carry out his own decision?

Before dawn one morning, Nuulaa told Felenkpeh about the planned ordeal with three white kola nuts. Felenkpeh had fainted, her body awash with perspiration. Zoe Nuulaa found himself confronted with the worst dilemma of his life. The creature he loved most was on the point of death! Forgetting his pride, he appealed to the Sande Zoes of Haindi for help. They took Felenkpeh's limp body to a sacred grove and poured water on her until she came to. Then, they bade her to honor her Sande oath by bearing the tragic news with courage on behalf of women. Her very life belonged to the Land, not to speak of those of her children. Felenkpeh had requested that she visit her mother before making a decision. When the women informed Nuulaa about her request, he did not only approve of it, he told her that he had, in fact, abandoned the sacrifice. He'd win the election by virtue of merit. Was he not the custodian of the traditions and life of the Land? He told his wife to take Korli with her and spend all the time she wanted at home, but Korli had insisted on remaining to help run his father's campaign. His father's victory, he thought, would give him an opportunity to become a Chief someday. Felenkpeh had spent a month in Gboryoimu and returned to find Korli in good health. She did not know that Zoe Nuulaa had planned a fantastic strategy to capture Korli for the sacrifice.

1

A DISTANT ROAD

ALTHOUGH NUULAA'S STRANGE MESSAGE struck him with disbelief and ruined his peace, Korli breathed a sigh of relief because the Gborlorkpili question did not arise. The revelation surprised him because nothing Nuulaa, Felenkpeh, Sister Moima, or anyone else ever said or did to him had remotely implied that he wasn't a legitimate member of the family. The youngest child, he had enjoyed the love and affection of the entire household. His "parents" and his two "brothers" (whom he remembered only vaguely because they had left the home when he was but a toddler) often shared their meals with him, even though Felenkpeh always gave him more than his fair share. Whenever they returned home from some errand, they brought him baby mice, bird's eggs, fruits, or honey—and always bought him new clothes for Christmas and New Year celebrations. The Old Man had slaughtered a goat, sheep, and flock of chickens for his graduation from the Poro—not to speak of the new clothes he had bought for him for the grand occasion. Korli was one of only four graduates who had worn leather shoes, long pants, and long-sleeved shirts on that memorable day. He learned that Nuulaa never conferred such honor on any of his "brothers." Hardly did Korli work. He loitered in town and wandered about the river and the forest for the fun of it, and went to the farm only when hungry.

"You people are spoiling this child," relatives and friends of the family often warned Nuulaa. "He'll soon have his own family. How will he support them if he doesn't learn to work? Besides, enemies bewitch the child you spoil with too much love."

Nuulaa usually dismissed the warning by saying that a child should enjoy love and leisure until it had grown up, for everything had its time. When Korli reached that bridge, he'd cross it. However, Korli got the hint eventually and distinguished himself as "hero of the cutlass and the ax", and he was a farmer of no mean ability. Blessed with a sturdy build and boundless stamina, he did in a day the work an average farmer did in a week. His gigantic height, broad shoulders, and strapping muscles had won him many a wrestling match on the riverbank, although he was modest, soft-spoken, and conciliating as becoming most strong persons. He'd go to any extent to avoid conflict and make peace, but once he took on an enemy, he made sure that enemy was no longer in a position to be a threat to him. Many boys bore scars for engaging him in fights. Korli was also an expert hunter; he once chased a groundhog in the forest and killed it with his bare hands amid the outcropped roots of a *beleh* tree where it had collapsed from exhaustion. Rumor circulated that he had a leopard *kaaseng*, which would demand his life one day as a compensation for making him brave, strong, and wise. Investigating his spiritual background, however, Zoes found no evidence that he had a leopard double; God had simply blessed him with strength, wisdom, and courage, they said.

Now this incredible revelation had disarmed him—had torn his world asunder, put his mind in utter disarray, and made him miserable. As if he had turned into stone or succumbed to witchcraft, Korli sat rooted and irresolute on the porch for a long time, feeling terrified and doomed. Then with immense will power, he mustered his ebbing strength and pried himself up from the creaking chair. "What a cruel world!" he thought as he staggered to bed in the dark room. He lay tense on his back staring up with teary eyes. Some of his peers who were orphans had known of their dilemma from childhood and had learned to live with it. Perhaps he could have even sustained the tragedy had he not played so crucial a role in it. His father's death he could accept, for men were made to die any time by accident, war, or the brutal attack of some wild beast while struggling to eke out a living in the hostile jungle. But the death of his mother, caused by his birth, was too heavy a burden for him to bear. He'd cling to life until he avenged his father's murder by killing at least one crocodile, then he'd join the ancestors by his own command to atone for his unpardonable crime against his mother.

Nuulaa left the town before sunrise to check his traps. After bathing in the river, Felenkpeh and Moima brought fresh water home, hastily packed their farm baskets with cooking utensils, and told Korli that they were about to go to the farm. They watched him with concern by the luminous sunrays pouring through the open door.

"Brother, are you sick?" Moima asked him. The early bird of the family, Korli usually woke up before dawn to check his traps and fish baskets. It was unusual for him to be in bed so late in the morning.

"No, Sister. Only tired," he admitted with a sigh and sat up, watching his winsome sister from the corner of his eye. "I'll stay in town today and rest." He stretched out again on the old bamboo mat.

Moima did not believe him. She felt that her brother was withholding something from her. She grew speechless—her dark brown eyes clouded with budding tears.

"Malaria has attacked you!" she said brokenly at length. "It makes one weak and tired—then comes that dreadful fever! Let's go to the farm for me to boil you some koyorokpoh."

"Moima, men get tired after harvest," Felenkpeh said in Korli's defense. "Korli alone built the new rice kitchen and filled it with the rice we harvested while busy hunting, fishing, and cutting palm nuts at the same time. That's too much work for one man. As you know, Nuulaa abandoned us again during the harvest to see after Poro matters. No human being is made of iron! Korli, stay in town today and rest well. We have nothing much to do on the farm but pound rice and cook. Cook the big black rooster and eat as much of it as you like. Rice, salt, dry pepper, and bitter balls are in a corner of the bedroom. If you don't want to cook, come to the farm by noon. I'll keep food there for you."

Korli, who had no appetite, said casually, "I'm not hungry. I ate more than enough last night. Bring me food this evening. Let's save the rooster for Christmas."

"The malaria has killed his appetite," Moima moaned and pursed her lips in frustration. "I'll boil the herb and bring him the water this evening. His stomach needs cleaning up also. *Koyorokpoh* can do both."

It was Nuulaa's astonishing revelation that was ailing Korli—not malaria or constipation. He wanted to ask Felenkpeh about it but demurred because a *kenamu* doesn't tell secrets to women. Besides, he had no reason to doubt Nuulaa's tale, though it seemed incredible. Because of his Poro oath, the Old Man couldn't afford lying about a matter so grave. Circumstances had waged war on him, and only he, Korli, could win that war, God and the ancestors being his helpers.

"Do you have clothes to wash?" asked Moima, lingering at the door. Felenkpeh was already in the yard waiting for her.

"I'll do some washing," Korli replied. "Rice pounding isn't easy, and you people will have to cook. Don't worry, Sister. I'm all right."

"Don't tamper with the river this month!" Felenkpeh shrilled in an effort to stop the conversation. She was afraid Moima's prodding might never end. They must hurry to the farm for they had many chores there to do. "Although the dry season is here and the tide is low," Felenkpeh told Korli. "It's dangerous to play in the river, especially when you are alone—and sick. Don't live on an empty stomach, Korli. A hardworking man should never go hungry. Cook the chicken soup and drink some to renew your strength to take care of yourself in case of danger. Moima, let's go."

After the women left, Korli took his father's spear and trudged to the "crocodile nest" in the river, located above where women bathed and fetched water. The deep, black, stagnant, forbidding reptile abode, covered with driftwood, leaves, and foam, spread mysteriously under the dense foliage of *kobeley*, *bheen*, and *kpano* trees. Observing it keenly awhile, Korli thought crocodiles might be in it after all, since nobody ever challenged their existence. Surely, they were guardians of the people as the elders claimed, or they'd have been killing people everyday. "Well, I'll soon understand that great mystery," thought he. "Once you're patient," he recalled the popular adage, "you see the inner workings of water witchcraft." He sat quietly on an outcropped root of a *kobeley* tree and watched the grim spot with an anxious gaze, his spear at the ready.

After failing to see a crocodile by midday, Korli walked up and down the riverbank, hoping to run into one on shore. He'd learned that they wandered on land during the day in search of animals or humans to spirit into the depths. He watched the torrential waters with amazement as if it were his first time seeing it. It roared fiercely at the cataract and lashed against the shore with unusual fury. He never tampered with the river as his friends did. He bathed and swam only in shallow cataracts and fished with a hook from the shore. His response to his friends' banter for his "cowardice" was, "Water has no bone to hold in case you're drowning, and nobody really knows all the creatures living in it." That was before he knew that a crocodile had killed his father. "Only when a cat is trapped," Korli thought of another adage, "does it display its fighting ability." Since he felt that his life was no longer worth anything much, he cast aside his fear of water and resolved to search for a crocodile in the river until he killed one. Then he'd become intimate with that boneless mass to atone for his unforgivable crime against his mother.

Korli's day was bleak indeed. Something relentless and indefinable was eating him inside. Overcast with mist that rapidly turned into drizzles, the sky rumbled and flashed piercing flames all around. A current of cold breeze swept over the river and fluttered the evergreen trees. Korli hastened home in the weather that matched his unhappy mood. It annoyed him to see birds squeak and frolic in bushes on the roadsides as if the sordid turn of weather was something to celebrate.

He met his uncle sitting stiff on the porch, dressed in a Vai cap and homespun gown, looking preoccupied with a scowl on his leathery face.

Nuulaa watched him with a surly challenge as he approached the house.

"Where have you been?" he growled with a booming voice. "To the river, eh? What are you doing with a spear? Looking for a crocodile to kill, eh? We're going to the farm right now!" He watched Korli with sober eyes as he entered the house. "You look disturbed!" he said softly. "I know it's what I told you last night bothering you. Forgotten my advice? *The Great One* will visit you tonight even if I must spend my last cent. Should he fail to lift your depression, you know the consequences."

Korli did indeed know the consequences of failing to please the leader of the Poro society, and he did not intend to risk them. Although his life was shattered beyond repair, he'd rather depart the world by either God's bidding or his own, not by the design of the Poro society. Since what he did about his problem mattered most, he wouldn't let Nuulaa's outrage disturb him. He put on a brave face and went with him to the farm.

Nuulaa was happy in his heart that the shocking tales he had told Korli were producing the desired effect. Indignant over the "loss" of his "parents", Korli would henceforth wander about the river in search of a crocodile to kill. Reinforcing his indignation by banning him from tampering with the river, Nuulaa believed that Korli would make the river his chief preoccupation because that which was forbidden was most attractive.

On the farm they met Felenkpeh and Moima butchering a huge red deer one of Nuulaa's traps had caught in the night. They helped with the butchering after which the women cooked. Thinking that plenty of rich food would make him feel better, Felenkpeh gave Korli more food than what three men could eat, but he ate only a little of the *gaigai* Nuulaa cooked and said he'd eat his food later in town. To please Moima, he drank the medicine she boiled for him.

The Great One came late that night as Nuulaa had threatened. He harangued the town with a doleful voice that rent Korli's wounded heart, mind, and the clear cold night. Terrorized as usual, women and children scrambled indoors for refuge. Soon the Great One and his retinue ran round the town, singing in loud voices echoing through the town and down the river into the forested mountains beyond it. When the townspeople felt the terror of his presence, the Poro Master and his followers gathered before Nuulaa's house where he seriously warned Korli to remember his Poro training and oath. Had he not died before and risen again into maturity, fearlessness, and wisdom? Why all this talk of depression, loss of appetite, and death?

"There's nothing like death," he declared. "Your parents are waiting for you in The Place of Truth where there's no sickness or dying. If you shed a drop of tear, continue to refuse food or fool with the river, you'll pay a fine of ten pounds and a bull."

The strains of the day's turbulent events having cast Korli into a dreamless sleep, he didn't hear the warning. He roused only when the Great One's "wife" sang her farewell song, which mimicked the cries of birds and deer and the sound of thunder. The nostalgic song stirred every fiber in his body:

The road is far
Gbaamu road is far
Vengeful sinner, give me your hand
My heartstring, give me your hand
The road is far to walk

It's a costly mark
Never obtained in vain
Brave saint to be, give me your hand
Heartstring of mine, take my hand
The town of men is far away…

The song reminded Korli of his initiation and innocent, resilient boyhood that primed him for any challenge. As the song tapered into silence and calm returned to town, he felt disgusted on hearing the animated Gborlorkpili song and its rattling *kono* accompaniment in the Evil Forest below the landing stage. The music stung him with mounting anger.

"Why is Gborlorkpilii heaping honor and praises on imaginary beings?" he said under his breath.

Before Nuulaa's astounding revelation, Korli had enjoyed the music of the water society, one of the few entertainments that enlivened the town, though he did not believe in the existence of water people. Now, even their music had become distasteful and offensive to him. He wished he'd never hear it play again in Haindi. In childhood, he had learned that members of Gborlorkpilii donned crocodile skins, spirited people into the river, and drowned them. He sincerely believed that they had a veritable hand in the killing of his father.

Korli wondered why the Master hadn't demanded his presence outside during his visit, for it was mandatory for all *kenablaa* in any town he visited to turn up, except those too sick or old to stand on their feet. Was it because the Mighty One did not wish to worsen his troubles? Why hadn't Nuulaa briefed him yet on details of the discussions held during the visit? Why was Gborlorkpilii, in violation of tradition, meeting in daylight? Certainly, something strange and ominous was afoot.

However, Korli was happy that the visit considerably relieved his depression. The blow had been severe and decisive—almost deadly. It had left an indelible scar on his heart he'd never discard for the rest of his life, but the music had revived his spirit and made him see his problem in a new light. He now felt that drowning himself was no solution to his problem. It was sheer cowardice, an admission of defeat, an escape from life. He'd stay alive and accomplish deeds of valor to put his enemies to shame, but he'd still kill at least one crocodile to avenge his father's death.

Realizing that spear could not easily kill a crocodile, considering its rocky skin, Korli took his razor-edge cutlass and Nuulaa's shotgun and hunting bag, which had been gathering dust under Nuulaa's bed, and hastened to the river. Happily, he found four cartridges in the hunting bag and loaded the gun with one. He didn't like hunting with a gun. He preferred to set traps. Nuulaa had warned that gun hunting was dangerous, but a gun was the only weapon that could kill a crocodile easily.

"My father died of a gunshot wound," the Old Man had told them many times. "He cocked the gun to shoot an antelope, but the deer had fled on hearing the cocking. Forgetting to uncock the gun, he took it home and placed it in a corner of the bedroom with a little more force than necessary. It fired and killed him on the spot. However, I keep a gun for war comes any time, anywhere. A man must always be prepared for it."

When he thought they were old enough, Nuulaa taught his boys how to use a gun. Korli had asked to learn how to shoot when he was only twelve. Afraid he might hurt or kill himself by accident, the Old Man had warned him sternly:

"You're too young to use this deadly weapon! You might kill yourself!"

"I've hunted with you many times and seen how you use it, Data," Korli had pleaded. "I'm no longer a child. Please let me try."

"You'll have to wait for a week then for me to accompany you," Nuulaa had said. "I still insist that you're too young to handle this weapon."

Korli had declined the offer, saying if he'd ever be a man, he must learn to stand on his own feet. The Old Man had accepted the brave reply in good faith. In their hostile surroundings, the sooner a boy learned to be a man the better were his chances of surviving, for the enemies they contended with were numerous, vicious, and sometimes invisible. Further, despite his age, Korli had matured greatly. He possessed nearly all the attributes of true manhood such as courage, agility, and a keen understanding of the jungle. He now needed a chance without the support of a guardian to mark his transition to manhood with a major prey, not the puny rats, squirrels, groundhogs, and monkeys he often trapped. Handing him the gun with his blessings, Old Man Nuulaa had directed him to places in the forest beyond the river where animals fed on fallen fruits. That day Korli had killed a young boar with the gun.

As he trudged to the river, Korli suddenly realized Nuulaa's tales of his parents' death was porous and invalid. His intuition pried them open effortlessly. Only an outright fool or *kpolowa*—a non-initiate—would believe them. For one thing, bad news doesn't hide. Had his parents actually died, the rumor would have reached his ears long ago. An enemy, a friend, or some circumstance would have thrown it in his face. Additionally, tradition ordained that death news be disclosed in the presence of at least one elder, the grave of the deceased be decorated with white sand and sprinkled with rooster's blood, and that a *gbon* Zoe cook the rooster with herbs for the townspeople to eat. A festival should be staged in memory of the dead, and, finally, the *gbon* Zoe should wash the bad omens from surviving members of the family of the deceased. Nuulaa had done nothing of the sort. Adding everything up, Korli felt that he was unmistakably his father despite his "confession"—and Felenkpeh was truly his mother. They had colluded with the water society to sacrifice him for fame, riches, or long life, the usual ploys people used for human sacrifice. Or perhaps the Old Man, who was a Gborlorkpili Zoe, was scheduled to provide a human being for the year's sacrifice to the river goddess—or he wanted to kill him for refusing to join the disreputable water society.

Too many conflicting thoughts made Korli lose track of time. Before he knew it, the sun had already passed overhead and he hadn't seen a crocodile. Going to the nearby cataract, he watched the vast expanse of azure forest on the western bank of the river, extending all the way to the horizon. Coveys of bluewings, *kpeyakpeya*, and hornbills hovered over it, proclaiming the dry-time, the happiest season of the year, with piquant cries. Eagles and hawks flew deep in the blue sky, their heads bowed sideways in search of birds and chickens to prey on. Monkeys barked and squealed in the treetops, recklessly gorging *sara* and *sorn* nuts and dropping some on the forest floor for deer. Below the cataract where the river flowed calmly in its wide and deep channel, fish popped to the surface, their white bellies reflecting the sunrays. Giving up his fruitless search, Korli now thought of hunting large prey such as boar or buffalo the town could feast on in celebration of his becoming a man. Since the day had gone, he decided to start exploring the forest by sunrise tomorrow. He'd bathe now and await his family's return from the farm.

Wisely tying the gun at the fork of a *kobeley*, he picked his way to the middle of the cataract where the water stopped at his knees, undressed on a wide slab of rock, laid his cutlass by his clothes, and plunged into the lukewarm water. He swam briskly—tumbling, diving, and drinking—until he felt rejuvenated. When he sat on a rock to dry off, Korli saw below the cataract what looked like a log floating on the river waves. It couldn't be a log, he judged, because it was moving against the current towards him. Fear gripped his heart when he realized that it was a crocodile!

Dressing in a flash, Korli bounced ashore and took the gun down, the crocodile lunging at him with amazing speed. The immense beast hit the bank and fell back into the water. Before it could clamber to shore, Korli squeezed the trigger. The aim was inexpert, and the gun jerked with a force that almost threw him off his feet. For a moment, a plume of acrid white smoke blinded him as the thunderous gun blast resounded down the river. Reloading the gun, he waited for his eyes to clear to see whether he had not missed. Some of the shots seemed to have hit the beast, he knew, for it had cried above the angry roar of the river with a human voice:

"Korli, you have killed your own father!"

Trembling from head to foot, his heart pounding his ribs furiously, Korli hurried to his father to try to save his life, but the old man dragged himself to a wide slab of rock, writhed in agony, turned over, and lay calm. He was dead. Korli gazed with consternation at Nuulaa's wrinkled deeplined face projecting under the jowl of what he had thought was crocodile! He couldn't believe his eyes. As he watched the astonishing sight, his mouth agape, a bitter taste welled up in his mouth. Surely, he thought, his Old Man wanted to sacrifice him to water witches. It accounted for the daylight Gborlorkpili racket in the Evil Forest. Now his own trap had caught him, and his tales had lost all credence!

Korli grew apprehensive. No doubt, Gborlorkpili men were lurking in the thick bushes on shore observing the drama. Since their plot had failed, they would certainly spring on him. Therefore, he must put Haindi far behind him immediately, for he was no longer safe in Kpelleland—or in neighboring Golaland, for the Gola too maintained the water society. Should they capture him, there was no other fate for him besides execution in the Evil Forest. Taking his cutlass with one hand and firmly holding the gun with the other, Korli ran home, tied his few belongings in a bundle, and escaped by a hunting path down the river, aiming for White Plains near the seacoast. He believed he'd be safe and secure in the *kwii* world, where nobody knew him—where he could settle with modern and civilized people and lead a happy, peaceful, and prosperous life, free from the menace of secret societies. Fortunately nobody had seen him. In fact, no one would be brave enough to pursue a man well armed with dangerous weapons.

2

DIVINE DELIVERANCE

KORLI'S MIRACULOUS ESCAPE and safe travel through the Gola forest convinced him that he was under divine protection. God and the ancestors must have some purpose for his life he couldn't divine. Had Nuulaa not been old—had tradition not ordained that only the next of kin capture a sacrificial victim—he would have been a dead man. Moreover, under Gorlorkpilii's very eye, he had killed their Zoe, a crime punishable by death, but they had inexplicably spared his life. Predatory animals like leopards, lions, gorillas, baboons, and apes that commonly attacked lone travelers or hunters in the dense forest, fled into the tangled undergrowth on scenting him. As he plowed through the ancient forest, Korli had no fear of anything—not even of the uncertain future towards which he was heading. He believed that all he had to do was place one foot before the other and his rugged path would lead him to a safe abode. What accounted for these favorable circumstances if not the mercy and blessings of God and the ancestors?

When the bluewings and *korkweh* birds started announcing dusk, Korli, who had avoided the main thoroughfare during daylight to evade possible pursuers, felt it was now safe to travel. He was not afraid of death, but he did not want to die for killing someone who would have killed him. It was fortunate he wasn't married, or Gborlorkpilii would have preyed on his wife and children. Now he understood why providence had stopped him from marrying even though he was old enough to support a family and had no problem falling in love. At the last moment an unexpected development always prevented his marriage from taking place. After going through the agony twice, he had put off marriage until he reasonably understood the problem and did something about it. Nuulaa was the culprit of his first ill luck. He had stopped his marriage to Gwanya, a childhood friend and first love because, as he said, they had the same allergies. Korli was surprised because they had made no secret of their love affair, which spanned over many years. Gwanya had initiated it by helping his mother with her cooking, washing, and other household chores, and he had returned her love by helping her father with his farming, gathering of firewood, and bearing some of the cost of her initiation into the Sande Society, where she would be trained to be a good mother and wife. The townspeople considered their marrying a foregone conclusion when they came of age, but she had returned his bride price upon Nuulaa's advice. Nuulaa might not be his father after all or he'd have supported his happiness. Gwanya's return of the three pounds he had paid her parents shocked and dismayed Korli beyond measure.

"What happened, Beauty?" he had asked her in a quivering voice as they watched a moonlight dance one night.

"Your father says we are brother and sister because we have the same allergies," Gwanya had said, her head bowed in dismay. "He says if we marry, the children won't live." Her eyes flooded with tears; she wiped them with the back of her hand.

"How come?" Korli had asked her. "We've been intimate friends for years and he never raised any objection!" Korli bit his fingernail and grew feverish. Perhaps he should have impregnated Gwanya to avoid this heartbreak, as some of his friends had done, he thought. "Unless you give a girl belly," the elders often advised boys, "she doesn't belong to you."

Casting her melancholy mood aside, Gwanya had told him impulsively, "When you became interested in marrying me, your father said he checked our backgrounds and made his astonishing discovery. Naturally, that canceled our marriage. But don't grieve, Korli. I still love you. You don't have to own the hen before eating its egg. Any time you want me, let me know."

Korli had walked away with his head bowed in distress while Gwanya watched him in anguish. No, it was too late for him to eat that egg, he thought. After Nuulaa's warning, there would be grave consequences. He'd only put to practical use two important lessons the experience had taught him: Nuulaa should never know about his next love affair, and neither should Felenkpeh—and he shouldn't wait until he married a girl before going to bed with her. By the time their affair became public, she might even be pregnant. Everybody concerned would have no choice but let him marry her.

The town's gossip soon spread the bad news around and even accused Korli of "eating *kai*," a crime carrying the death penalty. Fortunately, Gwanya ate *kperor* and survived the lie-detecting medicine, absolving Korli of committing incest with her. To prevent further intimate contact between them, however, her parents hastily found her a husband who married and took her to his home, a village far in the north. Korli went on hunger strike, not so much for the broken relation but for the waste of his time and Nuulaa's deception. Maybe he wanted the girl for himself, Korli thought.

"Many girls are looking for husbands," Felenkpeh had consoled him. "You did well to save your reputation and the family's honor by not taking her to bed. Boys who control themselves suffer disappointment, but people respect and trust them. Don't be surprised if they make you a Chief one day. Had you married Gwanya, you people might have buried one child after the other, or she'd have been a thorn in your flesh! Thank God for letting that bad wind blow over you safely. Don't forsake life because of her. Eat something—you're burning with fever!"

"Father was not fair to me," Korli had complained bitterly. "He should have told me about the problem from the beginning."

"Nobody expects first love to lead to marriage, Korli, because playmates don't take each other seriously, and sometimes the same blood runs through them. Don't worry. I'll find you a wife."

"I see a problem with that, Mother," Korli had said politely, hoping his disagreement wouldn't offend his mother. He'd tell her the problem only if she asked him.

"What problem?" Felenkpeh asked. "Many of your friends enjoy life with girls their parents found for them. Parents know the right partners for their children."

"If you choose a wife for me," Korli maintained, "she won't respect me because she might think you'll take her side in our disputes." Korli wondered if that explanation sufficed. Elaborating it was useless, for his mother firmly believed in tradition.

"You talk as if you've married before," Felenkpeh interposed sharply. "Look, the wife I'll find for you will love and respect you and feel welcome in her new home."

Felenkpeh had walked away feeling that her son's life was at risk because he was opposed to tradition. Korli always insisted on doing things his own way. Perhaps he needed the help of a Zoe, she thought.

A short while after that somber conversation, Korli had fallen in love with Korpu, another childhood friend, to avoid an arranged marriage. Korpu was just as beautiful and friendly as Gwanya. She was born a year after her parents migrated from Tulemu in Lorla to Haindi when Korli was but a toddler. Happily, her allergies were different from his and their love was mutual. Korli had served her and her parents with the same dedication he had served Gwanya and her parents. Korpu literally took over all his mother's chores. Felenkpeh was so relieved that she advised him to marry her before some other boy proposed to her. Korli had heeded the advice, but just before the marriage could take place, Chief Yakpalo Kining of Tulemu had brought Korpu's parents a lavish bride price of two goats, two gowns for Korpu's father and uncle, three lappa suits for her mother, ten pounds cash; five lappa suits, jewelry, perfumes, soap, beads, tins of powder, and a mirror for Korpu. He presented the bride price in the palaver house before Chief Fahn Goffah and the Elders who thanked him for the great honor he had bestowed on a daughter of Haindi.

Years earlier, when Paa, Korpu's mother, was pregnant with her, Chief Kining was traveling with a large entourage to the coast to sell coffee, had spent the night in Borkpai's house upon Chief Goffah's request. The hospitality had been elaborate. The Chief and his people had had more than enough to eat and drink throughout the four days they lived with Borkpai and his family. On returning from the coast, Chief Kining had brought gifts of soap, salt, tobacco leaves, towels, tins of powder, hair lotion, and a lappa suit for Paa, and a pair of short pants, a cutlass, Tshirts, and cartridges for Borkpai "to mark the pregnancy" and engage the baby before it was even born. To prove the sincerity of his intentions, he had given Paa a red kola nut and said, "If the child you're carrying is a girl, she'll be my wife." Then he gave her a white kola nut and said, "If it happens to be a boy, he'll be my son." Paa had presented "the marks" to Borkpai. The couple had thanked Chief Kining, considering his gifts a token of appreciation for their hospitality, for engaging a pregnancy did not entitle a man to marrying a girl without her consent, and boys must agree before their adoption in different homes.

Despite Korli's love for their daughter, Korpu's poverty-stricken, indebted parents had prevailed upon her to accept the Chief's proposal. Who else could be more generous in seeking her hand in marriage than such a wealthy Chief? They advised Korli to wait for her sister Lolia to grow up. She was more beautiful than Korpu, they claimed. She'd make him a better wife.

"How long does it take a girl to become a woman?" they said with conviction. "In three years Lolia will be marriageable! We'll keep her exclusively for you." Lolia was only five years old then, so Korli would have had to wait at least ten more years.

Korli made no contention over his loss of Korpu because he had failed to carry out his own decision. However, he did not blame himself altogether, for he had made an attempt, but Korpu had asked for a month to make up her mind before going to bed with him. Felenkpeh's advice that they marry without delay could have not been timelier; but then Chief Kining had denied him the opportunity with his bounteous bride price. Instead of mourning, Korli regarded his disappointment a challenge to plan a better strategy in finding a wife. After mulling over the problem four days, he decided to build and furnish his own house and save a substantial sum of money before proposing marriage to a girl. Entering the home of his in-laws through the back door, as he had previously planned, was ignoble. He'd distinguish himself as an eligible bachelor—a man of means—to earn his in-laws' consent honorably. Disgusted over the slighting, however, Felenkpeh had quickly engaged a girl of Genkema for him to marry. Nyenkole's beauty was extraordinary and akin to only that of a goddess and she had good character—friendly, hardworking, respectful, and self-possessed. Anxious to be Korli's wife, she literally became Felenkpeh's arms and legs. The townspeople congratulated Korli and thanked God for taking the shame from his face. Inexplicably, Korli turned down the engagement, insisting on finding his own wife. Felenkpeh had slapped her thighs and frowned her face in distress, looking forlorn and undone as if her son had confessed to a capital offense.

"Korli," she had said solemnly, "your friends are giving their parents grandchildren to hold. Why are you denying us this right? With death striking people down everyday regardless of age, it's important that you get your likeness now to leave behind when you are gone."

"Mother," Korli had said cordially but with much emphasis, "I want to build and furnish my own house and find some money before marrying. What I went through—"

"Nonsense," Felenkpeh had retorted sharply. "When your father and I married, we slept by fireside on a mat! Once you find the right partner, it doesn't matter what you don't have. You people can get anything you set your mind on. Son, when you become wealthy, that's when girls run away from you. They'll think some other girl might take their place any time since you're in great demand. Some may marry you just to get what they want and go away. Korpu will soon find fault with that miserable old man with one foot in the grave and come home to find a husband. You have a good point, however. Prepare before jumping into marriage, but hurry up because old age waits for no one."

To allay his mother's fears, Korli had commenced cutting sticks for his house right away and said he'd start its construction shortly after Christmas, which was only a month away. He set more than a hundred traps in the forest, which caught plenty of animals he dried and sold on the coast and bought clothes and household utensils with most of the proceeds. Girls began asking him who would take care of the home he was building since he had no wife. Korli had told them that he usually worried about one problem at a time.

So, since he had no family of his own, only the forest and the river Korli would miss—those sources of food, medicine, relaxation, and privacy. But he was happy he'd find forests and rivers in White Plains too.

By sundown, he left the bushes for the familiar highway, most travelers having reached their destinations by then. The Master, who loved traveling at night, might come after him, but he'd have great difficulty finding him in the pitch darkness. Climbing to the top of a steep hill, Korli heard drums and voices in the distance and judged that it was the Gola town of Kuntaa, where people were doing the evening dance until bedtime. He wasn't fond of dancing but he loved the music; the Gola were the best singers he knew. Korli was surprised to have completed half the journey in so short a time on empty stomach, traveling on a hunting path. The day's daunting events had killed his appetite, but not his ability to run for his life. Afraid that his enemies might take him captive in Kuntaa, he decided to spend the night on a farm and bypass the town the following morning.

Resuming the journey when his night vision became active, Korli took a narrow path in the shrubs on the roadside. After toppling several knolls and crossing a number of creeks and marshes, he arrived on an old farm with a ramshackle shed fitted with a wattle bench. West of the shed, near a hearth of boulders and cinders without a spark of fire, stood a half black metal drum by which lay several mortars and pestles. Behind the hearth, close to a cluster of banana trees, loomed a refuse pile strewn with fresh palm nut seeds and husks—crumbs of cassava, potato, eddo, and yam. Apparently, the farmers had made palm oil during the day. Entering the shed, Korli found a few embers on the hearth. Feeding them with thatch and bamboo splints he broke off the roof, he heated up and ate several mouthfuls of tasteless rice and soup he found in a small iron pot the farmers had left by the hearth for a hungry hunter or traveler. He put out the fire to conceal his presence. Laying the hunting bag and his cutlass on the bench, he sat on the front wall log of the shed and loaded the gun. Stars appeared in the sky but were inadequate to dispel the darkness. Round midnight, Korli saw the shadow of a large animal grunting and tramping towards the refuse pile. Quickly hiding in the banana bush as it came close to the shed, he observed that it was a buffalo coming to scavenge food crumbs. Praying in his heart, Korli aimed the gun at the buffalo's heart, held his breath, and fired. It did not fall; only gave a loud cry that sent Korli sprinting like a deer into the tall bushes beyond the edge of the farm where he hid in a thick bramble and reloaded the gun. "A wounded animal is vicious," Nuulaa's warning echoed in his mind. "It can tear a hunter to pieces!" When the beast stopped crying, he returned to the shed—but not too close to it—and discovered that it had escaped. He'd be a fool to follow a wounded animal without a headlight in the darkness. Hiding again in the banana bush, Korli waited patiently. When it did not come after a long time, he returned to the shed thinking that he had missed, but he remained on the alert because the beast had been too close to him when he fired. Unless it had vanished through witchcraft, it was likely wounded seriously and might return looking for him. Korli held the gun at the ready. At dawn, he relaxed his vigilance, thinking he had probably shot the animal's shadow, and decided to resume his journey.

The only way to travel without suspicion, he thought, was braving the highway. Should the Gola find him on a hunting path in their territory, he'd have plenty of explaining to do. He wondered about the safety of the highway. Brigands reportedly ambushed, stripped, robbed, and killed lone travelers on it. Well, he carried no bag of rice or coffee—no tin of palm oil or *kenja* of dry meat or fish they would want—and seeing him with a gun, they would think twice before attacking him. Besides, as a *kenamu*, he had the right to travel the countryside without molestation. Soon he'd be free from such problems when he reached the *kwii* world. But the lore of kidnapping, robbery, murder, and fraud he had heard about that world from people who had lived there, chased the assurance from his mind. However, he'd press on, for returning home was more dangerous than continuing the journey.

When pepperbirds announced the sunrise, which spread gradually over the forest, Korli surveyed the old farm for the buffalo, but saw nothing of it. Taking one last look at the farm, his eyes caught sight of the blurry figure of a limping old man with a cutlass coming towards the shed. The old fellow, who wore only a pair of short black pants and cap, stopped sporadically and looked around with suspicion as if searching for someone. Korli did not attempt to hide. He signed to him with his arm and a reassuring smile, trudging towards him. On sighting Korli with his rheumy eyes, the old man stood still, watched him steadily awhile, and began trotting to the tall bushes, beckoning him with nods. Korli understood. Walking rapidly, he caught up with him on the edge of the old farm; they rattled through shrubs to a tall palm tree under which lay the mountain of a freshly killed buffalo.

"You did the shooting?" the old man asked Korli in broken Kpelle, staring at him with delight.

"Yes," Korli said as he laid his hunting gear down. "Shot it by the old shed last night." This old man has a keen sense of recognition, Korli thought. He already knows that I'm Kpelle. His arms akimbo, Korli watched the buffalo corpse with amazement, wishing he had killed it round Haindi before his ordeal to dry plenty of it for sale on the coast. Well, the good fortune was timely, anyhow. The people of Kuntaa would befriend him regardless of what the talking drums might tell them.

"Two of us can't butcher this big thing," the old man said in his Gola-Kpelle, staring at the animal with widened eyes. "Men are coming to help. They should have come before dawn, but everybody in Kuntaa went to the Deyn yesterday, quite a distance away. I'm sure they heard the gunshot. It's fortunate the bushcow died, or it'd have put us in big trouble. We're already in plenty of trouble."

"What trouble?" Korli asked anxiously, for the trouble might change his itinerary. But the old man was reluctant to answer his question. Korli grew uneasy. However, he waited patiently for an answer to avoid suspicion.

Again, the old man beckoned to him with an upward swing of his arm towards a young palm. The first to reach it, he began cutting the fronds frantically.

"That meat will take at least ten *kenja*," he told Korli, who began plaiting the palm fronds to make the first long backpack.

They plaited ten *kenja* in all, making them sturdy with *seenin* saplings and *memeh* ropes.

"What is the trouble you were talking about?" Korli repeated his question. Perhaps his newfound friend, whose Kpelle was faulty, had not understood him. He was happy however that he had recognized him as Kpelle and could speak it somehow.

"My name is Bhea—Bhea Gootumo," the old man said. "The Chief will tell you the trouble. It's too big for my mouth."

"Is it about Gborlorkpilii or a fugitive?" Korli asked. Bhea glanced at him with sober eyes, wondering if the fretful young man wasn't the person whom the Kpelle drums had talked about last night. Perhaps a hint of the crisis in Kuntaa might put him at ease.

"The trouble has to do with soldiers—the Chief will tell you!" he said. "I wonder what those fellows are doing. They had better come for us to make haste and leave this area!"

To enjoy the old man's confidence, Korli tapped the nape of his neck with his left hand to assure him of his membership in the Poro, but the gesture did not dispose of Bhea's secrecy. He continued refusing to confide in Korli, an attitude Korli resented because it didn't conform to how one *kenamu* should treat another.

"I hope the soldiers are not holding them hostage," Korli said, hoping his solicitude might loosen Bhea up.

"They can't do it!" Bhea declared with irritation. "Let's start butchering," he said, abandoning the subject. "We could at least skin it before they come."

Old Bhea, who looked frail and decrepit with flaxen hair like an invalid, suddenly pulled a sharp knife from his pocket and began flaying the animal with incredible verve. Korli was amazed. Bhea was no longer the wizened old fellow he had seemed to be, but a vicious predator.

Meanwhile, the strident bell of a hunting dog sounded nearby. In a moment, a big black dog rattled through the shrubs to them, barking, wagging its tail, and jumping up and down round the buffalo as if it had helped kill it.

"Deimah, keep quiet and lie down," Bhea commanded the dog, patting its head. "Don't announce our location!" Deimah lay on its belly at a distance, looking around for the hunters it was leading. "Deimah is a good hunting dog," Bhea remarked as he resumed the flaying. "He's strong and sassy! Do you hunt with dogs sometimes?"

"Never," said Korli, his eyes riveted on the dog. "I set traps. A dog bit me once and I vowed never to bother with them again; G*bolo* hunting is dangerous. I also won't hunt with people who turn into animals. Sometimes your fellow hunter might turn into a deer and when you shoot it, it turns back into a human being. You find it impossible to absolve yourself of murder."

"That's true—you need a hunting charm to avoid that problem," said Bhea. "A hunter must be a Zoe to disappear when animals gang up on him in the forest." After a brief pause, Bhea asked seriously, "You came this far just to hunt? Fuama is full of animals including lions, leopards, bush cows, and elephants!"

Since Bhea was secretive with him, Korli thought he should reciprocate. Obviously, the old man had him under suspicion.

"I'm going to the coast to buy cartridges," he told him. "I spent the night on this farm because it was too late to knock door on people in Kuntaa."

"You made the right decision or you wouldn't have killed this bushcow in Kuntaa. Your journey has become sweet!" Pausing, Bhea looked at Korli inquiringly and said, "Be frank with me. I'm a *kenamu* like you. Are you running away from something or someone? The Kpelle drums sent a message—" The old man paused suddenly, not wishing to intimidate a man who had made so much meat available to him and his people.

Resolving to give him only a hint of his troubles, Korli said, "It's a long story, Bhea—a Land affair. I'll tell the Chief. Did the soldiers kill anyone?" he returned to his own query.

"They only put us at gunpoint and took our chickens, animals, and the little rice and palm oil we had in town."

"And you people left them in town and ran away?" Korli wrinkled his nose with disdain.

"You sound like a fighter. Can you fight the government?"

"They are not the government but soldiers—men like you and myself."

"Well, the Chief and some warriors set an ambush round the town. That's the only way to get them—shooting them with some secret spear or arrow." Bhea spoke in a low voice. "Four soldiers don't pose the kind of threat that demands rousing the Master from his sleep— My friend, you are a mango fly. You bite and blow, but you won't get any more information out of me. Let's talk about something else. Are you married?"

"No, I'm not," Korli said, wondering why the inquisitive old man who was so stingy with news wanted to know all about him.

"What are you waiting for? You're no longer a child, my friend."

"I know, but it isn't easy to find a wife. It becomes easy when you get ready for it."

"No girl has put you in trouble yet?"

"No. I had several opportunities, but I made the mistake of deciding to marry before going to bed with a girl."

"You certainly made a mistake. Only the belly ties down a young girl. She'd want her child to have a father. Another problem is that the people in all our villages are related."

"Yes. I faced that problem once."

"Love among relatives is risky. It's easier to find a wife in a village that is not yours. A Sande graduation took place in Kuntaa two months ago; the town teems with single girls. If you spend a week there, you'll surely get in trouble with one of them."

"You keep talking about getting in trouble with girls! Girls are men's best friends! Unless you have a wife, you can't be anybody!"

"That's what I used to think until life taught me that God is man's best friend. I had three wives and ten children, but I now live by begging. Do you see how famished and ragged I look?" Bhea stood still, looking gloomily at Korli. You could count his ribs under the thin wrinkled skin.

Korli found the conversation disquieting but held his end of it to befriend the brilliant elder. After much prodding, he might reveal the secret about the soldiers.

"That's bad," Korli said. "And you spent all your life bringing them up."

"And their children— My son, life is a trap for men. Both the married and un-married men are in crisis."

Before Korli could make a comment, four somber-looking men, armed with sharp bag-bottom cutlasses came upon them. Deimah greeted them with a wagging tail and several barks. They snapped Korli's fingers, thanked him for killing the buffalo and commenced butchering it madly.

"Let's make haste and go to the Deyn. The soldiers might still be in town," one of them, tall and husky, announced as he severed the buffalo's neck with a succession of blows with his heavy cutlass.

"Doing what?" asked Korli, standing still and watching him, perplexed.

"Your hunting charm is powerful!" the man told him, avoiding his query. "We've tried for years to kill this bushcow but couldn't. It avoided our traps—and no gun hunter could kill it. We thought it was someone's double or a witch turned into bushcow—if it could elude hunters so long— You must be a Zoe! What is your name and where do you come from?"

Korli wondered why the men were evading his query about the soldiers whose menace was all men's problem. Every man should know when they patrolled the interior to take necessary precautions to protect their families and themselves.

"I'm not a Zoe," Korli said. "I was only lucky to shoot it at a close range. I come from Haindi. My name is Gbamokorli."

"That's a Zoe name. Many times our hunting Zoe Dougbateeh tried to shoot it, but it always vanished from his sight in broad daylight! Now that it is dead, some dotard will soon die here."

"The one who is a witch," Korli rejoined. "I learned that you people are hiding from soldiers? Usually they leave a town once they get what they want."

"These don't want to leave Kuntaa because they want everything we have and expect us to carry our own properties to Haindi for them. We refused to serve them! They're waiting for hapless travelers to tote their loot to Haindi. Thank God they killed no one; we'll get more chickens and animals as long as we're alive."

"They hustled Gbakayu's two cows, not knowing that the black one is a *sala* cow offered to the ancestors so that he can have a long life. Sorry for those who eat it—they'll die immediately! The Chief used to keep his animals in his village far from the town, but leopards started eating them. Now he has distributed them in various towns."

"When they announced their entry to town with a bugle yesterday morning," said a man with an Adam's apple, "we fled to the Deyn. The women and children had already gone ahead. Because of soldiers, we go to our farms at dawn, but day before yesterday we had a funeral feast and drank too much. So they met many of us men in town. We gave them plenty of leftover foods and drinks. When their bellies were full, they went to sleep in the palaver house and we ran away." He pursed his lips and grunted. "They were sensible not to have followed us."

"They knew better than put a foot in the bush," said Bhea. "God will punish them for robbing us! He doesn't spare criminals, especially thieves!"

"You people should have collected their guns while they slept," Korli said.

"If the government sees you with a soldier's gun, it sends you straight to maximum prison. Soldiers might kill you on the way there and say you ran away."

"And where are you going?" a short bowlegged fellow asked Korli. Everybody looked at him with suspicion.

"To the coast to buy cartridges," Korli replied. The men looked at each other doubtfully but made no comment.

When the butchering was over to Korli's relief, they packed the meat hastily in six *kenja*, shouldered them, and hurried to the Deyn, traveling by a path the *gbolo* hunters cut. They arrived in a village lying within earshot of the river. It had three *zieh* houses and a large kitchen. In the kitchen lay an old man in a hammock, snoring with abandon. He woke up on their arrival and greeted them amiably, gazing at the *kenja* of fresh meat with a bright face.

"Bad luck and good luck always go together," he said smilingly and sat up. "So you people found the hunter and the hunted?" he said with delight as the men put their burdens down. They all laughed. Bhea came last, struggling breathlessly under his load. "A bushcow!" cried the man in the hammock. "Now our crops will have a chance to grow. For years this beast has been eating them! Killed by a stranger!" He stepped down from the hammock, waddled around the *kenja* for a moment, snapped Korli's fingers and thanked him. He loosened a *kenja* and started putting the meat on the dryer. "You're a godsend, my son," he told Korli and gave him an appraising glance. Pausing with his hands in the *kenja*, he looked at Korli with a dark frown and said, "I heard the Kpelle drums last night—"

"No, NanGwoi," someone interrupted. "It's for the Kpaan." Several men joined him to loosen the other *kenja* and put the meat on the dryer while the rest went into the bush for more firewood and sticks to build another dryer outside.

"Are we not *kenabelaa*?" protested NanGwoi as he resumed his task. "Let the young man get the news! He's one of us, isn't he? We can't give him away."

"Even so," said Bhea, "Chief Gbakayu is the person to give it to him. That's what makes him a Chief. And where is he, by the way?"

"Carried the women back to town," answered NanGwoi. "Says we should return home. Yesterday afternoon the soldiers forced travelers on their way to White Plains to carry their things to Haindi. Some of these travelers came from as far as Zorzor and Voinjama. I'm sure those soldiers are now torturing people in Haindi."

"One of them is Kpelle," someone said. "The Kpelle man in government uniform and armed with rifle has no regard for his own people. The man was on fire! He almost killed someone!"

"Making false impression! Put him on a battlefield and he'll run away." The others laughed.

"We're suffering because we don't know book. Any fool who can write his name on paper pretends to be king in this country. I'll send my sons to school."

"What about your daughters?"

"You wouldn't send your girls to an unknown land for school, will you? Boys can live anywhere on their own, but not girls who require great care. Were a school here, I'd send my girls there."

"We're suffering because we're cowards! The days have gone when real men dwelled in this land. Nobody could scare them with guns."

"Most Zoes had bullet-proof powers those days. But nowadays Zoes are impotent because they demand money before rendering service."

"Putting them in the bush with a downpayment for the medicine isn't bad. They have to live by their trade. The problem is, we don't know the good ones from pretenders to the trade."

"When a Zoe protected a town with *kpankpa* in the old days, anyone entering or living there with evil intentions died instantly! Witches and wicked people do as they please these days. The supernatural powers don't work anymore."

"Let's keep quiet, my people! Those idlers may be looking for us."

"May they fall in our ambush!"

"Gbakayu says we shouldn't tell anyone in town about this meat, nor take a piece of it there until he divides it tomorrow," said NanGwoi. "He doesn't want it to become soldiers' food. They travel a lot in the dry-time. Another group might be on their way to Kuntaa."

"They collect money, rice, meat, fish, palm oil, women, and *polortor*—men who will be forced to work for no pay."

They cooked half the *gaigai*, which filled a whole tub, ate much of it, bathed in the Deyn, tapped their wine trees, and proceeded to town, except two of them who remained with NanGwoi to mind the meat.

Arriving in town in moonlight, they met people conversing, singing, and dancing in knots and large groups while half-naked children shrieked and romped about the square. Korli was happy the highway divided the town in two, one-half inhabited by Gola and the other by Kpelle, as someone informed him. Thus, the people there were bilingual.

They took him to the Kpelle Chief Gbakayu who was then on the Stool, but he was absent. His oldest son Zolu lodged him in a round oneroom white house standing on the fringe of the square. One of his daughters, a girl about his age, lit an oil lamp on a wooden table standing against the wall below the only window in the house fastened with a bamboo board, then brought him food and a jug of drinking water. She kept his company until he had eaten and was about to sleep. Her beauty impressed Korli though he saw her only vaguely by the saffron light. Further, he was too weary to be alert. Happily, she cut her visit short, giving him an opportunity to rest, but he slept with open ears like a *kenamu*—just in case Gborlorkpili men came after him. After sleeping for some time, he jerked awake, tense with anxiety but heard neither rumbling voices nor footsteps outside. Remembering that it was illegal for people of a different town to arrest someone in another without the consent of its Chief, Korli grew relaxed and began reflecting on the events of the day.

Korli was struck that marriage and soldier problems were so important to people upcountry. "Early marriage is quite understandable because babies die too often," he thought, "but rushing people into marriage or arranging it for them won't solve the problem. Marriage will be happy only if people are ready for it and get into it willingly. And running away or hiding from soldiers is unmanly. The Chiefs should tell the president about the wickedness of his soldiers. The Poro should train and equip young men to defend the Land; only then will soldiers be cautious in dealing with people of the interior. The Gola drums might have told the Kpelle drums that no fugitive was in Golaland, which is true because they might have sent their message while I was in the bush. The good luck I shared with the Gola won't permit them to betray me. Anyhow, the sooner I leave Kuntaa the better off I'll be."

Before dawn, when the darkness was deepest, Korli heard four measured poundings on the door, signifying that eminent leaders of the Poro had come to welcome him formally to Kuntaa. He wondered if they weren't his enemies who had come with a pretense of friendship to spirit him away. Bouncing out of the creaking bamboo bed, Korli cocked the loaded gun, held it at the ready, and inquired in a voice that betrayed no fear or anxiety:

"Your servant is here!" No reply.

Korli felt the creeps. He blew out the flickering lamplight, drew a deep breath, bravely unlatched the door, and opened it with force, his finger on the trigger. A garish face with shiny eyeballs stared at him by the light of the bamboo torch he carried. He was a huge man of dark complexion that merged with the night. In the shadow behind him, he could see the profiles of three men. They were all naked to the waist.

"You don't need your gun," the gigantic man said companionably. "We're coming in," he added as he and his associates climbed the dirt steps. "Why, Leanya didn't light your lamp?" he said as he used his torch to light a black wick projecting from the stopper of a Schnapps bottle of oil. Then he and his men surrounded Korli who stood erect and calm in the middle of the room. "Are you a man?" he demanded, all eyes focused on Korli as if his visitors were primed to assault him should he lie to them. He disarmed them by tapping the nape of his neck with his left hand. They sighed with relief and, smiling now, snapped his fingers.

Three of them sat in rattan chairs while the youngest among them closed the door and squatted by it, a black bag at his feet. The dancing lamplight brightened the room enough for Korli to memorize their features. Assured that they were friendly, he uncocked his gun, laid it under the bed, and sat unruffled on the edge of the bed awaiting their "word."

The huge man broke the silence. "I'm Labhili Gbakayu, Chief of the Kpelle Quarters of Kuntaa." From his accent, Korli noticed that he was a Bopolu Kpelle who had settled in Gola country, probably because of marriage. "This is Dakena, the Big Thing's main follower," he touched the shoulder of the man on his left with fingertips. "This is Ballah the Poro Zoe of Kuntaa," he said, similarly touching the man on his right. Then he introduced as the Zoe's medicine carrier the young man at the door whom he called Kpanah. "What is your mission here?" he asked Korli.

"Thank you, Chief, for your kind reception," Korli began. "The food was good and the service splendid! Unfortunately you were absent when I called by your house, but your son took care of me. Many, many thanks!"

"I should have thanked you to start with," the Chief said, "but I'm not myself today. However, gratitude is like money; it's always a welcome guest. Thank you for taking that monster off our back and giving us meat. A brave and kind young man like you can make a good son-in-law."

Korli smiled wanly and said, "Chief, you own the Land, so I gave you only what's yours. It's God's doing, and I'm happy he did it through me. Gola and Kpelle people are one family. The Poro unites them—how far is Haindi from Kuntaa?"

"I should have come to the sound of your gun, but some warriors and I are in ambush for four reckless soldiers who raided this town yesterday—just in case they returned. My people might have told you of our troubles, I'm sure. I left the ambush to welcome you— Ballah, remember to *kpankpa* the town."

"I've already done so," said Zoe Ballah. "Any arrogant soldier causing trouble here will not live to tell the story, but he'll leave our town in good health so that we won't be responsible for his death."

"What is your mission?" the Chief returned to his query. They all trained their eyes on Korli curiously as if they already knew the answer he should give.

"I'm on my way to the coast to buy cartridges," Korli said. "We've run out of them and are starving for meat; animals are spoiling our crops."

"No," declared Chief Gbakayu, shaking his massive head vigorously and looking at Korli with unblinking eyes. "The Kpelle drums say you shot your own father Nuulaa Barsii while he swam in the Deyn yesterday afternoon, thinking he was a crocodile, and ran away. The water society of Haindi says the Mighty One should arrest and turn you over to them for punishment." Chief Gbakayu paused for a long time, every head bowed in somber reflection. "No, we can't let Gborlorkpilii gobble up a fine and kind young man like you," he finally said, breaking the intense silence. Everyone sighed with relief. "We Deyn Gola Kpelle save lives. Only criminals we kill. The water society is supposed to protect people from drowning and water witches, but your people have made it a plague. You're safe here."

"The Old Man was dressed in crocodile skin," Korli explained. "He was swimming against the current towards me as I bathed at the cataract. I was only lucky because I had a gun, for he chased me to the shore. Had I not shot him, I'd have been a dead man since yesterday. I fled because, once you shed human blood on the Land, even by mistake, you must die."

"We understand. We understand very well," said the Chief, nodding his head. "People never die of natural causes or accident in this country. Witch hunters always manage to find the culprits: usually, people perceived as witches or enemies of the deceased."

"Are you a member of Gborlorkpilii?" asked Zoe Ballah.

"No," Korli replied.

"That's the root of your problem. Once you aren't a member of a certain society, its members consider you an alien they can kill with impunity. Were you not a *kenamu*, they'd have killed you and claimed that you lost your way in the forest or drowned in the river. For your own sake, join Gborlorkpilii. Men who live by large rivers must be members of that society, otherwise they can disappear any time, and people will blame the rivers as convenient culprits for their death."

"I want to return home with a few Poro men from here, including the Master, to confront the Gborlorkpili people there," Korli suggested. "The only way to get to the other side of a river is by crossing it."

"A brave young man!" said the Chief, looking at Korli with an approving smile. "A seasoned *kenamu*, too, as indicated by the sign you threw at us when we entered here. Unless you return home as a Gborlorkpili initiate—a *zuuuu*," he stressed the one-syllable word lengthily, "they'll punish you because the wound you've inflicted there is still fresh and hurting. After you make amends for it by joining Gborlorkpilii, Zoe Ballah will cleanse you with herbs to make you indestructible before you return home. As you know, tribal laws excuse no one regardless of status. We can see to your initiation at no cost to you."

"Upon your recommendation then, I'll join it. I never wanted to have anything to do with it because it comprises a bunch of cutthroats and kidnappers."

"A *kenamu* doesn't talk like that. The reputations of some of these societies don't match what they actually stand for or do. You'll see for yourself. Secondary societies like Gborlorkpilii make you intimate with people and teach you valuable medicines."

"Once you join Gborlorkpilii, your crime will be forgiven," said

Dakena. "You killed in self-defense, didn't you? However, a wicked heart knows no mercy. Stay away from home for some time. You said you were on your way to the *kwii* world. Stay there for a few years. Are you a member of the snake society?" "Yes," Korli said.

"Good. We can initiate you into all the other societies that you may be entitled to justice, friendship, and mercy in the lands of the Gola, Kpelle, Loma, Gbandi, Kissi, Vai, Mano, and Mende in Liberia, Guinea, and Sierra Leone."

"Now we'll have you renew your Poro oath and give you protection against poison," said Zoe Ballah.

Fetching a lump of black chalk bedecked with cowries from the depths of his medicine bag Kpanah handed him, the Zoe laid it aside and told Korli to touch it with the index finger of his left hand.

"Repeat after me," he said. "I pledge to be strong, brave, and wise in all circumstances."

"I pledge to be strong, brave, and wise in all circumstances."

"I pledge to die fighting rather than run away from or surrender to my enemy."

"I pledge to die fighting rather than run away from or surrender to my enemy."

"If I renege on these pledges, may this medicine catch me."

"I'll never renege on these pledges by the grace of God." Korli jerked his finger from the medicine as if it were a snake. "Why should people who run away from soldiers make me take such an oath?" he said in his mind.

The Zoe's forehead creased and his eyes shone with consternation. Obviously, Korli's evasion of the last sentence of the oath disturbed him. He quietly put the medicine back into the bag and took a razor from it.

"Give me your left hand," he commanded Korli. Seeing that the Zoe was displeased, Korli gave him his hand without hesitation.

Zoe Ballah made four short parallel cuts on the back of his left wrist with a steady hand, took a small black gourd out of his bag, and rubbed into the wounds a pinch of black powder he poured from it. The wounds gave no blood.

"It's your protection against poison," he told Korli. "Poison is the worst enemy you may have to fight some day. This medicine has only two laws: Woman should never touch it, and don't ever touch lime. Breaking any of these laws will destroy its power. When you become somebody in the *kwii* world, don't forget the Land. May God and the ancestors be with you."

"That medicine is also a protection against witches and bad dreams," put in Dakena. "Sometimes your enemy fights you in your dreams or with witchcraft."

"Welcome to Kuntaa," Chief Gbakayu told Korli with a smile, snapping his fingers heartily. Zoe Ballah, Dakena, and Kpanah also snapped his fingers warmly. "I'm happy you have decided to plant your roots more firmly in the Land of your ancestors," said the Chief. "Even if you become a *kwii*, some day you'll travel upcountry; if you aren't acquainted with the traditional way of life, you'll be in grave danger."

After the visitors left, Korli hardly slept for the rest of the night. He reflected on the day's critical events and his future. He thanked his guardian angel for his narrow escape and the good fortune and friendship he'd met away from home. He had essentially become a citizen of Kuntaa. Perhaps life there might be ideal for him—but no, it wouldn't be much different from life at home. Nowhere but the *kwii* world would give him the best possible opportunity to lead a happy and successful life. He'd join the water society because it was active everywhere in the country, especially in the coastal region, which literally sat on water, as he had learned from travelers who had been there. He'd join the *gbon* society, too, to fight spirits and witches. Seasoned in the ways of the tribe, he'd be free from their harassment and intimidation. He also wanted to count for something in the *kwii* world. Not as a soldier patrolling the interior with a dangerous weapon slung to his shoulder to exploit his own people, but as a district commissioner or superintendent to protect them from exploitation. Was that too much to expect at his age? During one of his trips to White Plains to trade, a German merchant had praised him for his hard work and prudence and urged him to go to school.

"I see that you're a determined and ambitious young man," the white man had told him through an interpreter. "Nearly every month you buy clothes, farming tools, household utensils, kerosene, and soap. Are you doing business upcountry?"

"No, sir," Korli had told him. "They are for personal use. I'm about to build my own house."

"Are you married?"

"No, sir. I'm preparing for it by building a house."

"You're different from many country boys I know. As soon as they know themselves as men, they father numerous children even though they can't support them. Some day you'll have your own business or be somebody important in this country if you go to school."

Korli had pondered the idea of going to school for a long time and concluded that it was worth a try because he wanted to do much more with his life than simply find food to eat, have a house full of children, clash with soldiers, and die of old age. The German man had said that a person was never too old to learn.

3

A Happy Surprise

THE TOWN WAS UTTERLY QUIET, everybody having gone to their farms except Korli and his caretaker who remained to see after his bath and breakfast. She'd have wakened him at daybreak to bathe and eat something but for the strain and stress of yesterday's hefty activities, which had kept him under pressure until dawn. She wanted him to get enough sleep and gather strength. When the sun reached overhead, however, loneliness and the quiet of the town unnerved her. They were in danger! She especially! How would a sleeping man defend her and himself should soldiers come upon them? By the time he roused they would have killed, raped, or snatched her away. Checking Korli's door the third time and finding it locked, Leanya knocked it as hard as she could. Getting no response, she accompanied the knocks with the urgent cry, "Kpor-Kpor-Kpor!" Her voice strangely echoed through the town.

Korli bounced out of bed as from a bad dream. His heart shuddered when he saw tiny spears of sunrays with twirling motes pouring into the room through holes in the thatched roof. He was afraid day had broken long ago and he was alone in town. Surely his enemies had caught up with him, using a woman as bait. They'd have no problem spiriting him away. Dressing quickly and taking his cutlass to strike down at least one of them before his death, Korli heard several more knocks on the door accompanied by the feminine voice. He opened the door with force and was surprised to see a girl of mesmeric beauty, charm, and vitality standing on the threshold. She wore only a blue- and white-striped towel round her waist; her plump oiled body reflected the noonday sun like a pearl; her bulging bare breasts, like large oranges, rose and fell with her breathing. Three plaits of shiny black hair matching her ebony color stretched from the top of her forehead to the nape of her neck. Bushy brows and long lashes half concealed her sparkling brown eyes. The wisp of a smile played on her russet lips under a pudgy nose. Indeed, if there ever was a goddess, Korli thought, this was she.

"Good morning," she greeted him with a smile, exposing her even white teeth. Korli's heart trembled as he stared speechlessly at the girl. Thinking he still wandered about in a dream, she added loudly, "I didn't want to wake you up. I knew yesterday's troubles made you tired, but the sun has now passed overhead. You need to bathe and eat something for us to leave the town."

Still spellbound, Korli gazed steadily at the girl, searching his memory. She seemed familiar but he couldn't place her in a context. Exhaling a deep breath, he said Good Morning. Something in his lingering look must have communicated love to her, for she responded with coquettish gestures.

"Your bath is ready," she said with a grin and posed to lead him to the bath fence.

"Thank you," Korli said. "I'm sorry I overslept. I normally wake up before dawn, but yesterday's troubles wore me out, as you said. Give me a moment; I'll be with you." In spite of himself, Korli did not move. He continued watching the girl with fascination, wondering who she was. He recalled vaguely a girl fixing up his lodgings last night and bringing him food and water, but the day's events had made him so overwrought and sleepy that he hadn't focused his eyes on her. "What is your name?" he asked her.

"Leanya," she said with a bright smile. "And yours?"

"Good name!" Korli said. In their language Leanya meant 'Come near me.' "The lucky man who marries you must keep you at his side always, or he'll die of heartbreak. I'm Gbamokorli. People prefer Korli, the short form."

"Good name, too! Means you're strong like a leopard," Leanya said excitedly. Noticing that Korli couldn't take his eyes off her, she said, "Do I look like a stranger? Don't you know me? I prepared your bath and supper last night—kept your company until you slept."

"I thought I saw you last night, but it was too dark for me to make you out— I'm not brave, Leanya. They named me for my grandfather who was leader of a leopard society and a warrior. They thought I'd follow his footsteps, but I don't care for that society or warfare."

"Nobody wants war, but when it comes, or when you're put to it, you must defend yourself. You look brave— Hurry up; your bath is getting cold."

Leanya's words and the sidelong glance she cast at him sent a warm shudder through Korli from the crown of his head to the soles of his feet. He gazed at her with unblinking eyes, longing for a rejoinder that could excite a similar response in her, but Leanya was restive. She kept looking at him and at the way to the bath fence, waiting for him to move.

Quickly shoving the gun and hunting bag in the *zieh* ceiling and taking his cutlass, Korli walked behind her towards the outskirts, feeling exulted. If only he could pronounce the three words "I love you" with grace and charm in her ear and get the desired reply, it'd amount to killing another buffalo—no, an elephant—but it'd be risky and premature to say such words now. They had just met. He'd be imposing on her kindness and possibly putting his reputation at risk. Suppose she had a husband? Kuntaa had received him with love and honor; if he didn't behave himself, it might disgrace and expel him, his killing of a buffalo for the town notwithstanding. Even if she were single, what right had he, a man on traveling feet, to torment such innocent beauty with love? Leanya saved him the anguish by saying with a chuckle:

"You wisely carry a cutlass wherever you go. So I'm right! You are a warrior!"

Loosening up, Korli said casually, as if Leanya's compliments had no more significance than ordinary conversation, "All Poro men are warriors, ready for danger at all time."

"Your wife is well secured and provided for," Leanya said pensively. "Seeing those strong arms of yours, what man will mess with her? And you seem wise and hardworking."

Korli did not hear the compliments as he slipped into the circular thatched fence. Leanya hung a lappa at its narrow entrance and waited for him outside as he bathed—or flashed water on his skin to hasten out and continue the sweet conversation. Deeply stirred, his heart surged with love for Leanya despite his feeling that it was unfair and risky to fall in love with her.

After he had bathed, Leanya brought him a breakfast of boiled cassava and fish gravy spiced with hot pepper, sweet tomatoes, fever leaves, and *kelen* shoots. Desire having dulled his appetite, Korli ate only a piece of cassava he doused in the aromatic gravy. Though they often encouraged them to eat, he thought, girls usually despised men with big appetite. If he wanted to enjoy Leanya's love and respect, he should control his eating.

"My stomach is full," he told her.

"You only tasted the food!" Leanya said with a slight scowl. "At least eat the fish, Korli! I myself did the fishing."

To give him appetite, she smiled broadly. Apparently, his strategy had miscarried; Leanya expected him to eat to his fill. Perhaps her insistence that he eat was a test of his resolve, Korli surmised. If he failed it, she might not take seriously anything else he told her. He solved the dilemma with a distracting flatter he often used to assuage a girl's anger:

"Your beauty has filled my stomach!" The statement was really true. Korli was not accustomed to eating until he had "thrown cutlass." Early morning work always helped his appetite. Considering it a compliment, Leanya laughed a lovely laugh that further stirred his throbbing heart. He felt like walking in a cloud or in the shadow of a forest in the afternoon of a dry season, enjoying the songs of birds rather than suffering the painful restraint.

"I command you to eat," Leanya said amiably. "If you faint or suffer defeat in a fight, they'll say I failed to feed you."

Korli regarded this command as a test Leanya had devised; obeying it would betray his manhood. Thinking of another distraction, he said:

"Leanya, you're spoiling me. Men don't eat this early in the morning. It makes them weak and sleepy at the best time of day for work. Apart from that, when I go to the *kwii* world, who will make breakfast for me?"

This remark did not impress Leanya although Korli had intended it as a credit to her kindness. She only sat like a statue in the chair, staring sullenly at the rejected food she had prepared with so much care.

Inhaling the fragrance of the gravy, Korli said, "The soup smells delicious! Let me have some fish."

An expression of contentment on her face, Leanya said, "Korli, enjoy any opportunity you get and do not worry about tomorrow. The memory of a good day can see you through bad ones. Father wants me to take you to the farm. It's dangerous for one person to be in town during the day because soldiers, witches, and monsters prey on a single person they find in a town." She gave him some fish and a piece of cassava on the cover of the soup bowl. After he had eaten and drunk some water, Leanya tied up the soup and cassava bowls in a headtie and told him, "You'll eat when you're hungry."

"You made a good point," Korli reminded her. "It's good to enjoy any opportunity you get and not worry about tomorrow. But any man who hunts learns to be alone, Leanya. I can spend the day in town by myself with no fear. Soldiers, witches, and monsters mean nothing to me. But it's better to be with you and your family on the farm. You're friendly.

I'm afraid—"

"Of what?" Leanya asked. She wrinkled her nose and stared in his face.

"Of you."

"Why?" Leanya said with laughter as she stepped out to the porch with the bowls of food delicately balanced on her head. "I won't bite you."

Korli locked the door with a small padlock, stepped down with the gun on his shoulder and his cutlass in his hand. As he followed her towards the farm road, he said:

"Kpelle men are notoriously jealous over their wives. Your husband or boyfriend might—"

Leanya looked at him over her shoulder and said, "What man can beat a giant like you?"

"A man with a grievance is extremely dangerous, Leanya. He can kill a leopard!"

"I'm not married," Leanya said. "What married woman will expose herself like this? How could the Chief have somebody's wife care for a single man stranger? It's your wife you're afraid of, not me."

"I'm not married," Korli responded in kind.

After a long interval, Leanya turned her head round again and glanced at his face skeptically.

"I'm sure you have a steady girlfriend or trial wife," she said. "You're too handsome for girls to spare. I haven't seen a Kpelle man your age without a wife. So don't lie to me."

"Why should I lie to you? I could marry you even if I were married. Frankly, I don't have any girlfriend or trial wife."

Convinced that Leanya was in love with him, Korli told her of his terrible experience with Gwanya and Korpu to disabuse her of the belief that he was married. He ended the painful recollection by saying that he needed a powerful Zoe to cleanse him of the bad luck some witch or spirit had cast on him to stop him from marrying. Did she know of any?

"Are you sure someone is bewitching you?"

"Yes, I'm sure. They usually strike when I'm about to marry. I don't mind being in a Zoe's debt for life once he gets rid of them. I need a wife."

"No witch or spirit is after you. You don't have much experience with women. That's your problem. Finding the right partner is like hunting. Some hunters are lucky to kill a quarry without problem as it happened in your case with the bushcow. But most hunters rove the forest for days or even weeks before getting their luck. Be patient and keep your eyes and ears open; your luck is coming."

Korli admired Leanya's round undulating hips, shapely calves, and balmy voice. She had all the desirable qualities of the wife he wanted: beauty, foresight, vivacity, and a heart of gold. Were he not on traveling feet, he'd win her at any cost and spend the rest of his life with her. When they climbed to the crest of a hillock, Leanya pointed at a misty forest in the distance and said:

"Our farm is right behind that forest."

Korli stood enthralled, staring at the blue forest spewing spirals of mist into the sky. A flock of singing bluewings suddenly emerged from the mist, flew over them, and sat in a huge *sorn* within shooting distance.

Korli watched them with interest.

"You won't waste a cartridge on birds, will you?" Leanya asked.

"No," Korli said. "I don't kill birds. I'm enjoying their song." He heaved and resumed the trek with a weighty air.

"I love birds for their meat, not for their songs," Leanya said. "Bird meat is not only delicious, it is medicinal. It heals many kinds of sickness. My brother Dieley knows how to trap them. Whenever he gets some, I'll cook it for you."

"Fong, bluewings, *kpeyakpeya*, pepperbirds, wrens, and leopard birds are the best singers," Korli remarked. "Their songs have many meanings."

"Some of the fruits and leaves birds eat are medicines. If you eat birds regularly, it's hard for you to get sick. Most of the herbs my mother knows—she is a good herbalist—she learned from birds."

"Birds tell you when to wake up in the morning, when to go to and from the farm, when strangers are coming to you, when your faraway relative dies, and when danger is near."

"So birds communicate with you? You didn't listen to them this morning," Leanya said, grinning at Korli over her shoulder. When he made no response, she added, "That's expected of a good hunter, of course. Birds tell hunters where to find herds of animals and how to make their way home when they're lost in the forest."

"You sound like a hunter yourself!" Korli said with a chuckle.

They met Chief Gbakayu dividing meat among the Deputy Chiefs of Kuntaa while his wives were busy cooking venison with *kpaa* and fever leaves. The sweet scent of the stew pervaded the tiny village. Everyone warmly welcomed Korli with a smile and congratulated him for the exploit.

"You've put meat in our mouths again," the Chiefs told him, snapping his fingers by turn. "May the ancestors bless your gun."

Leanya commenced building a fire to cook for Korli and herself.

"*Demilahn*, take this seat," Dieley told Korli and yielded his stool to him. Korli noted his striking resemblance to his sister.

"It's too soon to call him *demilahn*," Leanya told him as she handed Korli a cup. Everybody laughed briefly, looking at Korli for a response.

As a diversion, Leanya's elder brother Zolu said, "Every single man is a potential *demilahn*."

Korli grinned, filled the cup to the brim and drained it.

"This is the kind of breakfast a man needs, Leanya," he said. Leanya smiled pleasantly but made no comment. Turning his gaze from his unresponsive caretaker to Chief Gbakayu, he remarked, "We don't make wine in Haindi for lack of piassava trees."

"Welcome to Kuntaa," said the Chief. "We have plenty here, full ones with strong wine! Deyn Gola is rich! Our forest is full of any species of animals you can imagine. Our traps and fish baskets are not catching anything these days because we have meat. In two markets, this village will overflow with meat and fish. The Deyn River and the creeks round here teem with all sorts of fish."

"Brother, we'll take you into the bush this afternoon," Zolu told Korli. "We have plenty of palm trees and fallow farmlands. As Father said, herds of monkeys, boars, antelopes, elephants, and many other animals roam our forest."

"Who told you the young man wants to live here?" asked Ma Gbavor. She was Dieley and Leanya's mother and the Chief's Headwife. "He is on traveling feet!" She pursed her lips and looked at the white clouds over the forest.

"Before settling in an area, a man makes sure it has a means of support for his family such as fertile farmland, hunting ground, a river or creek with plenty of fish," Zolu said.

"To me, what encourages a person to settle in a different land is the friendliness of its people," Korli said. "You people are kind and friendly. I won't mind living in Kuntaa for the rest of my life."

"You'll live here because you're in trouble with me," NanGwoi said with a chuckle. "Where is my gown? You've taken my wife from me!" Everybody laughed at the privileged badinage of Leanya's aged maternal uncle.

"The man has just come, NanGwoi," said Dieley in a loud voice because NanGwoi was hard of hearing. "He'll give us *cold water, cut the log*, and gown us. Let's be patient."

"There's no log to cut yet," Leanya declared and burst out with laughter as she dished out the rice. Afraid that badgering Korli for money might put him on his guard, she added with slight annoyance, "Let him eat something before the plenty talks. He only tasted his breakfast this morning."

"Korli has nothing to fear!" said NanGwoi, staring at Korli with sober eyes. "The boy who wanted Leanya ran away. He was too lazy, too thievish, and too talkative. The Bush Thing taught him a lesson one night. Since then we haven't laid our eyes on him. We don't even know his whereabouts."

"That's what happens when you force a woman on a man," said Leanya. "You people wanted me to marry that boy against my will." She gave Korli a bowl of rice and the gravy she had brought from town.

Korli invited the men to eat with him but they declined.

"Go ahead and eat, Brother," Zolu said. "We're mostly concerned about you the stranger. Our mothers are cooking plenty of food. The Deputy Chiefs will eat with their boss."

"Why didn't you cook meat for Korli?" Ma Gbavor chided Leanya when she noted that he was eating only fish. "With all the meat here, a man shouldn't eat fish bones! Maybe that's why his friends don't want to eat with him."

"I grew up by the river, Mother," said Korli, grinning. "I'm used to eating fish rather than meat."

"Gbavor," said the Chief, "if Leanya gives that man dry rice and palm oil to eat, it'll taste better in his mouth than the delicious meat stew you're cooking. We were protecting you, Leanya," the Chief returned to the previous conversation. "Young girls choose men by their looks, not knowing that looks are deceiving—or by their possessions. We didn't want you to make such a bad mistake."

"It turned out to be a mistake, anyhow," Leanya said. "I won't let you people make another one. It's men who choose women by their looks; women choose men by their character. Don't worry, Data. When I find the right man, I'll bring him to you myself and have him pay my dowry." Leanya sounded jovial, but her father's frowned face showed that he took exception to her straight talk.

Noting that her daughter's repartee was out of place, Ma Gbavor told her harshly, "Leanya, it's impertinent for a child to disagree so openly with its parent, even if it is intended as a joke!" The conversation returned to hunting, fishing, and farming.

That evening Korli joined the water society in the town's Kpaan. He was happy it wasn't as much of an ordeal as he had feared. The Chief simplified the rituals for him. A lover of music, Korli had no problem learning the water song sung in Bassa, the *kono* rattling, and the incantations. The Chief excused him from swimming in crocodile skin because "you're under my roof and have become a friend of the Land."

Then he gave him a small black gourd containing black powder. "Sprinkle some round any house you live in," he said; "and mix some with palm oil and rub it in your armpits to ward off evil spirits and witches." The Chief poured a little of the powder in his left palm, mixed it with palm oil, licked some to prove that it wasn't poisonous, and rubbed the rest in his armpits.

"That's a cure for victims of witchcraft," he told Korli. "No spirits or water witches will ever harm you if you follow my instructions." He showed him herbs for curing maladies such as migraine headache, heart and stomach problems—herbs of common plants found on the outskirts of towns.

Leanya cooked the most delicious dish she could for Korli that night, putting water herbs and aromatic spices in the meat stew. Because she was too particular about the cooking, it was nearly midnight when the food was ready.

"You cook very well," Korli told her as he opened the bowl of soup and inhaled its pleasant smell. "But it's late for me to eat. Anyone hearing me knock spoon in a bowl this late at night will say I'm greedy." He smiled at Leanya and stroked her hair.

"So what?" Leanya asked crossly. "You always worry about what people say. Do whatever is in your interest and forget what they say!" She sat in a chair with her face averted and her hands clasped between her thighs. Prepared for this sudden change of mood, Korli broke the impasse with another flatter:

"You resemble your mother, Leanya: the same eyes, the same lips, the same wavy hair, the same way of walking and talking. Unless strangers are informed, they'll mistake you people for sisters."

Though she enjoyed the compliments, Leanya did not respond to it immediately. She stretched and leaned back in the chair, accentuating the fullness of her breasts. Then she folded her arms across her midriff. Seeing that his banter had elicited only closed lips and nearly a frown, Korli put some stew in the rice and ate several spoonfuls. He smacked his lips with delight and drank a cup of water.

Loosening up slightly, Leanya said without looking at him, "Strangers often say Mother and I are sisters. Several times people in Gobataa market took me to be her. They couldn't believe me when I said I'm her daughter. Since then we call each other Sister."

"It happens to many firstborns and their parents because they grow up together. People who look alike should never commit crimes or owe debts, for the action of one is often binding on the other."

Korli had now eaten half the food. Buoyant once again, Leanya handed him more water.

"That's true—what you said," she told him. "We've paid each other's debts several times, so we've stopped borrowing. Tell me about your family. How many brothers and sisters do you have? What do they look like? What do they love to do?"

Clearing his throat and reminiscing, Korli said, "I have two brothers, but I know very little about them." He looked at Leanya's wrinkled neck and continued: "They left the home when I could hardly stand on my feet. Following Father's footsteps, they learned at an early age to be good farmers and hunters. Father says they spoiled me with food and toys. I wish I knew where they live. Lorkula, the oldest, inherited our father's looks and medical powers. The older one, Loryii, could sing, dance, and make the *samkpa* drum talk. He was a welcome guest at all festivals, Father says. My sister Moima is reserved. She has vowed to live in Haindi and take care of our parents until she buries them. She is very beautiful and friendly. She says I used to prefer riding her back than our mother's. My mother Felenkpeh came from Gboryoimu, a town under the shadow of the Bong and Zaweyeh mountain range half a day from Haindi. Mother used to run the home with Father's instructions. Moima inherited her beauty and devotion to duty. Because I'm the baby of the family, they all showered me with love, but they thought I was odd because I always insist on doing things my own way. I never joined Gborlorkpilii despite Father's relentless urging, and I turned down a girl Mother engaged for me to marry, insisting on finding my own wife. My father Nuulaa Bharsi, an expert swimmer, surprisingly drowned in the river. He taught me the importance of hard work and discipline—" Korli stopped speaking abruptly because his voice cracked. The words seemed to have choked him.

Thinking he was mourning for his father, Leanya pursed and twisted her lips one side as if she were enduring physical pain. Then she began to analyze Nuulaa's tragedy. It was unusual, she said, for a man who had grown up by the river to drown. Swimming was a diversion and a *must* for men of the Deyn River basin. Perhaps he had been drunk.

"We don't have piassava trees round Haindi, so people there don't do much drinking," Korli said. "Occasionally Father drank a shot of gin to go to sleep."

"Perhaps someone sold him to water people or he might have broken some of their laws. Was he a member of Gborlorkpilii?"

"Yes. The Chief Zoe of Fuama Chiefdom."

"That could have been the problem. Society laws are very severe. If you break any by indiscretion or mistake, you must pay the penalty in full. Sadly, the principal penalty for infringing society laws is death. To prevent frequent drowning, you people should move Haindi to a new location far from the river," Leanya suggested. "Water witches lure people in towns on riverbanks into the depths or kidnap them as they bathe in the rivers."

"Our people are shiftless," Korli said, sighing with resignation. "They prefer living only where their ancestors and navel cords are buried." He made a helpless gesture with his arms and laid them in his lap.

"The ancestors migrate with people," Leanya said with the assurance of a person well informed about the traditions. "Don't they know that?"

"They do, but they don't believe it, I suppose."

"Tell them not to listen to members of the water society. They are keen on convincing people to live on riverbanks in order to recruit them for their society—or sacrifice them. They collect plenty of money, liquor, and foodstuffs from new initiates."

"How can we convince the people to leave the graves of their ancestors and their navel strings and live elsewhere?"

"Tell them what I just told you: The ancestors will be with them wherever they go. The ancestors know that people have to move around; that's why God gave them legs. As for the kola trees—once a powerful *gbon* Zoe plants a new one with prayers wherever you go, you become part of the soil."

"The people need the river for food, bathing, washing clothes, and all that. This is the main problem, I think. The average man on the riverbank doesn't feel clean unless he swims."

"Tell your average man that life means change—movement! Any living thing with legs is expected to walk to some other place. We make farms and build villages by the river. So we do all our fishing, bathing, and washing in it and go home in the evening. Your average man can do the same thing. He should decide which is more important: saving his life by suffering slight inconvenience or living on the riverbank and drowning. There are creeks all over. Father says when Kuntaa was located by the Deyn, people drowned there too often. Murderers frequently killed people and dumped their corpses into the river, blaming it on crocodiles. Of course, some people drowned because they couldn't swim, yet they wouldn't leave the river alone. When they moved the town over here, the drowning reduced to almost nothing. Death by drowning is horrible! See how it has deprived a young man like you of your father!" Leanya gazed at Korli with pity. "There's good in suffering, it seems," she consoled him. "The loss of your father has made a man of you at a young age. You killed a full-grown bushcow by yourself in grim darkness! Only a grown man can perform such a brave deed. And you want to make a home in a strange land where you have no relative! Are you not afraid?"

"Of what? Death? Everybody has to die one way or another, Leanya. You can't run away from death. We suffer disadvantage and poverty because we don't use the legs God has given us due to fear. I never knew I'd meet friendly people away from home."

"People treat you as you treat them. Had you been mean and selfish, you wouldn't have shared your meat with us and become a friend of Kuntaa. Now the town belongs to you."

"People need one another; that's why it's good to be kind. My father used to say that no matter how strong, rich, or wise you may be, you can't make life alone."

"He was right; with all their seeming toughness, human beings can't survive alone."

Finding the conversation a little too gloomy, Leanya decided to strike a cheerful note. Sitting by Korli on the bed and leaning on him, she smiled and asked:

"What captures a woman's heart?"

Leanya's soft, warm body gripped Korli so completely that he became speechless for the moment. The riddle was simple enough; it posed no challenge. He wished she had told an inconclusive tale requiring debate to keep Leanya with him through the night. He laughed nervously and said, like a bowstring releasing an arrow:

"Love captures a woman's heart more than anything else."

"Korli, put your hand round me and hold me tight," Leanya said. Korli complied. "Many people who profess love harbor hatred in their hearts," she said. "True love is expressed by action and not words."

"A faithful husband captures a woman's heart," he said matter-of-factly. Leanya shook her head and said:

"No woman expects a man to be faithful to her. Men love variety. Try again."

"My father was faithful to my mother. She was his only wife," Korli said, stroking the titillating Sande scars on Leanya's arms.

"Do you know what he used to do behind her back? Rascal men often look innocent."

Korli thought of a rejoinder to prolong the argument before trying another answer. He was luxuriating in the sweet scent of Leanya's powdered neck, armpits, and hair lotion. The sensation stirred his mind, his heart—and blood. He became a bundle of feelings.

"I've never married before," he said quietly, "but I think men—or even women—who love variety don't get satisfaction from their partners. They always quarrel and fight. There's much more to married life than pleasure, I believe."

Leanya gave him another of her seductive smiles, raising her round face with its dimpled cheeks in his face. Korli couldn't believe his eyes, his ears, his feelings. It was a dream, he thought. He had thought love was but a succession of wounded hearts. Now he knew that it elicits joy, an incomprehensible radiance, a buoyancy that lifts one up to the heavens. Yes, Leanya is right—action and personal contact make love real. He pressed his palm in her soft body.

"If man and woman don't get pleasure from each other's bodies, do you think there would be anything like marriage?" Leanya said. "Hold me tight, Korli."

"Pleasure must be at the bottom of their relationship," Korli agreed, pressing Leanya harder and close to his body. "However, if there's nothing else to it, they get tired of each other. Every heart has a void. When the right partner fills yours, nobody else can get into it. I think that's why some marriages last for many years. "

"Stop dodging my question," Leanya said with mock annoyance. "You're talking about something impossible. Nothing can fill the void in the human heart except the God who made it."

"The things that capture a woman are good clothes, a beautiful home, household utensils—"

"Material things are good," Leanya interrupted, "but they don't give a woman lasting satisfaction. The happiest people in the world are poor, Korli. The answer to the riddle is simple. Maybe that's why you're struggling with it. Think."

Baffled, Korli cried out, "What then?" Leanya watched him with a smirk as he hung his head to reflect. Swarms of ideas whirled in his head until it began to ache. Coming to a decision, he said, "Two things capture a woman's heart, not one."

"I know of only one, but if you think there are two, I'd like to know," Leanya said without debate.

"If a woman's husband satisfies her in bed and gives her children, he has captured her." That should do it, thought Korli.

"You have failed the test," Leanya told him with laughter, holding his hand, their fingers interlacing. "True, a woman gets pleasure and satisfaction from her husband and children, but her husband captures her heart by eating her cooking well. Do you know why?"

"Well, then I'll eat your cooking everyday to your satisfaction!" Korli said, happy to know what mattered most to Leanya. He put his arm round her shoulders and held her tight against his side. She was trembling. "I thought women despise greedy men, for greediness impoverishes homes," he said. "My only problem is, I don't like eating alone. If you don't mind, I want to be eating with your brothers."

"Why not?" said Leanya. "It's our custom. Eat with them and other men as well. You're now part of our family and this town. I'll keep the rest of your food for tomorrow." Leanya tied the bowls of rice and soup in a headtie and resumed her seat. "How long will you be with us? One year? Two?"

"You didn't tell me why women love men who eat their cooking well."

"If a man doesn't eat his wife's cooking, it means one of two things: either he is angry with her or some other woman has fed him."

"Suppose a man eats your cooking well but doesn't do his homework, it won't bother you?"

"Men work hard, Korli; sometimes spend all their energy cutting down the forest, or hunting, or fishing. I won't hold it against my husband if he is tired as you were last night—and needs rest. But people have to eat everyday unless they are sick, worried, or angry."

"I've learned something new from you. You're a good teacher—Leanya, I'm on traveling feet. I might be here for a month or two to hunt before going. I don't want to go to the kwii world empty handed. Besides, strangers who overstay their visits become burdens on their hosts. It's better your hosts miss you than get tired of you."

"You're no burden on us," Leanya retorted. "We love you because you're brave and kind. We're praying for you to make this town your new home."

"You and who are praying?"

"Everybody in Kuntaa, especially my family. Do you think it's a small service you've rendered us? That bushcow made life hard for us. Without an armed man accompanying her, a woman couldn't put her foot in the bush. That animal consumed most of our crops, especially rice and cassava. We were starving!"

"You're spoiling me, Leanya," Korli said, tousling her hair and stroking her cheek with his fingers. "You make me feel like a married man. Your words are sweet and gentle, and you're deeply concerned about my welfare."

"Korli, no law decrees that you live on the coast. Don't you like it here? Are we not good to you? Live with us; I'll take good care of you."

"I like it here, and you people are very good to me, but it's only on the coast that I can fulfill my goal."

"What goal? Marrying a *kwii* woman? Women are the same regardless of where they live, how they look, or what languages they speak. It's better you marry one with your background."

Korli didn't like discussing his plans with people because they might get into the wrong ears. Denying Leanya's suspicion was enough.

"I won't marry a *kwii* woman," he dismissed her fears. "My wife must be a Kpelle woman. Why should I go to the end of the world looking for what is available at home?"

"Available in Kuntaa, you mean. Why are you going to the *kwii* world, then?"

"I don't like talking about my plans, Leanya," Korli said, feeling that only the truth would stop Leanya's inquisitive prying.

"Why? It's good you discuss them with someone who cares about you. You might get ideas that can help you fulfill them." As she spoke, Leanya trifled with his shirt collar and laid her head on his breast.

"Although we can't live without making plans, it's good to remember that God has a plan for everyone and only his plan works. So, it's risky to tell people your plans. You might not live long enough to fulfill them."

"Let's assume that you'll live to get gray hair. What would you like to do with your life if you were that lucky?"

Korli said, "Work for money. Go to school. Return home to help my people. No one will support such plans, especially my going to school at this age. It sounds foolish, but nothing is impossible to do once you are determined."

"You had better marry your tribal woman before going to the *kwii* world, Korli. You'll be tempted to marry a *kwii* girl if you don't. Women can live without men for a long time, but men can't live without women for a single moment. If you want to explore all the women in the world before marrying, you might end up with none or with sickness—or become too worn out to be of use to the one you settle with."

"Finding the right woman to marry is a problem. That's why some men go from woman to woman until they meet the one meant for them."

"That's an excuse to be promiscuous," Leanya shot back. "The right woman is the one who loves you. Men look for women who are beautiful, wealthy, or connected to eminent families. They're often disappointed. Beauty fades, and wealth can vanish within the twinkling of an eye. It's hard to live with people from influential families. Some consider themselves more important than others. Only the marriage based on true love lasts." Leanya yawned and laid her head in Korli's lap. "I'm sleepy," she said.

"Are you telling me indirectly that you want to be my wife?"

"I thought you were a *kenamu*," Leanya said crisply and laughed, then lay more comfortably.

Korli felt sleepy, too, but he was enjoying the conversation so much that he didn't want it to end. As a means of keeping awake, he caressed Leanya's braided hair with one hand and touched her firm breast with the other. She did not restrain him. The blood rushed to his heart, and he became a bit alert.

"You're right," he told Leanya in a steady voice, though a knot grew in his throat. He swallowed hard. "It's dangerous to go from woman to woman—or from man to man. I remember a pretty girl in Haindi whom many boys wanted to marry shortly after our graduation. She couldn't make up her mind to stick to one of them. She went from boy to boy until she developed womb trouble and ended up with no husband."

"Why not stay here with us, Korli?" Leanya repeated her invitation, raising on an elbow and looking at him from the corner of her eye. "I'll make a good wife for you. We have the same mind. The *kwii* world is dangerous! Here, we are poor but safe and happy." Sitting up and hanging her head thoughtfully, she said, "You're in love with me; are you not?" She gazed at Korli's face with a coy smile

"Do you mean it, Leanya?" Korli said, pressing her against his body with his left arm. It was his first time meeting a girl who wasn't shy about making her desire known. She knew what she wanted and went after it. "Yes, Leanya," he answered her question. "I love you from the bottom of my heart. Please marry me!"

Pretending not to have heard him, Leanya said, "It's unusual for a woman to propose love to a man, eh? Women have feelings, too!" Abandoning her playful look, she trifled with her towel for a moment and said, "It's you men who speak with double tongues. Maybe you never thought any other girl would love you after what Gwanya and Korpu did to you. Forget them. What belongs to you comes to you eventually. Although we're just meeting, I feel that you're the right man for me." Rising to her feet, she opened her towel before him long enough for him to see the little *bombor* she was wearing underneath. Then she retied it firmly and went to lock the door. Korli's heart jolted when she resumed her seat and laid her head in his lap again. Now she was completely in his hands. He could have her if he liked. No girl had ever been the aggressor in his love affairs. He always took the initiative but with caution, a mistake for which he had twice paid a heavy price. "This is a dream," his mind told him despite his physical contact with Leanya. "Though she is passionate, I'll behave myself because where people hold you in high esteem, don't take advantage of them. But maybe I'm worried over nothing. People normally lock front doors after dark." He looked over at her and was surprised to see she was already asleep. Talking aloud, he said, "Everybody has gone to bed, Leanya. Your mother might be concerned about you."

"What?" Leanya opened her mouth and yawned.

"It's bedtime! Your mother might be waiting for you."

Leanya sat up, faced him squarely, and said, "Do I look like a baby? Look at me, Korli, and answer my question." She clasped her hand in his. "I'm a grown woman. My parents want me to get a husband and a home of my own. Once Father has ordered me to take care of you, Mother knows that I have to be with you. Are you not afraid to sleep in this big house by yourself? Apart from all that, I hate walking in this town at night. Witches are flying all over it right now! I'll spread my lappa on the floor and sleep there if you don't want me to share your bed."

Korli had no more doubt that Leanya loved him sincerely. This was his opportunity to get a wife. He wouldn't let it go. How sure was he of getting the right girl after building and furnishing a house? When and where would he find a girl so astute, beautiful, and strong like Leanya? He'd cross this bridge tonight, right now! Otherwise, she might be for some other boy tomorrow. What should he tell her? How should he begin? At a loss for words or a method to break the impasse, he was happy when Leanya saved him the trouble by taking off her *bombor*, lying naked and full-length in the bed against the wall, and covering herself snugly with the thick wide homespun bed sheet. Undressing, Korli lay tentatively on the edge of the bed, then went under the homespun. Leanya sidled close to him, her fiery breasts touching his chest. They grabbed each other hungrily. Until pepperbirds woke them up next morning and they were on their way to the farm, Korli couldn't believe that he had slept with the most beautiful girl in the world and made love to her. Leanya went to their house and put on a yellow blouse and a lappa before they proceeded to the farm.

As if somebody else were whispering the words over his shoulder, Korli told Leanya on the outskirts, "Leanya, I love you. Please marry me." There was no reply. Again, he was afraid Leanya pretended not to hear him. Perhaps he should get another girl to liaise between him and her. Girls wanted men to get them through a third party, or people might think they had given themselves cheaply to men. Being a stranger, he knew no one to trust with the negotiation. In fact, it seemed unnecessary. Leanya had extended him an invitation and proved her sincerity by sleeping with him. Some evil spirit or witch must be the cause of his troubled relation with girls. It wasn't a matter to shrug off. He'd look for a Spirit Zoe to drive away the evil spirit haunting him and give him a love potion. Noting that his silence bordered on depression, Leanya rescued him with a question:

"How sure are you God made us for each other? I hope it isn't because of the little dream we had last night." She chuckled mildly.

Korli felt elated. He had been torturing himself with misconception. Leanya had been thinking about his proposal. What should be his answer to her question? If he says it was her beauty or kindness that inspired him to come to this conclusion, she might say that he was in love with her body and service, not with herself. After reflecting on possible replies, he realized that nothing justified love. Either it was there or it wasn't.

"I just happen to know that we're made for each other," Korli said. "Meet several other girls to make sure you really want to marry me. Until then we should be mere friends," Leanya said, to his dismay. He thought he *had* just made his choice after encountering several other girls.

"Passion is not love, Leanya," he said gently. "So the dream we had last night has nothing to do with my proposal. I need a companion, not simply a bedmate—someone I'll treasure in my heart, worship and serve for the rest of my life. Do you doubt me?"

"I have no reason to doubt you. I want you to be ready for marriage before I accept your proposal. I don't want us to marry and you go with other women."

"When a man meets the girl meant for him, their spirits agree," Korli maintained. "That's what has happened between us. You feel that she's the only girl in the world."

"You've met only three girls so far," Leanya said. "The first two disappointed you, so you didn't really meet them. I'm the only one you have truly met. How sure are you that our spirits agree? Why not befriend several others to be in a better position to make a choice?"

"Leanya, I don't pretend to know how spirits work. But they work."

There was a long interval of silence. Seeing that Korli had nothing more to say, Leanya decided to end the discussion.

"I see how difficult it is for you to explain the feelings you have for me, Korli," she said soberly. "Who am I to debate what the spirit decides? Korli, I'm yours. I agree to be your wife. Please be kind to me. I want to bear your child. I might already be carrying it. You never know. I'll tell Data this evening that we're going to marry."

"Thank you, Leanya, for healing my wounded heart," Korli said. "You've made me the happiest man in the world. Your pleasure and satisfaction will always be my only concern in life."

He laid down his gun and cutlass and Leanya set the food down. They hugged each other so passionately that they grew breathless. For a long time they stood hooked together as if they had grown that way. They couldn't find the words to express their joy.

"I wish someone were here to bear witness of your promise for the day you leave me for another girl," Leanya said at length.

"God is here," Korli said. "If I leave you for another girl, he'll be both the witness and the judge. Only death will take me from you.

Suppose you leave me for another man?"

"It'll never happen—only death would part us."

"I wish my mother were here to meet you."

"Don't worry about your mother, Korli. You're no longer a child. When conditions become favorable, we'll find her."

Korli had known all along that Leanya would accept his proposal. She had only wished to ensure that her love for him was mutual before making the final commitment. However, the speedy manner in which their love had progressed raised a question in his mind. Was she really looking for a husband or someone to help support her and her people? Her invitation to him to live in Kuntaa suggested this motive. Korli decided to give her a test to determine if love rather than mere convenience inspired her consent to his proposal.

"Leanya," he said, "my only concern is my journey to the coast. Taking you there won't be fair to you. I don't know what problems await me there. A man can withstand any hardship, but not a woman."

"What do you propose to do? Leave me here and go? Who told you I can't withstand hardship? Don't you know that women are tougher than men? The Sande teaches us how to survive in the most difficult situations. I can stand by you in any struggle. My love is not based on what you have or can do for me, but on what we can do together to lead a happy life. My parents love and trust you, Korli. So don't worry about them. Let's marry and go wherever you wish."

Korli wondered if Leanya had rehearsed that speech and the previous ones in expectation of this encounter. It was thoughtful, deep, and earnest. Her heated manner of speaking showed that she was angry because he had doubted her sincerity.

"I wanted to go ahead and prepare the way for you to make you proud when I carry you there—make me proud, too. A woman needs the nice things of life such as clothes, jewelry, enough to eat, money—and a decent home where she can live as she likes."

"Korli, those things will come later through hard work. Let's marry now and be together. I don't want some other girl to capture you on the coast—or anywhere else."

"No other girl will ever capture me besides you, Leanya. Let's marry tomorrow and fight together. Since we now belong to each other, I'll tell you my true story. I only highlighted parts of it for you until I was sure you are mine."

Korli began with his childhood antics up to Nuulaa's strange revelation and violent death and his painful parting with his homeland. When he came to the time he decided to drown himself for killing his mother in childbirth, which he had never told Leanya before, she stood nonplussed in her tracks, turned round slowly, and watched him with batting eyes. When the rueful story ended, her eyes were swimming and her lips were twitching, but words could not come.

"Korli," she said after a long pause, "I'll be everything to you: a wife, a friend, a brother, a sister, a mother, and a father." She wanted to say more but a knot grew in her throat and tears streamed down her cheeks. She wiped her face with the tip of her lappa, and they walked in silence until Korli stated that Nuulaa's story was like a fishing net; it couldn't hold water. He told her that it had occurred to him that he wanted to sacrifice him to win the chieftaincy election.

"As you can see, you're the only family I have now, Leanya," he told her. "I too will be everything to you. We'll work hard to raise a good family."

They met the women busy cooking and the men, including two Deputy Chiefs of Kuntaa, drinking palm wine Zolu had brought. Two big gourds foaming with the potent milky drink sat in the middle of the shed; some spilled down the gourds and made puddles on the dirt floor.

"Welcome, *Demilahn*, welcome! Join us!" cried Zolu who prided himself on making the strongest wine. Everybody smiled at Leanya, for the nice blouse and the lappa told everything. Zolu filled a big white cup and handed it to Korli, who sat comfortably on a bamboo *gbehgbeh* and drank to his fill.

Leanya made another fire to cook for Korli.

"The young love is on fire!" teased Ma Gbavor. Everybody laughed, embarrassing Leanya and Korli. "You mean to say the man won't eat from anybody else, including his mothers, but you?" Leanya only grunted selfconsciously, took a bucket, and went to the creek for water.

"She's learning how to care for a husband," said Nyanle, the Chief's third wife. "House keeping looks easy but it's difficult."

"She's really taking too much time to learn," said Maashu, the Chief's second wife. "She should remember, however, that there's farming to do. Preparing your husband's bath and fixing up the house shouldn't take half the day." There was more laughter.

"Who told you the young man wants a wife from Kuntaa?" said Ma Gbavor. "Young men come here to enjoy themselves; when they want to marry, they go home."

"Men get wives more easily from other lands than from theirs," the Chief said. Defending his daughter, he said in a deep voice, "Why this talk of marriage, anyway? Leanya is only doing a job I gave her. Our duty is to be kind to strangers, expecting nothing in return."

Feeling that the conversation had cast doubt on his integrity, Korli did not want it to end like that. Clearing his throat, he said solemnly:

"Chiefs, mothers, brothers, and friends, I have something important to say." The men adjusted themselves in their seats and looked at him attentively. The women abandoned the cooking, sat on low stools, and trained their eyes on him soberly. "I've fallen in love with this house and would like to be part of it," Korli declared emphatically. "I came to Kuntaa as an orphan, but God has given me a family. Chief Gbakayu, I'd like to marry your daughter Leanya. I promise to take good care of her." Giving the Chief a silver dollar, he said, "This is my word. It comes from the bottom of my heart."

Meanwhile, Leanya arrived from the creek with the bucket of water on her head; she placed it by the fire she had built. Noting the solemn expression on every face, she was afraid Korli had burst their secret.

"It's good you have come," the Chief told her. "The stranger you're caring for wants to be your husband." Leanya pursed her lips, sat on a stool, and turned her back to the crowd. Happily, the Chief did not press her further.

"Korli," he said, "thank you for your word. May this discussion we've started end in moonlight."

"Let it be so," everybody responded heartily.

"May God and the ancestors guide our deliberation and support any decision we make."

"Let it be so."

"Korli, I accept your proposal." Rousing applause and exclamations! "Welcome to my house! You needn't produce a father, mother, uncle, or anyone else to represent you. I'm certain you'll take good care of our daughter, for you are a faithful, strong, kind, and responsible young man. Before we go further with this matter, cut the log." Leanya made no objection this time, for Korli did indeed owe the family a fine for sleeping with her before their marriage.

"My cold water!" cried NanGwoi. "My gown! I'm vexed! Korli has taken my wife from me!"

Korli gave Old Man NanGwoi a dollar coin and said, "I owe you cold water and a gown. This is my word."

NanGwoi received the coin in a shaking, pallid hand, watched it in his open palm awhile, and slapped it on his forehead. It stuck—a sign of good luck. Putting it into his pocket, he thanked Korli, prayed that God would replace it with many more, blessed the expected union, wished them many healthy children, and promised to intercede for them in The Place of Truth. Then he wiped his moist eyes and hung his head moodily.

"Gwoi, hold back your tears," Chief Gbakayu told him. "This is a happy day for us. For many years we've been praying for it. God has answered our prayer. You'll soon hold Leanya's baby as you've always hoped." The Chief's soothing words did not lift NanGwoi's depression. He smiled only when the women fawned on him.

Diving into his pocket, Korli produced another silver dollar and displayed it in his palm for all to see. Then he handed it to the Chief and said:

"I hereby cut the log."

"Thank you," said the Chief. "The second bridge to cross is Leanya's mother. She brought this beautiful bride into the world. Gbavor, Korli says he wants to marry our daughter," he said. "The matter reaches you." Handing her the coins, he said, "This is his word and the cutting of the log. What do you have to say?"

Ma Gbavor looked at the coins for a long time and handed them to Leanya.

"Leanya," she said, "Korli says he wants to marry you. This is his word together with the cutting of the log. What do you have to say?"

"I agree, Mother," Leanya said without hesitation, to the hearty applause and laughter of the gathering. "Korli approached me on this matter this morning," she added. "I gave him my consent and planned to bring it to Data's attention this evening. Being too young, he isn't acquainted with some of our traditions, so he has done it himself. I fully agree to be his wife. I love him."

"Gbakayu," said Ma Gbavor with a bright smile, "since our daughter Leanya loves Korli and has agreed to marry him, I approve the marriage. May they live in peace, good health, happiness, and prosperity." "Let it be so," the crowd responded.

"May they have many children who will give us water to drink and put our old bones away."

"Let it be so."

"Thank you, Leanya, for giving us a prompt and positive reply," said the Chief. "Korli, we'll cross the next bridge in town. Neither Gbavor nor I own this child though we brought her into the world. Her owner is my eldest brother, Bema, who is too old to come to the farm. We'll see him this evening for his approval. Zolu, you and Dieley carry plenty of wine to town for the ceremony, and kill my biggest billy goat and three red roosters for the festival." Zolu and Dieley left immediately for their wine trees.

Dancing joyously, the women hugged Korli, telling him that Leanya now belonged to him. They thanked her for her speedy reply. Ma Gbavor pulled Leanya into the dance and prevailed on Chief Gbakayu to join it too.

"Some girls take weeks to say no or yes," cried Maashu, "because they think a quick reply might make people lose respect for them."

"If you love a man, you don't take much time to agree to his proposal," said Nyanle.

"All you need now is getting a big gown for Old Man Bema," Ma Gbavor told Korli. "For years he has been praying to live until he holds Leanya's baby. He'll approve your proposal without problem. He doesn't need anything much. A piece of kola nut or white coin will do."

4

PUNISHMENT

AS THEY PREPARED TO GO TO TOWN, Korli noticed that the flock of bluewings that had flown from the forest in the morning was returning there to roost, crying hysterically. Shortly after they disappeared, a wren, chirping strangely, flew over the Chiefs' heads in the kitchen and sat in a pepper bush near the rubbish pile. Korli knew that the birds were not only ushering in the dusk; a stranger bearing disheartening news was coming with great reluctance. To avoid alarming the people, he kept the birds' warning to himself, but his eyes flitted so frequently between the roadway to town and the kitchen that the Chiefs watched him with questioning eyes.

Dodos confirmed his fears when they began mourning the dying of the sun, at which time a disheveled young man appeared on the edge of the village with a bunch of green leaves in his left hand and the handle of a cutlass poking from his right armpit. The messenger's languid walk without eye contact and the green leaves he carried meant only one thing—a Poro Master was on his way to Chief Gbakayu. Always on the alert for a visitor from home, Korli was the first to see and recognize him. He announced in a guarded tone that the messenger was Kpenkeh, a home mate and childhood friend of his and a fellow initiate of the same session of the Poro society. Understanding what was afoot, the Chiefs stiffened and hastened to meet the messenger as the women scampered into a hut for refuge. A somber mood descended on the village. Korli was afraid his home Master whom he had tried to elude had caught up with him after all, and would put him under arrest. Despite his pounding heart, he walked calmly with the Chiefs to Kpenkeh who dropped the leaves and the cutlass at their feet and embraced him coldly, then bent down for the Chiefs to touch his back with their fingertips. Standing straight and gazing at Korli with level eyes, he said loudly:

"The Overlord of Haindi is coming to arrest you for the murder of Nuulaa Gbunakpele Bharsi, the Chief Zoe of Fuama Chiefdom and your father. I ran ahead to warn you of his imminent arrival. Gbanchon told the Land that you have made Kuntaa your new home."

The men stared at Kpenkeh speechlessly, their mouths open. A Master's visit, whatever the reason, always boded danger. After a moment of bleak silence, Deputy Chief Gboyo declared:

"This Gbanchon is careless indeed! Certainly, his mouth is not initiated."

"No! Not at all!" agreed Deputy Chief Bono. "He may have a grievance against Korli. You ever double-crossed him?" he asked Korli.

"No," Korli admitted. "I had very little to do with that man. I don't know what made him betray me."

"Regardless of what grievance may exist between men, it doesn't justify betrayal," said Chief Gbakayu. "It's against Poro laws." Staring at Kpenkeh's lean and hungry look, he tapped him on his bony shoulder and said, "Let's go to the kitchen for you to eat something, rest, and take a swim in the river. You look hungry, weary, and scratched all over! I'm Gbakayu, Chief of the Kpelle Quarters of Kuntaa. These are my deputies," he said, pointing at Chiefs Gboyo and Bono by turn. "Coming all the way from Haindi today by bush road?"

"I slept in Mawua last night and came by a hunting path," Kpenkeh said. "A rough journey it was—I must hurry back. If they meet me here, they'll consider me a traitor. I'm the only child of my mother, and I have nothing for ransom. I came to alert Korli because we died in the same session of the Poro."

Meanwhile, Zolu and Dieley arrived with the large gourds of wine they had been sent for. They stood with apprehension by the kitchen, watching the drama and wondering what had gone amiss. Their father beckoned them with his arm.

"The Big Thing of Haindi is coming to Kuntaa," he informed them. "Zolu, run to Zoe Ballah's farm and tell him to abandon whatever he's doing and come to me at once. Dakena should be in town repairing his house, so he'll receive and accommodate the Haindi Master and his followers until we go to town. Dieley, bring the messenger a piece of dry meat and some wine. He's going back immediately. Kpenkeh, thank you for the information. It isn't our fault you're returning home hungry. You're always welcome here. All men should follow me."

"Thank you for the meat and wine, Chief," said Kpenkeh. "Don't blame yourself for my hurried return. We've become one family because you've accepted my brother into your home. We'll see each other again. I hope all goes well."

As the Chiefs walked into a little Kpaan west of the village, Kpenkeh told Korli, "You were a fool to let a woman stop your journey in Kuntaa. Couldn't you carry her with you? Now you're in danger because of the betrayal of that talkative drunk. If I were you, I'd leave for the coast immediately. In four months the incident will become nothing but an amusing tale. Some wild boys accompanying the Overlord want your blood."

"Running away will only postpone a solution to the problem," Korli said. "They will forget it until the day I appear in Fuama. Besides, they might go after me with witchcraft. Kpenkeh, a *kenamu* doesn't advise another to flee danger. Let the Overlord come for us to settle this matter one way or the other. I stopped in Kuntaa to hunt before going to White Plains. I don't want to go to that strange world with empty hands. The girl Gbanchon is talking about is not only beautiful but hardworking, friendly, and intelligent. It's a shame that many of you who died with me in Poro are married and having children while I'm still single. We were just about to marry. I hope this trouble won't change our plans— What's new at home?"

"Korli, get out of the Master's reach until his anger cools down. He is dangerous, and you can't fight him! He's very angry!"

"Why? Because I was lucky to escape death? Let him come, Kpenkeh—let him come. A small ax can cut down a big tree, and a person dies but once. They'll meet a man like themselves. The sooner we settle this problem the better life will be for all concerned."

"You are an unusual man, Korli. I see danger looming over you to the end of your life. Brave men are admirable but they don't live long. Your trouble is the only news in Haindi. Afraid that war might break out between your family and Gborlorkpilii, many people fled the town yesterday. We buried your father without ceremony because of the way he died, and sent word for your brothers to come wash the blood from the Land. If they come repentant and give the Land white kola to appease the ancestors, all might go well although Gborlorkpilii is demanding blood atonement. Your mother and sister were beside themselves with sorrow and weeping after hearing of the incident, but Sande Zoes comforted them. Your brothers will have to carry them away for more comforting. We heard that four soldiers were on their way to Haindi, but they stopped in Mawua to collect provisions before reaching us—"

"They raided Kuntaa on their way," Korli cut in. "Made everybody run away from the town. I didn't witness the raid, but I heard all about it. It's strange, Kpenkeh, that people who consider themselves civilized love living on the blood and sweat of other people."

"They'll be disappointed in Haindi, for they won't find anybody there. A dozen of us young men took cover in the Kpaan waiting for them. We missed you because you and Bhiliwoo were the only ones who could handle soldiers. He alone can't do much. Well—goodbye, my friend. I can't tarry here long. I have to go back to the bush. Some of the Master's haughty followers may be on their way here. You're old enough to take care of yourself. There're plenty of forests round here to hide in— and there's the river too."

As he went to the assembly, Korli felt aggrieved. Circumstances might again deny him the opportunity to marry; this time he might lose his life. But he'd stare Fate in the eye and affirm his right—fight for it if necessary. When he was a child some of his peers always found fault with his looks and doings. They said his eyes were too big, his nose too large, and his ears too wide. They scorned him for being a recluse who shunned men's company and feared danger. He had overlooked the malicious provocations for years, but they persisted until he fought his attackers. He winced when he thought of the heavy blow he had sent into Napa's mouth costing him a tooth and much blood. Now as a man he was subject to the same torment. What had he done to deserve it? One thing he knew: If he was going to die, he wouldn't die alone.

He met the men standing under a huge *beleh* surrounded by a clump of trees farmers had spared for a mini Kpaan. They were engaged in a heated debate, making wild gestures as if preparing for war. There was no measure to their discontent.

NanGwoi was speaking presently, waving his thin arm in the air. He'd have Korli escape by crossing the Deyn and going to a settlement such as Millsburg or Arthington—or Monrovia itself—to get out of danger. Retreat, he said, was not defeat but a strategy for victory.

"If the Master follows Korli to the *kwii* world, he'll get into serious trouble with the government," he declared. "Years ago the government confined the Poro society to the interior."

"It is not advisable for Korli to run away," said Deputy Chief Gboyo. "The Master already knows that he is with us. If he catches us in a lie, we'll lose our self-respect and status as full-fledged *kenablaa*. In fact, he won't rest until we produce him. Were Korli wrong in this matter, perhaps he could go undercover. But even then, that won't be advisable. How can you say you're a man if you're afraid to bear the consequences of your action? We shouldn't let the Master destroy an innocent man. If he can't settle for anything less than war, we should fight!" "Yes, we should fight!" cried the gathering.

"The Owners of the Land," Korli addressed the Chiefs, "I don't want the blood of anyone else but mine to flow for this matter. This war is my war. As Chief Gboyo said, I'm innocent. If the crocodile I shot turned into a human being, nobody should blame me. Let them shed the blood of an innocent man if they like, but they'll pay a heavy price for it."

"You are brave but badly mistaken," admitted Chief Bono. "You can't fight the Master. No man can. His decisions are final. The Chiefs were talking about a fight between Zoes and Masters, not ordinary men like you and me. Besides, once you're in this land, any war that comes upon you is our war. Yes—you were on your way to the coast, but Fate ordained that you stop here. So Deyn Gola must fight for you. If we fail to protect you, you may take matters in your own hands."

"Let's go to town," said Chief Gbakayu. "Who knows, the Haindi Master might already be there waiting for us. Korli is not a stranger in Kuntaa any longer. He has become my son—a son of the soil, not by birth but by love. We will protect him with our blood if necessary."

"Two men should remain here to guard the women," said Chief Gboyo. "We might meet the Master or his envoy on the way."

"No," said Chief Gbakayu. "The women are going with us! The Haindi Master never told us in advance that he was coming to Kuntaa. If we meet him there or on the road, he'll have to excuse the women."

Korli looked round the kitchen for his gun and cutlass but saw neither of them. Thinking that someone had put them in the kitchen attic for safe-keeping, he climbed up there and fruitlessly searched all over it. "I'm keeping your gun and cutlass until this matter is decided, if they're what you're looking for," Chief Gbakayu told him. "In your disturbed condition, we can't let you handle weapons. You're not the type of person to think twice before acting. After the bad wind blows over you, you'll have your gun and cutlass. Don't worry. Your head will not remain in this trouble. The Master will only exact a heavy fine from you because he knows you're now part of my family."

Fortunately for Korli, they soon learned that the Master changed his mind at the last moment and would not come to meet them in town. He didn't want to cause a disturbance, and, since tribal laws did not back criminals, he trusted the Chiefs of Haindi and Kuntaa would see to it that justice was done. If they failed to handle the crisis, it would become a problem for the Masters of the two towns.

In the meantime, Chief Goffah led a delegation of four elders and four young men to Kuntaa. They retired in the town's Kpaan almost at sundown and sent a messenger to Chief Gbakayu to inform him of their arrival. Zolu caught up with the Chiefs on the outskirts of the town and said that Zoe Ballah could not come because a *seney* thorn had pierced his foot, but he was with them in spirit and power. A reputable upriver Zoe, Ballah exercised greater power when he was absent from the scene of a crisis. With this assurance and Dakena's presence in town, the Chiefs were confident that nothing would go amiss. A bunch of fresh leaves lying across their path on the edge of the town informed them that they had eminent visitors in the Kpaan awaiting their arrival. By sending a deputation, the Haindi Master did not want the case to explode, the Chief thought. They went straight to the Kpaan and met Chief Goffah and his delegation.

"You didn't see my messenger, then?" asked Chief Goffah as he embraced his colleagues.

"Probably lost his way," said Chief Gbakayu as he and his deputies snapped fingers with members of Chief Goffah's delegation. Early stars appeared in the sky and playing commenced in town, to Chief Gbakayu's delight. The sound of drums and voices would take much of the tension from the delicate meeting.

The conciliatory manner in which the discussion began and proceeded disappointed Korli. The two Chiefs and their retinues had snapped fingers amiably; Chief Gbakayu had presented Kuntaa to Chief Goffah with wine and white kola and lengthily introduced his deputies to him. Chief Goffah reciprocated by introducing members of his delegation to him. Korli considered these courtesies necessary, but when the Chiefs began telling jokes, myths, and legends interspersed with laughter, he smoldered with anger, for he had expected them to engage each other immediately in a heated discussion of the case at hand. Had Chief Gbakayu forgotten its urgency and the stern position he and his deputies had taken on the farm?

In reporting his mission to Chief Gbakayu, Chief Goffah had initially emphasized the unity of the two tribes by blood, culture, and history. Then he went on to explain how intermarriage had made a majority of them bilingual.

"We are one people," Chief Gbakayu agreed. "It's *kwii* people who have divided us with arbitrary boundaries. In some cases, members of the same family or tribe live on both sides of a boundary!"

"Do you know that the best singers in Kpelleland sing in Gola?" said Chief Goffah.

"The same thing happens here in the reverse," admitted Chief Gbakayu. "When we get our freedom, our children will correct this mistake."

"Don't talk about freedom," warned Chief Goffah. "The government will not like it because white people have never ruled this country."

"The black people ruling it are doing exactly what white people did in Sierra Leone, Guinea, and the Ivory Coast—but what is your mission?"

Clearing his throat Chief Goffah, who looked tipsy, said, "We came to confer with you about your son Korli who took the life of the Chief Zoe of Fuama Chiefdom Nuulaa Gbunakpele Bharsi." Goffah spoke without emotion. "When a life is lost, people wait to see what happens because death has a claim on everyone. Korli overreacted to a threat, so he must make amends for the murder. A crocodile was swimming in the river at noonday. It did nothing to him, but he shot it out of fear."

"Thank you for bringing this matter to our attention," said Chief Gbakayu. "It's another proof of the unity of our two tribes. You could have simply walked into our territory and captured your citizen, but out of love and respect for us, you have put the case in our hands. May it end in harmony."

"Let it be so," everybody responded.

"May this discussion further strengthen the friendly ties existing between our two tribes."

"Let it be so."

"May whatever decision we make be consistent with the will of God and the ancestors."

"Let it be so."

Korli was pursing his lips, biting his fingernails, burning with impatience, and wondering when the dreamy old men would come to the problem at hand.

"What I understand from my son is that the crocodile chased him to the shore," said Chief Gbakayu. "He was only lucky to have shot it. Had he not done so, the story would have been different. I don't think a man with sound mind will wait until a wild beast attacks him before defending himself." Chief Gbakayu paused for Chief Goffah to respond but there was none. "Since we're all full-fledged *kenablaa*," he continued, "I can expose the secret behind this incident: We heard that Nuulaa wanted to sacrifice this fine young man to win a chieftaincy election. Had Korli seen a palpable human in the open and shot that person, his action would have been indefensible. But crocodiles are just as dangerous as leopards, lions, snakes, and all other predatory beasts. Will you let a leopard attack you before you shoot it?"

"Whatever happened can't be undone," Chief Goffah said. "Someone has died by the hands of someone else. This is the problem. The circumstances in which the death occurred do not matter. The blood of a human being has tainted the Land and is crying for atonement. This matter is certain to reach the ear of the government. They'll want to know what we did about it. If they learn that we took no action against the killer, we'll be in great trouble. The ancestors too must be appeased; otherwise, accidents, sudden death, and every conceivable disaster will plague the Land. I needn't explain these problems to you."

"Quite true," agreed Chief Gbakayu. "But now that Korli is a member of Gborlorkpilii, should he bear the full weight of the law?"

"That reduces his sentence," said Chief Goffah with a relieved smile. "He did well by joining it. For years his father urged him to join it, but he refused, saying it was a waste of time. Since he is now one of us, he'll enjoy the mercy of the Land, but he must appease the ancestors with one cow, four billy goats, and ten pounds cash."

Korli heaved involuntarily and looked at his father-in-law with anxious eyes. He wanted to make a statement but the Chief waved a restraining hand at him and placed his finger across his lips.

"We can't dispute a decision of the Land," declared Chief Gbakayu. "The Land has the right to require anything of us, whether we commit a crime or not. But this punishment is too heavy. We bow to the knees of the ancestors for mercy."

"In addition," Chief Goffah went on, indifferent to the appeal, "Korli will be confined at the Shrine for four days, eating only raw cassava and kola nut. That should satisfy the ancestors and the government. Since Nuulaa is now beyond recovery and he died by accident—the government might even punish us for maintaining the water society—we can't execute a man for his death."

"We're going to *hang heads*," said Chief Gbakayu beckoning to his deputies and Korli with a shake of his head towards the town.

On their return from the brief consultation, Korli fell face-down to the ground and stretched out his arms as he had been advised to do. The Chiefs and Dakena placed their hands on his back.

"I appeal to the spirits of my ancestors to forgive my crime against them," he cried out. "Who am I but a poor, fallible human being made for the dust. My father-in-law will present what I could afford for the fines."

Chief Gbakayu gave Chief Goffah ten kola nuts in place of the tenpound fine as an appeal to the ancestors for mercy, two billy goats (which he said represented four), and five pounds cash in place of the cow to wash the blood from the Land. Then he added another pound to redeem Korli from the four-day confinement at the Shrine.

Chief Goffah stood up and declared that he was but a servant of God, the ancestors, the government, and his people. As Chief Gbakayu knew, no Chief could alter their decrees, which he had been appointed to carry out on pain of death. If the appropriate fines were not paid, the Land would live under a curse and suffer unexplained deaths and disappearances; devastating storms, floods, lightning; and wild animals' attacks. Even Golaland would not be spared for harboring the offender. He'd rather execute Korli than subject the Land to such dangers. So, if Korli actually regretted his crime, he should pay the fines in full and bear the confinement to save the Land needless misfortunes.

"Elders and men of Haindi, is this not our word?" he cried.

"Yes, it is!" cried his delegation.

Korli suddenly rose from the ground and pushed aside the men touching his back. Several staggered and almost fell. Flexing his muscles and looking at the gathering with a grim face, he said, "If the Land is not satisfied with the compromise we have made, I have nothing more to say or do about this problem. I shot a crocodile, not a human being. If the crocodile turned into a human, it is not my responsibility. Is there a law in this country that forbids killing crocodiles? I regret the incident, but it isn't my fault at all."

Before Korli could say another word, the four young men of Chief Goffah's delegation attacked him viciously, each trying to hold one of his limbs. But, having planned in detail what to do in case of attack, he knocked one of them down with a succession of blows that stunned everybody. The fellow fell in a turf of grass as Korli kicked another attacker in the groins. He fell to the ground with a heavy thud holding his stomach and moaning piteously. Seeing the harms inflicted on their mates, the other two attackers, who were small in stature, withheld their participation in the fight. They stood aside watching Korli with apprehension.

"Stop!" cried Chief Gbakayu, grasping Korli by the arm. "You have spilled dirt on the Land. That's another fine you ought to pay. If you keep on fighting, we won't defend you anymore. You'll have to settle your problem with your homeland before we resume further relations with you."

Gravely disappointed, Korli collapsed on the ground and cried like a baby. The Chief and his deputies had failed to support with action the brave talks and promises they had made on the farm. He put up no struggle when Chief Goffah's men tied him to a cross they hurriedly made from young trees. Unable to bear the sight of his son-in-law as a bondman, Chief Gbakayu tapped his counterpart on the shoulder and said:

"No execution."

"No execution," Chief Goffah replied as he gestured to his men to start the journey to Haindi. But then he suddenly changed his mind and said, "No, let Korli stay while I accompany the Chief to town."

Chief Gbakayu ordered Dakena and two other men to help guard Korli. The Chiefs and their elders went into the palaver house to deliberate until daybreak.

At sunrise Gbakayu turned the town over to his guests with white kola and feasted them with plenty of rich foods and wine. While they were conversing, Maashu came in, bent double, and pinched Chief Gbakayu. The Chief went with his wife to his house and met Leanya lying unconscious in her mother's bed, Ma Gbavor dabbing her with a wet towel. A crowd of Sande Zoes who had been administering all sorts of herbs stood around in a somber mood staring at her helplessly.

"She fainted since we arrived from the farm last night," said Ma Gbavor. "She thought they had killed her husband. We told her that it wouldn't happen as long as you were around, but she didn't believe us."

"Leanya! Leanya! Leanya!" the Chief called his daughter loudly. There was no reply. Thoroughly shaken, he sat down to keep steady. "Zoe Wua," he called the Chief of the Sande Zoes who stood at the head of the bed, "take her to your Kpaan and make sure she recovers. Tell her they won't kill her husband. I won't permit it! We'll only pay a fine. They'll take him to Haindi to be back in four days."

On his return to the palaver house, Chief Gbakayu informed his guests of his dilemma. They sympathized with him but demanded full payment of the fines and Korli's four-day confinement before his release.

"Your son-in-law will be in our hands until he meets the demands of God and our ancestors fully," said Chief Goffah. "Sorry for the inconvenience, but, as you know, tribal laws have no exception. Our administration of them is done under the eye of God and the ancestors. So we'll imperil the safety of the Land if we let a violator of any of their laws escape punishment. Further, your son-in-law wasn't repentant. We came in peace for reconciliation, but he fought people I authorized to arrest him. That offense we can forgive because it was meted on us, but that which was done in violation of tribal law can't be forgiven."

Despite Chief Gbakayu's pleas, Chief Goffah and his men took Korli to Haindi that night.

Zoe Wua and her deputies succeeded in rousing Leanya with herbs. They explained the entire situation to her and urged her to be brave. Nothing would happen to her husband, they said, for the killing was an accident. Her father would only wash the blood off the Land. But Leanya was unsatisfied. She went on a hunger strike, vowing not to drink a drop of water or eat a grain of rice until she saw Korli. Chief Gbakayu had no choice but give up one of his two remaining cows and four of his billy goats, which Zolu and Dieley collected from remote villages the following day and took to Haindi with the required ten pounds.

Upon his release, Korli met his mother in a state of collapse on the porch, two Sande Zoes holding her by the arms and several other women standing around, looking on with concern. A group of men stood below the porch expressing amazement; they were unable to look each other in the eye. Two of them peeled from the group and greeted Korli without words as he approached the house. He had fond memories of his home despite the pall of gloom that descended on him. Climbing to the porch, he saw his mother sitting on a mat, wet all over with herb water; her hair tousled and littered with scrambled herbs. Looking stunned and mute, her eyes closed, she was leaning forward, her outspread hands resting on her knees. One of he Zoes shook her by the shoulder and shouted in her ears:

"Felenkpeh, Korli has come! Open your eyes and see him!" A Zoe fastened her lappa over her dangling breasts. She opened her pallid eyes languidly, breathed a heavy sigh, and stared at Korli with disbelief.

"Is that you, my son Korli?" she said weakly.

"Yes, Mother," Korli said, laying his hand on her shoulder. "I'm sorry you are sick, but everything is over. Don't worry, Mother. I'm all right."

Felenkpeh shuddered, gasped, and fell backwards in a faint. Gathering her in her arms, Zoe Wua tried unsuccessfully to make her sit upright. She let her lie still while two of her assistants dipped towels in a bucket of herbs and dabbed her from head to toe. Korli's brothers pulled him gently away when his eyes closed and his breathing became labored. He collapsed below the porch in the sand. With the help of several other men they took him to the Kpaan as voices cried for Poro Zoes. It was round midnight when he emerged slowly from the coma, speechless. They took him to some other house, telling him that his mother was going to be all right. He wouldn't see her until the following morning because Sande Zoes were tending her. Felenkpeh remained in the Kpaan with the Zoes until daybreak when she came to and they took her to her house. She asked for Korli but they wouldn't let him in the room. He stood at the door and told her not to worry. His brothers would take care of her while he continued his journey to the coast. It wouldn't be long when he'd come back to see her.

"Mother, I now have a wife," he called in a loud voice. "Her name is Leanya, the daughter of Chief Gbakayu of Kuntaa. We'll come to see you before we go to the coast."

Korli left with tears in his eyes. Kpenkeh accompanied him to Kuntaa while his brothers saw after their mother. Everybody feared that any encounter between him and his mother would result in their death. Some people commented that their love for each other was overwhelming, while others maintained that they probably shared the same *kaaseng*.

Korli and Kpenkeh arrived in Kuntaa late in the afternoon. Finding no one in town, they went to the village where they met Leanya sleeping on a *gbehgbeh*, her mother and stepmothers pounding rice for the next day's meal. They were relieved and joyful on seeing Korli, though he looked lean and haggard. They hugged him warmly, and thanked Kpenkeh for bringing him to them alive. They took them to Leanya.

"Your troubles sent our daughter to bed since yesterday," said Nyanle. "As you can see, she is sleeping well; the worst is over. She almost crossed the river last night. Prayers have power, my son. They saved her life. She thought they had killed you despite the Chief's assurance that they wouldn't. You had better marry her and take her to the coast right away."

Ma Gbavor called her daughter who only twitched and resumed sleeping until she announced that Korli had come. Immediately she sat up and smiled. Korli hugged her with warmth and said:

"We're marrying tonight and going to White Plains tomorrow. God has let the bad wind pass over us safely, so don't worry. All will be well with us. I wanted to take you to my mother for her to see you, but I don't think we'll have time for that. Besides, when she saw me, we both collapsed. When she learns that we're out of danger, she'll recover. My brothers are taking care of her."

"They almost killed you, it seems!" Ma Gbavor told Korli, staring at him aghast. "You look like someone from the grave!"

"I too almost killed two of them," Korli said. "They recovered, but they'll always remember the lesson I taught them."

"They were lucky you're good, or they wouldn't have survived those deadly arms of yours," said Maashu.

"Why did they set upon an innocent man?" said Ma Gbavor. "Thank God for sparing his life. I need grandchildren. We had planned to sleep here due to Leanya's illness, but I think she can walk now. Her brothers brought her here in a hammock for fresh air. They and their father have gone to their wine trees. They'll follow us to town. The Chief said when you come, you may have your weapons. They're in the attic."

Leanya, Korli, and Kpenkeh ate some food Ma Gbavor gave them, and they all went to town, taking their time in light of Leanya's condition. The moon was up, so they had no problem traveling the narrow path. Since it was late, the marriage was postponed for the following evening. When the Chief and Leanya's brothers came to town, however, playing commenced immediately. The people were happy for Korli's narrow escape from death and the marriage that would take place the following day. Happy beyond measure, Chief Gbakayu spent lavishly. The people had more than enough gin and palm wine to drink. They played until sunrise when the Chief killed three goats and a sheep for the marriage festival. After eating to their fill, the players bathed, dressed, and resumed the dance.

By sundown, in the presence of elders, the family, and friends of the family gathered in the palaver house, Korli gave Old Man Bema ten silver dollars for his gown, another ten to NanGwoi for his, and ten pounds to the Chief as Leanya's bride price. He promised to do more for them when he began working in White Plains.

It was a simple ceremony, which Chief Gbakayu performed on behalf of his infirm brother. Splitting a kola nut in halves, he gave onehalf to Leanya and the other to Korli. Leanya gave hers to Korli and Korli gave his to her. They ate and drank to the rousing applause of the crowd.

"Give me my kola nut," Korli told Leanya.

"I can't give it back to you," Leanya said.

"It means you'll always be my wife," Korli told her amid rousing applause.

"Give me my kola nut," Leanya told Korli.

"I can't give it back to you," Korli said.

"It means you'll always be my husband," Leanya told him. Another applause.

Speaking in a solemn mood, Chief Gbakayu said in a cracked voice, "We are entrusting our heartstring to your care, Korli." His wives wiped his neck and face with their headties, smiling in his face and dancing around him. "Never let hardship, sickness, or wicked advice separate you two. May God and the ancestors bless you people with beautiful, healthy children."

"Let it be so," everyone answered.

"Any man or woman, young or old—who causes confusion, witchcraft, or trouble in your family—may we walk on that person's grave."

"Let it be so."

Drum and *geeh* players roamed the town in honor of Korli and Leanya all night. Drinks were overflowing.

Despite his desire to leave Kuntaa right after his marriage, Korli was constrained to spend two months there hunting because he had spent nearly every cent he had and was indebted to his father-in-law. He was happy he had married at last and that his trouble with Gborlorkpilii was settled.

A week after the marriage, Korli took his wife to Haindi for his mother to see her, but he learned that his brothers had carried her and their sister beyond the river to Lorla Clan. Leanya gave two lappa suits to Chief Goffah to send to her mother- and sister-in-law by anyone who went up to Lorla. They returned to Kuntaa the following morning.

"I want to continue my journey to the coast," Korli told Chief Gbakayu one evening when the two months had ended, and he had acquired a substantial quantity of meat. "Since I'll work on a farm, it's good I go now because the rainy season is almost here. I don't know how to thank you for all you have done for me. Leanya will be coming back occasionally to bring you something and see how the family is faring."

"I wish you well and God's many blessings, Korli," the Chief said. "I'm sure you'll make it because you're brave, determined, and young. We need a son of ours in the *kwii* world to fight for us. It'll be a hard struggle, my son, but with God, the ancestors, and Leanya on your side, you're bound to succeed. Don't worry about paying back what I paid for you. Once you take good care of my daughter, I will feel more than repaid.

"Ask for General Diamond Jackson in White Plains. He's a great sugar cane farmer and longtime friend of mine. He womanizes and drinks too much, but don't mind that. He's kind and friendly. Tell him you're from upcountry looking for a job to get money for your hut tax. Always sleep with a sharp cutlass under your bed in that Congo country, and never put your foot in anyone's yard without invitation. They sacrifice human beings in the *kwii* world as a matter of course."

5

THE SONGS OF BIRDS

WISHING TO MAKE THE JOURNEY to White Plains in one day, Korli and Leanya had planned to start before sunrise to avoid much of the day's blistering heat, but inexcusable delays made it impossible. Three times Leanya remembered something else she had forgotten to include in her bundle: a pair of earrings and a bunch of neck beads her mother had kept for her in her raffia bag, a lappa suit and two headties her father had stowed for her in his wooden box, a silver spoon and a glass mug she wanted to carry for Korli's use. Her mother and Maashu further prolonged the delay by going to the farm for a bucket of rice and a gallon of palm oil for them to carry. On returning to town, they cooked an elaborate dinner for them to "carry the water of the Land in their bellies" so that they would remember their homeland. Taking advantage of the delay, Korli checked several traps near the town, two of which caught a wild cat and a foulintonger. He turned the animals over to his mother-in-law.

"The journey is fruitful from the start!" said Ma Gbavor. "I pray that you people find happiness and good luck in the *kwii* world."

"We will, Ma," said Korli with the assurance of a diviner. "The worst thing that could happen to us has happened. We're going to live with people like ourselves. It shouldn't take long for us to know the secrets and temper of the place. Once we put our mind on what we're going for, everything will be all right."

"That's true, my son," said Ma Gbavor. "People usually get what they expect—what they work for. Don't let the ill-advice of friends distract you from your goal. It's good you drink only palm wine. Liquor breaks up family and puts people in trouble."

The Chief prevailed on Zolu and Dieley to help their sister and brother-in-law carry their loads and remain with them until Korli found a job.

"Help them until they settle properly," he said. "Or 'black boys' might rob or kill them. Strangers are their favorite prey."

"We'll be with them until they're properly settled, Father," said Zolu. "Making a home in a strange land is difficult and risky."

Their instant acceptance of the request was understandable, for the adventure of traveling to the coast was always a temptation for young men. They took two of the three large *kenja* of dry meat and Korli took the third. Besides Korli's bundle and hers, Leanya carried the bucket of rice and the food her mothers had cooked, which they couldn't eat because of anxiety for the journey.

The journey finally commenced by midday. Leanya's large family and friends, almost half the town, took them partway, asking them for keepsakes and admonishing them to be on their guard for the infamous 'black boys.' Korli gave them the few coins that remained with him. Exercising prudence, Leanya gave only a coin to her five-year old niece Worlikemaa who cried to go along, and a used headtie and lappa to old Zoe Wua, her initiator into the Sande, the first gift she received in the year. The wrinkled old woman had pressed the clothes to her bosom like a baby, thanking God with tears rolling down her cavernous cheeks. Multiple voices advised her to hold back the tears to avoid casting a shadow on the travelers' path. Leanya promised the rest of their well-wishers that she'd bring them gifts on her return. Those who were taking them part of the way would have to *cross water* before returning, otherwise, according to their beliefs, the travelers would find it impossible to cross the river of the death when they died. So the crowd walked until they slouched through a shallow creek below an incline, quite a distance from town. There, they exchanged farewells with the travelers and began to retrace their steps. Ma Gbavor stooped, covered her face with her careworn hands, and shook with stifled sobs. Several women and Chief Gbakayu held her by the shoulders, admonishing her to "send the children off with cheers and blessings rather than tears."

"Don't give them bad luck," the Chief told her. "A mother's tears are dangerous unless they're shed for joy or real misfortune. Let them remember smile and laughter on your face to give them courage in times of trouble."

"Leave them with God, the best caretaker," said Maashu. "This journey will be safe and sweet, for the day is bright and birds are singing."

"If I see tears on your face, you'll pay a heavy fine," said Zoe Wua in a tremulous voice.

Gbavor's weeping ceased only when the traveling party walked swiftly up the incline and bent a deep curve. She wiped her face with the tip of her lappa and gradually resumed her composure.

Leanya's toughness impressed Korli and her brothers. Although she was pregnant and carried the biggest load, she led them by many yards on the hilly deep-rutted path. Several times, she waited on the summit of a hill as they struggled up under their heavy *kenja*, grunting, panting, and perspiring. At sunset Zolu recommended that they spend the night in Gbojei, a short distance off the main road. Everyone agreed, given the strain and stress of the journey and the fading of the sun.

"Darkness is upon us," he explained, "and we are traveling with a woman, so we shouldn't try to make it to White Plains today."

"I have legs to walk on, my friend," Leanya retorted sharply, lengthening her strides. "You men are the ones wasting time." She raised her large bundle to let her neck rest.

"We can't do that to you," said Zolu, glancing at the sun. "We might meet up with the Master on the way. He loves traveling at night."

"Tell your Master the road is not for him alone," Leanya said boldly. "When it's overgrown, we women feed the men as they clear it."

Dieley and Korli took no part in the dialogue. They cleared their throats, a sign that Zolu was going a bit too far with talk about the Poro Master with a woman even though she was his sister. His tongue might slip, a mistake that could cost him his life. To save his brother's neck, Dieley changed the subject.

"White Plains is but half a day from Gbojei," he said. "If we leave early in the morning, we'll reach there by noon and do all the trading we want before dark."

"Why the big hurry?" Leanya said. "Selling the meat is a whole day affair. If you buy or sell things in a hurry, they cheat you. Let's take time and reach White Plains tomorrow evening, rest through the night, and do the trading the next day." No one debated Leanya's suggestion.

"Are the people of Gbojei hospitable?" Korli wanted to know. "I've never been there. Only this trip compels me to sleep on the way. I've always traveled with men, and we usually took one day to get to White Plains and another to be back."

"The closer you get to the coast, the more people are inhospitable," Zolu informed him. "Travelers sleeping in Gbojei must feed themselves and give its crabby old Town Chief much of their goods for lodgings." Zolu spoke in the high-pitched voice of an angry man.

After a long pause, Dieley declared in a similar tone, "People living in the coastal region don't make farm, hunt, or fish because they think they're civilized. So, they have nothing to offer strangers."

"We treat them like Chiefs when they visit our towns and villages— do everything for them free of charge!" Leanya said. "Why should they refuse to accommodate us?"

"Father says the coastal tribes used to be slavers," Zolu put in. "In the olden days, they waged war on the interior tribes, captured most of the young men and women and sold them to white people for salt, tobacco, clothes, guns, and gunpowder. They live by sugar cane farming, claiming that rice can't grow in Liberia."

"An excuse to be lazy! The coastal region is more suitable for growing rice than the interior," said Dieley. "It's rich in swampland. Rice loves water. They despise rice farming because it is difficult. They make cassava, eddo, potato, and sugar cane patches and rubber farms because they don't require much care."

"Coastal people live on eddo, bananas, plantain, potatoes, plums, oranges—but we of the interior prefer rice," said Zolu. "Perhaps the coastal people are afraid to offer us the foods they eat. We might not like it."

"They are simply mean and selfish," said Leanya. "They could offer strangers whatever they eat."

"Most travelers are not choosy about the food they eat," said Korli. "Their main goal is to survive until they complete their journey and return home."

"Sister is right," said Dieley. "Coastal people don't bother with strangers and people who aren't their relatives. Unless the blood running through your veins runs through theirs, expect nothing from them. They'd rather take the little they see with travelers than offer them aid. If things don't work out as we hope, we should go right back home. We didn't burn Kuntaa."

They arrived in Gbojei at twilight. The sky was dark and rumbling, so the people were indoors except a group of half-naked boys who watched them inquisitively as they walked to the palaver house. Two of the boys, the oldest ones, ran to the largest house on the southern edge of the town while the others stood round the palaver house, their eyes pinned on the *kenja* of meat. Zolu and Dieley threw knowing glances at each other, watching them closely. In a short while a tight little old man in a flowing white robe and skullcap, a surly expression on his face, breezed into the palaver house and slumped in a rattan chair a boy brought for him. It now drizzled and breeze was blowing; the rumbling of the sky turned into an occasional thunderclap.

"I'm the Chief of this town," said the puny man gruffly, viewing the strangers with a sidelong glance. "What do you people want?"

"We're on our way to White Plains," Zolu said politely. "We wish to sleep here and continue our journey tomorrow. Please give us lodgings."

Korli offered the Chief a deer haunch, a *teyli*, and a silver coin Leanya handed him. The Chief turned a sullen face from the meat Korli had placed at his feet as if he were insulted.

"Chief," Korli said calmly, "if the meat were ours we'd have given you more than this. Please take this little offer and give us a sleeping—"

"Don't lie to me!" the Chief broke in. "The meat belongs to you people! I know hunters when I see them! Is this not your gun?" he pointed at the gun leaning against the low wall of the palaver house by Korli. "One deer haunch, a baby *teyli*, and a dollar are nothing for our hospitality!" He paused to catch his breath. "We on the trade route always shower travelers with great hospitalities," he continued, "but after selling their goods in White Plains, they take a different route when returning home, forgetting about us. Let me have three more deer haunches." As if that settled the case, the Chief hung his head morosely, awaiting compliance with his demand.

Korli glanced at his in-laws and Leanya; they nodded. Speaking to the Chief in a conciliating tone, he said:

"I'll give you one more, Chief. Soldiers took most of this meat from us on the way, putting us in trouble with their owners. We are your children. So please accept our small offer and give us a sleeping place."

The "hospitable" Chief lodged them in a dilapidated, one-room house on the edge of the village. It had neither a bed nor chair. He gave them nothing to eat, nor kitchen utensils to do their own cooking. It was fortunate Leanya had brought food. Zolu and Dieley fetched firewood on the outskirts and built a fire in the house, where Korli and his wife slept on a lappa on the dirt floor. The brothers slept in the palaver house not only because it was forbidden for them to sleep in the same room with their sister but also to watch over the house. Occasionally, a boy acting like a scout would stalk round it but bounce away when Zolu or Dieley coughed. Gradually, the drizzles ceased after midnight and the moonlight bathed the countryside.

"I wanted to ask the Chief to let us spend at least a week here while I look for job in White Plains," Korli said when they began the last leg of their journey early next morning. "But it's better we go. That grumpy old man looks mean and wicked."

"We had to keep an eye on the house all night," Zolu said. "Had we not done so, they'd have sneaked in because it doesn't lock. Several times a scout came by to find out if we were sleeping. Brother," he told Korli, "always be vigilant in the *kwii* world."

Walking faster than the day before, they arrived in White Plains by mid-morning as Dieley had predicted. They sold the meat to market women from Monrovia for a good price. Korli gave Leanya money to buy cooking utensils, clothes, and other materials for herself and her people. He also gave his brothers-in-law substantial amounts to buy whatever they wished for themselves and their families. Leanya cooked a hasty meal on the crowded market ground. After eating, Korli told them a new plan he had made.

"From our experience in Gbojei, I see for myself that the coastal region is dangerous," he said. "I don't want to expose you people to its hazards, especially Leanya. Let me remain here to find job and lodgings, then go for Leanya. You people should return home and expect me in a month." Giving the gun and hunting bag to Zolu, he said, "Take them to the Old Man as an assurance that I will come."

"Korli, are you sure you'll come for me?" Leanya said, wiping her eyes with the tip of her lappa.

"Leanya," Korli said, placing his arm round her shoulders, "I know I'm hurting your feelings, but I don't want any harm to come to my beautiful wife whom I've just married. Were this place upcountry, we'd have no problem. Whichever way they beat the drum we'd dance it. I'll come for you before the end of the month."

"Brother is right," Dieley told Leanya. "He has a good plan for you people, but he must fight to carry it out. He won't win the fight with you on his back, especially in your condition."

"In case of anything, come to us," Zolu told Korli. "We'll explain everything to our parents. They'll understand. You'll need the gun to defend yourself!"

"If they see me with a gun," Korli rejoined, "it'll give them excuse to kill me."

"Whatever happens, we must reach home tonight," said Zolu, looking at the slanting sun. "I bought a flashlight. Sister will walk between us. The Master will give way once he notes that we're traveling with a woman."

Overtaken by emotion, Korli took his bundle, tore himself from them, and walked hastily down a double-trail, grassy road leading to a distant sugar cane farm on the riverbank. He did not look back.

As he walked through the sparsely inhabited old settlement with dilapidated framed houses, Korli thought his father-in-law was right in proposing caution for a stranger living in these environments. The houses stood far apart with thick, thorny bushes between them as if their residents were natural enemies. Built with plank and corrugated zinc, each one sat on pillars of huge boulders, three to six feet high, and stood on a three-acre plot of land. Each front yard had a colorful flower garden, and plum, butter pear, guava, and banana trees occupied the backyard. At one house, some dozen concrete steps led to a windswept porch on which sat the potbellied master of the home, dressed in black pants with suspenders and staring around—doubtless on the watch for trespassers. Korli wondered which house was General Jackson's but judged it prudent to find his farm and get advice from his workers on how to approach him.

Quickening his strides on the gravel road that wound through tall bushes, Korli climbed atop a hillock and saw plumes of gray sugar cane flowers covering both banks of the Deyn and stretching inland. Shimmering in the noonday sun, the river looked wide, deep, and stagnant. White seagulls with long yellow legs and beaks hovered over it. Surprising to him, he did not see a single canoe on the river, or a rice or cassava farm on its banks. Below the hillock, he ran into a short brawny boy. Awash with perspiration and panting under a large bunch of firewood on his head, the boy was crossing a sagging corkwood bridge with tentative steps. Dressed only in a pair of ragged short blue pants, the fellow held the firewood firmly with both hands, carefully taking one uncertain step after another, lest he fell in the squalid creek with its croaking frogs. Korli waited until the boy had crossed, placed his heavy burden on the grassy roadside, and taken a deep breath.

"Please direct me to General Jackson's farm," he asked him cordially in Kpelle.

The fellow looked at Korli darkly, took a rolled-up empty sack off his head, shook it out, and re-rolled it slowly. Korli wondered if he understood Kpelle or if he had unwittingly offended him. When he posed to continue his journey, the fellow greeted him in correct Kpelle.

"Good afternoon, my friend," he said with a smile that exposed a gaping hole in his upper teeth where two were missing.

"Oh!" Korli remembered his etiquette. "Since you look tired, I didn't want to waste your time with plenty of talk," he told the fellow. "Good afternoon, Friend! Are you well?" Korli greeted him formally and extended his hand to snap his fingers, but the boy ignored it.

"I'm fine, thank you. And you?" he said.

"Quite well. Will you please show me the way to General Jackson's farm?"

The boy now reached out to shake hands and snap Korli's fingers.

"See that cotton tree?" He pointed at a tall cotton tree on a hillcrest swarming with chattering *soya* down the riverbank.

"Yes." Korli had never seen so many yellow rice birds in one place.

"That tree is in the middle of General's farm," the boy continued. "You'll meet his workers." Placing the wrapped sack on his head, he lifted the bunch of wood with a grunt, laid it over the cushion, and set off.

"Thank you," Korli told him. But the boy did not reply. He was too busy climbing the hill, his bare feet pushing gravel behind him.

Sauntering to the cotton tree, Korli met ten well-fed men lounging near it on a turf of soft grass under the shade of a Christmas bush. They were engaged in a heated conversation, emphasizing their points with frantic gestures that bordered on hysteria. When he greeted them, they stared at him coldly and continued with their conversation, which competed with the chattering of thousands of rice birds in the cotton tree. Korli could not understand them because they spoke English. As he awaited their convenience, a bearded middle-aged man with grizzled hair peeled off the group and staggered to him.

"Those men are a mixture of Gola, Kpelle, Bassa, and Kissi," he told Korli and snapped his fingers, smiling amiably. "They speak English because anyone speaking a native language in a settlement is considered a bushman." The old man laughed wanly. "They're arguing over the advantages and disadvantages of living in a civilized country."

Nine pairs of interested eyes now focused on Korli. Another member of the group, sodden with liquor, the only one wearing long pants, leather shoes, and a torn long-sleeved shirt, joined Korli and the old man. Staring at Korli with dilated eyes, he drawled in broken Kpelle, thumping his chest with fingertips in concert with each word: "I'm Gbatulu, manager of this farm!"

The other men watched quietly as Gbatulu extended his hand to Korli for finger snapping. "What do you want, Friend?" he asked Korli as he slapped his callused hands into the visitors'. They snapped fingers roughly.

"I came from upcountry to General Jackson for a job to pay my hut tax. They say his farm is in this area. Will you please direct me there?" Korli spoke standard Kpelle in one breath, arousing the interest of several other men who joined them.

"Brigadiya? You're standing on his farm!" declared Gbatulu. "My

real name is Seward Daitumoi, but the fellows here call me Gbatulu—
bull's whip—because I make them work hard. I don't like laziness." There
was a brief concerted murmur of protest from the group. "I'm Kpelle,"
continued Gbatulu. "I don't speak it too well because Congo people
raised me. They forbid their wards to speak native languages. We have
plenty of work here for strong men. Are you prepared to work hard?
When do you want to begin?"

"No man looking for job will say he's lazy," a slim man with a
sheepish face remarked. "The man looks strong and determined. If he
could leave his family and come all the way here—"

"My question is for the stranger!" snorted Gbatulu, giving the slim
man an angry sidelong glance. "My friend, put your bundle down and eat
something. You look hungry! Musu, bring some leftover food! We have a
stranger!" Gbatulu called in a loud voice. "What's your name?" he asked
Korli.

"Gbamokorli," Korli said, laying his bundle in the grass and sitting
by it with raised knees. He ran his hand through his tangled hair and said,
"They named me after my grandfather. Korli is the short form I'm known
by."

"Was your grandfather a Zoe?" someone asked.

"Yes, but I didn't inherit his medical powers."

"Brigadiya went to Monrovia this morning on government
business," Gbatulu said. "But once you see me you have seen him. Here
is the cane farm—as far as you can see on this side of the river—we're
harvesting." With a sweep of his arm, he showed Korli the extent of the
farm, which covered the sky and bordered the river and the horizon. Piles
of harvested cane littered half of it.

A young bare-breasted girl with a beaming face emerged from behind
the Christmas bush with a bowl of rice crowned with palaver sauce and
placed it before Korli. Korli thanked her, watching her beautiful curves
curiously.

"I'm going for spoon and water," she said and left. In a moment, she
was back with a spoon and cup of water.

Five men, their arms riddled with marks of cane leaves, stood round
Korli as he ate. The others sharpened their cutlasses on granite
whetstones.

"You'll like it here," a youth of his age told Korli in fluent Kpelle
while his co-workers listened as if he were speaking on their behalf.
"General pays his workers good money—ten cents per day—and gives
them plenty of food," the fellow continued. "If you get in woman trouble,
he pays the fine and doesn't deduct it from your pay. I came all the way

from Kpatawee in Zorkwelle country near Gbarnga. Fled from soldiers who frequently looted every chicken, head of cattle, grain of rice, and drop of palm oil we had. Now what soldier is foolish enough to mess with me?" He assumed a militant posture and flexed his muscles.

"And there's no witchcraft here," the Kpelle old man said. "If anyone tries to kidnap or threaten you with witchcraft, tell them, 'I'm General Jackson's son.' The person will run away. He's known as General Pepper because he's responsible for many disappearances. Now he is a bornagain Christian—kind, friendly, and generous—attends Church regularly." At this, the other men murmured disapproval. A bitter taste welled up in Korli's mouth, and his heart pounded. He listened to the old man for more information, but he only chuckled and said, "Old men are immune from prosecution, aren't they?" exposing a cluster of tobacco stained teeth. "So, I can break any law with impunity and say what I want to say. With my two legs already in the grave, they're welcome to kill me. I'm looking for someone to bury me."

"Sleep in my *konko* tonight," the Kpelle youth said, diverting the conversation to everybody's relief. "You come from——?"

"Haindi, Fuama Chiefdom," Korli said.

"We're one family, then! My name is Saki Takparaya. I come from Sanoyea Chiefdom—Sanoyea town itself—the town of lawyers! Do you have a family?"

"I married only two months ago. My wife is staying at her home until I find a job. Since I now have one, I'll soon go for her."

"Where is her home?"

"Kuntaa."

"Went all the way to Gola country to find a wife?"

"She's Kpelle."

"Kuntaa is not in Gola country?"

"Kpelle people occupy half the town."

"Returning home after getting your tax money?"

"Saki, I'd rather live here to escape witchcraft and the menace of soldiers upcountry. What brought *you* here?"

"I was searching for a better life. Soldiers don't fool with people where I lived because the men there are hunters, so they have shotguns. My problem had to do with in-laws. They took nearly everything I earned. Marriage is slavery."

"If you want to know what slavery is, stay single," someone interposed.

"And there's no school or hospital upcountry," Saki continued. "The Zoes do well with herbs, sometimes curing diseases hospitals can't cure, but finding them is difficult, and there are many charlatans pretending to be Zoes. Here, when your children are ready for school, you can send them to some civilized family in Monrovia, and when you're sick, you get treatment from Public Health."

"It might sound foolish if I tell you I want to go to school at my age," Korli said. "That's the main reason why I came. I won't enjoy my education that long, but it'll pave the way for my children."

"A good decision, Korli. It's never too late to learn, as they say, and education pays. No one takes advantage of you, and you get a good job. Nevertheless, I'd rather help my children with their schooling. Once a month I take a few dollars to them to buy their copybooks and pencils. They're in Monrovia."

"I have an advantage over you. My first child will be born in seven months. Is there a school round here?"

"A government school is here, but the teachers hardly go to work. They don't get paid. I suggest you hire a teacher in Monrovia to help you. You can't sit with five-year old children in the same class."

When the girl collected the dishes, Korli watched her every movement until she disappeared in the Christmas bush. Observing his wistful look, a worker scoffed at him and said:

"Congo people have a song that says, *If you see my girlfriend you better pass by, for I ga' my razor bottom my shoe.*" There was hearty laughter from the men. Saki translated the song for Korli and he too laughed.

"A man has but one woman even if he marries a hundred," said the old man. More laughter. "Marrying more than one wife is taking responsibility for other men."

"This man has a good plan for his life," said Saki. "I don't think he'll let women spoil it. Which one of us doesn't admire the looks of a beautiful woman?"

"Time for work!" cried Gbatulu. "Da woman palaver your talking? We finishin' de task before quittin'! Korli, here you cutlass." He handed Korli a worn cutlass with an old black handle held together with black tape. "I want to see how you work before taking you to Brigadiya." He spoke the last sentence in Kpelle.

"Why do you welcome the stranger with a cutlass?" someone asked him. "Who says he speaks English?"

"No man is ever a stranger to cutlass, my friend. A man looking for a farming job must prove his ability to handle a cutlass. If the man is going to live here, he must learn English. The only way to learn how to swim is by jumping into a river." Gbatulu, whose Kpelle was improving with use, spoke mostly for Korli's benefit.

"Kpelle people live by the cutlass, anyway," the protester remarked as Korli began sharpening the cutlass. "Prove to him that you are a Kpelle man, Korli."

Korli admitted that he loved cutlass work, but the long journey had drained his energy. However, he said, he'd do his best. Though he began late, he cut as many canes as any other worker. All his co-workers admired him except for the old man who told him:

"Take it easy, my son. Even if you do ten men's job, Jackson will give you only one man's pay. This work looks easy but it makes you old before your time."

"For some men hard work is good," someone remarked. "They get sickly and unhappy when they don't work."

Korli spent the night at Saki's home, which was located by the river. Some wives of the other workers brought rice and crawfish to his wife "for the stranger." At six in the morning, Saki took him to a wine tree, where the workers gathered each morning for "tea" before going to work. In an animated conversation, Korli learned the history of White Plains as well as the names and reputations of its prominent citizens, including businessmen, lawyers, legislators, and pastors, many of whom Saki said were 'black boys.'

"Who are these black boys?" Korli asked, believing that he'd finally get an answer to that question, now that he was in the land of black boys. "I often hear about them, but I haven't seen any."

"I don't think you want to see any," Saki said. The workers laughed briefly. "They are kidnappers and cutthroats! But they only prey on strangers, so you have nothing to fear since you've become one of us."

"If you are drunk," someone told Saki sternly, "take your cutlass and go to the farm to sweat the liquor out. You may take over the stranger since you people are of the same tribe, but don't lie to him. Who says we have cutthroats and kidnappers here?"

"Under a wine tree, men are free to say what they like, and whatever they say remains there," someone said. "Let the man talk."

"Evil is everywhere," someone said. "Upcountry they have the Poro, Sande, spirit, snake, leopard, *gbon*, and water societies; down here, we have the Masons, the UBF, and IOGT. Korli," he said seriously, "have a cutlass in hand wherever you go in this settlement, and keep your eyes and ears open always."

After assigning the day's tasks to the workers, Gbatulu took Korli to General Jackson's moldy two-story framed house standing under a plum tree at the southern end of the settlement. The General sat slouched in a wide wicker chair browsing over a copy of the *Daily Listener* when Gbatulu and Korli entered the porch which was badly in need of repairs. He wore a pair of brown pants with black suspenders and a pair of black leather slippers.

"Ha!" he cried, whisking his head up to look at Gbatulu and Korli. "The Speaker is dead! I can't believe it! The man was with us at last night's society meeting! He wasn't even sick. How can he be dead this morning? We're in it again for the next two weeks. I'll soon be going to Monrovia… Gbatulu, what's the matter? You caught the rogues? Is this one of them? I won't get one bottle of liquor from that farm again!" He looked at Gbatulu and then at Korli with suspicion, smiled cryptically, and shook Gbatulu's hand, the chair creaking under his massive weight.

Placing his hand on Korli's shoulder, Gbatulu told the General, "I'm bringing you another strong worker; he wants a job to get hut tax money. He's Kpelle."

"Good!" said General Jackson whose smile broadened, displaying a huddle of crooked teeth. He appraised Korli with inquisitive eyes and snapped his fingers. "Your name?" he asked him in labored Kpelle.

"Korli," Korli said shyly, "from Haindi, Fuama Chiefdom."

"This is your home, son. Don't be shy. You're a fine-looking young man. If you have good ways in you, I'll tie you to this farm."

"I gave him a cutlass when he came, and he worked like bushcow!" said Gbatulu.

"Good," said the General. "Try him for one week. Start him with five cents and one cup of rice a day. Give him place to build his *konko*. When will you people finish cutting de cane, Gbatulu? And don't tell me one more moon. My gin finished." The general's tone turned somber and a scowl appeared on his face.

"Why you never tell me before?" Gbatulu sounded remorseful. "I will borrow one gallon from Jimmy. Before dis weekend we will finish cutting, sir. I'm on de boys dem back like hell! We will start brewing week after next."

"Fine. Give them hell! A country man is like a turtle: if you don't put fire on his back, he won't move."

Gbatulu gave Korli a two-room unfinished framed house some fifty yards from the river. Though incomplete, Korli loved the accommodation because it was near the Deyn, which reminded him of home even if it happened to be wide, stagnant, and deep at this point. He couldn't tell how life would turn out for him in White Plains, but he believed that his kind reception promised a bright future.

The following week, he ran to Kuntaa for his wife. He carried gifts of cash and articles of clothing, salt, soap, slippers, shotgun shells, and the like for his father- and mothers-in-law. They thanked God and the ancestors for the gifts, his success and good health—and staged a festival in his honor.

"Leanya was worried to death for nothing," Chief Gbakayu told Korli at a family meeting on the eve of their return to White Plains. "She had the Zoes of this land *cutting sand* to see her future and making sacrifices to ensure you'd come for her. She couldn't be comforted despite their reassurance. Thank you for the gun. I'll take good care of it until you need it. It's a lucky gun. I killed the male bushcow the other day with it. He was obviously looking for his wife; they move in pairs."

The Chief gave Korli two *kenja* of dry buffalo meat. Zolu and Dieley once again helped him carry them to White Plains where they remained and completed the construction of the new home. They expanded it to a four-room house, daubed and roofed with thatch.

Korli soon became the most productive worker on General Jackson's farm. The birth of his first son Junior bolstered his commitment to hard work. Puzzled by the workers' disdain for fishing, hunting, and farming, he set traps all over the cane farm and its surrounding bushes as well as dozens of fish baskets in the river, which caught no less than ten groundhogs and five buckets of crawfish per week, respectively. Each Saturday morning he gave the general at least three groundhogs and a bucket of crawfish—two groundhogs and some crawfish to Saki and Gbatulu. He sold the remaining catch to market women from Monrovia. At times when his job permitted him, he traveled by bush road to Dualah market in New Kru Town, Monrovia, to sell them at better prices. Korli also made a farm in the swampland at the northern end of the sugar cane farm, which Leanya always planted with rice, corn, potato, cassava, and pepper, most of which she marketed in White Plains. When he acquired substantial funds, Korli hired a mason and carpenter to plaster his house with cement, roof it with zinc, and furnish it. Once every three months, he sent Leanya home with gifts for her people and money to repay his father-in-law for the expenses he had gone through to release him from the custody of Chief Goffah. Nearly every week he invited his workmates to dine with him. They admired and praised him for his hard work, although Saki told him that some of them circulated rumors questioning his intentions. Saki said they referred to him as "that pitiful, illiterate, native boy," and wondered if he wanted to be a representative or senator for a Congo settlement. "The people say those Congo people will soon teach you a lesson," Saki told him.

No threats deterred Korli from working to the best of his ability and taking good care of his family and himself. In fact, they inspired him to work harder and be more generous than ever. After spending a year on General Jackson's farm, he decided he wanted to go to school, although he had no idea how it would happen. He knew of no Kpelle who had ever been to school, but he was convinced that it was the most practical means of fighting the aggression and injustice the *kwii* world unleashed on his people and himself. The general might expel him from his farm for the bold step, his co-workers warned him. They said it wasn't his policy to let any of his workers attend school even at their own expense. However, Korli hoped to convince him that education would make him a better worker. It'd enable him, for example, to keep records of the workers' production and pay. He'd then pay them according to their work rather than by their mere presence on his farm.

For two weeks Korli kept his catches of crawfish and groundhogs to present to the general the day he'd make his appeal. He made the appeal a day after the general became Chairman of the Deacon Board of Mt. Sinai Baptist Church. It was a Saturday. The night before, the general had drunk heavily in celebration of his elevation on the Deacon Board. He came home dead on his feet and dropped into bed after having his favorite dish, *dumboy* and groundhog stewed with palm butter. Waking up at noon on Saturday, he took a warm bath, had a bowl of *dumboy* and crawfish stewed with bitter leaf for lunch, and sat in the chair on the porch "to catch breeze." He skimmed an old copy of the *Liberian Star* apathetically, repeatedly taking lusty draughts from a large bottle of gin on bitter roots, which the elite called "the Constitution." When the eighty-proof spirit made him half-insensate, he took a dull look at the paper's political headlines.

"These boys are crazy," he exclaimed, laying the paper aside and looking away. The excitement revived his jaded spirit. "Who told them democracy means many parties? A single party can be democratic! Many parties can be despotic! They'll get in trouble with the Old Man. I'm sure this treasonable statement will come up in Monday's cabinet meeting, and these know-it-alls will be banished to Camp Belle Yallah, never to return."

Meanwhile, Korli, who had been awaiting his convenience for an hour under the plum tree, climbed to the porch and placed before him the tub of crawfish and ground-hogs he had brought for him.

"This is for you, General," he said and stood at attention several yards off.

"My faithful son!" the general declared, staring at Korli with a benign face. "May God bless you." Then he shouted, "Bendu!" A girl of seventeen appeared instantly. "Take these things inside," he said to her. "I'm swallowing *dumboy* again tonight!"

"Too late for *dumboy*, sir," Bendu said. "I finish cookin' collard greens and snappers. You swallowed enough *dumboy* this week."

"Whatever you say," the general said. "You de boss." Turning to Korli, he said, "What's on your mind this morning?" Korli was standing like a sentry, his tight lips suppressing a statement he was anxious to make. Usually he left immediately after delivering the general's meat. "Tell me what's on your mind, Son. You want another wife?"

"No, General, I want to go to school," Korli said with apprehension, scratching his head.

Growing sober, Brigadier General Jackson watched him with bloodshot eyes. Thinking he had offended the general, Korli posed to go.

"Stay," the general ordered him. "You didn't offend me. I hope you aren't planning to leave the farm, Korli, are you?" he said with a slight frown.

"No, no, sir!" Korli cried, shaking his head vigorously. "I'll be here while going to school. You've made me somebody, so I'll be with you until you're tired of me. When I go to school, I'll be of better service to you, sir."

General Jackson's face eased of its strain. He sighed and took another draught of the Constitution.

"Tired of you?" he said and belched. "Nonsense. Sit down. Maybe I should put you in the army. You stand like a soldier." Korli sat in a small rattan chair and clasped his hands between his knees, staring at the watering old eyes with entreaty. "Do you want to be a soldier?" the general asked him. "You'll make a good one—with those strong arms of yours— to go on patrol upcountry now and then to get us all the foods we need instead of torturing yourself hunting and farming."

"I might join the army after going to school."

"You're an unusual man, Korli," admitted General Jackson. "Ambitious—hic—determined—ho!—Bendu, bring me a cup of water!" The general gulped the water in one swig. "You have a vision for the future," he continued. "Education will help you get a well-paid job, but I'm afraid when you know book, you'll despise me and you'll leave this farm."

"No, sir," Korli said seriously. "Where else could I get the nice treatment you're giving me here? You've become a father to me!"

"That's good to hear, Son. I can't afford to lose you; you're doing for me what no other worker has ever done. Boys round here don't like work—and they steal! They tote my cane elsewhere at night while I'm sleeping, grind and distill it, sell the gin, and pocket the money. The farm really belongs to them. When they hunt, fish, or make a garden—a few of them ever bother with such—they don't give me a bite of meat, crawfish, or greens. They run away after getting what they want. God sent you to help me. As of today, you are my new headman. I'll get rid of that drunken fraud Gbatulu who joins the workers to steal my cane. Your new pay is twenty-five cents per day! I'll give Gbatulu something else to do lest he blames you for taking rice from his mouth. He'll run the old truck between here and Kakata. Yes, that's it! Transportation makes plenty of money."

Love for the old man mellowed Korli's heart as he gave his pathetic speech. Life had not treated him too kindly, Korli remembered Saki telling him. Inheriting the farm from an indulgent father who had inherited it from his indulgent father, the general had never run it profitably. It wasn't the job for a civilized man, he said. The managers he hired to operate it took most of the gin for themselves, only giving him enough for his root bottles. While his father Immanuel Jackson lived, he had no money worries. A committed farmer, his father gave him whatever sum of money he requested. He lavished it on clothes, women, and liquor. When he completed eighth grade, his paternal uncle, who was Secretary of Defense, created a sinecure for him in his Department. Diamond Jackson had no problem climbing the military ranks. On the nation's 100th Independence Day, the president commissioned him Brigadier General and decorated him with the nation's highest medal of honor, Knight Commander, *Order of the Pioneers of Liberia*, although he had never had any military training nor done anything to deserve such honors. For weeks the family celebrated the promotion with sumptuous parties notable for numerous brands of expensive imported liquor, abundant rich foods, and crowds of elegant merrymakers. Then the wind of independence had swept over Africa with its consequent power struggles and civil wars. The UN mandated Liberia and some dozen-member states to restore peace in the former Belgian Congo. Much to the family's delight, the president appointed Jackson commander of the Liberian contingent, but something unseemly happened. While giving the president and his Cabinet the farewell salute at BTC military barracks, Jackson had collapsed. Exceedingly angry, the president appointed another commander on the spot and imprisoned him. Jackson nearly died in confinement. Unable to bear the shame, his wife and children had gone to America where they had been living since. After his release the general remained in White Plains to fend for himself. A few of the native children he had collected for schooling, more than half of whom never saw the inside of a classroom, took care of him. Most of them had grown up, married, and left. He had had children by several of the girls, but they had gone with their children. Only the latest arrival, Bendu, still lived with him. So Korli understood why he was bent on retaining his services and would not let him go.

"I agree to your terms," Korli told General Jackson obsequiously. "Thank you, sir. I'll never neglect my duties, sir."

Smiling broadly, the general took a swig of the Constitution and said, "I believe that you mean what you say, Korli. You're a godsend. I'll stand for you if you want another girl. How many children you have?" His lips stretched with a smirk.

"One—a boy."

"How long have you been married?"

"One year."

"You're on schedule with your wife, but you married late." Korli smiled blandly. "You are behind schedule in having children. At your age, you're supposed to have at least three. You need another girl to help you. You may have Bendu. She's good. I'll get another girl to replace her. I don't sleep with girls any more. I get them mostly for my workers."

When a reply wasn't forthcoming, the general continued his prattle:

"I don't blame you for marrying late because everybody in the village is related: this girl is your sister, that one your auntie, and the other one your mother— I don't know why country people make life so difficult for themselves. It isn't your fault you were born in the village, however, but I'll blame you if you refuse to have enough children."

"Had I not fled my home, I won't have been married by now," Korli said. "I met my wife on the way here."

"What do you think of Bendu? She's well-trained, beautiful, hardworking, and friendly. Come here by nine o'clock tonight to know how good she is in bed. She has her own room. If your wife doesn't accept her in the home, she could be here for you. Try her for a week and see. Bendu!"

Bendu appeared again, looking beautiful, genial, vital, but Korli looked at her with unseeing eyes. Bubbling with joy for the opportunity of going to school, his mind was fully focused on how he'd blend his schooling with his job and other activities. He'd get a tutor as Saki had suggested. He couldn't afford to sit with five- or six-year olds and take the same lessons. He'd do at least two or three grades per year to catch up.

"This is your new husband," the general told Bendu matter-of-factly. "He is strong, hardworking, handsome, and sound of mind. He doesn't drink, he doesn't smoke, he doesn't run around with wild women—since he's been here, I haven't heard of a single woman calling his name and confessing a relationship with him. I don't want some foolish boy to make you pregnant and run away as it happened to Gbarnlee and Sata."

Bendu looked surprised. General Jackson's benign smile calmed her somewhat, but her eyes remained wide and vacant, her mind plunged in disarray. She had lived with the General for three years. He had promised to send her to school, but it hadn't happened. She was happy, however, that old age and liquor had worn him out, so he had never taken her to bed. A matter by far more serious struck her as she waited for Korli's response. She had befriended Leanya to make her feel at home. She did not want to put a wedge between her and her husband nor lose her friendship. She was happy Korli did not so much as snap her fingers. He looked withdrawn like one embarked on a long mental excursion. It was her first time seeing a man incapable of saying no or yes to a proposal.

"I have a pot on the fire," Bendu said after vainly awaiting a comment from Korli. Switching her stare from the general to him, she said, "When you're ready for me, come to the kitchen."

Astonished, the general told Korli when Bendu was out of earshot, "Don't tell me you're afraid of that fine girl. You seem to be the kind of man a woman has to chase—and force into bed. If you go with Bendu for six weeks, you'll see her belly bulging with a baby." He paused. "Tell me, why did you run away from your home?"

"My own father tried to sacrifice me to water people, but he fell in his own trap." Korli went on to explain the incident in detail, happy that the conversation had shifted to something else.

"Good for him," cried the general when Korli reached the climax of the story. "When the Kpelle man's stomach is full, he engages in mischief. Fear nothing in this settlement. You're under my umbrella. It's a good idea—going to school. You could attend an afternoon school in Monrovia. I hate night school. Get a canoe. Traveling by bush road, as you've been doing, is risky. Heart-men might catch you, and before you know it, you're finished. You could also use the canoe for fishing and trading in Dualah market. Bendu will always be here for you whenever you're ready."

"It's dangerous to be on the river everyday, sir, because of crocodiles," Korli said.

"I understand, given your narrow escape from your crocodile father.

Real crocodiles flee when they see people. It's Gborlorkpilii and *Niji* men who dress in crocodile skins that kill people and dump their corpses in the river, blaming it on crocodiles. But I'll get you a gun; when you kill two or three of them, they'll run away whenever they smell you. Korli, I'll see to it that you get a Christian marriage to become a pillar of this community. You have ambition! You need encouragement. Many country boys I know are only concerned with women when they become mature. After getting plenty children, they force them on other people to rear. You are different. One day you'll become somebody in this country."

Leaving quietly, Korli hastened to his wife with the good news. He felt greatly relieved, for the fulfillment of his long dream had begun. He appreciated Bendu's grace and charms, but he believed that marrying her was a hopeless prospect. General Jackson was drunk when he made the offer, so it was conceivable that he'd forget it when he sobered. His fickle position on the number of children a man should have supported this conclusion. At one moment he'd encourage him to have many children; at the next he'd denounce men who fathered many children. Besides, his offer was useless because polygamy was restricted to the interior where households needed many hands for the tedious task of farming. The economic problems of the *kwii* world and the teachings of the Church made monogamy more practical in that world. Saki had told him that General Jackson used women to trap workers on his farm. Once he gave you a wife, you were obliged to work for him forever because she'd scream objection in your ear if you as much as mentioned the word "leave." No—he had no desire to be in bondage. He wanted to leave whenever necessary, although as matters stood, he had no plan of going elsewhere. Life on General Jackson's farm made him happy, secure, and prosperous. His education would make that partnership even more advantageous and meaningful for him. Who knew? If he became literate and well informed about government operation and acquainted with people with political weight, he might get a well-paid job in the government. He hoped General Jackson would be alive to see that day. His greatest fear was hurting Leanya, to whom he had promised fidelity until his death. The impulse of the moment might be grand, intense, and radiant, but it was nothing but an impulse. It would pass away, leaving disaster in its wake. Gathering women under the same roof compounded troubles. He was a living witness to the problem. Perhaps if Leanya came up with the suggestion he might try it, but with the utmost reluctance and the clarification that she wouldn't leave him. A man can easily take in any child as his and bear all the expenses to raise it, but not a woman. He had seen many instances and heard many stories of child abuse and neglect by stepmothers. Should something go wrong—say an exchange of insults or a fight between Leanya and her partner—Leanya would definitely desert the home, perhaps leaving the children with him, making them vulnerable in the hands of a stepmother. For the present, the friendly relations developing between her and Bendu were good enough; he wouldn't let a competing interest mar them.

Korli withheld the good news from Leanya until the day's work was over and they had eaten supper and gone to bed. Leanya was more than happy to hear it. She congratulated him and said that she had been praying for his success. She asked him to pass to her whatever he learned. An educated man, she claimed, should have an educated wife; otherwise, they wouldn't be able to communicate.

6

THE PRICE OF SUCCESS

KORLI'S SUCCESSES AROUSED HATRED and jealousy among the workers and even among pillars of the community. Their grounds for complaint were his "accumulation of wealth", the "unusual privileges" General Jackson accorded him, his "phenomenal" rise to the position of headman, and his exercising of powers that had not been available to Gbatulu—powers not even the general used on them, as Bendu and Leanya informed Korli. Granted, the general had been constrained to remove Gbatulu from the headman position because of excessive drinking and other misdeeds, but he should have replaced him with a worker of long standing, not with "someone employed yesterday." As far back as they could remember, the general had been quite content with his regular supply of the Constitution, leaving the operation of the farm up to them. Now he had given Korli a shotgun to mind his farm, consequently closing a means of supplementing their meager wages. Korli lived in a commodious house like a government official and had a canoe for fishing and taking meat and crawfish to Monrovia for sale. The general had given Bendu, his only caretaker, to Korli as his second wife. Her close ties with Leanya were a concrete proof of the deal. Crowning their many grievances, General Jackson had sponsored a Christian marriage for Korli and held the reception in his house, something he had never done for any of them. All these went to prove that he did not appreciate their many years of diligent service. The scant pay and provisions he gave them were nothing compared to what he had given Korli. If he did not expel him from the farm, they would sabotage its operation. Leading members of the community also resented General Jackson's support and protection for Korli. They said Korli was pulling him by the nose. The president, who was courting the natives for votes, might make him a representative for White Plains even though he was illiterate and constitutionally barred from citizenship.

When the workers began carrying out the sabotage, Korli and the general became gravely troubled, for they paralyzed the entire operation of the farm as they had threatened. For two consecutive months a majority of them failed to report to work, claiming to be sick, although they wandered along the river and in the bushes setting crawfish baskets and groundhog traps. Most of the catches of Korli's baskets and traps were stolen. The sugar canes already cut went to waste because parts of the mill were either missing or worn out; the remaining canes ready for harvest were overgrown with weeds. Many of the workers, especially those who worked the hardest, left the farm secretly, and nobody knew where they went. Korli could not find replacements for them, for his damaged reputation dissuaded job seekers from applying to him. The farm was a total loss that year, but Korli redeemed it with a wise strategy. With the general's approval, he raised the workers' wages to twenty-five cents per day, increased their daily food rations to two cups of rice per person, built a tuition-free primary school for their children, and hired a nurse once a week to see after their health. These incentives attracted scores of employees who worked beyond the call of duty. They increased the size of the farm, helped Korli with his hunting and fishing, and safeguarded the sugar canes. Before the next harvest, Korli repaired the mill and gin production resumed on a grand scale. General Jackson's farm became a major supplier of liquor in the lower Deyn River basin.

The failure of the sabotage left the town council with no choice but to give General Jackson a strong warning. At a secret meeting to which he wasn't invited, they advised Township Commissioner Johnny Howard, who was infamous for brutalizing natives, to appeal to his drinking partner to "stop making that poor illiterate country boy frisky." Gbatulu, who engineered a campaign to expel Korli from White Plains, volunteered to accompany Howard to General Jackson's house.

With Gbatulu at his heels, the seventy-year old commissioner pulled together his scattered wits and fleeting energy at sunset and made the mile-long trip from his house up a steepening grade to General Jackson's home, arriving there, spent and breathless. When Bendu saw them entering the yard, she gave them seats on the porch, climbed the shaggy stairs to inform the general of their arrival, and returned with the information that he was indisposed.

"What happened to him?" asked the Commissioner. "Drunk?" He wrinkled his face.

"He hasn't been feeling well these few days," said Bendu. "His stomach bothers him a lot."

"It's the liquor!" cried the Commissioner. "Tell him we—I won't be long. Just a word or two—and I'll be on my way home."

Bendu sighed with resignation, climbed the stairs again, and came back with the general's root bottle and glasses for his guests. She filled the glasses with the fiery spirit. Gbatulu drained his immediately and asked for more. The Commissioner only sipped his drink.

"Take time how you drink this liquor," he advised Gbatulu, gazing at Bendu's shapely figure as she went upstairs the third time. "You're putting too much pressure on your heart and liver. This liquor is very strong—I believe it's eighty-proof!" He took another sip and coughed lengthily.

"The bitter root takes away the edge," said Gbatulu, clearing his throat and pursing his lips after swallowing a large dose of the throatburning drink.

Bendu clattered down and said the meeting would have to take place the following day. The general couldn't sit up in bed despite his effort, and he could hardly breathe, she explained.

Exactly at the same time the following day, Commissioner Howard and Gbatulu met the general slumped in the wide chair on the porch, skimming back issues of several newspapers.

"Ho! Mr. Commissioner!" he cried, straining to rise. "How you do?" He warmly embraced his drinking mate, and when they knocked heads together, he said, "You look pale! How is the malaria treating you?"

"The Constitution took care of it," the Commissioner said and sat down. "My trouble is lack of appetite. It's the booze I think. I'm trying to control it."

"You better control it! We tired burying people. Coffins are too dear nowadays. Cigars carried the Speaker to the great beyond and if you don't look out, booze will carry you there, too."

"I finish buying my coffin. I hope you've bought yours. You're nearer to the grave than I am," the Commissioner joked.

"Some people believe if you buy your coffin you live long. Others say you won't. Who is right? It's all superstition. When I give the matter a second thought, I tend to believe that you die soon if you buy your coffin."

"Why?"

"Because you think of nothing else but death," the general said. "You become miserable. Worry kills fast! I expect to live to be a hundred."

"Not at the rate you're drinking. Control your drinking, or you'll soon go to the great beyond. Liquor is the cause of your stomach trouble."

"Everybody has their appointed time to die. When your time comes, you must go whether you drink or not."

"You can shorten your time with drink. We who drink are gambling with our lives, my friend. In your case, you like women too. That makes it worse. I hope it isn't Bendu hastening you to the grave."

"Ha!" The general laughed in a self-abasing manner and belched. "I've retired from worshiping women," he said. "I'll never bow down to them again— Gbatulu, how's the truck?" he changed the subject.

"It needs repair, sir," Gbatulu wheedled. "Broke down in Kakata a week ago. A mechanic charged me one hundred dollars to fix it. The man taking care of it charged me twenty-five dollars."

"Hmm. Gbatulu, this is my last time giving you money to fix that truck. I gave it to you to make me money, not for me to give money to you. If I employ some other driver to run it, you'll say he wants to kill me." General Jackson told Bendu to bring one hundred and twenty-five dollars for Gbatulu. "Add five dollars to pay his way," he added as an afterthought.

The general trifled with a newspaper awhile, and then told Gbatulu, "You know what? The truck is now your truck! That's what you want to hear, isn't it? Take it and get rich! When a Liberian opens business it belongs to the employees. That's what you people did with my farm. Took it as your personal property. I was only lucky Korli came around. The day he leaves I'll close it— What brought you people to my poor little *konko*, Mr. Commissioner?" The general smiled companionably as if nothing disturbed him.

"Poor little *konko*? You're living in a mansion! We came to advise you about that son of yours—what's his name? Korli!" said the Commissioner. "The citizens say you've made him frisky! Get him out of here, or he'll disappear."

"I dare anyone to put hands on that boy!" the general blasted in anger. "I have no family and Korli is the only person helping me! He helps nearly everyone in this township, including you! Is this the 'thank you' you people want to give him? If something happens to him," the general jabbed his finger at the Commissioner, "you'll be the first to go. Why are you people after Korli? Because he is a country man? What's the crime he has committed? Giving you people groundhogs and crawfish? Has he killed anyone, lied on anyone, stolen from anyone?" General Jackson was sweating and panting. Bendu brought him a wet towel. He wiped his face and neck roughly with it and laid it aside.

Commissioner Howard and Gbatulu, who had not expected the stormy outburst, did not know what to say or do. After a long pause, the Commissioner stroked his bald head and tried to reason with the general.

"We're concerned about your welfare, too," he said quietly. "A man with ambition is dangerous. Korli is ambitious. He sees that your family isn't here, so he's using the opportunity to take over your property and enrich himself. If something happens to you, your children won't have anything to inherit. You brought all this trouble on yourself and the community. Why did you conduct a Christian marriage for an idol worshiper and hold the reception in your house, which you spruced up for the purpose as if you were having a party for the president of Liberia? You made him the headman of your farm; gave him a gun to guard you. What next? Are you going to make him our representative? That will happen only over our dead bodies."

For months General Jackson had been hearing rumors that leading members of White Plains wanted Korli expelled from the community, but no one had confronted him with the grievance until now. Prepared with ready answers, he decided to make short work of the case and be done with it, for hatred was like a disease; if tolerated, it festered. The general took a long drink, cleared his throat, and, calmly spacing his words, tried to reason with the Commissioner:

"The fellow is kind to everybody!" he said. "Your hatred for native people once denied you an opportunity to become vice president of this country. Get it in that gray head of yours that the country belongs to them also. Those proposing his disappearance want me dead. It will not happen. Johnny, let's talk of something else." The words had escaped his lips against his inclination, for the subject was like crab, which one can't eat with shame.

When neither the Commissioner nor Gbatulu put in a rejoinder for a long time, the general tried again to control his temper and clarify his position. Anger would only tip the scale against him.

"You people seem to know more about me than I myself," he said softly and took another swig of rum. "I need no bodyguard in this settlement or anywhere else. As a soldier, I expect to die any time. I gave Korli the shotgun to protect himself from crocodiles while fishing. If you're a member of Niji, you had better watch out. He also drives thieves from my sugar cane fields with the gun. Do you hear of groundhogs eating cane on any farm in this area nowadays? I'm sure those who profited from the theft are the ones engineering his expulsion." Gbatulu heaved, twitched in his seat, and averted his face in embarrassment. "If Korli worships idols—let's suppose it is true—if he is an idol worshiper, how will he turn to Christ if we don't expose him to the Church? God does not belong to the Jews or to the Americo-Liberians alone, or to white people alone. He is for everybody!"

"General," said Gbatulu, thinking that his intervention would bring the storm under better control and put out the smoldering fire before it blazed, "Korli intends to kill you—"

"Gbatulu," the general interrupted, "the Bible says everybody is appointed to die. Let him kill me if he likes. That's none of your business!" Annoyed, he took another swig of the Constitution.

"The fellow has been putting *juju* in some of the meat and crawfish he has been giving you!" Gbatulu continued undeterred. "How else could he win your love and trust so thoroughly? You don't listen to your old workers anymore! We have become your enemies!"

"What should I do to Korli? Kill him? Was his employment not based on your recommendation? Stop talking rubbish and be serious."

"You'll die of unexplained sickness one of these days!" the disgruntled former headman warned. "Imagine, you knew nothing about sickness for many years, but these days you suffer from heart trouble, stomach trouble, breathing trouble, bone trouble, bad fever, and so on. You've done more than enough for that poor country boy, General. Let him leave the farm—in fact, let him leave this settlement, as the Commissioner suggested! I never knew he was a leopard in human skin."

General Jackson coughed, took a long drink of the Constitution, looked askance at Gbatulu, and said, "Gbatulu, let me be frank with you. If something happens to that boy, you too will be killed. What makes you country people so jealous of each other? Your condition will never improve if you continue acting like that! Look, if that fellow wanted to kill me, he'd have done so long ago."

"General, we still need you around. If you die, the farm will become a ghost land."

"Gbatulu, my doctor told me that life becomes difficult when all is well with you. Now I'm getting more than enough to eat and drink—thanks to Korli—so I've grown too fat and lazy. That's why I've become sickly, but I'll soon resume my walking. I see nothing suspicious about Korli. I trust him with my life and the safety of this community. I trust him with everything! He has made me prosperous! Nobody's hatred or jealousy will make me expel him from my farm or from this settlement."

General Jackson was happy to have stood his ground against the threat Commissioner Howard and his cohorts had schemed for his favorite worker. It was no guarantee, however, that their position would change. Perhaps his militant stance might reinforce their determination to carry out their plan. With Johnny Howard, that drunken, heartless, indiscriminate killer, spearheading it, there was no telling what might happen. A man with one foot in the grave would not hesitate to carry with him anyone he perceived as his enemy. The animosity was undeniably directed against him personally, not Korli. Was his farm not the most productive in the settlement? Was it not well protected from pillage? Indeed, he had cut off the supply line for cheap liquor in the community, and nothing could they do about it. Howard and his cronies would have to pay the right price for his liquor for a change. He was beyond their atrocities, for he belonged to the Masons, the UBF, the IOGT, and the Church, holding responsible positions in all four. He was an old government official and a descendant of the pioneers just like they were. Their consciences wouldn't permit them to violate the oaths, traditions, and faiths those institutions represented, but poor Korli needed protection. The new corps of workers could help him. They loved and trusted him for the improved working conditions he had provided them. He'd put Korli, his family, and properties in their care.

The frank discussion showed that Korli's position was unshakable, Gbatulu knew, because the boy had succeeded through earnest labor. Even though Korli was headman, he did more than his fair share of the farm work, stopped the pillage of the sugar canes, encouraged the workers with better pay to work harder, and built a tuition-free school for their children, among other achievements. As a result, the farm yielded much more gin than ever before. The general would never get rid of him, no matter how persuasive arguments for his expulsion may be. Some other means must be employed to eliminate him.

After accompanying the Commissioner halfway to his house, Gbatulu bade him goodbye and took the road to Monrovia, where he had lived since his removal from the headman position. Nothing was wrong with the truck. He had hired a driver to run it, but, for several weeks he had neither seen the truck nor the driver. He was happy the general believed his lie the third time. As he now had full possession of the truck, he needn't undermine Korli or eliminate him. Korli had many enemies and so someone else would do that dirty job.

When the Commissioner was near his house, he slipped and fell in a deep gutter, blaming it on the strong liquor General Jackson had offered him. Had he put poison in it? The general had said he'd be the first to die should anything happen to Korli, but nothing had yet happened to Korli. The Commissioner fell asleep right there in the gutter and many people, including Americo-Liberians like himself, passed him by, turning their heads in a different direction. Why rescue a drunkard who'd be in the same gutter by tomorrow? The cantankerous man only held the post of Township Commissioner by inheritance. His father had been a friend of White Plains, so, upon his demise, the township had passed the position to him. His ruthless atrocities against the natives had drawn world attention to Liberia's human rights record and many Western nations withheld aid from Liberia because of him. So he was now outside the inner circle—the sons of "the pioneers" who ran the country.

Fortunately for the Commissioner, Korli, who was on his way to see the general, caught sight of him and went to his rescue. Perhaps nobody had noticed him because the gutter was deep, Korli thought. Only close inspection could have assured a passerby that it wasn't trash but a human being lying in it. Korli shook the man's delicate spare frame until he exhaled an exhausted sigh and opened his watery eyes. Then he led him by the hand to his house.

"Thank you, my son," mumbled the Commissioner. "Most people in this town go to Church but aren't Christians."

"Don't mention it," Korli said in the little English he had gleaned in the street. "I myself would have passed by you had I not bowed my head while walking. Whenever you want me to do anything else for you, send for me." With that, he left the Commissioner and resumed his walk to the general's house.

"How is my boy?" General Jackson shouted as Korli entered the yard. "You look concerned! Coming up with another proposal? You have my approval already, so don't worry."

"I'm thinking about the Commissioner, sir. I picked him up from in the gutter on my way here. He needs help, or we'll have another funeral on our hands."

"What help can we give him? His problem is private; he alone must wrestle with it. The fellow loves drinking although it doesn't agree with him. He and Gbatulu were here a while ago threatening to kill you for the good work you're doing for me. Howard is better off in the gutter than on his feet. In fact I think he might be better off in the grave."

"Father, everyday I hear rumors that some people here want me expelled from the community, but I have no fear. I feel safe under your umbrella. The Poro teaches that the first weapon your enemy attacks you with is threat. If you surrender to it, they conquer you with no problem."

"If you don't surrender to it, they go after you with a gun or witchcraft," said the general. "Because they know that you're my favorite worker, they'll always be after you. We have to nip their wicked plot while it is in the making. I advise you to join a Church and a society. They're the backbones of this country. Once you are active in them, you are one of us regardless of your origin. You enjoy the influence and protection of the government and civilized people worldwide. As it is, you stand naked! But let me first hear what you came for."

"I want us to build a shop from which the workers can credit, but not in excess of their wages. Some of them often ask me for salt, bath soap, palm oil, and so on. I don't always have money to help them. The shop will be a means for them to maintain their self-respect and another incentive for them to do good work."

"You already have my approval, as I told you. You always come up with brilliant ideas. That's one way we can share with the community the profit we're making from the farm. But who will run it? Certainly not you or Leanya. Your hands are full and Leanya is too busy with her farming. Perhaps Bendu could run it."

"She reads and writes and is friendly," Korli agreed. "She would make a good businessperson."

"And a good wife too. The girl is all yours, Korli, but you're wasting time! If some other man picks her up, don't blame me. She and Leanya could take turns running the shop. That's one way in which their friendship will deepen. Korli, this farm now belongs to you," the general smiled with pleasure. "When I go to bed, I sleep well because I know you're in control. As of now you are my heir. My days are now numbered, Korli, and I know it. A servant who takes good care of you is more important than a faraway son. I'll write on a piece of paper that in case I die you may have the mill, the still, and this old house. As for the land, that has to go to my children. It's the tradition. If they want to maintain the farm, they should buy their own equipment and build their own house. I don't want to leave you here with empty hands. By the way, find a lot somewhere and I'll buy it for you. Try to build a house on it—at least a foundation—to have claim to it. Don't wait until you get all the money needed before starting its construction. You can start with one dollar. That can give you a bag of cement which can make thirty blocks. I don't think you're safe here. When I die, my children will not let you stay on this land. Most children in this country are only interested in inheriting their parents' property. When I die that's when rats will crawl from holes saying they are my children. They'll want everything I own, but they won't ignore my will."

"Thank you very much, Father," Korli said, his voice loaded with emotion.

"Keep this a secret. And let Bendu help you run the shop," the general repeated. "It'll be another source of income. Don't dump goods in it and forget. Keep checking on her. Men are quick to hook onto girls who run shops to get free money and liquor. If you don't use your head, people ride your back like a horse."

"That's true," Korli said, his head bowed in deep contemplation. General Jackson may be a playboy, a drunkard, and a sniveling old man, he was thinking, but he is no fool, and he is kind.

"After cooking, Bendu has nothing much to do round here but sleep or worry," continued the general. "The shop will keep her busy and in touch with you. She has been visiting your wife regularly and they seem to be good friends." Korli nodded.

"Have you tested the engine yet?" the general asked with a smile.

"No, sir. I see them together on the farm planting rice, greens, and cassava. Maybe Leanya is trying to see how well they can get along before making up her mind about her. I don't want to interfere now. She might be afraid I'll leave her. A Kpelle man's first wife usually decides if her husband should have another wife. She makes sure she and the incoming woman are good friends before inviting her into her home."

"Suppose she doesn't invite her? Will you let that jewel go? Korli, you're a fool to think your wife will give you permission to go to bed with another woman. Women don't do that. Perhaps the Kpelle women upcountry are different from women down here."

"If she doesn't suggest the idea to me, I'll try some other way after talking with Bendu to know what she thinks of it."

"Bendu will put up a big argument to convince you that it is wrong. The only time she will think it is right is when you're between her legs. I have already talked with her. What would make me turn her over to you had I not consulted her?" The general paused for a long time to reflect. "Korli," he said quietly, "I'm not trying to bind you on my farm by giving you a woman. I know that's what people tell you. Many workers I've hooked up with girls have left the farm. This is a free country. You can't force people to live with you, but when I meet a good worker I try to help him become somebody. You love farming. It's a tedious and lifelong task.

I don't want your wife to wear out herself too soon. She has a home to see after, and she's still having children. She needs help and company."

After another long pause, the general continued: "Since we have a new group of workers, I want to talk to them for your protection. With enemies plotting against you, you need friends to protect you. You've done well to befriend the workers. However, I need to assure them that I too am their friend; that they shouldn't believe the lies people are circulating about you. Don't travel at night without your gun. Hatred takes many forms. You need an assistant to be in charge when you go to school. Let the people here miss you sometimes— By the way, how's the school going?"

"Fine, sir. I've bought books for grades one to three and hired a teacher—a Kpelle man like myself—to help me with the lessons. He told me to get a bicycle instead of a canoe. Canoe is good for daytime travel. At the rate we are going, I'm sure I'll complete the third grade by the end of the year."

"I'll buy you the bicycle. Go to school by noon each weekday and come back before dark. Don't ever stay in town until nightfall."

"General, you did well to let me go to school. You don't have to bear the expenses."

"Why not? When you go to school you'll become a better worker. We don't keep records here. That's why we fail in business. When you learn how to read and write, you'll be keeping records. We won't be playing this music by ear anymore. The bicycle will be my contribution to your education. I have money. People here don't know that the government gives me a pension. I have an uncle in Millsburg who helps me with cash sometimes. His cane farm is bigger than mine. Fight for your education. It's the best property you can have because nobody can take it from you. I know you want to catch up with the lessons, but after the third grade, I suggest you take one grade at a time. When you learn everything you need to know in a grade, the next one becomes easier. I tell you what—education doesn't depend on how many grades you complete, but on constant reading, writing, and thinking."

"Thank you, sir."

"Go now and pass the word around: I want to meet with the workers this Saturday afternoon."

On the Saturday of the scheduled meeting, the workers were treated to a sumptuous *country cook* before they assembled in General Jackson's yard. The general did not touch liquor that day so that they wouldn't take his speech as drunken talk. He put on a coat suit, a hat, and dark glasses. Speaking softly in the friendliest voice he could command, he thanked them for the good work they were doing. He said the little feast he had had for them was a token of his appreciation. He asked them not to listen to the gossip of the miscreants who had turned the community against him and Korli for taking good care of them. He asked them to work in harmony with Korli for he would make their life better. Any of them could replace Korli when the opportunity came, the general said, so if they joined his enemies to bring him down, they would be bringing themselves down too.

"Korli is your friend and brother," the general declared. "I didn't choose him for this position. His honesty, hard work, and kindness gave it to him. Now your children go to school without charge. You get more pay and will take goods on credit from the shop he's about to build. A nurse visits the farm once a week to see after your sick children—and even yourselves. Which other farmer round here is doing such things for his workers?"

"None, whatsoever!" cried the workers.

"Because they don't take care of their workers, they hate us who do. Protect Korli and you'll be protecting yourselves. Destroy him and you have destroyed yourselves. I'm old now—about to cross the river—"

"No! No! No!" the crowd roared.

"You'll never die!" some shouted.

"God won't permit it!"

When the cheering ceased and the old man found his voice, he thanked the workers for their love for him, but added that their hard work rather than their shouts would be the best proof and expression of their love.

"Anyone can say anything," he cried, "but it's a person's doing that counts. If you observe anything wrong, tell me. I'll do my best to make it right. If I can't, you'll at least see that I tried my best. Any questions?"

Raising his hand, Korli said he had something to say. The general granted him permission.

"I came to this farm in peace, looking for a job," he began in a mild voice, addressing the crowd. "God agreed for me to find a job here, and he put the idea in General Jackson's heart to give me this position. My only concern is making life better for all of us. If I do anything wrong to anyone, please let me know. I'm not too important to hold your foot and beg for your forgiveness. Whatever I can do for you, please let me know. If my best effort can't solve your problem, I'll appeal to our father General Jackson for help."

The workers dispersed gradually, laughing and feeling contented. Their pay was good. Their fringe benefits were good. Their bosses were good. They had nothing to complain about.

7

A Trap?

IT WAS LATE IN THE NIGHT. There was no trace of moon- or starlight in the sky. A breeze that promised rain swept the river and fanned the ancient zinc shacks. Korli had no problem winding his way surreptitiously through the tall grasses to General Jackson's house and to the privacy of his bedroom. The general gave him a blue denim purse containing a large bundle of money. Pocketing it, Korli thanked him, and promised to do his best as always. Leanya was asleep when he arrived home, giving him a chance to figure out how to handle the money. The general had only told him that each bill was ten dollars. Korli pulled the money out of the bag but couldn't count it in the dim light of the hurricane lantern. If each bill was of such a high denomination, he thought, the general had probably given him the wrong purse or he had other intentions for the money besides running a shop, for it was too much for an ordinary shop. Perhaps General Jackson wanted him to use some to build the foundation of his house or rebuild the school with cement blocks. Korli fastened the purse securely in a coarse sack and locked it up in his wooden box, planning to ask the general for clarification before using a cent or even informing Leanya about it. The following day the general assured him that the money was for building the shop.

"You think it's too much for a shop?" he asked him. "As a shopkeeper, you're expected to supply the community with nearly all their basic needs. So you'll have to keep that shop well stocked. I don't want you to run into money problems at the very beginning of the business. That's when you either gain or lose your customers' confidence. Have you thought of where to build it? I recommend a place near your house to keep an eye on it."

"I'll build the house later, sir, when profit from the shop begins coming," Korli said. "I want to use this money to get enough supplies to start with, as you've recommended. I'll use a room in my house as a shop in the meantime."

"Good. You are thoughtful. The building might take half that money, and since the workers will be taking things on credit, you need all the supplies you can get."

That evening Korli told his wife about the money. They checked it and were shocked to discover that it amounted to three thousand dollars. Leanya looked at the cash with wide eyes and open mouth. Sighing deeply she told Korli:

"This is a trap General Jackson has set for us. A test of our honesty. Bendu told me that he tests people he confides in. She says when she began living with him, he used to put money in the pockets of his pants and ask her to wash them. She always gave him his money, which sometimes amounted to a hundred dollars. Many girls were caught in that trap and had to go home. He did the same thing to the workers by leaving the farm up to them. Gbatulu paid the penalty for their roguery. We shouldn't keep this money with us here. The house doesn't lock. Even if it does, what will stop thieves from breaking in when we're out? I suggest we start the business on a small scale—a gallon of kerosene, a carton of soap, a bag of salt—"

"If you jump in a river, don't be afraid of getting wet," Korli said. "We've already told the people about the shop. They'll be looking up to us for everything because the Germans have left, and shops round here sell mostly liquor. So, we must get enough goods to win the people's confidence. It's bad the Germans left the country. One of them was my customer. I hope he comes back. Had he been here, I'd have given him this money and got all the goods I want—and money too when necessary."

"The Germans left long ago, so we have to make other plans. You told me of Lebanese traders—"

"They are different, Leanya. Totally different. If you give them money for safekeeping, you get only goods in return. Sometimes you might need cash— I never thought the old man's trust in me would go this far. I've never handled this amount of money before. As you said, it is a test. With your backing I'll pass it. Keep half this money in your waist purse while I buy goods with the balance."

"How will you run the farm, do this business, and go to school at the same time?" Leanya said as she rechecked the money by the lantern light. She made two equal piles, put one in her stringed leather purse, tied it deftly on her waist, and stared at Korli for an answer to her question.

"You'll be in charge of the business," Korli told her. "You can make it because you know the importance of money, and you're afraid of trouble as I am. Besides, business is not difficult. Your presence in the shop is the most important thing. Make sure to lock it whenever you go out. If you'll stay away for a long time, let me know in advance for me to take over."

"The people go to work during the day, anyway. So, most of the business will be done in the evening. I might lock up the shop during the day and open it at night."

"Keep it open all day and half the night. That's another secret to success in business. The Lebanese open their stores daily except Sunday. Some days they sell little or nothing, but when their good luck comes, people buy nearly everything. Let the people be sure to get what they want at all times."

"This is a big responsibility, Korli. The old man should have started with a small amount of money—say one or two hundred dollars—what you will be able to pay him without problem in case the business fails. Suppose we are robbed, from where will you get three thousand dollars to pay him back?"

"Don't ever go into business with the idea of failing. Think of success. Once you have what people need and you're nice to them, they become your customers. Here's another secret of business success—smile at the people even if they don't buy from you, and believe in what you're doing. For a long time, the old man has been looking for someone to trust because his family has deserted him. Money flies! If he doesn't put the little he has in business, he might get broke. Friends and relatives help you in times of trouble. Most times you have to see after yourself."

"In fact, people help you only when you're in a position to help them also, Leanya said. I'll try with the business, but its success or failure depends on you mostly. You're too openhanded. Giving money and things to people doesn't guarantee their love for you. Some people ask you for things not because they need them but because they know you have them. It's their way of greeting you. The more money you give people the more they demand of you, and the less they appreciate it. As their headman, be fair to them and you'll enjoy their love and respect."

"The general suggested that Bendu help run the shop," Korli said, hoping his suggestion wouldn't create suspicion. "She could keep records of the credits. The workers will be our main creditors, and whatever they take should not be more than their pay. In other words, if a man earns three dollars, he's welcome to credit the same amount in goods."

"Let Bendu help with the shop as the old man suggested," Leanya said. "She is friendly and reliable. I'll continue with my farming, for food takes too much money if you have to buy it. When Bendu goes to bed, I'll take over the shop until midnight."

"We should make *kuu* to do the farming; otherwise, it'll make you old before your time. That shouldn't be a problem. The workers are all farmers. I don't know why they abhor farming when they come down here."

"Let the people credit on a special day—say each Saturday—or they might take nearly everything on credit, and we won't have money to buy more goods. Liquor makes money, but it takes time to sell because there are too many liquor shops here."

"That's a good point. Remember not to credit members of the community without the general's approval. Always make it clear to them that the business belongs to him, not to us. We are only supervising it for him."

Leanya smiled, then said, "Bendu is interested in you, but you're too blind to notice it. Korli, I need another hand. Our responsibility seems to increase from year to year. I'll soon have a young baby—most of the time you're either on the farm with the workers or in Monrovia for school. Bendu says the old man likes the idea of her keeping my company and helping me with housework. She doesn't have much to do at his house after cooking. We could even cook together and take his share to him."

"The decision rests with you, Leanya. My interest in Bendu is no more than the interest I have in the workers. Anyone inclined to hard work is good to have around. If two of you are agreeable, I'll put her on my payroll. The old man takes care of her, but a little cash on the side won't hurt. She needs something to send to her people."

"You're dodging the issue. Who is talking about pay? Look, Korli, you're a young man. You need many children, and—"

"My main concern is our security," Korli broke in as if he had no desire for Bendu. "Bendu has lived in this settlement for many years; she knows all its ins and outs. She'll help us avoid danger. Women are the best security. Now we're about to build a large shop, which will rouse the jealousy of our enemies more than before. After men get drunk, they tell women their secrets. She'll make a good informant for us."

"That's true, but no woman will render you that kind of service unless you sleep with her. Don't you have feeling for Bendu? She's young and pretty and she loves you."

Korli watched Leanya from the tail of his eye, smiled, heaved a sigh, and studied her girlish face with amusement. Leanya smiled at him too, and blinked.

"Despite your belly, you look beautiful," Korli told her. "A year's inconvenience is not too much sacrifice to make for our child. Are you sure you want Bendu to help you in that way?"

"This is the last month you'll have something to do with me before I deliver," Leanya said, nursing her bulging belly. "I know how hard it was for you when I had my last two children. It's better you get someone to take care of you—someone I know—someone who respects me. Bendu is that person. I trust her. I don't want you to go through another yearlong agony. You might yield to temptation. A sassy girl might break up our family."

"You're not suggesting that Bendu become my second wife, are you?" Korli said. "The old man might not like it. Bendu is his back scratcher."

"Bendu says he has retired from bedding women, but she wants to get her children. The wealth of the poor is children. Let her come into the house. I've tried and tested her in many ways and found her to be singleminded, hardworking, and trustworthy."

"I'll talk with her, then. I want to assure you, however, that I still stand by my word: never to leave you for another woman. My father might have had his way with women, but he kept only one wife, my mother. You alone are quite sufficient for me. Had farming been the only question, I wouldn't risk bringing another woman into the house, but this security problem is serious. Leanya, sometimes I regret leaving home and coming down here. Life is fraught with danger everywhere, especially for those who want to be somebody. We should have remained in Kuntaa as you once suggested."

"You're the first man I see who is so honest when it comes to women. Most men I know do their thing secretly until the belly betrays them. Women love keeping their business secret. Remember we are married legally in the Church. Let people speculate if they might, but don't confirm their rumors. Whatever happens between you and Bendu should be top secret— Korli, I want to go home to have this baby. My last delivery was difficult, as you know. I want my mother to be around when I deliver this time. Bendu will take care of you and the children until I come back. I've talked to her about it. My brothers sent word the other day that they're coming here next Saturday to trade and buy Christmas things."

"I'll hurry to Monrovia this afternoon, then, and buy the goods so that you may carry things for the people. Tell Bendu what we have decided. That will be the best approach. She'll believe your words faster than mine. Some women consider men liars when it comes to love negotiation."

"You're a strange man, Korli," Leanya said. "You've had no experience with women, yet you seem to know all about them. I'll talk with Bendu. Everything will be all right. Look for my cold water."

Korli was happy that the question of Bendu had been resolved wonderfully, not only because of the pleasure and honor of having a second wife but also because she would be valuable as security. He had no reason to fear for his life, for only a devil incarnate would destroy a person who wasn't engaged in underhand deals. Any man worth his manhood wouldn't abandon a goal because of fear. His greatest concern was securing his family; that, he wouldn't compromise. Bendu would help him solve that problem.

With Saki accompanying him, Korli went to Water Street downtown Monrovia and chartered a pickup, loaded it with things required for everyday living such as stockfish, smoked fish, rice, palm oil, sardines, soft drinks, soap, petroleum jelly, kerosene, mosquito coils, blankets, cutlasses, axes, cartridges, fishing hooks, matches, T-shirts, lappas, and headties. As for rum he had plenty of that. The workers and other members of the community greeted them on their return, helped unload the pickup and packed everything in the room adjacent to the porch. Korli had wisely added this room to the house for a future shop. He had furnished it with shelves, a counter, a double door opening to the porch, and a single door opening to the center room. Leanya had urged him to begin the business with liquor, but he had cautioned patience.

"Many people sell liquor round here," he said. "If we sell only liquor we won't make much profit. Let's wait until we get a good bit of cash. A profitable business requires a full shop."

Korli was delighted that the shop experiment proved successful from the outset. The workers did not wait for the goods to be completely packed before putting to use their unusual privilege. They took up to half their earnings for the month. Bendu was more than busy keeping records in a nickel copybook by the bright light of a gas lantern. The serious expression on her face showed her determination to put her education into practical use and conduct the business professionally. Leanya too was busy overseeing the transactions. Some members of the community stood around, their hands hooked behind them observing the incident with misgivings, making snide remarks and sneering.

"How long?" they were saying. "Everything will soon fail. Do Liberians know how to do business?"

"Is that girl really recording all the debts?"

"The fellow has really bewitched the old man. For ages we have been here and never has he thought of building a shop. This Kpelle man's witchcraft is extremely powerful!"

"Instead of keeping the money for his burial, he's making a big show!"

The next Saturday Dieley came along with other traders who accompanied him to the shop they had heard about. They watched the commodious house and the large quantity of goods with much admiration. Korli bought their produce, and they bought things in the shop. Dieley, who brought half a bag of rice and dry meat, gave his sister a haunch of deer and thanked her and her husband for the progress they had made.

"Zolu remained with Data to engage next year's farmland," he told them. "The rate at which farmers are preying on fallow farmland is alarming. Data decided to mark off our share now."

"You look lean and feverish!" Leanya scanned her brother with worried eyes. "What caused that scar on your jaw?"

"Malaria knocked me down for a week," said Dieley. "And the scar came from setting a trap; the tension sapling misfired, almost bursting my eyes. Our parents miss you people. If they were not too busy preparing for the clearing season, they would have come for a visit."

"Leanya has been waiting for you and Zolu to take her home to deliver," said Korli. "It's good women came along to help in case she gets pains on the way."

"But I thought it would be better for her to deliver here. The *kwii* people can handle delivery better than Kpelle people," Diely said.

"It's true but I want my mother to be around when I deliver this time," said Leanya.

The traveling party slept with the Korli family and started off early the following morning after eating *puwan*. It was Bendu who cooked the rice with okra, bitterballs, and palm oil for them. In addition to a few items he bought for himself, Dieley carried a bag of goods Korli sent for the family. He did not permit his sister to tote anything but a small bundle containing her clothes and three new lappa suits for her mothers. Korli and Bendu took them partway—Bendu carrying Leanya's bundle while Korli carried his gun and cutlass.

"Brother, I see a new face in the house," Dieley told Korli on the way. "I'm afraid!"

"She was employed to take care of the shop," said Leanya. "He'll be a fool to bring another woman in the house while I am there."

"We have to walk fast to get near a town," Dieley said. "By God's help we'll reach Kuntaa before nightfall."

"Dieley, don't worry about me," Leanya said. "If I couldn't make the trip, I'd have said so. I'll deliver in another month. The walk will do me some good."

When they reached Harrisburg, Korli and Bendu bade them farewell, and turned to head back home.

On their way back, Korli, who thought he had control over his feelings, threw his gun and cutlass aside, grasped Bendu roughly, pressed her to his chest, and touched her all over. She grew limp in his arms and moaned, then suddenly sobered and said:

"This is the wrong place, Korli—the wrong time!" Korli released her gently. "If people meet us so engaged, they'll think you're raping me." They resumed their trek. "I thought you weren't interested," Bendu said. "The old man welcomed you to my room, but you never so much as looked in it. We could have crossed this bridge long ago."

It took some time for Korli to catch his breath and sober up. Then he said at length:

"I wanted to make sure the general was serious—and that you and Leanya would agree. The settlement is small. If we got together without her knowledge and consent, it would have been dangerous."

"Most men I know are not afraid of their wives. They jump into the hole and then try to fight their way out but often find it impossible. I respect your restraint."

"I'm not afraid of my wife. I only respect her. I wanted to know how you'd feel about the whole affair before touching you. Leanya says she talked with you."

"I accepted her proposal in my heart, waiting for you to make a move. That woman is brave. I consider her my big sister."

"The day the old man gave you to me, I couldn't think straight. It was the same time he agreed for me to go to school. I couldn't think of anything else."

"Many boys have been after me, but I declined their proposals because they live under other people's roofs. They're the kind of boys who give a girl belly and deny it. But I know you won't act like that to me. Korli, I am an orphan. I have no mother or father to help me with a child. I've been looking for a man to take care of me and any child I get. My parents died when I was an infant. I don't have the faintest idea how they looked. My uncle who was taking care of me died suddenly one day of snakebite. His widow—I must say this for her—his widow was good to me, but how could a woman without husband care for so many children? She kept her lastborn, a girl, and sent the rest of us to civilized families. I was lucky to go to a missionary as a housekeeper. He was the principal of the mission. The problem arose when my breasts came out in full. By then I had completed the sixth grade. This man was huge and full of desire. He couldn't keep his hands out of my clothes whenever we were alone. Then one day his wife went to Sinoe—" Bendu ended the sentence with sobs.

"Don't cry, Bendu," Korli told her. "You aren't responsible for that. Thank God you came through without a child. That would have been embarrassing."

"I had a child for him—that's what brought me here. He said General Jackson is his brother, which is a lie! He is no relative to the general. When it became clear that I was pregnant, he sent me to him."

"What happened to the child?"

"When I delivered the general sent my baby—a beautiful boy—to his brother in Millsburg who was childless. He told me, 'Bendu, you're the only family I have now; everybody has gone from me. Please don't leave me. Live with me until you get a good man to take care of you.' It's true that he is through with women. Sometimes I sleep with him—the most he does is fondle me occasionally when he isn't too drunk."

"Do you sometimes visit your son?"

"No. I don't," Bendu said sadly. "If I do, they'll trace him to me naturally—and they'll trace me to that missionary. It might cost him his job and a breakup of his marriage and the mission. Without the support of the mother Churches in America, none of our missions will survive. General Jackson often tells me, 'Your son will find you when he grows up. Children have more feelings for their mothers than their fathers.'"

"Did Leanya tell you about the shop?"

"The old man did. He says he has made you his heir, so he was turning the little cash he had over to you for business. There's nothing much you'll inherit from him, but it's an honor to be connected to a

Congo man in this country. It opens doors for you. When you start living in Monrovia, you'll know what I'm talking about. Perhaps when you become somebody, you'll build me a little *konko* somewhere. I can't live with Leanya in the same house. It'll spoil our friendship. Korli, the arrangement you people have made is good—that I keep the shop. Now and then you can take a bite when Leanya is not around. Don't come to me in the old man's house. It won't disturb him but the people in this community will eat you raw if they see you in my room. You made the mistake of marrying in their Church. Besides, if the boys who tried unsuccessfully to get me discover that you are the lucky man, they might harm you."

"Everybody already believes that you are my wife. They say the general has given you to me. Perhaps you have heard the rumor."

"Certainly, but I don't care. Rumor is nothing but rumor. The people here have very little to do but gossip. Their imaginations run wild and they believe what they imagine. The most they can do to you is expel you from their Church. One day you'll move down to Monrovia where you'll be free to live your life as you like. There people mind their own business."

"Bendu, I can take care of myself. I'll tell you my story some day. I'm happy God has put us together in order to help each other. If having more than one wife was sin, why did God come down from heaven and befriend King David and King Solomon who had hundreds of wives? It's better to be bold enough to take responsibility for the children you have by the women who cross your path than to throw them out pretending you have one wife."

The children were still asleep when they returned. Gbaaseng, Saki's wife, who had been taking care of them, said only Junior had woken up and asked for his mother, but went back to sleep when she told him that she'd soon be back. Right away Bendu went to the river for water. On her return she went to Korli in the master bedroom. Undressing hurriedly, they grasped each other savagely and fell into the bed.

As Korli got between Bendu's shuddering warm thighs, he was amazed at what he had been missing. Bendu received him with pleasure and tenderness, and he felt the satisfaction of a starving person who had just had a rich dinner.

Afterwards, Bendu cooked in a hurry and took some food to General Jackson who had just roused from sleep. The old man bathed, had his lunch, and asked Bendu how the shop was going.

"Fine," she said with a radiant smile.

"From the happy expression on your face, you must be enjoying it," the general told her. "Remember, business doesn't mix with pleasure. Some lazy louts might tempt you to get what they want from the shop and use you on top of it. We put much money in it, hoping it'd be our mainstay of support. We pay the workers with half of what we get from the farm and live on the other half. The shop should be our profit if you run it profitably. Make sure to mark all the debts."

"Korli has already advised me about that," Bendu said. "The workers will get their credits only on Saturdays when Korli himself is present. Anyone else who wants credit will have to get your approval."

"That boy is prudent," said General Jackson. "Take care of him, Bendu. Another girl is coming to help with the housekeeping here. That will give you a chance to do your job well. Sarah comes from Gbonoi, a short distance from your village. You have done well for me; that's why I found you a good man. Korli will take good care of you. Don't listen to this nonsense about one-man-one-wife. Every husband in this country has a second or third wife. Korli is welcome to meet you here or at his house. You love him?"

"Yes, I do," Bendu admitted.

Sarah came the following day, and the general introduced her to Bendu. About the same age, they became thick friends immediately. Whenever she was through with her chores, she spent some time with Bendu in the shop and helped to take care of the children. Nobody could tell which one of them was Korli's lover, and when they inquired of them, Bendu always maintained that she was employed to run the shop, and Sarah would say she was taking care of the Old Man. They took their duties quite seriously. Bendu never gave a shot of liquor or a pinch of salt to a beggar, and she was always in the shop exactly at eight in the morning until eight in the evening. Sarah served the general with dedication.

Leanya returned home with good news: the safe birth of her third child, Liimu, a bouncing baby girl, and the report that all was well in Kuntaa.

"Let's choose the name of our next child," Korli said. "Liimu is a good name."

"How many children do you want?" Leanya said. "Three should be enough."

"We need an even number, or they won't get along. Why are you in a hurry to stop having children?"

"If all three were of the same sex, they wouldn't get along," Leanya explained. "One of them would always be an outcast. But if one is a girl, she'll be a mother to her brothers. If a boy, he'll be a father to his sisters. For us upcountry, a large family is an asset, but here it is a liability. It's better we have a few children and take good care of them than have many we can't support. How is Bendu? Did she receive you?"

"Bendu is doing a good job, but as you said, it's good for you to take over the shop when she goes to bed. People come for liquor up to midnight."

"Have you put Bendu on payroll?"

"I've put two of you on payroll," Korli said, noting the happy look in Leanya's face.

"That is good. Did she let you—" Leanya ended the sentence with laughter and a sidelong glance.

"You aren't expecting me to confess to you, are you? Bendu has given me her consent. She has great love and respect for you. Perhaps she has told you her story. It's a sad story. By bringing her into the house, we are doing her as much good as she is doing for us. She has given me the names of key people who are our enemies. You know about Gbatulu and Commissioner Howard. But there are some boys—mostly the Old Man's old workers—who plan to ambush me on my way from Monrovia. I wanted to ask my teacher to be coming here instead of my going to Monrovia every weekday, but he could be in danger once they know he is my teacher."

"I suggest that we continue living as usual without fear. Fear alone can kill a person. You have done nothing bad to anyone in this settlement or anywhere else for them to be after you. In fact, you have improved the condition of life here. People who don't work for the general send their children to the school you built. Now you're running a shop for the community— I wanted us to return home, Korli. Upcountry, people live for each other. Your relatives, friends, and neighbors come to your aid in times of trouble. But my last visit there convinced me that living there will be equally dangerous."

"Why? Home is the best place to be!"

"The only problem upcountry is that people burden you with their troubles. Once they give you a cup of rice, a piece of kola nut, or keep your company, you are obligated to them all your life, especially if you're successful. What is annoying is that they don't try to help themselves as long as you're around. So, everybody is always poor. I don't like country life."

"To beat the poverty plague upcountry, everybody should work, not only for food or clothes but also for money. Hardworking people get all that they need—and much more besides."

A long silence ensued, for the subject was becoming thorny. Tradition was too painful to abandon.

Leanya broke the silence. "I never wanted to tell you this, Korli, so you won't be discouraged or angry, but our present situation demands that I do." She paused significantly, bowed her head, and averted her face. Korli watched her in suspense. "As of now, I'll visit home only during *Twenty-Sixth* and Christmas seasons. Too many visits are bad for the people—and for us."

"Why?" Korli asked, perplexed. He looked at her for an explanation. When it wasn't forthcoming, he asked, "What have the people done to you—to us?"

"We shouldn't continue giving things away as we get them. That's courting poverty and hatred. Now that we have children to support, we need every cent we get." Leanya sounded uncompromising.

"Those are strange words, Leanya," Korli told her. "Our people own part of whatever we get, no matter how they treat us. Sometimes I wish to see my mother and sister despite all that happened."

"I don't want you to go home now. Our children are too little for them to lose you. Don't let the same flooded river make you take off your pants twice. When all is well, your mother, sister, or one of your brothers will come and let us know. They spared you for Father's sake. If you return there with the reputation of being rich, you'll not come back to me alive, so let me say it again: don't make the same mistake twice."

"You're always giving me sensible advice, so I agree to what you have said. But you have no reason for staying away from your home. Nobody is after you there. Maybe I should be going there since it is my home also. I might get news about my people."

"Don't go to Kuntaa, either. Let me tell you why. Since we came down here, I have been visiting my people nearly every two or three months, as you know, making sure each family member, friend, or neighbor gets something, if only a piece of bath soap. I never knew I was digging my own grave."

"If they bewitch you for your kindness, don't carry anything for them when you go there again."

"They'll do worse things to me if I go to them with empty hands. They believe that we are rich! Except for my parents, most of those who received gifts from me bore us malice. Sometimes I don't blame people who only find food to eat and clothes to wear. If you try to be somebody in this world, you make many enemies. I never believed it until my niece Kpelinweni attacked me with jealousy during this visit. I gave the girl a whole lappa suit as her Christmas present. Do you know the 'thank you' she gave me?"

"What" Korli asked, looking at Leanya with surprise. "She refused the gift?"

"She needed it. While her husband was cutting palm nuts to make oil to sell and buy Christmas things, he fell from a palm tree and broke his leg. I didn't want her to be in old clothes among her friends during the season. She might destroy herself with sorrow. She grabbed the clothes from me with her callused hands and said rudely, 'Is this all you're giving me for my Christmas? Leanya, you are too mean! We hear that you people have become rich in White Plains, but you don't care about your people! Don't you know that we are mates? That man belongs to me as much as to you.'"

"What did she mean by that?" Korli asked, rising to his feet. "I don't even know her!"

"That's why I didn't quarrel with her or tell you about it. She was in Zaraimu when you were in Kuntaa. And she made her jealous remarks with laughter; people sometimes tell you the evil in their hearts with laughter and jokes. I wasn't worried, too, because I didn't take you from some other woman, and we happily left Kuntaa. Had we remained there, that girl would have taken you from me."

Korli laid his robust arm round Leanya's neck, drew her to him, and said, "Nobody will ever take me from you, Leanya—or you from me. How many times I have told you this? I have only one heart and you have taken it."

"The leaves in the bush work wonders, my dear," Leanya said. "If someone puts a combination of them in your food, you do exactly what they want. If they want you to hate your wife, you won't want to lay your eyes on her or even the ground she walks on."

"They do it to weak-minded people."

"Bendu's case is different. You didn't go after her. I did. Whatever we give her she earns with her sweat. But these women who do nothing for you usually want everything you have."

Korli laughed and said, "Don't worry. Every experience is a lesson, and God pays you for every good deed you render people."

"The old man has finally had his way, eh?" Leanya said, laughing. "He's good to us, anyway, so there's no harm living on his farm. He should have been a Paramount Chief—to have all the women he wants. Bendu tells me that he's making arrangements to bring several other girls. When he noticed that you were reluctant to take in Bendu, his idea was to have something to do with me. Many times, he sent for me, but I never entered his house. Had he tried to force me, I'd have told you."

"I knew all about it," Korli said calmly, "but I didn't worry because I trust you, and his womanizing days are over. It was good you remained in Kuntaa until I started working for him. They say when a man applies to him, the only way he gets the job is by sending his wife to him for a reply. Once he makes love to her, he controls him through her. You are right. That's how our paramount chiefs do; own all the girls in their domains to enslave boys who fall in love with them."

"How did you know about what happened between us?"

"Saki told me."

"My brothers asked me to bring their children for schooling—all five of them. I told them that it wasn't possible because we're still unsettled. We might take two of their boys when we see our way clear. They walked away frowned up. You know why? Because they helped bring our things here and build this house."

"We gave them money!" Korli said.

"As far as they are concerned, we're indebted to them for life. Father advised them to be reasonable. 'Your sister and brother-in-law are just beginning life,' he told them. 'If you overburden them now they might not accomplish anything. Further, with the danger of "black boys" widespread on the coast, we shouldn't be in a hurry to send children down there.' They knew better than argue with the old man. I'm telling you, I won't put my foot in Kuntaa except during the Twenty-Sixth and Christmas seasons."

"Your brothers told me about their children when we were building the house. I told them exactly what you told them and added that they should see you because you'd be the children's caretaker when we take them in."

Korli had no illusion that solving a problem mentally disposed of it. Unless he took concrete actions to protect his family and himself, the threat to them remained real, immediate, and dangerous. He could sense Leanya's inclination to return home despite her resentment of the family pressure. The country had its problems and plenty of them, but the people there were honest and just. Once you conformed to the norms and mores of the place, you were secure. Beneficiaries of ritual killings, for example, sacrificed members of their own families, unlike the *kwii* world where killings were indiscriminate and widespread. But returning to the country without accomplishing his goal would be a disgrace. How would he face the people? Bendu had many eyes and ears, but plotters were adept at concealing their motives until they carried them out. With his popularity among the workers, he could raise a secret army for protection. But no—it would cause needless alarm and estrange his friends. Leanya was right. He'd go on living as usual, but with vigilance.

PART 2

8

A VICIOUS ATTACK

THE MORNING AFTER Korli and Leanya made a vow to protect their family from harm, the relentless sunshine was joined by a soft breeze rolling over the river. Korli gave the workers tasks that included carving a third canoe out of the cotton tree in the center of the farm for the fermentation of cane juice, which had overwhelmed the farm's two canoes. Sonny Boy warned him of the danger of hewing a cotton tree in or on the outskirts of a town. A loquacious fellow whose right arm was longer than the left, Sonny Boy said he was a descendent of Zoes, his uneven arms being the evidence. He claimed to be well acquainted with the traditions, and everybody believed him. Korli had dismissed his fears as idle talk and demanded immediate compliance with his order, reminding him that a fierce wind had once broken a bough of the cotton tree. Had the incident occurred when the workers were at work, it would have killed someone. Perhaps him. Korli joined a group of men to hack away at the huge, ancient tree.

Korli had no fear because he had grown inured to his insecurity. "What we often fear doesn't happen," he was fond of saying. More than a year since opposition to his presence in White Plains became an issue, he'd been walking the streets of the settlement and going to and coming from Monrovia for lessons without fear. His courage and service to the community made him popular with the people, especially the old folks who encouraged him with inspiring remarks:

"A cowardly man would have run away long ago, but you did well to stay and fight."

"When God is on your side, your enemies become your footstools."

"People who fight for progress always meet opposition, but in the end they put their enemies to shame. With the Germans gone, had you not come to our rescue we'd still be suffering. Carry on, Son; we're on your side."

"Nowadays we don't send our kids to relatives in Monrovia for schooling, nor do we go there for salt or chicken soup. Are these the evils you have done to justify your expulsion from here?"

The young boys hated Korli for his popularity and for taking Bendu who had rejected proposals from many of them. One of them called Solomon Day, a ward of Chief Justice William Wright, vowed to fight him. Solomon had offered Bendu large sums of money to marry him, but she had refused because she knew that Solomon had stolen the money. He implored General Jackson and many influential women of the community to intercede for him—to no avail. As a last resort he had tried to rape Bendu one night when the general spent a weekend in Monrovia. Bendu's cry had drawn a crowd, and Solomon had fled after Korli gave him a good flogging. That grim encounter, long forgotten, convinced Korli that his popularity had overridden the hatred some elements of the community harbored against him. The gradual departure of those who had engineered his expulsion reinforced his conviction. Commissioner Howard had departed, and Gbatulu was tottering on the brink of the pit. But Korli maintained the precautions he had taken for the protection of his family and himself: Saki helped him watch his house at night; he abandoned nighttime hunting and went to Monrovia before noon for his lessons to make sure to be back before dark.

As he came home from Monrovia today, one tire of his bicycle went flat. It took an hour to repair it at Bernard's Farm. Just before he resumed his journey, rain began to fall. The rain was brief but heavy. It was dusk when he reached the rubber farm between White Plains and the highway. His head grew heavy and the hair stood on his head. Such things had never happened to him even when he hunted at night. Unable to ride the bicycle on the muddy road in the pitch darkness, he rolled it at his side. After every few yards of progress, he stopped and listened keenly for noise or footsteps. All of a sudden a rubber tree fell across the road ahead of him. A bright light flashed in his face, making him blind and dazed. "Who's that? Saki?" he said weakly, pushing the bicycle aside and bracing himself for attack. On second thought he turned round and started running to a little village at the junction with the highway for help. But another rubber tree fell before him and another powerful beam of light blinded him. A voice bellowed, "You've been wishing to know black boys. You'll know them tonight." Korli felt a blow on the back of his skull. He saw stars and fell in a faint. On rousing he found himself lying half-naked to the waist in a makeshift lean-to on an old cassava farm, four hooded men with cudgels surrounding him.

"What have I done to you people?" he said weakly as he fought for his breath.

In answer to his question, a ruffian hit him on the head with his cudgel, another hit him in the stomach, and the others kicked him. After beating him senseless, they scrambled away in the bushes.

"Had it not been for our secret oath," Solomon shouted over his shoulder as he went, "today would have been your last day on earth for taking Bendu from me." Korli recognized Solomon's resonant baritone.

Dragging himself to the shoulder of the path, he tried unsuccessfully to make a sound to secure the help of a passerby. The blood that had oozed from his head wounds blinded him and clamped his hair. Swollen whip welts and bumps littered his face and body; his head split with pain. By sunrise a boy going to his traps discovered his mangled body lying motionless in last night's mud. He ran shouting to the village, and a group of men quickly followed him to the lean-to. Recognizing Korli, they carried him in a hammock towards White Plains.

Saki and a group of workers met them on the way and took over the burden. The settlement gathered at Korli's house where General Jackson, Leanya, Bendu, and the children sat helpless on the porch, looking at the road to Monrovia. Under the general's supervision, the workers bathed Korli, tended his wounds, and dressed him.

"Take him to the highway and get a taxi to carry him to Public Health for treatment," he instructed them. "I'll be there this evening. I know who did this wicked act. He will pay for it double."

Nobody had to tell General Jackson that it was Solomon's doing. He ordered his black boys to arrest him and his accomplices. They really paid for their mischief double. After their arrest the general had them confined in an underground jail, and they were never heard of again.

It took a whole month for Korli to recuperate. After spending two weeks in the hospital, he went home. Sympathetic neighbors brought him eggs, fruits, vegetables, crawfish, and other edibles to console him and his family. After his recovery, General Jackson held a thanksgiving party for him, which the workers and their wives, and prominent members of the community, attended. The party was elaborate. Under the competent supervision of Leanya and Bendu, the workers' wives cooked nearly all the choice Liberian dishes: *fufu* and soup, *dumboy* and palm butter and crawfish stew, check rice and gravy, *torborgee*, and *puwan*. Eating with the general in the dining room were Chief Justice and Mrs. Wright; Police Director Col. Nathaniel Gabriel; Rev. Allison Williams of St. Paul's Methodist Church; and Hon. Abel White, Land Commissioner of Montserrado County; Korli, Leanya, and Bendu. The workers, their wives, and other invitees ate on the green outside.

Addressing General Jackson, Chief Justice Wright said, "You're really fond of this country boy." He swallowed large balls of *dumboy* and palaver sauce and washed them down with palm wine. "He's now part of us—but he must join the UBF or the Masons; otherwise, he'll disappear."

"My son doesn't have time for that," said the general. "He says the Poro is enough for him. Korli, how is your schooling?"

"Fine, sir. I am now fighting with the fourth and fifth grades."

"Are you helping Leanya to learn something?"

"Yes, sir. She is taking the second grade now," he said, even though Leanya had not started school yet.

"Marvelous!" said the general. "In two years, you should complete the eighth grade. If given the opportunity, the country man performs well."

"The president is building schools all over the country," said Commissioner White. "Pretty soon the native people will take the country from us. That Negro is not thinking about the future of our children."

"Your Honor, what is your opinion about majority rule?" said General Jackson.

"If the majority is illiterate," said the Chief Justice, "they have no right to rule. It's unjust to give people responsibilities they can't handle. That's one bad mistake the Old Man is making: putting illiterate people in the Legislature. They're nothing but rubber stamps."

"Well, we are responsible for that," said General Jackson. "For more than a hundred years we failed to educate them. They are the majority, you know. Without their support the Old Man won't stay in power. The only way he'll continue enjoying their support is let them take part in the government. It's good he's trying to educate them."

"I forgot," said the Chief Justice. "You're a lawyer for the country people. Maybe I should exchange my chair with yours. But I warn you—the educated country man is more dangerous than the uneducated one. The average country man or woman is quite content getting something to eat and a place to lay their head. But the educated one wants everything including the Executive Mansion."

"And why shouldn't they get it? Is Liberia not their country? Let me make my last statement about this subject," said General Jackson. "We have done a bad job at nation-building by excluding 95% of the people from citizenship and by failing to develop the country, yet we have millionaires—millionaires who bleed the natives and the country to death to enrich themselves. We practice segregation among ourselves. Those with light skin color think they're better than those with black skin. We don't accept our president because he doesn't have light skin color and he didn't come from America."

"Barbados is no distance from America," said Director Gabriel. "This question of color makes no sense to me. Once you have a drop of Negro blood in you or your ancestry, the world considers you black." "It has worked in the Old Man's favor," said Chief Justice Wright. "He has cast his lot with the natives who know nothing about discrimination. They love him and vote for him; they'll soon appeal to him to succeed himself the fourth time. It'll happen because they are the majority."

"The natives too practice segregation among themselves," said Commissioner White.

"Not by reason of color but tribe," said General Jackson. "Once you speak their language and practice their culture, you become one of them, but not we civilized people. We say we believe in law and the brotherhood of all people in Christ, yet we look down on our fellow creatures because of the color of their skin. What can people do about their color? The Bible says everything God created is good."

"Well, that Negro has become part of the tribes. He once had the fancy to tie lappa round his waist and do war dances with them," said Commissioner White. "He loves women and the Constitution, and they offer him plenty of them."

"As we all do," said General Jackson. "And why do you keep rudely addressing him as 'that Negro'? If you are drunk, go home and sleep it off. I don't want my house to be under surveillance. I'm planning to go to America to get medical attention, not to South Beach. Junior sent for me."

"If you forget about women and booze, you'll recover," said Chief Justice Wright. "How many young girls have you initiated this month?"

"Your Honor, we are not alone. Respect the women."

The Chief Justice laughed. "Is there a secret about men that women don't know?"

The general ignored him and turned to Korli. "Korli, I want to see your report card sometime this week. If your teacher lets you fly through three grades in a year, you must be an excellent student. I hope he's not deceiving you."

"I brought it with me, sir."

Korli pulled the card from an old plastic bag and gave it to General Jackson who helped himself to a large portion of *dumboy* and crawfish stewed with palm butter before skimming it. He winked at Korli with candid admiration, nodding several times. Korli grinned; Leanya smiled.

"The lowest grade I see on that card is ninety percent! I was wrong to suggest that you do one grade at a time after the third. In a year or two you should complete the eighth grade. Make haste and catch up; the president is looking for country boys with good education to give them big jobs. The Old Man is thinking ahead. If we don't let the country people get education and take part in the government, we're in for trouble. Is Bendu doing a good job?"

"Yes, sir. She's doing very well. When I was away, she took care of the shop."

"You're a strong man, Korli. She's already loaded! I can see why Solomon almost killed you. He's jealous! A faint-hearted boy would have run away. I want to talk with you and Saki after the dinner."

"Diamond, I must go," said Justice Wright. "I thank you for all that is within me."

"Goodnight, Friend," said General Jackson. "Take care of yourself—and the family—and the job."

Everyone stood up as the Chief Justice and his wife left. Shortly thereafter the others left one by one. The people outside were dancing in the moonlight to a mixture of Gola and Kpelle songs.

"Korli, I held this dinner not only in honor of your recovery but also to inform you that Junior has sent for me. I'm leaving for America in August."

"How long will you be away, sir?"

"I don't know. Maybe a year or two. I'm leaving the farm with you and Saki. Of course you're fully in charge of the shop. My suggestion is that you build a zinc shack near where you are constructing your house and move in it. Transfer the business there. It's still my business. Keep a bank book; when you get enough cash on hand, send me some. I'll leave my address and phone number with you. Go on with your education. Some day your enemies will come to you looking for jobs."

The blow was heavy. Everybody stopped eating and bowed their heads solemnly. Leanya sobbed.

"Monrovia will be the best place for you people," the general told her. "It's the head to everything in this country. Stand strong behind your husband, and you people will get somewhere."

"What do I do about the farm, then?" Korli said.

"Sell the mill and the still and the sugar cane heads and clear out.

You don't want to live here while I'm gone. They'll kill you. And you Saki, help this man. I should have made you his deputy long ago. Be a brother to him, and you too will be better off. Korli is friendly and kind."

"Thank you, sir," said Saki. "I'll be with him until he goes to Monrovia; then I'll go home. My parents are too old. I want to be with them until I bury them."

"I suggest you go to Monrovia with Korli. Not to stay with him but to help him until he gets settled. He could help you start your own business. Now and then you could take something to your people upcountry."

"Thank you, sir. I'll do my best."

Turning to Leanya, the general said, "Leanya, thank you for taking good care of this man for me and for receiving Bendu in the house." The general washed down his last mouthful with a large dose of the Constitution and wiped his face and neck with a wet towel Sarah handed him.

"How far have you gone with your construction?" he asked Korli.

"Not very far, sir. My builders stole most of the materials. However, they made a thousand blocks."

"Put police on them!" the general said. "Most so-called builders in Monrovia build a house for themselves each time they build one for somebody else. Don't let them get away with it. With another thousand blocks you can build a three-bedroom house."

9
Ineffable Gifts

AS THE OLD SMOKING FORD PICKUP CRAWLED on the bumpy laterite road to Monrovia, Korli thought of the happy country life, especially nature's beauty and enduring vitality such as fragrant evergreen forests teeming with squeaking birds, barking deer, screeching monkeys, dace swimming in luminous waters, and crops growing in their seasons. These ineffable gifts had given him full joy and contentment despite the odds. However, he felt that the key to a prosperous and secure life resided in the *kwii* world, not upcountry. This new life entailed difficulties and dangers, but happily he had prepared for it. His uphill struggle at home had taught him the importance of discipline, hard work, and vigilance—qualities that had paid off immensely in White Plains. He had been fortunate to marry a beautiful girl who had borne him three wonderful children and stood with him in his struggles. He had enjoyed a secure life in White Plains despite his brush with Solomon and his gang.

During his last few weeks in White Plains, he had suffered a great disappointment with Bendu. She had carried their son Sewo to Millsburg on a visit, promising to join him and the family in a week or two, but she didn't return. Investigating the case, Korli discovered that she was living with Solomon in Gbehzorn—Solomon who was supposed to be dead and buried. The deception was unsettling, but Korli quickly rose above it, for it wasn't his first time experiencing disappointment in love. He hoped Sewo would fare well in the hands of his enemy. After seven years he'd take custody of his child in keeping with the law.

Korli had sold all the farm implements and the goods in the shop and paid off the workers. He retained a fair sum of money to accommodate him and his family until they settled in Monrovia. His fifth grade education should enable him to find at least a messenger job to get additional income. He hoped to exert himself in the capital city with the same determination he had demonstrated in White Plains. Many rural young men plunged into the *kwii* world out of vengeance and the desire to live on their people's sweat. They joined the army to avenge atrocities soldiers had committed against them or some relatives of theirs. But he'd rather use any influence or fortune he acquired there to help defend and support his people and his family.

A week before moving to Monrovia, Korli sought his good friend and customer Joshua Obadiah to give him information about life in the city. Obadiah had painted a bleak but hopeful picture of city life and promised to help him adjust to it.

"In six months you'll be a master of this town, and nobody will be able to handle you," he had told Korli with the assurance of someone knowledgeable about the city. Korli had listened to him with rapt attention.

They first met at Dualah Market in New Kru Town one Saturday afternoon while Korli walked home disgruntled, holding in one hand an empty tub that had contained the dry meat and crawfish he had sold in the market. He was making wild gestures with the other hand, talking to himself emphatically and bobbing his head. Having seen him haggle with market women over the prices of his commodities, Joshua surmised that the women had cheated yet another poor, innocent country man of his goods, and he was grieving over his losses. Market women set the prices for all produce farmers and hunters took to market in Monrovia. The prices were always more favorable to them than to the hunters and farmers. For instance, they would buy a haunch of deer for a dollar or two at what they called "wholesale price" from a hunter and sell it for ten or fifteen dollars in his very presence. The poor hunter would have no choice but accept the unfair deal since he had nowhere to stay in Monrovia until he sold his meat by retail for a better price. Some fought the injustice by sleeping on the market ground to sell their commodities the following day—only for robbers to steal nearly everything from them, and they would be lucky to return home alive. Additionally, the marketing association made them pay heavy fees for the right to do retail selling in the market, which the government had built for everybody free of charge. Those who couldn't withstand the raw exploitation carried their produce back home and consumed them. Thus, even marketing could not break the cycle of humiliating poverty plaguing rural dwellers.

Joshua had helped many hunters and farmers caught in such predicament to get much more for their commodities by reducing his own margin of profit when buying from them. It had been a mutually rewarding business, and he had many customers. Running to Korli, he extended a friendly hand to him and said:

"Hello, my friend! What happened?"

Korli hastened his strides—almost jogging—for Saki had warned him to be wary of anyone stalking him in the market because such a person could be a robber. Joshua's solid muscles and elegant dressing (a white long-sleeved shirt, gray long pants, and black leather shoes) fitted the description Saki had given him of such crooks. "Whenever a well dressed young man trails you or potters round you in the market," Saki had admonished him, "fasten your eyes on him and keep your hand on your money until he goes away."

Judging that the fellow might attack him at some dark deserted place on the bush road, Korli paused, set the tub down and braced himself for a fight. Perhaps he wasn't fair to the young man after all, he thought, because he didn't look like someone in a fighting mood. He looked intelligent and walked with grace. Korli thought he might be an official of the marketing association assigned to Dualah wishing to do business with him. However, he must be on his guard, for crooks often posed as gentlemen to get hold of their victims.

"What's wrong?" Korli asked gruffly, assessing him with piercing eyes. "I'm only hurrying home for it's getting late."

"Where do you live?"

"White Plains. What wrong have I done?"

"I came to help you," Joshua disarmed Korli with a friendly smile. "I'm Joshua Obadiah, a representative of the marketing association assigned to this market," he said, extending his hand to Korli. They snapped fingers warmly. Korli's suspicion reduced markedly.

"I think I've seen you before," Korli said, "but my memory fails me. Anything I can do for you?"

"The women initiated you today, eh?" Joshua said. "I saw you haggling with them over the prices of your meat and crawfish."

"It's not their first time cheating me," Korli admitted angrily. "What hurts is that they sold my meat and crawfish in my presence at more than five times what they paid me for them. How can you help me?"

"How much did they pay you for the meat?"

"Two dollars for a haunch of duiker," Korli said and sighed dejectedly.

"I can give you ten! What about the crawfish?"

"Twenty-five cents per dozen."

"I can give you one dollar per dozen. To prove that my intentions are earnest, I'm giving you forty dollars for meat and ten dollars for crawfish." Joshua took a bunch of fresh banknotes out of his pocket and gave Korli the correct amounts.

"But you don't even know me!" Korli cried as he received the money. "Suppose I don't come back?"

"You'll come back," Joshua said with confidence. "I see you in the market every Saturday selling meat and crawfish. I've been hearing about you for a long time. You're Kpelle, aren't you?"

"Yes," Korli replied cheerfully. "This is my first time taking a contract, but I won't disappoint you. I hope we'll do business for a long time. My name is Korli. I'll be here before noon next Saturday by the grace of God. Thank you very much."

"Thank you, too. Hurry home, for 'black boys' lurk in every corner of settlements in this country, several of which you'll pass before reaching home."

Since then Korli had complete confidence in Joshua, although some marketers told him that Joshua made great profits from the business deal. Korli had argued that a businessperson who wanted all the profits was doomed to fail. He was happy to have a partner who took the meat and crawfish off his hands each week. Their relationship became so close that people unacquainted with them would think they were blood brothers. Joshua, who was born and bred in Monrovia, became Korli's chief informant and adviser about the city. Korli could not buy a piece of cloth or soap in the market without consulting him first.

For this last business deal with Joshua, Korli had brought him two groundhogs, four duiker haunches, and plenty of crawfish. Joshua turned everything over to his customers.

"I hope you'll be more successful next Saturday."

"Joshua, I have a problem. I need your help."

Growing sober, Joshua watched Korli with troubled eyes and asked with apprehension, "What problem? Are you in trouble with the Congo people? You were a fool to live in White Plains. Just thank God you've escaped with your life."

"I'm moving to Monrovia next week. I want you to find me a room in a community free of thieves and ruffians and killers. The old man I was working for has gone to America. I must now fight for myself."

"I'm finished, my people! I am finished!" Joshua cried, looking so crestfallen that Korli became concerned. "How will I live now?" Raising his arms to the sky, Joshua gazed up in distress. Recovering quickly, he commented, "However, it's better you come down here. You won't amount to anything in this country unless you establish roots in Monrovia. Let's go to the beach for privacy to discuss this matter."

They sat under a plum tree between Fanti and Popo Beach, looking at fishers casting their nets from canoes in the deep sea.

"Your request is difficult to grant, Korli, because you're looking for a place that doesn't exist," Joshua remarked. "However, I'll find you a home in a good neighborhood where you'll have no problem. I know every corner of this town." After a long pause, he continued: "Life in Monrovia can be bitter or sweet depending on how you live it." In preparation for a long lecture, he reclined on his back with his fingers interlaced under his head.

Sitting straight like a statue, Korli watched him steadily and said, "What do you mean? By the way, the meat and crawfish I brought are my farewell gifts to you. You've been a good customer. I hope our friendship lasts for a long time."

"Yes, it will. Of the many customers I have, you're the most faithful. I can bet on you— You wanted to know why life in Monrovia can be bitter or sweet. First, to live here successfully you have to get a job to rent a place to stay and support your family and yourself! Second, make sure you live in a safe neighborhood. Many parts of Monrovia are unhealthy and full of witches and criminals. Since you are Kpelle, I'll take you to Sinkor Old Road. The area is clean and crime-free; many Kpelle people live there. You might even find someone there from your home. Third, make friends with the right people, and never join a gang!" Joshua paused to see the effect of his advice on Korli.

"What kind of job would you recommend that I do in Monrovia?" Korli asked him.

Joshua sat up, put his arms around his knees, and said, "I'll tell you the ones I don't recommend: Don't be a taxi driver. I tried it twice and almost lost my life. One night I picked up a group of bad boys who said they were going to New Kru Town. I didn't normally go to that crowded town at night, but one of them showed me a twenty-dollar bill. So I was sure I'd get my money. When we reached Point Four, they hijacked me to Caldwell Road, whipped me thoroughly, and took the car from me. On another occasion—"

"That town must be a dangerous place, then," Korli interrupted.

"It's dangerous at night because thugs from all over Monrovia go there to carry on mischief. Seldom do its residents engage in criminal acts. When the slums are replaced with well-lighted urban communities,

Monrovia will be safe."

"Did the police arrest your hijackers?"

"Police seldom venture across the bridge at night. They'd rather guard bigshots or harass drivers for handouts." Continuing with a smirk, Joshua said, "When a police officer inspects your driving license, he expects at least five bucks in it. They get such tips mostly downtown and Waterside. Once I gave one my license with nothing inside; he flipped through it and asked pathetically, 'Is this the license you want me to inspect?' I felt sorry for him; doubtless, he didn't have a grain of rice at home. Though I hate corruption, I gave him a ten-dollar note. To be fair to them, however, enforcing laws in cramped dark alleys of slums full of criminals is impossible."

"I see why the taxi business doesn't pay," Korli said. "With the large number of police officers in town, how will you ever make money for yourself if they constantly ask you for money? The government pays them, doesn't it?"

"How much pay do they get and how often?" Joshua said. "Sometimes they get a month's pay after working for six months—something like seventy-five dollars. How can a man with a family live on that kind of money? That's another job I don't recommend—police work."

"Why does the government treat its law enforcers like that?" Korli was amazed. "It breeds corruption!"

"The thinking is if they're paid regularly, they won't go to work, and criminals would have a field day. But let's go back to your problem. The very ground we're sitting on has ears, and I don't need a jail term."

But Joshua's story about the police stirred Korli's curiosity so much that he pursued it:

"They say there's a partnership between some police officers and criminals in this town."

"Do you know why?" Joshua asked.

"No," Korli said. "But if it's true then we're in trouble!"

"Big, big trouble," Joshua said. "I won't blame the police for this but the authorities. Thinking that it takes thieves to catch thieves, they recruit prisoners and people with criminal records into the force. You can imagine why crime is rife in this town. These prisoners turned into police know where the thieves live and what they steal. Those who steal auto parts live in a certain part of town; those who steal clothes live in another part, and so on. The police have no problem finding and arresting them, but they usually share the stolen goods. Let's go to your problem—the day is far gone.

"The other job I won't recommend for you is selling market. It's a waste of time and effort because the profit is too small and thieves are always at your heels to rob you."

"I heard some soldiers complaining the other day—but I think it was a joke—saying that the police enjoy corruption and the army should take over the country so that they too may get their share."

"It's no joke when soldiers talk about overthrowing the government. Not a single year goes by when soldiers don't take over the government of some African country. Military coups have become contagious on the continent. Don't be surprised when the same thing happens here. The average Liberian soldier's monthly pay is no more than fifteen dollars."

"They should go into business as we are doing. When the government finds it difficult to get soldiers, it will have to give them better pay. But the soldiers enjoy hanging guns on their shoulders and going round the country harassing people for money and food. Should war break out in this country, they too will suffer."

"That's for sure, but what will encourage them to do business when government officials get all the money they want without sweat? Our elites get a foothold in government and pocket the country's money. Our soldiers don't have the education needed to get office jobs in the government, but they have guns. They can take over the country anytime and loot everything."

"They don't have to do that; it will spoil the country for everybody. If they go into business, they'll get all the money they want."

"That's true but our people don't like business; I don't know why. Most of the market boys you see down Waterside with trays slung on their necks full of petty goods like cigarettes, candies, matches, kola nuts, and so on, only pretend to be marketers. They rob the real marketers, especially the Lebanese traders."

"The Lebanese don't guard their goods?" Korli looked surprised.

"They do, but they don't worry when they're robbed."

"Why?"

"Because they pass their losses onto their customers, especially the government which is their soup pot. There's no price control in this country, so shopkeepers quote any price they fancy depending on what they think of a customer. I swear to God the Lebanese know all the money people in this country!"

"I wanted to run a shop in Monrovia, but from what you're saying, it seems risky."

"The shop business is good, Korli. It's difficult for robbers to break into a shop. Since you'll go to school, your wife could manage it. Women do business better than men. I can supply you with goods at very reduced prices."

"Joshua, I'm puzzled," Korli said, looking at the rolling waves of the blue Atlantic and the fishermen in their canoes far out to sea.

"What puzzles you? Corruption?"

"Yes, Joshua. Why doesn't the government stop it?"

"The best answer I can give you is, nobody is complaining. Our journalists have tried to address the problem, but most of them end up in prison. Those who want to live only praise the politicians. So corruption is here to stay. Our book people can't straighten up our politics because they all work for the government. How can you criticize an institution that gives you your daily rice? You've seen for yourself how a market woman buys a deer haunch for next to nothing and makes a fortune out of it. There used to be a shoe store on Camp Johnson Road—Bata, I believe was the name—selling leather shoes for two to five dollars a pair. The business went slow. Someone told the Lebanese owner of the store the secret, and he more than doubled his prices. The lowest price for a pair of shoes there rose to fifty dollars. People fought over the shoes. Our people think the higher the price they pay for a commodity, the more durable it is."

"How come you don't run a store?"

"I don't have the money, Korli. It's impossible for a Liberian to get into business because the banks prefer lending money to foreigners—and politicians."

"Maybe it's because they pay their debts."

"Not the politicians! That's the root of our problem. Let's not go into that. We have run out of time. I'm sure your family is expecting you to go to them tonight, not to end up in South Beach Prison."

"How will you supply me with goods if you don't own a store?"

"Suppliers of goods don't own stores. They either manufacture or order them for retailers. I get my supply from Freeport. These ships come here regularly with plenty of things to sell for little or nothing. You can buy a bottle of Gordon gin or a radio with a tape recorder on a ship for five dollars or less and sell it to a Lebanese trader for ten dollars or more. Before doing business with the ships, you must have a lot of money and good contacts with the security."

"You could run your own shop, then!"

"I prefer supplying customers. It is more profitable. I'm doing this hand-to-mouth business because I don't have the money to buy supplies. Business with ships requires at least five thousand dollars to start with. I don't have even half that amount."

"No problem. Find me a house; when I move to town we'll go into business."

"You need a three-room apartment—at a good price. Fifty dollars per month is reasonable. That will give you a chance to save money and build your own house. You're lucky you're coming to town with money in your pocket, and you've met a friend like me to help you. Trust me. You'll become a rich man, especially when you finish school. They'll give you a big government job for you to eat your share of the big government money."

"How far did *you* go in school?" Korli asked.

"I stopped in the sixth grade. I had no support, Korli. For a country man to make it in this country is next to impossible. One bigshot, a money man, visited Sinoe County on government business and met my mother who was a young girl then. Her parents urged her to sleep with him, hoping he'd help the family, but he didn't. The man brought my mother to Monrovia and had her live in a rented room in Buzay Quarters, that congested, swampy, mosquito-infested slum. After I was born, he forsook her for virgins. My mother supported me by selling in the market; that's why I love it. Mother still makes market. Some men wanted to marry her, but they were afraid of the bigshot who helped her with the rent even though he no longer paid her visits. To me, the country man's best bet is to remain upcountry and fight to survive—but these government people and their soldiers won't let us live there in peace. They collect our foodstuffs from us and force us to work on their farms. I learned that they used to sell our people to plantation owners on one island called Fernando Po. You'll learn about that in history books. Many country boys do well in Monrovia and sometimes take money and goods to their people upcountry. From the age of fifteen up to now, I've been responsible for myself in this town."

"Thank you very much for the information, Joshua. When and where do we meet again? I'd like to move to town next Saturday."

"Don't worry. I'll charter a truck and go for you. Just find fifty dollars for the driver."

A week later, they sat on wooden benches in the old pickup Joshua had chartered, Korli did not feel the effect of the bouncing roaring vehicle as it moved at a snail's pace on the washboard road because he was intimately conversing with Joshua, who was giving him more information about the new life he'd soon lead. Leanya and the children sat opposite them on a similar bench, their things cramped between them. They held the dilapidated wooden frame of the truck firmly as it leaned sideways precariously in deep gullies and ravines. The twenty-mile journey took two full hours, as the driver had to stop frequently by a creek for the truck boys to pour water into its overheating engine or revive it when it cut off. Several times the truck broke down altogether and he had to repair it. Villagers along the way gathered on the roadsides and stared at the open vehicle and its weary passengers and their goods.

"I'm taking you to Old Road, a good community, as I told you," Joshua told Korli. "I was lucky to find a concrete house belonging to one of my own tribesmen from Grandcess, Mr. Nah Seton. He and his family have lived so long among the Kpelle that they speak the language very well—just like Kpelle people. It's good your landlord isn't Kpelle. Whenever you live among your own people don't live with them in the same house. They dig up your secrets and make their problems your problems. Mr. Seton is a gracious old man. He retired from the Freeport years ago. People will scare you by saying that Kru people are fussy and love fighting, but it isn't true. If you don't take advantage of them, you can live with Kru people all your life without a problem. They will even fight for you if someone takes advantage of you. You'll see for yourself."

"That's good news, Joshua," Korli said. "Tell me something. Why is the community called Old Road?"

"It's the first road the government—or America, I should say—built to the interior. It winds through Sinkor and Congo Town. The new road leads directly from the city to Mt. Barclay and upcountry, bypassing the old one. America also built that one for us. Numerous bigshots live on Old Road and so it's not as congested, unhealthy, and quarrelsome as Sinkor Airfield, Soniwein, Waterside, West Point, and many other places in Monrovia where country people live."

Korli was surprised. "Parts of Monrovia are earmarked for country and Congo people, respectively?"

"Your pocket decides where you live. Where will country people get money to live in Sinkor or Mamba Point?" Joshua answered. "Most country people live by selling goods in the market, so they love the crowded areas. Old Road Market is small but popular because people from Bassa, Bong, Nimba, and Lofa Counties bring their produce there for sale. Like Dualah Market, it supplies the big markets in town. Now, let's talk about the problem at hand. Monrovia is dangerous! Never fall into deep sleep at night; keep your lantern burning, your radio on, and your cutlass under your bed while sleeping. Happily, your windows are secured with rogue bars. Thieves prowl about this town, day and night. They attack mostly at night when people are sleeping. Always remember to lock all your doors when you and your family leave the apartment."

"Joshua, thank you for the information and advice," Korli said, feeling that he had had more than enough information and admonition about the city. "I'll try to be wise, vigilant, and strong."

"One more thing—you need a Christian name to get respect in this country. If you put country life aside and live like a *kwii* person, you'll be surprised at what becomes of you. Pay your rent in advance—say, three to six months—to get a chance to build up your business. If rogues visit you, they'll be disappointed. I'll get you radios, tape recorders, fans, flashlights, cigarettes, soaps, Coca-Cola, beer—you want to sell auto parts? They make quick money. All the vehicles in this country need repair."

"Bring me whatever you think will sell," Korli said.

Just then, the driver, who was dressed in threadbare overalls with tools in every pocket, parked the wobbly old truck off the narrow street half a mile of its destination and said he couldn't go any further.

"If I go beyond this point, this *duazeh* will hitch in the sand," he said, jumping down and signing to his boys with a shake of his head to come down and unload the beat-up old truck. "To repair this *duazeh* will cost me more than the money you people will pay me," he told Joshua.

"Thank you, Jack," said Joshua, coming down. "My people, hurry down let's carry the things to the house," he told Korli and his family. "The weather is having mercy on us. November is a rainy month and it's getting dark."

The baby pressed against her shoulder, Leanya alighted with a grunt, followed by Korli who put Junior down and shouldered Famang. Joshua and the carboys took what they could and they all went to the house.

Leanya and the driver remained to watch over the things. Occasionally a group of boys stopped by, looked at the furniture and kitchen utensils with inquisitive eyes, and asked if they could help tote them. The driver would decline the offer and keep his eyes on them as they walked away with hesitation, looking over their shoulders in anger.

"Such boys can take a chair and vanish without a trace," the driver would tell Leanya.

It was a great relief when Joshua and Korli returned with several boys and girls from their new home to help carry the things.

"The landlord is not at home," Korli told Leanya, "but his wife is there. Our apartment is ready—clean and freshly painted. There's a well in the yard."

The new community impressed Korli and Leanya. The zinc shacks were not as congested as those he had seen in New Kru Town, Logan

Town, and West Point. Scattered among them were modern concrete houses roofed with high quality aluminum sheets painted red. Pit latrines, rarely found in the average slum, stood behind some of the shacks. Unlike the alleys, the sandy streets were relatively free of trash and puddles. While some children played football in yards, others shrieked and chased each other in crooked alleys littered with banana and orange peelings, assortments of cans, bottles, and pieces of planks. The new home was a voluminous white concrete building standing alone in the center of a twoacre plot of land fenced with barbed wire. Neighbors gathered in the yard to welcome the new arrivals and see their belongings. Attached to the back of the building, the apartment had its own door and porch, much to Leanya's delight. She asked Joshua and Korli to help her set up the furniture in the vast living room and pack the cooking utensils in the kitchen.

"Let's greet the people first," Korli advised her.

In a spacious lounge, furnished with two sets of leather-cushioned furniture, they met the landlord's wife, a chocolate-colored skinny woman with three plaits of grizzled hair extending to the middle of her shoulder blades. She wore a blue calico lappa suit printed with images of the president and of bougainvillea flowers. Her beady eyes shone brightly under bushy brows and long lashes.

"Welcome! Welcome!" she greeted her new tenants with outstretched arms and a broad smile. She hugged the children and Leanya and snapped Korli's fingers. Surprising Korli and Leanya, she said in correct Kpelle, "This is your new home! Feel free here! My name is Bornyonoh Seton, from Sasstown. The bossman is visiting a sick friend. He'll soon come; he knows you people are coming today. Please sit down."

"Thank you very much for the kind welcome," said Korli. "And thanks for building this wonderful house. We are happy to be here and hope to live with you people as long as possible." Then he introduced members of his family.

"Wonderful children!" exclaimed Mrs. Seton. She took the baby from Leanya, cuddled her lovingly, and they sat on a large brown sofa. Junior and Famang squeezed themselves between them, while Korli and Joshua sat in another sofa. "Borwulo, bring us a bottle of Gordon and ginger ale," Mrs. Seton called. Then she told Korli, "We are honored that Joshua chose our poor home for you people. We built this house ten years ago when Old Road was so-so bush. Nah used to hunt deer and monkeys here. Now the place has become a modern city. The market is but a tenminute walk away, and it has a bus stop. Rogues don't bother us because bigshots live in this community. The Secretary of National Security lives just a stone's throw behind us. Therefore, the security are always patrolling this area. The bigshots love the suburbs—and many Kpelle live round here, too. We're surprised you people didn't pick a Kpelle family to live with."

"People are the same, Ma'am," Korli said. "Only our languages separate us. I thought you people were Kpelle; you speak it very well."

"Before my husband started working for the Freeport, he worked for the Forestry Development Authority for twelve years. We lived in Ziansu, Bong County, during those years. The Kpelle are friendly and kind. After living with them so long, we were bound to speak their language. I have many Kpelle friends."

"Living with your own people is a problem," Joshua said. "That's why I brought them here."

"It's true," said Mrs. Seton. "Had we built this house among our own people, they would have taken it from us. Not by force, of course, but by claiming it as theirs because we are related. All the tribes have the same problem."

Borwulo brought a big bottle of Gordon gin, several bottles of ginger ale, and glasses on an aluminum tray, and set it on a center table. Then, filling the glasses, she placed them on small trays and took them to the guests and Mrs. Seton.

"Let the strangers drink to their satisfaction, Borwulo," Mrs. Seton said. "But let me taste it first to take out the witchcraft." She sipped her drink.

"Don't talk about witchcraft," Korli protested mildly. "You have given us this beautiful home with a pure heart, and I have full confidence in you and your family. We'll eat or drink without fear whatever you offer us."

"It's our custom, Korli," said Mrs. Seton. "No matter how familiar we are with *kwii* customs, we can't forget ours. If your own mother gives you something to eat or drink, she must taste it first."

"Trust is the best security," Korli said. "When you trust people with your life, they're bound to take care of you. For five years I lived with Congo people. Tell you what—they treated me better than my own people ever did. I was a darling in White Plains. Another reason why I feel safe here is that one of your daughters has a Kpelle name. 'Borwulo' means 'small friend.'"

"Kru people love their tribe, but they also love and respect all other tribes. One of my Kpelle friends lives in the big brown house you people passed on your way here; she named Borwulo for herself. So, we consider ourselves Kpelle people, and, as you can see, we speak it somehow."

"You'll teach my wife English, then, and we'll learn Kru. I learned a few words of it when I was doing business at Dualah. It's true what you said. You learn a language fast when you live with the native speakers."

"Women learn languages faster than men. In six months, Leanya will speak English—perhaps Kru also. I'll teach her. You people are not drinking! The liquor is not for holding in your hands! Borwulo, bring us another bottle of Gordon. Wait, let's drink half of this first."

"We have plenty of packing to do, Ma'am," Joshua said. "And Leanya has a baby."

"Baby or no baby, she doesn't drink. Period!" Korli said, sipping his drink.

"Drink and eat something before packing," said Mrs. Seton who wasn't doing much drinking herself. "My boys will see to the packing in the morning. The girls are about to bring you some food. You'll eat Kru food tonight: *fufu* and palm butter with *kiss me quick* and grouper. We cooked Kpelle food, too: rice and cassava leaves with red palm oil and *yanga boy*."

"Monkey meat!" Leanya exclaimed with delight. Everybody laughed heartily.

"Korli," Joshua said, "you are now in good hands. I'll come tomorrow afternoon to see how you people are faring and for us to complete our discussion."

"Joshua, don't tell me you're leaving without eating!" said Mrs. Seton. "You're sleeping here tonight." She went to the kitchen and, in a moment, Borwulo and another girl brought in the food.

"This is a feast!" Korli said delightfully.

"We're happy you people made it safely here," said Mrs. Seton. "So let's celebrate."

As they ate, Mr. Seton bustled in. He was a fat baldheaded man with light skin. His puffy face, dilated eyes, and unsteady gait suggested that he had been drinking.

"Hello! Hello! Hello!" he cried thickly, his face beaming. "So our strangers are here and the Madam is seeing after them! Thank you Bornyonoh! Welcome! Welcome! Welcome!" He shook hands with the guests and sat at the table by his wife. Immediately he pulled the bowls of fufu and palm butter and started helping himself. "You people are eating only rice!" he said.

"That's what the guests are eating," said Mrs. Seton. "Kpelle people can't go without rice for a single day." There was general laughter. "When famine comes to them, it isn't due to lack of food. The people of Bong

County grow plenty of bananas, oranges, cassava, corn, potatoes, and eddoes but don't consider them as food."

"Each African tribe has its staple food," said Mr. Seton. "The Fanti of Ghana love corn; the Igbo of Nigeria love yam; the Swahili of East Africa love corn too—they call it millet. When you work for the Freeport, you go round the world. The British and the Americans love bread and potatoes, though they eat other foods also."

"We the rice eaters of the world are the majority," said Joshua proudly.

"That's true," said Mr. Seton. "We'll finish this food! You people will learn how to eat all these dishes—Bornyonoh, please send me that bowl of *torborgee*. Before good food wastes, let belly burst!" He ate and drank to repletion and looked at Korli and his family. "You are blessed with fine children, Korli," he said, "and a beautiful wife. My name is Nah Seton."

"The old ma welcomed us warmly and told us your name. In fact, Joshua told me a lot about you people. He did well to get us in your modern home. Thank you for accepting us and for this delicious dinner."

"We have much to talk about," Mr. Seton said, breathing with difficulty, "but you people are tired from the day's activities; bathe and go to sleep. We'll see you in the morning. Goodnight." Rising with much effort, he staggered on the marble floor to his bedroom.

"We'll give you people rooms to sleep in tonight, Mr. Korli," Mrs. Seton said. "Joshua, you know where to sleep."

"Of course! This is my house! If my old lady jumps on me tomorrow, you'll settle the palaver," Joshua bantered.

Mrs. Seton laughed quietly and said, "Martha is fighting a losing battle; she'll soon get tired of it. Men love variety." There was no comment on that. To rouse a response, she added, "They often leave the best women at home and go after the worst ones in the streets." Nobody made a rejoinder to that, either.

"Leanya and the children should sleep here, while Korli and I sleep by the things," Joshua said, winking at Korli. "We're afraid of nothing. We only want to chat. We have much to talk about."

Feeling that the question Mrs. Seton had raised shouldn't be left unchallenged, Korli said, "Love is like food. When you get enough at home, you won't go out looking for more."

"I used to wonder," said Joshua, "what makes a couple stick together for life. Now I know why. If people marry for love, they can't imagine living without one another."

"I hope so," laughed Mrs. Seton. "Don't dig a new hole for Korli. That's my advice to you. What men say and what they do are not always the same."

"The man loves his wife, Ma'am," Joshua said, laughing, "and his hands are full. I'll keep this family together—you and I. Leanya is my sister; I won't let her suffer. If this man plays tricks on you, Leanya, let me know. I'll pepper him." Everybody roared with laughter.

"I sometimes wonder what men mean by love," Mrs. Seton said. She rose and added, "You people may go to bed. You're tired after that long bumpy ride. We'll complete this conversation tomorrow."

Korli and Joshua went to the apartment; Borwulo and Leanya and her children went to the girl's room, a spacious room with a big mahogany bed. Three girls who were lying in the bed left the room when they entered.

"We'll sleep in the living room on the sofas," Borwulo told Leanya, following her sisters.

"No, Borwulo, let's sleep together—all of us," Leanya said. "The bed is large enough."

"Those children fight in bed, Ma'am," said Borwulo. "After a hard day, you need good sleep."

"Borwulo, Liimu doesn't let me get good sleep. She wakes up to suck when I'm ready to sleep."

Borwulo called her sisters back.

An hour after they went to bed, Korli, who was keeping vigil over their things, heard some noise at the door. Someone was prying it open with a crowbar. Taking his cutlass, Korli tapped Joshua lightly on the shoulder and whispered:

"Someone is breaking in, but let's wait until they get inside for the law to be on my side. My cutlass is ready."

"No, Korli," Joshua whispered. "When you kill him, everybody will turn against us. Further, he might have a gun." Then he declared loudly, "My friend—you who are breaking in here—we are not sleeping! When you come in, you'll meet men like yourself! We'll burst your nut bag! We're not afraid of you!" The thieves scampered away. "They think we are stupid," he told Korli. "Who will bring these plenty things in a house and sleep elsewhere?" Advising Korli, he said, "Don't ever let rogues break door on you. They usually come in groups—with dangerous weapons. Knowing that they will be killed once they're caught in a house, they kill anyone who wakes up. Hire an old man to guard your door at night. Of course, he might invite rogues to rob you and share your property with them. You have to be your own security, Korli. Keep a shotgun under your bed. Don't make alarm about what has happened tonight. Let's pretend that nothing happened; someone will get in your trap one of these days."

At daybreak, they busied themselves setting up the furniture in the living room and packing cooking utensils in the kitchen. Before ten, everything was in place. When Leanya came to the apartment, she was surprised that there was nothing left to do. After a brief inspection, she called Korli to the tiled bathroom.

"Your drinking cup is missing! The glass one with handle!" she told him, her voice quivering. "And I don't see one of my bundles! The one with my good clothes!"

Korli hugged her affectionately and whispered, "We'll get more of those things. Don't worry. Let them have the eggs. When we have the hen, we'll get many more eggs. Should we complain about robbery, the people might think we came with bad intentions. As of now, let's be careful. I don't want to keep money here."

"Where will you keep it, then? It's risky to give it to someone for safekeeping. They could use it and claim that it was stolen. If you put it in the bank, you won't get it when you need it. That's what Joshua told me. Let me have some to make market. I'll tie it on my waist. Before they steal it, they'll have to steal me, too. Keep the rest in your box, and get one more lock for the front door."

"A good idea. Joshua told me to give him money for him to bring me goods to sell—things like radios, watches, and car parts—at very low prices. I want to build a shop here."

"Give him a little amount and see what happens. Selling is not easy. Don't let him pile goods on us we might find impossible to sell." Korli opened his small wooden box he had hidden in the bathroom. In it was six thousand five hundred and fifty dollars. He gave two thousand to Leanya, two thousand to Joshua who was waiting in the living room, and kept the balance.

"I'll see you by the end of next week," Joshua told him on receiving the money. "You have courage—I could run away with this plenty money."

"You won't do that to me," Korli said. "Besides, that money won't solve all your problems for life, Joshua. You taught me how to trust people."

10

A Dream World?

THEIR GENEROUS RECEPTION by the Setons and the sound
business deal he had made with Joshua assured Korli of a good future in
Monrovia. Interestingly, the people of the *kwii* world were not much
different from those of the tribe. While some had improved their lot like
the Setons, most of them were struggling for survival like himself, living
entirely on menial labor. Joshua had excluded some categories of work
from the jobs a gentleman should do, but all jobs were demanding and
fraught with dangers, Korli thought. He'd do any job he might get to
support his family and himself.

Korli was happy that Leanya, who had initially opposed moving to
Monrovia, now felt it was the best place to be. She loved the beautiful,
secure, concrete house and the freedom from family interference in her
personal life. When Korli asked her after their first night in the new home
whether she liked it, she exclaimed with delight that she loved it and
thanked him for bringing her to such a dream world.

"Look, Korli," she added, beaming delightfully, "I'll go to school.
You've been doing well for me, but I need a teacher because you'll be too
busy. A *kwii* house is not a place for a country woman. If you can make it
at your age, I can too."

"It'll be a great help to the family in the future, but don't blame
yourself if you can't make it," Korli told her. "It isn't your fault that there's
no school in Kuntaa. You have children to raise. How will you manage to
go to school?"

"A teacher could come here in the evening two or three times a week and give me lessons. It wasn't possible to get one in White Plains, but here there should be many of them."

"We'll see."

"It's time we made some plans, Korli. I want to begin my business tomorrow, but I can't afford the license fee. The marketing association charges four hundred and fifty dollars for a little spot on the market ground to build a stall. And then you must pay them ten dollars per day as you make your market."

"I'll ask Mr. Seton to let you build a stall in the yard. Why does the government let them rob the marketers like that? The money they collect doesn't go into the treasury but into their pockets! I'm sure Mr. Seton will let you make your market in his yard for a small fee. It'll keep you at home to mind our property and save the women round here the trouble of running to and from Old Road Market for common things like greens, chicken soup, pepper, kerosene, and toilet tissue. I'll use the money that remained with me to pay school fees, buy modern furniture for the apartment, and pay six months' rent in advance."

"Pay the school fees, but wait until Joshua brings the goods before spending more money. Don't let your pocket run dry. To get food in this town, you don't go to a farm but put your hand in your pocket!"

"I can't help but buy modern furniture for the apartment, Leanya," Korli said. "Rattan chairs don't belong in a modern house. Visitors don't come only to keep your company but to see the inside of your house! My dear, you don't get in leopard skin and act like cat. We must make the sacrifice. I'd rather spend my money on my family than let thieves steal it. The day we moved here, they tried to break into the apartment. I didn't want to alarm you with the news. They thought nobody slept by the things."

"What?" Leanya shook with surprise. "Joshua told us that this area is crime-free!"

"He means as compared with some other areas in Monrovia. Nowhere is safe in this world, my dear. If you don't defend your properties and yourself, thieves will take everything from you. Try to feed the family with the money you have. I'll soon get a job to help you."

"How will you do a job and sell the things Joshua will bring at the same time? Are you sure he'll bring us anything? Do you know where he lives?" Leanya looked doubtful.

"The things will be part of your business. Joshua won't deceive us. He looks honest. He gets the things through contacts, as he told me, so it'll take him some time. Leanya, business means trust and patience. The

Lebanese have partners who supply them, and they have those that *they* supply. Let's be patient. If he brings us nothing, we'll still make it."

That evening Korli took the rent to Mr. Seton who was lounging in the sitting room in pajamas. Sitting with him on the large sofa, Korli handed him an envelope containing six months' rent. Mr. Seton carefully opened the envelope with his mottled hands, took out a bunch of fresh banknotes, and cast a questioning look at Korli.

"For safe-keeping?" he asked.

"No, sir," Korli said quietly. "For rent."

"But you're required to pay only one month's rent at the end of each month! The month hasn't ended yet! Your first time paying rent? Don't press yourself too hard. I don't put renters out for owing me unless they refuse to pay. Anyhow, thank you. You really mean to live with us for a long time."

"I should thank you, sir!" Korli said. "We want to live here until we build our own house. We're paying for six months in advance to have a chance to get into business. Business takes time to grow."

"You're a good man," said Mr. Seton, leaning on the backrest of the sofa. "Some renters don't like to pay rent, not knowing that what they pay is nothing compared to the cost of building the house they live in."

"I'm sure it took you many years to build this big house—and much money."

"It's what I got out of the twenty years I worked for the Freeport of Monrovia. I had eight children in school and more than ten mouths to feed when I was building this house. Mind you—I had only three children of my own. The rest were for relatives. We lived in New Kru Town those days. My family knew nothing about this house until the day we moved in it."

"You did well. It's exactly what I'd like to do. Once you have your own roof over your head, you have settled."

"I bid you to keep it secret. Don't let even your wife know about it. This is the second house I've built in Monrovia. I played the fool to have built the first one on a Vai girl's lot. A beautiful girl with long hair but sweet-mouthed." Mr. Seton bowed his head in reflection and continued: "Land isn't dear here, but the tricks! Some landowners make you buy the same lot four or five times! When you build a house on it, someone with an older deed claims it and your house. If you don't stand strong, you lose everything. What is sad is that nothing happens to the crook. Corruption will bring war to this country," said Mr. Seton. "Never buy land from someone you don't know, or you'll be throwing your money away. I was happy to build on a lot my future wife's father had given her. I firmly believed that she wouldn't play any tricks on me. When I finished building, Miatta told me not to put my foot in the house, or I'd go to jail. I thought she was joking. We had lived together for five years and planned to marry as soon as the house was completed— It's good you have a wife. Don't let Monrovia women make you leave her— When I moved into the house, a police officer, her lover, jailed me; I was released only when I signed a statement under duress turning the property over to her. She and her police lover are living in that house today. I almost died of frustration, but I thank God I built another house to prove to her that when a big tree falls, it's still higher than the grass."

"That was too bad," Korli said. "Were you not a good man, you'd have done something bad to her! Why should another man enjoy your sweat?"

"When I became Deputy-Managing Director of the Port, Miatta often went to my office and asked me for money. I used to give it to her, though not as much as before."

"Did she have a child for you?"

"No. I suffered in vain. If she had had a child for me, it wouldn't have been a total loss. My child would have enjoyed that property, too."

"Did you sue her?"

"My lawyer told me that the judge would have ruled in her favor. I had no business building a house on somebody else's land. Am I not living in a house?" Mr. Seton looked round his luxurious sitting room.

"People take advantage of good people," Korli said, remembering his own experience with Bendu.

"Do you know why iguana doesn't have craw-craw?"

"No, sir."

"Because it has nails to scratch it. Good people don't revenge, so people take advantage of them. Who will take advantage of a crook, thief, or murderer? The last renter I put in the apartment you're in left owing three months' rent. The fellow had sweet mouth. After paying two months' rent, he started paying me with empty promises. At the end of the third month, he asked for a two-week grace period to get a ten thousand-dollar check from the government. Then something went wrong: the government didn't have enough money in the bank. He asked for another two weeks to collect debts. But the debtors hid themselves from him! After three months, I grew tired of his lies and put him out. I found out that he had been living like that in Monrovia for years!"

"Old man, thank you for your good advice," Korli said, standing up. "Before buying any more land in this town, I'll let you know—and I'll never build on somebody else's land. Please give my greetings to the

Madam. You need your rest. I too need rest; I'm beginning my hustling tomorrow."

"You already own land in this town?"

"Yes, sir. One lot. Not far from here."

"Who sold it to you?"

"One Joseph Dennis."

"Oh, I know the man—he's good. Make haste and put a foundation on it."

"I'm doing so, sir."

"I wish you good luck. How is the family?"

"Everybody is fine, thank you, sir. Leanya wanted to begin her business tomorrow, buying and selling produce. She wants to build a stall in the market but the license fee is prohibitive."

"She could build her stall in this yard to save the women round here the trouble of walking back and forth to Old Road Market. The big markets are usually full of confusion and thieves. Let her start her business here since she is new in town."

"Thank you, sir. I'll let her know."

"She'll make money because she'll have no competition. Let her get her supplies from wholesalers, people who bring produce from upcountry in pickups, instead of buying them from retailers. Time will come when she'll charter a pickup and buy produce directly from the farmers. That's when she'll make the most profit."

"Thank you, sir," Korli said. "Good night."

"One more thing—After you get a good bit of money, don't be tempted to run a taxi. Taxis make money but you have to be your own driver to get it."

"Joshua gave me the same advice; in fact, he told me that the taxi business is dangerous. Some bad people might take you to an isolated place, beat you up, and take the car from you. Even if that danger didn't exist, I won't bother with taxi because we don't have good roads and car parts are very expensive. I might buy a car for private use some day." Korli yawned and stretched.

"If you are sleepy," said Mr. Seton, "we'll discuss other matters later. Good night. Sleep well."

"Good night, sir. We'll see you in the morning."

11

A STORM

THEY HAD INTENDED to carry out their plans the following day, but a severe rainstorm and lightning made it apparent that they would spend the day indoors. Korli opened the curtains at seven and watched the translucent morning with dismay. Laden clouds with patches of pale light hung low over the city. An ocean wind was blowing them upland, but they crawled at a snail's pace although the wind was so severe that it sent debris flying in all directions. Korli returned to bed disappointed; he had wished to take applications round the town and buy furniture. His instructor had helped him prepare an application with great care and was certain it would produce a positive result.

"A messenger job is easy to get," Teacher Kpenkpa had assured him. "Due to lack of telephones and a good mail delivery system, messengers are the most practical means of communication in this town. However, increase your chances of getting a job by making at least ten copies of the application and take them to the various government departments."

Mr. Seton had given him the names of assistant secretaries for administration of ten departments and told him to address his applications to them.

"People pay close attention to letters addressed to them personally," he told Korli. "Tell them you intend to make their duties your career. Tell the assistant secretary of information for administration, for example, that you want to be a journalist in the future. He'll most likely employ you.

Due to a shortage of trained workers, some departments employ students as cadets. In some cases, they even give them scholarships. Have some messengers recommend you to their bosses. People hardly read letters of application in this town."

"I want to apply to the Department of Education for a scholarship," Korli said. "A messenger's pay can't support my family."

"Scholarships are reserved for high school and college students. Besides, it's almost impossible for a native boy to get a scholarship in this country. The bigshots give them to their children, wards, and girlfriends who never sit for the exams. You might stand a small chance of getting one when you complete at least the eighth grade."

"Unless the government builds schools round the country, getting an education will always be a problem for people upcountry," said Korli. "Down here, children start school early, but upcountry, they usually start it late because they must first grow up and go far from home to live with relatives or friends of their families to send them to school. Civilized families adopt some of them, promising to send them to school, but the boys often end up as farm workers and the girls as mistresses of masters of the homes."

"They think by keeping the country people in darkness, they'll cling to power forever," said Mr. Seton. "It's a bad mistake. One day the blind country people will take power by force. Power in the hands of the blind is dangerous."

Just then, a bolt of lightning struck, and the cries of people running home for safety made Korli open the front door to see for himself what was going on. The wind pushed him so violently that he closed the door immediately and returned to his seat.

A moment later, fully dressed in a lappa suit, a puny umbrella in her hand, Leanya came to him and said she was going to the market. "Listen out for the children in case they wake up," she said. "There's a bottle of milk on the bedroom table for Liimu. I'll soon be back."

Amazed, Korli told her, "Let the rainstorm stop before you go. Flying objects might hurt you and you might catch cold!" Leanya hastened to the kitchen for her market basket.

"If you mind rainstorms," she said over her shoulder, "you won't do a thing in this town. The rainy season begins here rather early and lasts until the end of the year. Korli, money is breeze. Unless we do business, we'll soon go broke."

Korli walked her to the door and opened it. The storm had become more intense; people were running about in disarray for cover. Pieces of zinc and planks were flying all around.

"You see what I was talking about?" Korli told her. "This storm will turn your tiny umbrella inside out." Thunder crashed, rain pounded the roof, and the wind blew with a mighty force.

"I'm no sugar or salt to melt," Leanya said with a faint smile. "When it rains, marketers sell their produce for little or nothing and run home. It's bad we can't hear from Joshua. His two weeks have turned into a whole month. Were he to bring the things, we'd build a shop. Shops make more money than market."

"Mr. Seton says you may build a stall in the yard. He's not charging any fee. You won't have competition, so it's an opportunity for you to make more profits. Don't worry about Joshua," Korli said with a tinge of anger. "When you put money in business, forget it. Business is gain and loss." Lightning flashed and thunder boomed doubly.

"If the loss is more than the gain, you have to do something about it, or you waste your time. I'll thank Mr. Seton, but I'll wait until the business takes shape before building a stall. We used good judgment in White Plains by not using the little money General Jackson gave us to build a shop there. Where would we have been today had we done that?"

Covering her head with the wicker basket, Leanya leapt out of the house into the rainstorm; Korli closed the door with a sigh of resignation. Though concerned for her safety, he was proud of his wife. Very few women would risk their lives to support their families, he thought. The burden of support was always on the shoulders of their husbands.

Korli was tense with anxiety as the storm gathered incredible momentum, tore roofs from houses, and flattened zinc shacks. He could hear the racket outside. Rushing to the door, he called Leanya back, but she was gone. He dropped in a chair and held his head in his hands, planning to deliver his applications as soon as the rainstorm ceased. Though he wasn't born in Monrovia, he knew the city well. He was healthy and ready to apply himself to his duties with dedication and commitment. Leanya's motivation challenged him. To accomplish anything worthwhile, one must endure a little inconvenience. He watched the raging rainstorm through the window, and now saw people fleeing their broken shacks, seeking shelters in concrete buildings. A sudden pounding of the front door drew his attention. Thinking it was his wife, he promptly opened it and saw instead an old woman, soaked to the bone, standing on the threshold, trembling with cold and dripping.

"My son, please let me in," she whimpered in Kpelle. The wind flashed the rain on them. Korli quickly led her in by a thin wrinkled hand and pushed the door with all his might and closed it. "The wind has knocked down our *konko*," whined the old woman. "They say you people are Kpelle."

"Yes," Korli said. "We've been so busy settling down that we haven't had time to visit our neighbors. They told us that Kpelle people live here. You're welcome, Mother."

Taking her to the girls' room, Korli brought her one of his wife's lappa suits and returned to the sitting room. Despite the turbulence, the children slept sound. Soon the old woman came to him with her wet clothes, which he hung in the bathroom.

"Thank you, my son, for saving my life," she said with a deep bow and sat by him.

"God saved your life, Mother—our lives. I only helped. Leanya will soon come. She went to the market."

"I wanted to come over and welcome you people, but I decided to let you settle first. God wanted me to pay the visit without further delay. I believe he sent this rainstorm because he is vexed with the *kwii* people. I've never seen a rainstorm this bad."

"The sun will soon shine. I saw it behind the clouds."

"Too many wicked deeds happen in this town—things unheard of upcountry: murder, rape, stealing, lies— I had thought such things didn't happen in the *kwii* world."

"People are the same everywhere, Mother. The *kwii* people think they're better than us because they speak English and have money. But they behave exactly the way we do—sometimes worse."

"It's true! Women here offer themselves to men for money! Of course, most of the women who do such things come from neighboring countries, but our children are quick to adopt foreign ways. Some get pregnant and don't even know who the father is."

The rain stopped abruptly. Liimu squealed. Korli went for her and put the bottle of milk to her mouth. Junior and Famang woke up and called their mother, clinging to their father.

"So the rainstorm put you people to sleep," Korli told them. "Mother will soon come; she went to the market to buy food." Korli sat at the dining room table with Liimu in his arms, while Junior and Famang held onto his knees, staring at their visitor with curiosity.

"Fine children!" said the old woman, lightly pinching Liimu's cheek and smiling at her. Liimu was unresponsive. "Which Kpelle country you people come from?" she asked Korli, abandoning her playfulness.

"I come from Haindi, Fuama Chiefdom. My wife comes from Kuntaa, Deyn Gola Chiefdom."

"I come from Gbarnga, Zorkwelle Chiefdom. Many Seghai Kpelle live in Gbarnga. One of them is a close friend of mine, a great market woman. Noai says she has a sister in Deyn Gola. I've forgotten the name of her town."

"Kuntaa?"

"Something like that. Oh, I remember. Zaraimu!"

"Zaraimu is no distance from Kuntaa. My name is Korli and my wife's name is Leanya."

"My name is Gonmaah. I can't invite you to my house because it's gone. We'll have to move to some relative's house. I want to meet your wife."

"She'll soon be back from the market."

"What is she doing in the market in this kind of weather? Please advise her not to go anywhere in a rainstorm. The children need her!"

"She'll get under somebody's roof, I'm sure."

"Brave, strong-minded woman! She'll make plenty of money if she goes upcountry to buy produce. Monrovia market women make everything too expensive. In Zorkwelle country, food costs little or nothing. Fruits and vegetables such as oranges, bananas, plums, pawpaws, potato greens, and cassava leaves are not for sale in our villages. You pick what you want and give the people anything you like. The only problem is bringing them down here. Whenever your wife decides to go to Gbarnga, let me know so that I may give her my people's names and direct her to their houses. They'll help buy her produce at low prices—give her some free of charge."

"Thank you, Mother," Korli said.

Another knock on the door. It was Leanya, wet and shivering, who came with a basket of potato greens on her head. Junior opened the door for her and gasped. She entered with laughter and took the greens to the kitchen. Korli inspected them and said they were good.

"I was lucky," she told him. "The market women gave their greens away for whatever they could fetch and ran home from the rainstorm."

As she went to the bedroom to change her clothes, she paused and looked questioningly at the old woman.

"The rainstorm broke down her house, and she came here for refuge," Korli told her. "She's Kpelle."

"Welcome, Old Ma," Leanya snapped her fingers. "I'm going to take off these wet clothes and come back."

On her return she sat by Ma Gonmaah and said, "The rainstorm knocked down many stalls—and houses! Fortunately, nobody got hurt."

"I saw everything from the window," Korli said as he handed her Liimu who raised her arms to go to her. Leanya put her nipple in her mouth.

"After this girl drinks a whole bottle of milk, she sucks the titty before she's satisfied," she said. "I don't think she'll ever leave the titty."

"It's the best food for a baby," Ma Gonmaah told her. "Don't take it from her mouth by force. She might get sick from grief or disease."

"How much did you pay for those big bunches of potato greens?" Korli asked Leanya.

"Five dollars for all," Leanya said. "My profit should be twenty-five dollars and three bunches. I'll sell some round the neighborhood."

"Our *konko* broke down, my daughter," the old woman told Leanya, gazing at her with watery eyes. "Don't go in the rain again. Monrovia rain is full of dust, disease, and smoke. The rain drives them into your skin and makes you sick."

"Ma Gonmaah comes from Gbarnga, Zorkwelle Chiefdom," Korli informed Leanya. "I gave her one of your lappa suits. She came here wet and trembling with cold."

"Thank you for helping her," Leanya said. "People were running for their lives as their zinc shacks broke down! We're lucky to be in a concrete house."

"Don't be playing in the rain, my dear," Korli told her. "The children need you. Sickness wastes time."

"You too need me," Leanya said smilingly. "It doesn't rain everyday, Korli. Once in a while I'll brave the rain and the storm to buy markets at reduced prices."

"Ma Gonmaah says produce is inexpensive in Gbarnga. She knows your Auntie Noai who is now a big market woman. Says they're friends. Whenever you decide to go up there, let her know. She'll show you where your Auntie lives."

"One day I'll go to Auntie. She left Kuntaa when I was a baby, they tell me. I took cover in some Bassa people's house on my way from the market. They gave me a seat and fufu to swallow, but I only tasted the soup."

"You'll buy produce at better prices up in Gbarnga, Ma Gonmaah says. Kpelle people are good farmers and the land upcountry is rich."

"Ma Gonmaah, this is your home," Leanya told the old woman with a smile. "I've been wishing to visit the Kpelle people round here, but I couldn't get the chance."

"I know how busy you've been. Thank you, my child," said Ma Gonmaah. "Settling in a new home is hard work, especially in the *kwii* world. You have to do everything for yourself."

Giving the baby to Korli, Leanya lit two charcoal stoves for cooking rice and soup; she started cutting up a bunch of greens.

"You people will soon eat," she said. "I don't know why people get so hungry during the rainy season—when they do nothing but sit round and talk."

The sun was now up and the day became clear and bright. Korli opened the front door. People were going to their broken shacks to see what they could salvage from the ruins.

"Old Ma, you may live with us until they rebuild your house," Leanya told Ma Gonmaah who was helping her fan the charcoal stoves. "Trouble isn't for one person. The same thing could happen to us. When I see you, I think of my mother. Korli, hang her clothes out on the fence to dry." Korli carried Liimu who was sleeping to the bedroom and hung the old woman's wet clothes out on the fence.

"Thank you for the change of clothes," Ma Gonmaah told Leanya, watching her with grateful eyes. "I hope the wind didn't carry the rest of my rags. When I get dry clothes to wear, I'll send yours."

"They're your clothes now," said Leanya. "I don't take used clothes from old people. It's bad luck."

"Really? They belong to me?" The old lady's eyes sparkled under the electric light. "I can't believe it! I can't believe it!" She danced for joy and hugged Leanya, tears running down her cheeks.

"Mother, don't cry on me. That too is bad luck. We should thank God for saving us."

There was another knock on the door. A teenage girl dressed in a blue skirt and white blouse entered and said greetings. Ma Gonmaah recognized her.

"Musu," she called her with apprehension, "are you children looking for our things? Where did you people take refuge?"

"In this house, Grandma," Musu said. "Mother brought us to Ma Seton's house for refuge. Ma Seton gave us bread and tea and we're cooking rice and soup. Mr. Seton said we may live here until we rebuild ours. Our house broke down completely; the boys are looking for our things in the ruins."

"God is at work, Child. He has passed through the heart of a different tribe to save us."

Borwulo knocked the door and entered breezily. "Is everybody all right here?" she said with curious eyes. "Papa says if someone is hurt, I should tell him."

"We're all right," Korli said. "How are the people back there?"

"All right. I'm running back to tell them not to worry."

When everybody had eaten, Leanya put half the greens on a wide metal tray, placed it on her head, and said she was carrying it round the community to sell. Junior insisted on going with his mother.

The following morning as Korli carried his applications around, he ran into Ezra Boimah at the Department of Treasury. Boimah was a student of Demonstration School in Bassa Community where Korli went for his lessons. After telling him about his application, Boimah advised Korli to find a goat for the Secretary of the Treasury.

"It's the only way you'll get the job quickly," he explained. "Do you have people following up your applications in the other departments?"

"No. My letter contains everything they need to know about me. A messenger job is not that big for people to run after. If I give the Secretary a goat, he might think I'm not qualified for the job. I learned that some government officials eat your goat or money but never give you the job."

"My brother, you are dreaming. Job placement doesn't work that way in this country. I've been a messenger in the Department of Finance for nearly five years. You have to put something in somebody's pocket or belly to get a job—girls have no problem once they give the bosses what they want."

"Does it not break up their marriages?"

"People are trying to survive, and you talk about marriage? Some husbands actually want their wives to have Godfathers to support them and their families. They wouldn't have to work; their wives would get them any amount of money they want. You'll be surprised to see a man take his wife to you, saying she is his sister, once you are in a position to give her a few dollars at the end of the month."

"Boimah, Liberian men are jealous over their wives! I don't think they'll do such a thing."

"That's true for the country people because they marry for love and take responsibility for their wives and children, but down here some people marry for money and to appear together at social functions such as Church services, banquets, birthday parties, and so forth. I had a friend whose wife was secretary for a certain government Secretary. The woman was literally the official's wife. She always went home late at night with the poor excuse that she had worked too hard all day, so she was tired. She wouldn't let her husband touch her in bed, but as soon as she heard the sound of the Secretary's car horn, she'd go out with him without telling her husband goodbye. Once he made a protest; the following day police jailed him for a traffic violation. They kept this fellow in for two weeks. When they released him, he grew very depressed. He died before the end of the year. Amos was a fool. He should have rented a room for a young girl to enjoy himself while living with Josephine just for the money— I'll see about your application, or it'll be filed for future reference."

"But my letter is addressed to the Assistant Secretary for Administration! Don't you think we should take the goat to him?"

"All letters of application go to the Secretary himself regardless of whom they are addressed to. If they remain with subordinate officials, they employ their friends, some of whom know nothing about the jobs they're given."

"Thank you, Boimah," Korli said. "When do I bring you the goat?"

"This Saturday at noon. When the Secretary's executive assistant gives him that goat, you'll hear from the department in two weeks. Marie is a good woman. Likes fine young men and has a strong connection with the Secretary. He doesn't sleep with her nowadays because he has had two children by her. She is looking for a husband."

"That excludes me."

"Why? You're a fine looking young man!"

"I have a wife and children, Boimah, and I'm not that educated."

"So what? Some of these women only want enjoyment. When they marry a country boy, he keeps his country woman. They wouldn't care. Once you satisfy them in bed and accompany them to social functions, no problem."

"It seems you're loving to one of them yourself," Korli said, laughing.

"What to do?" Boimah said. "That's the only way a native boy can make it in this country. I almost forgot. Get a big billy goat. Billy goat, you understand? You look surprised, Korli. When you go to Rome, you live like Romans. Maybe missionaries brought you up. Or some holy ghost church has pumped strange ideas into your head. Korli, I've lived long enough to know about human beings and their conceit. When they tell you what they know or think, you are impressed, but they live by their feelings, not ideas. When a government official—or even a preacher— tells you about love of country, he is talking about selfish-interests. When you join the club, you'll understand what I mean."

"They often dismiss corrupt officials for administrative reasons."

"You're dismissed only when you go off-track," Boimah said. "That is, when you stop praising them and attending their functions. That's being disloyal, unpatriotic, and treacherous. Many good people have lost their lives or languished in prison for such reasons. So, most citizens who acquire good education go to Europe or America to put their learning into good use and live a decent life. Well, let's keep praying and doing our best for our children. No condition is permanent—change will come. It is already on the way."

"Running away from a problem doesn't solve it, Boimah. Westerners didn't wake up early one morning and discover progress. They suffered and died for it. By destroying our countries and running to other nations, our conditions will never improve."

"You're right on that score, Korli, but I beg to differ. I think every man and woman on this planet has the right to live a happy and comfortable life. If you can't make it where you happen to have been born, go where it's available. The white man will not hesitate to live on the moon if life there is better."

"Boimah, you're a first-rate pessimist."

"No, I'm a realist. For more than one hundred years, we have been chanting about progress, but nothing has happened. Our leaders tote all the resources of our country abroad. Not even ten percent of the country has roads or clinics or schools. And there's no electricity outside of Monrovia. What is sad about our problem is that we expect other countries to develop ours. It will never happen."

"Look, my friend, I know that things are bad—very bad. The only way they'll improve is by remaining here to fight. But again, it's hard to win a battle if those you're fighting for don't support you."

"Go find the Secretary's goat let's take it to Marie on Saturday, okay? I want to be happy today because it's my daughter's birthday. Goodbye."

This irregular manner of getting a job disturbed Korli. If Joshua brought him what he promised, he'd build a shop and be his own boss.

12

THE BRIBE

KORLI BOUGHT AN overpriced chubby billy goat with reluctance and took it to Boimah as he had promised. It annoyed him to bear such unnecessary expense because he saw no need of bribing someone for a messenger job for which he felt more than qualified. Additionally, with the help of his instructor he had worked hard on his letter of application to ensure that the English was correct and the contents to the point. Indeed, he deserved an interview to give it the practical support it needed. However, he was hard pressed for the job. After furnishing the apartment and paying his instructor's fees as well as six months' rent in advance, he was low on cash. Therefore, he had no choice but submit to the doubledealing.

When Boimah told him at the last moment that he would take the goat to Marie all by himself, Korli grew doubtful of his motive. He wanted to go along in the hopes that Marie would interview him right away to get first-hand information about his circumstances and, consequently, attach some urgency to his application. Nothing could substitute for personal contact on the job market. Obviously, Boimah was up to something fishy.

"If you go with me to Marie, she will think we're putting her under pressure," Boimah had argued vehemently. "She'll get angry, and you won't see head or tail to your application. Marie knows that bribery is bad. Therefore, she's afraid if people see someone looking for job at the department bringing a goat to her, they might spread the news, putting her job in danger. She told me to take the goat to her sister who will give it to her later."

Korli wondered if Marie would actually get the goat, for Boimah's sudden change of mind and contrived explanation were suspect. Getting a reply to his expansive letter of application from the Department of Treasury seemed improbable. He had heard numerous stories of fraud in Monrovia but regarded them as fairy tales meant for diversion, not credulity. Now he was beginning to believe them. After receiving the goat, Boimah had told him that he'd hear from the department in two weeks since he had "put Marie in the bush." She had successfully processed job applications for many friends of his; however, when the two weeks became two months and there was no reply, Korli thought it wise to inquire for replies at dispatch offices in the other government departments to which he had applied, but he got none, nor did he get a single acknowledgement of any of his applications. Making matters worse, Joshua had not yet delivered the goods, which had exacted nearly half their savings. Korli grew wretched and confused but still hopeful that everything would be all right.

Although Leanya was doing her best to support the family, Korli felt embarrassed for being unable to make a contribution. He was fortunate his wife was energetic, hard-working, and imaginative. Considerations for her health and safety did not stand between her and the business. She was at it from dawn to dusk daily, rain or shine, showing no sign of strain or weakness. Customarily, men provided for their families. Women saw after the children, household chores, planting and harvesting crops, but Leanya ably assumed the role of provider for her family without protest. It wasn't only because the *kwii* world permitted it and the power and freedom it gave women but also because she had a strong sense of responsibility and love for him and the children, Korli thought.

In three months, Leanya's business grew substantially. She now joined other market women and chartered a pickup truck each week and traveled upcountry as far as Totota, the end of the paved road where the president made his farm, and spent two to three days there buying produce. Old Lady Gonmaah's report that food was inexpensive up in Gbarnga persuaded her to catch a ride on a private pickup and go there for a week. A popular market woman, her Auntie wasn't hard to locate. Her five-bedroom concrete house stood near Ganta Parking Station, which every driver and car loader knew. Getting directions from a car loader, she went there and introduced herself to Noai's large family. Noai's oldest son Flomo gave her a seat and regretted their mother's absence.

"Mama went to Jenepilitaa market this morning," he told her. "She'll soon come." Then he called to his eldest sister, "Nyamah, make hot water for your mother's bath and give her something to eat."

All eight of Noai's children gathered round Leanya and greeted her amiably. The youngest, a year-old boy, sat in her lap and toyed with her neck beads.

It was a happy reunion that night when Noai returned home. She had never expected a member of her family to visit her in faraway Gbarnga, and Leanya had never expected to see her. They embraced her each other tearfully, for the joy of reunion was overwhelming.

"I'm sorry my husband isn't here," Noai told Leanya. "If you marry a driver, he's not for you, my child. Daniel drives for LAMCO. The company gave him a house in Yekepa, but I'd rather live here with my children and make market. Daniel comes here every weekend with the truck he's driving, goes to Monrovia on Monday mornings, and returns on Tuesdays to Yekepa."

As the children brought bags of dry meat, cassava, palm nuts, eddoes, potatoes, cassava leaves, potato greens, and tins of palm oil into the house, Leanya watched them with consuming interest. Her Auntie glanced at her yearning stare and said:

"Food costs nothing much up here. The only problem is transportation. A deer haunch, no matter how big, doesn't cost more than five dollars. A tin of palm oil costs no more than seven-fifty. As for fruits and vegetables, you pick what you want and give the villagers kola."

"I too have become a market woman, Auntie," Leanya said. "I come to Totota nearly every week to buy produce. If the road were paved up to Gbarnga, you would see me every Saturday. Drivers refuse to ply unpaved roads, unless you charter their vehicles for a fortune."

"Daniel will take your market things to Monrovia," Noai said. "He carries the truck there empty, and on his way back he loads it with company things."

Leanya thanked Noai and told her about Old Lady Gonmaah and the rainstorm. Searching her memory, Noai remembered the old woman. "I'll take you to her quarters," she said. "She's a good friend of mine. She went to Monrovia to live with her oldest daughter Gbeehnga after her husband died. She couldn't bear to lay her eyes on their house because it reminded her of her late husband. Some of her grandchildren live in it. The bad luck has followed her to Monrovia. I told her to join a prophet church to get blessings, but she said a Zoe was seeing after her."

"The churches have made our Zoes impotent. If you don't bend on your knees and pray to God, nothing happens."

"I'm sure she'll find a prophet in Monrovia. We don't have any here."

For a week Noai took Leanya to the major markets round Gbarnga including Bariila, Jenepilitaa, Forekwelle, and Suacoco, where she bought bags of dry meat, cassava, plantains, vegetables, and tins of palm oil at very low prices. The following Monday, Daniel took them to Monrovia for her in a long Ford truck, which she almost packed to capacity.

After introducing her Auntie's husband to Korli, Leanya hired several hands to help unload the truck. Some buyers who stood by the fence helped with the unloading.

"My name is Korli," Korli told the huge Mano man who was dressed in a LAMCO uniform.

"My name is Daniel," he said. "I'm Mano from Ganta."

"I'm Kpelle from Fuama Chiefdom," Korli said. "Thank you for your help."

"Don't mention it. Any time she comes up for produce, I'll bring them down for her. I travel to Monrovia every Monday."

The dust had hardly settled after the truck left when customers bought nearly half the commodities. After serving them and taking a haunch of deer to Mrs. Seton for their soup, Leanya, who was dead with fatigue, bathed and ate the food Borwulo had cooked for her.

"Had the president made his farm round either Gbarnga or Sanniquellie, marketing would have been most profitable," Leanya told Korli and the children who gathered around her as she ate.

"He doesn't have to make a farm somewhere before extending a road there. He's responsible for the whole country," Korli said.

"Don't talk like that. The man has ears all around. Do you know that he is the first president to open up the country? The rest of them lived only in Monrovia and its surrounding settlements, where they carried out the little development you see in this country."

"They say between here and Totota, people plant rubber trees mostly," Korli said. "You hardly see rice or cassava farm."

"That's true, but in the bushes behind those rubber farms, there are rice and cassava farms. I buy most of my produce from farmers who bring them to the highway. Auntie is a big market woman; her husband buys most of her produce on the highway between Gbarnga and Yekepa. They've built a big concrete house in Gbarnga! She has eight children; seven of them attend mission school. She told me, 'Why don't you people live up here with us? You make more money in Monrovia and know all the important people in Liberia, but that city is dangerous. You and thieves must always fight over your life and properties. Here, we are poor but safe: we leave our doors open and go wherever we like and come back to meet everything in place. People don't disappear here to be killed for ritualistic purposes.'"

"Living in Gbarnga is a good idea, but if you chase too many frogs into a swamp, you might drown in it. No matter what you become up there, people from down here take advantage of you. Here, you get redress when someone offends you, so people think twice before attacking you."

The conversation had ended on that note. Leanya wanted to continue it, but she knew that convincing her husband to live upcountry was impossible. Many times Korli had told her that hardworking people could make it anywhere and that it was risky for her to travel up and down the winding, narrow, broken highway too often. Interestingly, he had confessed that he relished her absence from home. It strengthened his love for her, he said. Each time she returned home after spending two or three days in Totota, he told her how he missed her and the dreams he had had of her. However, he complained that taking care of the children alone gave him no chance to see about business.

"When I'm gone, let Borwulo help you take care of the children, so that you may have a chance to go to town and see about your business. She could even sleep with them. I've talked with Mrs. Seton about it, and she gladly agreed to the arrangement."

Korli wanted to mention an incident that took place one night when Leanya was up in Gbarnga, but he felt it was too risky to tell her about it. Yes, Borwulo was good at taking care of the children and doing household chores. The girl had good training. She literally took over the house whenever Leanya was away. The problem occurred when he had left her in charge of the house and gone to town to see about his applications. On his return late that night, Korli saw Borwulo lying flat on her back in his bed, completely naked under the bright light bulb hanging from the ceiling. He couldn't believe his eyes. When he tried to wake her up to go to the baby in the girls' room, Borwulo, who was fifteen, lifted her head languidly and stared at him with squinting eyes; then spread her legs wider apart and went back to sleep.

His heart speeding, Korli shook her vigorously until she awoke, put on her clothes, and went to the baby. Sitting in a sofa with his cheeks cupped in his hands, his elbows planted on his thighs, Korli said to himself, "This is not her own doing. She is too young and inexperienced to do such a thing on her own. Some adult is manipulating her to get money from me. They think I'm rich. But if Borwulo desires money from me, she can ask for it as a child asking its father for favor. Perhaps she is pregnant and is looking for someone to take responsibility for it. It'll be impossible for me to establish my innocence should she accuse me of molesting her! But as long as I know that I'm not guilty of any wrongdoing, I won't worry unless someone brings it up. No—I won't conduct an investigation. If you pull rope, rope pulls bush. I'll let the matter drop. As of now I'll lock the bedroom door before leaving the apartment."

After six months of waiting without seeing Joshua or hearing from him, Korli felt that his assurance to Leanya that he'd fulfill his promise had somehow amounted to betrayal. If he did nothing about it, Leanya might think he had connived with him to use that large sum of money for some other purpose under the guise of a business deal. Besides, he would suffer severe heartbreak because the money had come from years of relentless hard work, sacrifice, and trust, not corruption. Leaving it with Joshua in such an irregular manner was unfair and inexcusable unless a valid mishap beyond Joshua's control such as sickness, bereavement, or ill luck had caused him to use it, life in Monrovia's impoverished slums being vulnerable to such mishaps. Even then, Joshua, a man of integrity as he seemed to be, ought to bring the problem to his attention for them to look for a solution rather than put himself under needless suspicion. Therefore, it was crucially important for him to find Joshua to know what had gone wrong. In searching for him, Korli decided to cause no alarm to avoid disgracing or sending him under cover. Who knew? His good friend might be putting together a superb consignment of cargoes for him.

Korli did not remember any signposts to Joshua's secluded cubicle located deep inside Logan Town. He had gone there hurriedly with him but once. After walking on a sinuous path, Joshua had told him all he had to do to find his place was trek a hundred yards on the slum's muddy Broad Street to the first coconut tree he'd meet and ask anyone round there for him. When confronted with problems, Korli remembered his math teacher telling him, tackle the easy ones before dealing with those that are difficult. Thus, he decided to go to Dualah Market instead of bothering with the cramped slum and commence his search for Joshua.

Dressing in a sturdy outfit—a pair of khaki long pants and longsleeved shirt, a pair of black boots, and a brown cap—Korli took a rickety Dirty Joe overcrowded with shrieking passengers, and proceeded to Waterside. The discomfort of the ancient bus made him squeamish. He wished Dualah were within walking distance. Gratefully alighting at Waterside, he took a better one that carried him to his destination swiftly. The noisy market overflowed with the usual milling crowds, shouting, quarreling, and fighting. Korli shouldered his way among them to the western end where hunters sold their spoils. Joshua was not there. Walking aimlessly round the market, he casually pawed trifles of merchandise such as bath soaps, briefs, T-shirts, flashlights, slippers, and dry bonies, haggling with marketers over their "high" prices but not buying any. Growing weary of an inspection tour that tested his patience, Korli went to Popo Beach. Ostensibly angry, the sea sent mountainous waves crashing against the sordid shore, a dumping site and restroom for beach dwellers. Had it not been a strong wind blowing from the ocean leeward, Korli would have died of the asphyxiating stench. Popo fishermen were busy pulling dragnets ashore. Idlers always helped them with the demanding task as a diversion or an exercise, but in appreciation for their help, the fishermen usually gave them some of the catch. Korli loved the sight of swimmers, big and small, riding the high waves by the shore. Some were girls! Fanti fishermen, standing in large canoes like statuettes, cast their nets in the deep sea, while lone Kru fishermen paddled small dugouts towards the horizon where Lebanese trawlers plowed the sea. The canoe fishermen usually returned to the beach late in the afternoon with diverse species of fish such as snappers, bonies, cassava fish, barracudas, and groupers, which they sold to a crowd of waiting customers. Joining a group of Popo fishermen, Korli helped to pull their net so well that several of them expressed admiration for his strength. When it came to shore, they gave him a cassava fish larger than what they gave the other helpers. Korli left his fish with them and ran to the market to check for Joshua once more, but didn't find him. On his return, he helped with one last pulling and collected another fish. Korli carefully wrapped his fish in old newspapers, put them in a plastic bag, and went home.

After failing to find Joshua at Dualah Market three more days, Korli concluded that he had probably stopped making market or left the town. Could it be that he now lived on his money? Korli didn't want to believe it. He'd check his residence; if he didn't find him there, he'd ask the police for help.

One place to look for a resident of Logan Town was at the Cinema. People often gathered there around seven o'clock in the evening for movies and other entertainment. Thus, on a Saturday evening, Korli dressed in the best clothes he had and boarded an express Toyota bus plying between Old Road and Dualah Markets. Although he paid a little more for the ride, it was faster and safer than a ride on a Dirty Joe.

Alighting at the Cinema, Korli stood transfixed on the unpaved sidewalk, watching the raucous crowd meandering about and marketers displaying arrays of wares. Market women on stools fried fish and roasted skewered meat under streetlights on the sidewalks and at two nearby gas stations; sizzling oil sent plumes of aromatic mist into the sky. Beside them sat market girls on small rattan chairs by wooden trays loaded with cigarettes, candies, candles, bitter kolas, flashlight and radio batteries; boiled eggs, *kanyan*, *kala*, fritters, and other snacks. Hawkers, mostly Fulah boys, moved about with similar items arranged in wooden trays slung to their necks or carried on their heads. Legions of young girls and boys consumed these commodities as they wandered around, some entering and leaving the cinema building, which resounded with cheers for winners of gun- or fistfights. Lovers hungrily hooked to each other and disappeared in the narrow, dark, and winding alleys between zinc shacks or sped away to Point Four, Nyornpatorn, or Waterside in taxis to find motels.

Two girls, well dressed in calico with cleavages exposing half their breasts, walked jauntily to Korli, stared at him patronizingly, and moved on, looking at him over their shoulders.

Korli bought a well-seasoned piece of roasted beef. As he munched it, looking around for Joshua, another well-dressed girl came by and asked him for a dollar, her open palm raised to his face with entreaty. Korli obligingly gave her the dollar; she left haltingly, watching him over her shoulder. "Thank you, my friend," she said. "My name is Sarah. Sarah Flomo. You good man. Some other man will have to lay you down before giving you this dollar. If you want me, come with me." Korli did not go with her; only stared speechlessly at her until she disappeared in the anonymous crowd. Noting that standing on the same spot too long invited intruders, he mixed with the sweltering crowd, moving about with his head up. The people spoke Kru mostly, so it was difficult for him to make any contact or query. On the wide pavement of the gas stations, a ragged, pale-looking boy—probably ten or twelve years old—raised his tray of commodities to Korli's chin and yelled:

"My friend! My friend! Bitter kola! Bitter kola! Cigarettes! Sweet cigarettes! Buy some! Buy some!"

"I don't smoke," Korli told him politely. "I don't eat kola." He looked far away, thinking that his indifference would send the boy away. It didn't.

"You can smoke and eat kola," the boy insisted with a sneer. "You just don't want to buy from me. My friend, buy bitter kola so girls won't eat your money for nothing! It'll make you a man."

He again raised his tray until it almost touched Korli's nose. Irritated,

Korli walked away with wide strides, but he spied the boy over his shoulder running after him. Halting abruptly across the street, Korli turned around and, shaking a finger at him, said:

"Move from behind me! I don't want anything from you! Leave me alone!"

"Big man like you don't have ten cents to buy kola?" the boy sneered at Korli again. "You too cheap! When you die, that money will be for somebody else. Somebody you don't know."

"The boy wants to put you in trouble-o, my friend!" a moviegoer told Korli. "Find somebody else to buy your market!" the stranger yelled at the boy. "Leave the man alone!" But the boy stood his ground.

Korli walked down the street and stood some ten yards away. Another girl of exquisite beauty walked to him and asked for fifty cents, raising both palms in his face, her lips pouting invitingly. Korli gave her a dollar and she thanked him. "My name is Titi, yah," she told him. "What is your name?"

"My name is Gbamo," Korli told her.

"Goodnight, Gbamo. You look fine." "Thank you. See you later."

"What about now?" the girl asked.

Before Korli could say another word, the persistent boy he had confronted earlier was back with his tray of goods.

"Ehn you say you ain't got money?" the boy cried. "That girl finish eating your money for nothing. If you go to bed with her, she'll eat all your money and put you in trouble. Buy something good from me and enjoy yourself."

"You boy, why you behind dis man?" It was another moviegoer coming to Korli's rescue. "My friend," he said to Korli, "if you don' fight for youself, dese children will not stop bothering you." He turned to the boy again. "You humbugging dis man because he's a stranger? Is he de only one with money? Go away!"

"Is it your business?" the boy yelled as the man turned to walk away. Then he raised his wooden tray to Korli's nose again, so close this time that Korli couldn't breathe.

Korli pushed the tray aside gently and, before he could take a step, the boy deliberately dropped it to the ground. Its contents scattered and the boy began yelling for the police. People were already fighting over the items as he stood crying, stamping his foot, his fingers interlocked on his head.

"Pay for the little boy's market!" yelled the hustlers at Korli as they pocketed kola nuts, candies, packets of cigarettes, matches, and so on. "Big man like you want steal de little boy things?"

"Rogue! Rogue! Rogue!" cried spectators running to the scene, two police officers among them.

"Officers, your carry dis man to jail!" someone declared, pointing at Korli.

"He look like country man," someone else scoffed at him. "What you doing in the city? You better go back to your bush!"

"What happened?" one of the officers asked.

"Dis man knocked my market down," whined the boy, pointing at Korli. "Dis man nah put me in trouble, my people! My Ma will kill me tonight!"

Speechless, Korli only stared at the boy with opened mouth and widened eyes.

"The boy meant to drop the tray, officer," he said at length. "When he put his tray too close to my nose, I only pushed it aside and walked away. Then he threw it to the ground. He has been following me more than an hour."

"I saw everything," the girl to whom Korli had given the second dollar testified. "I know dis boy. He's full of trouble. He followed de man around with his tray as if he owed him something." Then she turned to the boy: "Why don't you sit or stand one place with your market? If someone wants to buy from you, dey will come to you!"

"Pick up your things and go home," one of the police officers advised the boy.

"Everything gone!" the boy cried in desperation, tears running down his cheeks.

"Let him pay for de boy's things," cried a hustler. "Man like dis suppose to be home with his wife and children at this hour. What is he doing in de street?" He sized Korli up and decided that he'd be better off taking to his heels.

"Don't talk like that, my friend. The street for everybody," someone put in.

The crowd dispersed as no fighting occurred to entertain them. Some were already smoking the boy's cigarettes, chewing his kola nuts, and sucking his candies.

"My friend, we'll have to take you and the boy to the station to judge this case," said the other officer, a tall man with a scrawny neck.

"My friend, you know what?" the short officer told Korli. "Small shame is better than big shame. Pay for the boy things and find something for your officer dem and go home." Addressing the boy harshly, he said, "How much for your things? Don't lie to me! Tell me the truth!"

"Twenty-five dollars," cried the boy.

"You lie!" came a harsh denial from a spectator. "Those things ain't even worth five dollars!"

"Da your business?" asked the tall police officer. "Beat it!" he bobbed his head toward the street. The speaker hurried away.

"Give him his twenty-five dollars to save your good name," the officer told Korli. "Anyone looking into this case will say you took advantage of him because he is small."

Korli checked his pocket and found only one dollar and fifty cents. He remembered putting two ten-dollar notes there plus three dollar-coins. Someone had picked his pocket! Fortunately, he had put a ten-dollar note in his sock. Taking it out, he handed it to the officer and said irritably:

"This all I got."

The officer took a five-dollar note from the breast pocket of his uniform and gave it to the boy and told him, "I'm going with him for the balance. I got to pay my way. See me here tomorrow evening."

Just then another excitement began. Fighting had broken out between two lovers. Enthusiastic spectators encouraged them with jeers and cheers. The other police officer ran there while Korli and the tall one walked towards Broad Street, knocking against pedestrians for the right of way.

"You're just coming to town, eh?" the officer asked Korli in a friendly tone.

"I've been in town for some time," Korli said, "but I live on Old Road Sinkor. I don't know this part of Monrovia very well."

"That's why that boy initiated you tonight." The officer laughed. "They have eyes for strangers. When you come to Cinema again, don't stand by yourself or carry much money in your pocket. Bad boys will attack you or pick your pocket. Why are we going this way? You said you live on Old Road."

They had reached the junction of Broad Street and Inside Logan Town. Korli led the police down Broad Street a few yards, and they halted before a large puddle sitting in the middle of the street, a result of last night's downpour. The rim of it used for bypassing was deep and muddy. Thinking that the rustic fellow wanted to run away, the police touched the handle of his gun and repeated his question.

"You needn't worry, sir," Korli told him cordially. "You came to my rescue, so I consider you a friend. I have a problem, officer. Please help me solve it; I'll take care of you."

His curiosity stirred, the police asked, "What problem? Somebody robbed you? Or claimed a lot you bought? What happened?"

"God brings people together for reason," Korli said pensively. "A friend of mine and I have been doing business for years. I don't know what has happened to him. It has been six months since I saw him. He's supposed to be living somewhere up this street, but with this lake in the way, we can't go there."

"We can take a different road to bypass it, but let me warn you; once I'm with you, someone will pinch him to run away when they see us. They'll think you want me to arrest him. Does he owe you anything?"

"Yes, but I'm more concerned about his health than the money."

"If you don't need the money, I can help you make use of it," the officer laughed slyly. "No, I'm joking. How much does he owe you? What is his name?"

"His name is Joshua Obadiah, a Kru boy from Sanquin."

"Oh! I know the fellow. He's a crook with sweet mouth, but friendly. I hope you didn't give him much money. Always keep your money in a bank until you need it—a Lebanese bank. Don't give it to anyone for safekeeping. I can get him for you, but it will cost you something." The police hung his head, waiting for Korli's reaction.

"Cost me?" Korli was surprised.

"I need a little cash to pay my way while looking for him," the police said, looking at Korli. "OB doesn't stay one place long. Maybe he has moved to some other part of Monrovia. I might have to chase him all over this big town—maybe all the way to Sanquin. It'll cost money."

"Let's hurry to my house, then, for me to see what to do. Doesn't the government pay your way when you're on duty? I see many police cars around town."

"The government gives us a few cars, but our director and his deputies use them. When they send you on a mission, you must put your hand in your pocket and pay your own way. The complainant is supposed to give you a refund."

Walking back to the Cinema, they took a taxi and arrived on Old Road round midnight. Korli offered the officer a bottle of beer and thanked him for agreeing to find Joshua for him. The officer gulped the beer with speed.

"If he has used my money, he should let me know so that I may see what to do about it," Korli told him. "Bring him to me."

"I need to know how much money he owes you," said the officer. "When he knows that I know what he owes you, he won't deny it. Did he give you a receipt?" The officer looked at Korli in suspense.

"No. I'm just getting into business, so I have much to learn. My first lesson is to put every deal on paper and keep a copy. I gave the fellow two thousand dollars to find goods for a shop I want to build."

"My God!" cried the officer, slapping his thighs. He drained the remaining beer and sighed deeply. "Why did you give him that much money? How long has he been gone?"

"Six round months, as I told you!" Korli sighed dismally.

"Well, let's hope and pray for me to put my hand on him. If he doesn't bring your money, he'll get rotten in jail. Had you given that money to a Lebanese trader, he'd have given you all the goods you wanted and become your customer. However, you didn't know. Now that you know, don't repeat that kind of mistake."

"How much do you need for transportation?"

"First, let me give you my name to show you that I'm not a crook. My name is John—Captain John Mark. I'm assigned at Zone Five Police Station at Point Four. Most of my friends charge victims of robbery little or nothing, but they share the stolen properties with the thieves and lie to the victims, saying they didn't see them."

"That's unfair," Korli said. "If those we depend on for protection are corrupt, to whom will we go for redress?"

"Their excuse is that government seldom pays the police, and the police have families to support. I don't think the citizens are responsible for that. If you don't get paid for the job you're doing, find something else to do. I can leave the Force any time I like. I'm doing this job because I love it. I only ask victims of robbery to give me twenty percent in cash what has been stolen from them and I take full responsibility to recover it."

"That's fair enough," said Korli. "You have to spend money to get money. It's better to lose four hundred dollars than two thousand."

"As long as you keep your side of the bargain, I'll keep mine. I won't bother you for more money even if it costs me much more than this to get the thief."

Korli went into his bedroom and brought the four hundred dollars to the captain.

"This is my wife's market money I'm borrowing," he informed him. "Please don't let me down. If I don't hear from you soon, I'll be in trouble."

"My friend—what is your name?"

"Korli."

"Korli, don't worry. Your landlord knows me very well. I was once assigned to him when he was working at the Freeport as deputy managing director. If you mention my name to him, he'll tell you the kind of person I am. I like people to laugh and thank me when I eat their money, not cry with my name. Bad luck follows you when people cry with your name.

Trust me, Korli. You'll get your money, or Obadiah will spend the rest of his life in jail. Oh, we forgot about the little boy's balance."

Korli gave him fifteen dollars, wondering whether he wasn't giving money away in vain once again. John Mark—was it really the fellow's name?—slipped out of the apartment like a phantom. Korli resolved not to upset Leanya with information about this transaction. It would discourage her. While she was putting her life at risk to make money, he was giving it away in vain. It occurred to him that his problem derived from pressing his luck too hard, by believing that any departure, any arrangement or initiative would work even if glaring evidence showed the contrary. No—providence doesn't work that way, he thought. It comes to your rescue when a miracle is your only means of deliverance, not when you jump into danger with open eyes. Another serious fault of his was relying completely on the advice, opinions, and decisions of others, as if he wasn't endowed with a mind of his own. Where was the advantageous *kwii* world? Certainly, it wasn't the squalid, cramped, disease-ridden, ramshackle villages he had seen round Monrovia, which were but an extension of villages upcountry except that upcountry villages stood on high grounds, free from puddles and refuse. The people were the same— innocent, beautiful, and happy despite their incomprehensible and chronic poverty. No amount of politicking, perfidy, or fraud could free them from the menace of poverty, disease, and ignorance, only discerning hard work and respect for the national interest. He was happy his wife had caught the vision soon enough; he'd work with her, encourage her— be her teacher to avoid unnecessary expense. He had bought his experience at a costly price; he would make full use of it.

13

JESUS THE SAVIOUR

"KORLI, LET'S HAVE a prophet sanctify our home," Leanya told her husband late one night in bed. She had just recovered from malaria and body pains that had kept her in bed for a week. "God has been good to us," she continued, "but we seem to have forgotten about him. You need a job and the goods from Joshua. I'm coming down with sickness these days. God is telling us indirectly that we can't make it without him. The other night I saw a weird owl sitting on our window ledge in the starlight. My scalp crawled, my heart missed a beat, I became weak and tongue-tied; I collapsed on the bed without closing the curtains! I thought I'd die, but the Lord's Prayer saved me. It sent the witch soaring through the cold night air." Leanya paused and took a deep sigh. Beads of perspiration stood on her round forehead. "Beggars have ruined us!" she said breathlessly.

Korli put on his clothes, switched on the light, and paced the room slowly, looking at the ceiling and the pictures on the wall. Leanya sat up and placed an elbow on a raised knee, staring at him.

"What do you think about what I said?" she asked him.

Korli sat down by Leanya. "In spite of everything, we had a good time in White Plains!" he said, trifling with her smooth black hair.

Liimu who lay at the foot of the bed groaned and smacked her lips. Leanya placed her in her lap and put a nipple in her mouth. She sucked greedily, rubbing her minuscule rosy feet against each other.

"You woke her up by putting on the light," Leanya chided Korli.

"Had old man Jackson not gone to America," Korli said, "we'd have prospered by now. It's been a year since we came here. I should have heeded his advice—built a zinc shack and run a shop in it." Korli sighed helplessly.

"Those good old days have gone, Korli, never to return. You live in the past and trust everybody. That's your problem. Now we are penniless. My business is coming on fine, but it can only feed us and pay our rent. We need a miracle, Korli. I've heard of a prophet with unusual powers, a famous faith healer and preacher. Doesn't charge much. You only give him something for a candle, white cloth, white bucket, holy oil, and a white sheep for sacrifice. When he solves your problem, you give him whatever you can afford."

Korli took his wife's hand with tenderness. Liimu, now sleeping in her lap, suddenly rubbed her eyes briskly, twisted her pursed lips one side, yawned, and resumed sleeping.

"When will you take the titty from her mouth?" Korli asked Leanya quietly.

"I've tried to stop her from sucking, but she won't," Leanya said with slight annoyance. "After I stuff her with rice water, she sucks the titty on top of it."

"When you aren't around, she's quite satisfied with bottled milk."

Leanya said, "Girls usually take a long time to leave their mothers' milk. It's their right, anyway. Makes a child behave like human being. That intimate contact with the mother is important. Children who drink cow's milk often act like cows."

Korli laughed and said, "It's the lack of proper training that makes children misbehave, not the food they eat."

"You want another child, Korli?" Leanya said with a smile and poked him in the ribs with her elbow. "In six months Liimu will give you water to drink. Then—"

"Two and a half long years!" Korli said. "If God sends us another one, I won't mind. Children are a blessing."

"You won't mind because you won't tote it for nine months." Leanya laughed quietly. Korli caught the laughter and grew serious.

"Don't worry, Leanya," he said. "We have plenty of time. Let Liimu enjoy herself. Girls usually suck titty longer than boys."

"You're a brave man, Korli—that's why I love you. You've never weaned any of our children until I was ready, so they're all living. I'll give you one more. Let's attend the prophet Church this Sunday to conquer our enemies and give back to God some of what he has given us. That's the only way we'll get rid of the bad luck."

"We should do that. I saw a Catholic Church round the corner—"

"With the missionary priest?" Leanya said abruptly, wrinkling her nose. "No, Korli, they don't have the spirit in them, nor do they prophesize or speak in tongues."

"Do you believe that our prophets tell the truth? Prophets of the Old Testament used to be in direct contact with God, but not those of today. Our prophets have too much of the spirit in them. The deafening drumbeats, the frenzied shouting, the speaking in tongues, and the finger pointing distress me."

"Those activities fill people with the Holy Ghost! You never enjoyed church service in White Plains because of them, I noticed; you used to enjoy the sermons and go home a different man."

"Next Sunday we meet the prophet, eh? We needn't join his church. It's better we join the Catholic Church. They don't beat drums, and they have schools, hospitals, and clinics, though not free."

"The churches our prophets establish don't have schools or clinics! What do they do with the offering?"

"After giving something to God, you don't worry about it. Your reward is his blessings and a place in heaven. The Catholic Church gets its money from America, so their priests don't depend on the offering plate to build schools or hospitals."

"After the poor scrape and starve to raise money for the church, the preachers should give them something in return. At least pencils and copybooks for their children—and teach them the ABC. However, we'll go to your prophet. Jesus says if the devil preaches the word of God, listen to him."

"Ahhh, Korli the thinker!" Leanya again elbowed his ribs. "Too much thinking leads to the wrong conclusion and makes you unhappy. Don't worry about the expenses; I'll pay them. You've used up all your money—I'm sure. Anyhow, you did well to spend it on the family. If we don't get goods from Joshua, we'll say what we gave him is a sacrifice."

"No—an offering," Korli corrected her. "Jesus has already made the sacrifice on the cross."

"An offering, then," Leanya agreed.

"By the way, I bought copybooks, pencils, and a Reader for you," Korli said. "Let's start your schooling now. A whole year has gone in vain. You should have been speaking English small-small by now, knowing how serious you can be when you decide to do something." He fetched the *Let's Learn English* Reader from the cupboard and presented it to Leanya. She opened it and gazed at the pictures of familiar objects in it.

"This is a pan," she told Korli excitedly, pointing her finger at the picture of a pan. Korli nodded. "This is a spoon; this is a bird; this is a girl; this is a boy; this is a house—" She named other objects such as, bed, cup, shoe, rat, mosquito, chicken, cow, sheep, goat, cat, and dog.

"You're halfway in learning how to speak English," Korli told her with delight. "You know the names of things in English! What remains is spelling and writing them and tying them together to say something. We'll work on the ABC tomorrow."

"No. Right now!"

Korli brought a copybook and pencil and they went to the dining room table. He wrote the alphabets and read them slowly while she repeated the letters after him. Then he taught her how to hold a pencil and write the first three. Leanya was so absorbed in writing that she didn't pay Liimu attention when she awoke and cried. Korli carried her in his arms and rocked her until she went back to sleep, but not for long.

"When you study, let the titty be in her mouth," he told Leanya, briefly inspecting the writing she was doing. He nodded approval. Liimu raised her arms for her mother, moaning.

"It's good you're going to school during the day," Leanya said without taking her eyes from her writing. "We'll do most of our work at night when the children sleep."

"I'm happy you are a willing learner. You learn faster if you keep at it whenever you have a chance. In six weeks you should be writing a letter to me."

"Ha!" Leanya laughed and glanced at Korli without debating what he said. "Korli, we are cheating the night!" she said, taking the baby from him. She gave her titty and Liimu sucked with abandon. "I've noticed it's better to sell greens and pepper in Old Road Market than around here," Leanya said. "They sell faster back there. Borwulo can help sell some around here after school in the afternoon."

Korli reserved comment on the subject. Becoming concerned, Leanya asked:

"Don't you want Borwulo to be part of the family?"

"Leanya, the clothes you borrow from others are not yours. Borwulo is now part of our family, but her parents may need her service sometimes."

"The boys could help sell but they are too playful."

"You needn't worry about selling, Leanya. Do your best. You have two hands but you can do only one thing at a time."

"The next time I go home I'll ask Mother to teach me her birth control medicine for us to space the children. It will give me time to make market until my hands catch something. I learned that doctors can stop women from having children after they've born the number they want."

"Nobody should ever tamper with God's plan," Korli retorted and yawned. "I need plenty of sleep for the early morning waking," he said. "The buses wait until they're full before going. If you want to be in town early, be at the bus stop by six o'clock to take the first bus. School begins at eight in the morning."

"The same is true of the market. Fresh greens come by seven in the morning. To get some you have to be in the market at six. Poor Liimu had better learn to ride my back half the day."

From the time Leanya told him about the owl, Korli always remembered to check every window before going to bed, but he still had never sighted one himself. Now, he opened the curtains at each window, closed them, and retired to bed.

"Don't let that witch of a bird drive you crazy, Korli," Leanya told him as she laid the baby beside him. "It'll never come here again. The Lord's Prayer has driven it away from here."

"You can't defeat the devil with one blow, Leanya. Fighting him is a daily struggle. Let us pray." Korli said a prayer and they went to sleep.

The following Sunday the entire family, dressed in their best, went to the prophet church, an impromptu structure of old corrugated zinc sheets standing on a strip of laterite ground surrounded by sandy soil deep inside Old Road. The shack fronted sparse knots of vegetation, tall coconut and palm trees, and tufts of wilting grass struggling to survive in the arid soil. Old Lady Konah, a pious neighbor, and Ma Gonmaah had recommended the shabby little church to Leanya because, they both said, "the bishop performs miracles!"

"Don't mind the look of the church building," Ma Konah had said, nodding her head. "Good churches are not showy or full of bigshots. You find them in out-of-the-way places, administered by poor preachers full of the Holy Ghost. Bishop Aziyah heals sicknesses of all sorts, including those hospitals cannot cure."

"When the Holy Ghost gets into him," Ma Gonmaah had explained, "he stiffens and becomes transfigured. The playful, smiling, middle-aged, gray-headed man grows fiery and perplexed. He sweats profusely like a man at war. After he's thoroughly spent, the spirit leaves him half-dead but alert. He mumbles everything about your past, present, future—and what you should do if trouble hangs over you. With prayers, fasting, holy oil and water, he cures madness—binds evil spirits, makes the lame walk, the blind see, and the deaf hear. I'm telling you something I've seen with my own eyes, not what somebody heard from someone else."

"My daughter," said Ma Konah, "tell your husband to take the whole family to Prophet Aziyah to see for yourselves what we are talking about. You'll not be disappointed."

"Let him free your house from sickness, quarrels, hardship, and bad luck," said Ma Gonmaah. "When he prays over your market, it will grow until you won't know what to do with the money."

The service was in progress when Korli and his family arrived at the prophet church that Sunday. Leanya had dressed the boys exquisitely in new calico shirts, blue denim long pants, and black sneakers. She braided Liimu's hair in cornrows and dressed her in a pink dress and blue bonnet. Korli wore a pair of gray pants, a white long-sleeved shirt, brown hat, and a pair of black leather shoes. Leanya wore a green lappa suit with floral designs and a pair of red leather slippers. The Bishop, who was dressed in a black robe, white collar, a silver cross on his potbelly, was preaching about the sick man whom Jesus had healed at the pool, the congregation listening with rapt attention. The women were dressed in white lappa suits and headties, the men in white short-sleeved shirts. Whenever the Bishop touched a keynote in the sermon, the congregation sang one stanza of a gospel song and he would resume preaching.

As soon as Korli and his family entered the church, the Bishop digressed from his subject and said he had seen Satan following the family. That Satan was following but ran away when they entered God's mighty fortress. Jesus had redeemed them! He added that the people who would go to heaven with Jesus after his second coming were those who attended church regularly and paid their tithes. Prosperity without Jesus was disaster, for circumstances eventually wipe everything away and leave troubles in their wake. Then he burst into a gospel song. Though most of them didn't understand English, the congregation sang along, clapping their hands with the rhythm of the inspiring song that implored them to *Come to Jesus*—some jumping up and down and crying with Jesus' name. A fat woman fainted. A group of women grabbed her as she collapsed to the floor and with great difficulty deposited her limp body before the altar. The Bishop swung a white cow tail over her with force. A girl poured perfumed burnt oil from a small white bottle on her forefinger and made the sign of the cross with it on the woman's forehead. The congregation raised their hands to heaven and murmured prayers. The Bishop laid a

Bible on the woman's belly and she sat up, looking around with amazement. Everybody clapped their hands, shouting:

"Praise the Lord! Praise the Lord! Glory Alleluia! Thank you, Jesus! Thank you, Jesus!"

Bishop Isaiah Zachariah waved his sleeved arms like the wings of a dove, and the church grew quiet. He offered a prayer, mostly for "the young man and his family who had just entered God's Mighty Fortress." God had great plans for them, he said, but they needed prayers, sanctification, and the word of God for protection against Satan. Two worshippers led the revived woman back to her seat, and the ushers began collecting the offerings while the Bishop cried that the redeemed of God should give and give until they could give no more. God would multiply a thousand-fold whatever they put in the offering baskets and give it back to them. After receiving the offering and blessing it, the Bishop placed it on the altar, then gave the benediction. Before leaving, he put the offering in his pocket. Then he marched to the door of the church to bid members of the congregation goodbye and God's blessing. He made the sign of the cross on each member's forehead.

"I want to see you people," he told Korli and Leanya as he shook their hands. He smiled at Liimu in her mother's arms and pinched her chubby cheek lightly. Liimu turned her face away from his smiling lips and reddish eyes. "The devil is a liar," he said. "We will root him out of your house and life," he told Korli. "Only Jesus can defeat him. What can you, a poor sinner do to him?"

After the congregation left, the Bishop took the couple and their children to his office, a shabby little room at the back of the church. In the middle of the room stood a rattan chair behind a plank table before which were two long benches. Bottles of holy oil and dozens of empty white buckets cramped the room. One white bucket of holy water covered with white skirting sat under the table, which served as the Bishop's desk. Korli and his family sat on the front bench and tried to show a pretense of well-being in the sultry, stifling room.

"Welcome to Church of the Redeemed!" Bishop Isaiah Zachariah declared so loudly that a girl put her head through the door as if she were summoned. The Bishop's frowned face made her recoil and retrace her steps. Wiping his perspiring face with a white towel and laying the Bible on his belly, the Bishop leaned back in the chair and told Korli:

"My son, you have a good future waiting for you, but you must give yourself to the Lord. He loves you and wants you to be somebody in this country; that's why he has taken you out of many dangers. Imagine, your own father trying to kill you in the water society! You escaped safely and killed a bewitched bushcow professional hunters had failed to kill! A poor country boy like you lived for five round years with Congo people and enjoyed their hospitality without disappearing! Let's thank the Lord on our knees."

Korli and Leanya looked at each other, speechless at the man's accurate account of events in Korli's life.

The Bishop condemned, denounced, and bound with Jesus' blood all evil spirits, owls, crooks, and sickness that had attacked or threatened to attack Korli and his family. He prayed that happiness, prosperity, and peace be in their home. Then he asked them to join him in the Lord's Prayer.

"Jesus has already redeemed you and your family from Satan's claws," he told Korli. "What you should do now is give me an offering so that I may sanctify your home next Sunday—temptations are piling up on you and festering. Conquer them with the blood of Jesus. You need a job, a thriving business, a double promotion in school, for you're too old to be in the eighth grade. You should hurry up and complete college to see after your children. God has two more children for you."

Leanya smiled faintly and shook her head without comment.

"You can't stop the will of God, my friend," the Bishop told her. "My son, find me six white buckets, a white sheep, a black goat, six packs of candles, two sheets of white cloth, and a hundred dollars cash," he told Korli. "Make white suits for the family. We'll hold next Sunday's service at your house and sanctify it; the family will bathe and put on the white clothes here, leaving the old ones in the church—with all their bad luck—and return home reborn in the blood of Jesus. I'll take a ten-day dry fast for you people because the problem I see coming to you is not small. My fee is fifty dollars, just to replace the blood I'll lose from the fasting. Let us pray."

As she had promised, Leanya provided funds for the sanctification, including the cost of the new clothes. Bishop Zachariah brought the entire congregation to the apartment the next Sunday. Neighbors joined the celebrants after they cooked the sheep, the goat, and a whole bag of rice. Members of the church burned incense and sprinkled holy oil and water all over the apartment. The deacon board preached and prayed in tongues for the safety of the Korli family. Finally, everybody marched to the church singing. The crowd increased in size and temper as the marchers proceeded on the sandy path in the sea breeze. Again, crowds accompanied Korli and his family as they returned home from the church, dressed in white.

A week after the sanctification, Boimah brought a positive reply to Korli's letter of application to the Department of Treasury. Korli was out. Boimah only told Leanya that the letter was a reply to Korli's application but did not say whether it was favorable or unfavorable. When she gave Korli the letter on his return, he quickly opened it and was surprised to see the name and signature of the Deputy Secretary of the Treasury for Administration. A government official of such high rank signing a letter of employment for a messenger was beyond his comprehension. Korli sat in a sofa, leaned back, and took a deep breath, then read the official letter slowly. The deputy secretary stated that he was happy to learn that Korli, an eighth grade student, wanted a messenger job at the Department of Treasury with the hope of becoming a revenue agent in the future. If he did a good job, the Department would put him on scholarship until he completed college. Korli read further:

Before replying your letter, I got in touch with Central High concerning your performance in Math and English. You came through excellently. You will therefore be employed as a cadet in the economic department. It's a waste of time to use someone with your brilliance as a messenger. Your employment takes effect on September 1. Congratulations!

Astounded, Korli laid the letter aside to recover his senses. "Is this a dream?" he muttered. "The sanctification must have something to do with it!" he thought. Our troubles are over! I'll contribute my widow's mite to building the Church of the Redeemed in concrete. Bishop Zachariah is powerful indeed! Leanya may be unschooled but she is wise. If such a girl becomes educated, our family will prosper." Korli carefully put the letter away and ran to Leanya in the bedroom.

"Guess what?" he said with a bright smile.

"What?" Leanya looked at him in suspense.

"I have a job! Not a messenger job, but a real job! I'm supposed to start working in September but I want to try and see if I can start earlier."

"As of now you'll believe me whenever I tell you something," she told him as he hugged her with all his might. "Bishop Aziyah has power! Korli, read the Bible to me before we go to bed each night."

"Let's find something for the Bishop to buy blocks for his church," Korli said. "Even though he's been building that church for ten years and still hasn't completed the foundation, it's the least we can do for him."

Leanya laughed. "If your hands are dry, you could wait until you begin working," she said.

Korli ran with the letter to Mr. Seton who read it and said, "This is good news, Korli. You applied for a messenger job and they employed you as a cadet. That's one step from full employment. Congratulations! The ball is now on your half of the field. Try your best to keep that job, and don't put your hand in corruption. The Bible says a good name is better than riches. If you steal a million dollars, people will eat it from you and spoil your name. Write a letter of thanks to the Deputy Secretary and assure him that you'll measure up to his expectations."

Korli spent the whole night drafting the letter. To save his self respect, he didn't want to sound enthusiastic about the job. After all they had seen some merit in him. A self-abasing letter would compromise the esteem they had for him. If he could start immediately and work for three months without pay, he'd enjoy more of his boss's confidence.

"Only one change I recommend," said Mr. Seton when he looked over the letter. "Thank the Deputy Secretary for his consideration, not his 'kind' consideration. He isn't rendering you kindness by giving you the job because he admits that you're more than qualified for it. Don't sell yourself cheap although you need the job."

On his way to deliver the letter on Monday morning, Korli stopped by Marie's office on the ninth floor of the Department of Treasury to thank her for the part she might have played in his employment. A police officer gave him a seat in the well-furnished air-conditioned office.

"The executive assistant is with the Secretary," he told Korli. "She'll soon come out. Are you her relative?"

"No, sir. I came to thank her for helping me get a job here."

In an hour an extremely beautiful young woman opened the Secretary's door, looking at Korli with long-lashed eyes. Her black hair, coiled around her head, accented her height. After a moment, she smiled amiably, calming Korli's anxiety. Sitting in a swivel chair behind a well-polished mahogany desk crammed with files, she gazed at Korli darkly as if searching her memory.

"Hello, my friend," she greeted him.

"Hello, Ma'am," Korli said.

"This man did not come for appointment," explained the police officer. "He said he only came to greet you."

Korli rose, made a slight bow, and with hesitation, said:

"My name is Sumowor Gbamokorli. I came to thank you, Ma'am, for your kindness. Had it not been for you, I wouldn't have gotten a reply to my application. The Deputy Secretary has employed me as a cadet in the economic department."

"I know nothing about your application!" Marie said pointedly.

"Congratulations, anyway. I wish you the best!"

"My friend Ezra Boimah who works with you, told me that you helped to follow it up for me."

Korli did not know if he was betraying his friend or conferring honor on him by giving him credit for his assistance. Marie made no comment. After sorting out documents on her desk for a moment, she pulled out several files and returned to the Secretary's office at the sound of a bell. Korli decided not to make further reference to Boimah until he had seen him. Perhaps he had not given Marie the goat, and if he did, the matter should be kept secret as Boimah had advised him.

When Marie came out of the Secretary's office, Korli obligingly rose again. "I have a letter for the Deputy Secretary I wish to deliver, Ma'am," he said.

"Sit down, my man," said Marie, leaning her beautiful head one side and looking at him studiously. "Why do you call me Ma'am when we're almost the same age? And why are you in such a big hurry to go? You're lucky the officer admitted you here. People make appointments, sometimes a week or two in advance before coming to this office."

"I didn't want to take much of your time. I see that you're very busy."

"You were employed as what?"

"A cadet in the economic department."

"We use college students as cadets, not elementary or even high school students," Marie said and paused. Korli's mouth grew bitter; the blood rushed to his heart. Perhaps the letter had been mistakenly addressed to him. "But it's your luck," Marie said with a whiff of a smile and paused again. Luck? Korli could not believe it. He waited for an explanation. "Secretary Johnson sees something promising in you," she continued. "Report to my office when you start working in September. We have plenty of work here. You could help us since you're a cadet. Cadets don't have special assignments."

"I want to start working on Monday, if possible."

"Your name is not on the payroll yet," Marie said. "If I were you, I'd look for something else to do to get some cash. You have a family to support, do you not?" The Secretary's bell rang again. This time it was the police who went in.

"I'll make use of the time to learn."

"That's a good idea. If we drop or fire a cadet, we'll give you the person's check."

"Thank you very much," Korli said with a deep bow. "I'll be here by eight o'clock on Monday morning."

"Are you married?"

"Yes, Ma'am."

"How many children do you have?"

"Three."

"A responsible man, then. That's the kind of worker we want. Oh yes, I saw your letter of application and sent it to the Secretary's special assistant who handles such letters. He says it was well written. You were employed because of merit, not for any other reason. Congratulations again! The job here is not hard. All it takes is time and effort. In case of any problem, you have the whole Department to consult. You'll be working on this floor. Since you are a cadet, I'll make use of your service at times."

"Thank you very much," Korli said appreciatively. He did not bow this time.

"My name is Marie Tarjibo. You may call me Miss Tarjibo, not Ma'am. Don't make me old before my time." Marie laughed, straightening the frown that contorted Korli's face.

"Miss Tarjibo, will you please direct me to the office of Secretary Johnson?"

"Sorry, you can't see him now, but I will be happy to hand-deliver your letter for you." She rang a bell and the police emerged from the Secretary's office. "Kebeyor, Korli will be working with us starting Monday. Please escort him out for now."

"Yes, Ma'am," said the police officer. "My man, let's go," he commanded Korli. When they were out of earshot of Marie, he told Korli, "I'm sorry I forgot to tell you about your friend Boimah. His father died in Buchanan two weeks ago. He went there to see about his funeral. That's why you didn't see him. He says I should tell you not to mention anything about the goat to Marie or anybody else. Keep it a secret. I heard that Boimah might not come back. He has found a job at LAMCO; the company pay is better."

On his way home, Korli pondered Marie's reaction to him. Her free way of addressing him did not augur well. Kebeyor might get the wrong impression that he was Marie's intimate friend, morals being so loose in town as he had been told repeatedly. Should Secretary Johnson or his Deputy get such news, his job would be in danger. Certainly, Marie had a hand in his employment but was reluctant to admit it. Was she afraid he might mention the goat? On the whole, it was a happy encounter because it had ended on a happy note. Until he became acquainted with this new setting, it was premature for him to draw any conclusions.

14

A Farmer's Son

PRIOR TO HIS EMPLOYMENT at the Department of Treasury, Korli had never dreamed that the son of a poor farmer and hunter could work in one of the highest offices in the country. He had always considered important government jobs an exclusive domain of *kwii* people and their children and wards, as people always told him. Now he enjoyed the miraculous conveyance of an elevator, the comfort of an airconditioned office, a handsome check at the end of each month, and, above all, working with people who mattered. However, he didn't let his elevated position alter his decorous attitude in dealing with people. He continued exuding a spirit of humility and friendliness towards people regardless of their status, and extending to them a helping hand whenever possible.

He had never divined a reason for his successful move from one constraint to another in triumph. Initially he thought this particular one was due to his understanding of English, for he had put much time and effort in writing his letter of application to make it clear and precise. Marie admitted it. No! He had never written a sentence that pleased him, not to speak of a composition. The blank page was his enemy; whatever he wrote on it only approximated the meaning he wished to convey. Perhaps Marie was simply being polite. "Am I not berating myself?" Korli wondered.

They say success in Liberia depended on who in the upper echelon of government knew you and not on what you knew. No government official knew him except his retired landlord, yet he had obtained an enviable job in one of the most important public offices with a simple letter of application. No. Mr. Seton had told him that they seldom read letters of application in the country. Could it be the goat? No. Boimah never delivered it to Marie, or he wouldn't have made it a forbidden subject. What advantage would a goat be to people who handled an abundance of cash? Or to people who seldom ate local food? To bribe a government official you needed thousands of dollars, which he couldn't afford.

Marie by no means accounted for his success, for she had confessed that merit was the only ground for his employment. Korli believed her simulation of friendship was but a bribe meant to exploit the little potential she had seen in him. City boys, who prided themselves on dressing well and having good connections, seldom bothered with meticulous studies in school. They often boasted that whether or not they did well in school, their jobs waited for them. But native children, who depended only on their academic achievement for success, had to do exceptionally well in school. Consequently, they became the brains in workplaces although the lucrative positions and emoluments went to city boys. Maybe it was his humility and hard work that continued to pay off. He kept company with messengers, drivers, and sweepers as well as with honorables if they, too, were so inclined. He did not like barriers between other people and himself. He helped people solve their problems. But no: Humble, brilliant, kind, and hardworking people were disposable drudges needed only for their service, Korli thought. He saw no discernible merit in himself or his circumstances that accounted for the privilege he enjoyed.

Because people, including his wife, told him to be careful about what he said or did at Treasury, he decided to live above suspicion to avoid the crippling effects of fear and anxiety. As long as he did the right thing with a clear conscience, the people could say, do, or think what they may. Of course, to maintain the trust reposed in him, he wouldn't be careless with confidential information. Mr. Seton would be his only confidant because he was frank, broad-minded, brave, secretive, and prudent. He valued his secretive attribute the most. The Kru who did not conduct Poro or Sande society, notable for their secrecy, seemed to keep secrets by far better. There was virtually no secret kept in Kpelle- or Golaland.

"What you should worry about," Mr. Seton advised him one night in his office after he had told him of his success at Treasury, "is saying and doing the right thing. Nearly everybody in this country is a PRO—a public relations officer listening for the slightest slip of tongue to report to the authorities who will dismiss you from the job or imprison you for expressing an unfavorable opinion about the government. Once the government sacks you, you won't get a job in this country again and your life will be in jeopardy. If they suspect you of political ambition, you disappear or find yourself in Belle Yallah before you know it. It is better, I believe, to be true to your conscience than compromise it for a job. My way of handling this problem is remaining silent. If I can't tell the truth, I keep quiet. They accuse us the silent majority of cowardice and betrayal, but prudence demands that you speak only if your speaking will accomplish something worthwhile. You're a fine young man, Korli. There's no limit to what you will achieve if you exercise patience and common sense."

"Those are my views, too, Mr. Seton," Korli said. "Except I don't feel the government alone is responsible for the chaotic order of things. Good governance is impossible without a population committed to excellence, hard work, and honesty. Besides, what passes for criticism in Liberian society is mostly propaganda, jealousy, envy, and malice. Critics opposing the government become its loyalists when they get public offices that afford them a chance to line their wallets with banknotes. Criticism is good only if it identifies problems and suggests possible solutions."

"You have a point, but without good government, nothing works," Mr. Seton observed. "True, our critics are not sincere." After an interval of contemplation, he added, "In this country, enemies become friends overnight depending on which way the wind blows. As long as the government is the only employer, we'll never have good critics. Those who form part of it will always praise it, and those who are not part of it will always condemn it until they get their share of the cake."

Korli walked to the door, poked his head out, quickly surveyed the yard, and closed it. Then he closed the office window. As he returned to his seat, Mr. Seton, who had been following him with curious eyes, said:

"You needn't worry about informants, Korli. They'll drive you crazy. Don't be surprised if your own wife or child is a government spy!"

"You're kidding," Korli said.

"I'm not kidding," Mr. Seton rejoined. "Since we're in the pool, we needn't worry about being wet." He trifled with papers on the desk and passed his hand through his wiry hair.

"What do they get from betraying their own people?" Korli asked.

"Power! Jobs! Money! Often the jobless in this society are far better off than the employed because, as undercover agents, they get any amount of money they desire to do their jobs! They commonly build an expensive house in six months—ride the most expensive cars, build houses for girlfriends, and go to Europe and America for weekends! As watch dogs for the government, they lock up innocent people who get in their way! Only when they fall from grace do you hear about their corruption. So, be on your guard at Treasury! Don't talk about all that you see happening there. Before signing a document, read it! I need not advise you about women. They brought us into the world; they can take us out of it any time. An honest, intelligent country boy beginning government service in the highest office of its key department is a target."

"I bare my heart to you without fear because you're wise and courageous, Mr. Seton," Korli said. "I seldom talk about political issues with people. I pray the Lord's Prayer and recite the Twenty-Third Psalm each time I go to work."

"Have you met Hon. Johnson?"

"Yes, sir. He said I should work with the Secretary's executive assistant."

"What kind of work does she give you to do?"

"Drafting letters. She tells me what to put in them, making my job easy, but I have problems with English."

"Knowing what to write doesn't make writing easy. Most people don't like to do it because it is tedious. That's why they're dumping everything on you. Nevertheless, the act of creation is rewarding. Your job is sensitive because you have access to people's secrets, so you have to be tight-lipped. English is everybody's problem because every rule of its grammar has an exception and it is difficult to do original thinking. But the English language is so flexible that it can accommodate any shade of thought. Read a grammar book and master the rules. Have a dictionary at hand when writing. Write something every week for your English teacher to inspect. If he underlines a sentence or a word, let him tell you why so that you won't make the same mistake again. Read good literature. Pretty soon you'll be able to write the perfect sentence."

"Do you know that you have become a father to me?" Korli told Mr. Seton soberly. "I lost my father ten years ago and left my home, but I've never suffered for want of advice or anything I need."

"We're one family, Korli. Only our languages divide us, but we have the same culture. If I go to Bong County right now, they will turn it over to me with white kola. The same thing will happen in Lofa or Nimba County. Nkrumah once said all of West Africa should be one country. He was right. You're my son, a brother to my children. Don't hesitate to consult me on any problem."

"I'll keep you informed of every development in my life."

"Take good care of that job. I look forward to the day *you'll* become

Secretary of Treasury."

Korli smiled. "I'll try, although that day is far in the future."

"That's a good attitude."

"In college, I'll major in literature to master writing skills. I have many interesting ideas but putting them on paper is difficult. The blank page is terrible! You ever went to school abroad?"

"In Ghana."

"That's what I thought."

"Ghana has a large Liberian community. I was born there and I went to school there. They use the British school system. The British don't believe in making learning a pleasure. They make you sweat and bleed, but you come out solid like a rock. I have a good library; you may borrow some of my books if you like. Majoring in literature is good, but don't slavishly follow any writer's style. Do your own thinking and make experiments with words to express your ideas according to how you perceive them."

"Thank you, sir. I'll look at the library tomorrow. Goodnight."

"Look at it now. Don't get in the habit of putting things off for tomorrow. Let me give you a book all educated people ought to read—*Tales From Shakespeare*, by Charles and Mary Lamb. You learn much from Shakespeare about human beings and their attitudes."

"What about the plays themselves?"

"You'll appreciate them better if you first read the summaries." Mr. Seton pulled out the much-handled book from a shelf and gave it to Korli. "Have you read any of Shakespeare's plays?" he asked him.

"Our literature teacher told us about one called *Julius Caesar*. He did the reading and told us the story."

"Read the summaries and then come for the plays."

"Thank you, sir. Please give my best regards to the Madam. She always seems to be out when I come here."

"With nothing much to do, she visits friends for their company. I always deliver your message to her. How is Borwulo doing?"

"Fine. Leanya tells me we already have our fourth child—Borwulo. She takes care of the house while Leanya sees after her market."

"Does she help with the market?"

"Oh, yes! She has become a serious businessperson. You should hear her discuss market strategies!"

Mr. Seton laughed. "Our children are brilliant and serviceable, but they lack the opportunity to learn."

"That's true, unfortunately. Well, goodnight Mr. Seton. See you in the morning."

"Goodnight, son. Give my greetings to the Madam. Sleep well."

Korli mulled over Mr. Seton's words of wisdom nearly all night. It was his first time seeing a library in someone's home. Other well-off people he knew affected to be connoisseurs of drinks, music, clothes, furniture, cars, money, government jobs, women, and the like, but not of books. Here, thought Korli, was a lonely man dying for discussion about things of the mind. He'd die without committing to writing his rich knowledge and experience because the country lacked book publishers—and nobody cared. Yes, he remembered the story of *Julius Caesar* as told by his literature teacher. The story dramatizes how the average person is self-centered, proud, and manipulative. "That's what ails our society," Korli muttered.

15

THE RETURN OF JOSHUA

NOT FOND OF PICNICS or outings, but in keeping with his promise to Leanya and the children, Korli took the family to the beach during the weekend for them to see the sea. He hoped to use the opportunity "to wash" his new job, as the saying was. A cadet job was nothing to celebrate, but it was an important step to full employment, as Mr. Seton had said.

They took a long walk to ELWA Beach early Saturday morning. The sky was clear and bright, the sea calm, the air unsullied. A wren hovered around them on the way, squeaked and chirped into the tangled bushes on the roadside. Korli was so absorbed in his own reflections that he didn't hear the bird.

"A stranger is coming to us," Leanya told him, staring absently at the blue sea and tying Liimu more firmly on her back.

Junior and Famang romped in the tall grasses on the way and decorated their sister's hair with wild roses they picked on the roadside.

"Don't swim in the sea or even go near it," Leanya warned them. "It's deeper than a river. If something sinks in it to a certain point, it can't come back to the surface."

"Oh!" Junior cried, looking at the immense body of water in wonder. "It's also wider than a river. It ends in the cloud!"

"The clouds are far from it," Korli said. "The sea ends in America. People swim in it—even little children, but you have to learn how to swim before jumping in it. I'll get swimming trunks for you boys, but you are too little to fool with the sea. Right now you should only look at it."

The beach was bare and breezy, for beachgoers usually visited it on Sunday afternoons, which was just as well, for Korli wanted to be away from everything and get complete rest. He and the boys stood on the edge of the foaming waves rolling towards the massive expanse of sand and watched with fascination a ship gliding at the horizon towards the Freeport of Monrovia.

"It's a whole house, Father!" cried Junior, pointing to the ship.

Famang only stared at it with unbelieving eyes and went up-shore with Korli, while Junior let the approaching waves spread at his feet.

"Come up here!" Korli called him when an enormous comber heading towards him gathered speed. Junior waited until it came close to him before running up-shore. Where he had stood soon disappeared in deep angry waves.

"You see?" Korli told him. "Those waves could have carried you away, and you wouldn't have come back alive! Forgotten what Mother told you?"

Leanya held Liimu by the hand as they stood further up, looking at another ship moving along the shore. When Liimu saw it, she grew frightened and raised her arms for her mother who picked her up and tied her on her back. Junior sighted a Liberian flag fluttering on the ship and pointed at it excitedly.

"That's our ship!" he cried. "I want to ride it and go to America!"

"No, it's not our ship," Korli said. "Liberia doesn't own ships."

"But our flag is on it!" Leanya said. "A Liberian flag belongs on Liberian property."

"We take care of ships for other countries," Korli said. "That's why you see our flag on other countries' ships."

"Why don't we own a ship?" Junior asked.

"Because we don't have enough money to buy one," Korli said. "We used to have ships long ago, but they became old and rusty and couldn't go out to sea."

"Too bad. They should have fixed them. Papa, how long does it take a ship to go from here to America?"

"Two weeks. Maybe three, if it doesn't stop in other countries to put down cargo. People go to America by airplanes nowadays, not by ships."

"Why?"

"Airplanes are faster. Take only one day to get to America."

"Really? Liberia has an airplane?"

"Yes, but they are too small to go to America. They fly only in Liberia. If an airplane leaves Liberia at six in the morning and goes straight to America, it arrives there before six in the evening."

"Let's go to America, Papa!"

"We don't have that kind of money, Junior."

"We can work for it."

Leanya smiled. "You know how long it'll take to get enough money to send one person to America? Five years or more."

"What do you want to do in America, anyway?" said Famang, his eyes fixed on the ship as it faded into the distance.

"Get plenty of money and buy clothes, cars, watches, and radios," Junior answered, his eyes glistening at the thought.

"All the money in America is locked up in big houses with iron doors," Korli joked. "The only way you can get some is by finding a job and working hard."

"I can work hard!" Junior declared.

"The kind of work they do in America requires schooling. Every job has its own school."

Leanya spread several lappas on the sand and sat on them with Liimu. Korli and the boys raced down the beach. Famang and Junior soon left him behind. With her mother's help, Liimu was busy building a sand house. She'd pile the sand on top of her foot, press it with her palms until it became compact, and then withdraw her foot. She built a house for each member of the family. Her mother's house was the biggest. As she and her mother waited for the others to see their houses, they watched a dozen canoes with fishermen casting their nets before them. The ship had now disappeared round Cape Mesurado. Junior and Famang ran back to their panting father as he jogged wearily towards them. They spied the fishermen as they ran.

"If we had a canoe, we could go fishing," said Junior when they reached their mother and Liimu.

"These are the houses your sister built for us," Leanya told them. "This one is for you Junior; this is for Famang; that is for Papa, and this is for Liimu and me."

Korli took Liimu in his arms and thanked her for the houses.

"You're no more a baby, Liimu," he said. "You have built houses for us!"

The boys broke down the houses to build better ones. Liimu cried on seeing her handiwork being destroyed. Her mother took care of the problem by putting a nipple in her mouth. She no longer paid attention to the houses. Korli suggested that they all eat and go home.

Liimu got a piece of bread and butter and insisted on sitting in his lap to eat. She leaned her head on him, and rubbed her bread on his chest.

Korli gently put the bread in her mouth and smiled.

"You're not able to wash my clothes yet," he told her, "so don't get me dirty."

"Won't the sea swallow us if we swim in it?" asked Famang. "They say it can swallow a canoe—" Famang paused abruptly when he saw a group of seagulls hovering over the sea, some sitting on the waves.

"If you learn how to swim, the sea will become your playground," Korli told him. "You'll know how to tackle the waves and ride them. The next time we'll go to New Kru Town Beach for you children to see Kru and Fanti children swimming in the sea."

As they ate in the cool breeze, another wren chirped over their heads and shot into a nearby bramble. Junior looked after it with longing, wishing he had a rubber gun.

"Let's go home now," said Korli. He rose, put Liimu on his shoulders, and started the journey. "Strangers may already be at the house waiting for us," he said. Everybody followed him.

"This is not the first time the wren has cried on us," said Leanya as she gathered her lappa. "It cried on us as we came, and it has been crying on us since we arrived."

"I hope the stranger or strangers are bringing us something good," said Korli. "I don't like empty-handed strangers."

As they had expected, they met people in their yard unloading a green pickup truck under Mr. Seton's supervision. Brown tarpaulin hung on either flank of the pickup. Mr. Seton's children, the driver and carboys were taking down cartons of beer, cigarettes, sneakers, car parts, radios, powder, soap; crates of Coca-Cola, gin; bales of cloth, T-shirts, shorts; fans, a small icebox, and so forth. They packed everything on the apartment porch. Partly hidden behind the pickup, Joshua was busy paying the driver his fees and shouting at children who were gazing at the goods to go away. When the driver pulled off, Korli ran to him with outstretched arms and a smile.

"Oh!" cried Joshua as they embraced. Leanya, beaming, stood waiting her turn to embrace him.

"My friend, what happened to you?" Korli drawled as they hooked together urgently. "I thought the goods were for Mr. Seton!"

"I didn't run away with your money as I joked I would," said Joshua. "You didn't see me for so long because I was in trouble."

"What trouble?" Korli asked solemnly. "Were you sick? Jailed? Somebody died?"

"My mother nearly died of some mysterious sickness no hospital in this town could treat or even diagnose. We ended up in Sinoe! The sickness was so serious we had to travel by air. Then someone took me deep inside the county to one Bodio—what you people call Zoe—living in a small Nefu village—a two-day trek. The Bodio said witches had sold my mother to a wizard. In ten days, she was supposed to have been sacrificed. We were lucky to have consulted him soon. He came with us to Greenville and cured her." Joshua broke off speaking and hugged Leanya so passionately that Korli had to look away. "Had you people not given me that money," he said, "Mother would have died! I used every cent I had plus half your money. Thanks very much. After Mother got well, we vowed to find your money before coming back to Monrovia. Let's carry the things in. We have invited thieves again! Let them come! When I am finished with them, they will know who born dog. The first time I only warned them, but this time I'll shoot." He surveyed the crowd with a weighty face as he spoke. The crowd, comprising mostly boys, cowered away.

"You people may pack the things in the big warehouse," said Mr. Seton. "Borwulo, go and call your Mother. Tell her that Joshua is here."

By the time they were through packing everything in the warehouse, it was around seven in the evening and Mrs. Seton had set a table. Borwulo called them to eat.

"Oho!" Mrs. Seton shouted for joy on seeing Joshua; they hugged fiercely. Her shiny hair and face sparkled in the light over the threshold. "You got us worried!" she cried, holding Joshua back by his shoulders and staring in his eyes with a smile. "Why did you desert us so? You brought us strangers and refused to come back and see how they're faring!"

"Ma'am, don't blame me. I got in trouble."

"What trouble? Woman confessed your name? Not tired of women yet?"

Joshua smiled blandly and said, "Let's sit down for me to explain everything to you." Everybody sat down except Mrs. Seton, who stood watching him.

Joshua scratched his head roughly and leaned back. His face assumed a solemn, gloomy look.

"Police nabbed you?" Mrs. Seton prompted him impatiently. Joshua seemed to be struggling to hold back tears.

"His mother almost died," Mr. Seton said. "Hospitals in Monrovia couldn't help her so he had to fly her to Sinoe. You're a man, Joshua. You'll pay a heavy fine if you cry." Joshua wiped the budding tears with a cambric handkerchief he pulled out of his side pocket.

"Mothers are the dearest people in children's lives," Mrs. Seton said, sitting down next to him. "Your mother's sickness seems to have made you ill, Joshua. You've lost weight! You should be glad she made it. Cheer up, my friend."

"I'm glad, Ma'am," Joshua said. "This Bodio is powerful. He gave Mother a simple leaf to eat with kola nut. In a week she was on her feet again, sound in health as ever."

"Our native doctors have curatives hospitals know nothing about," remarked Korli. "The ones that amaze me are the bone-joiners. Your bone may break into a thousand pieces, yet they join it; if they can't, they replace it with deer bone. Nobody will notice the difference when you're well. Kwii people call them witchdoctors."

"The witchdoctors are the psychiatrists," said Mr. Seton. "They heal people who are bewitched or possessed. They do some evil things also but only to their enemies and criminals."

"That's common all over the country," said Mrs. Seton. "I mean the bone-joining. In my village, we had a bone-joiner who didn't have to touch the broken bone. He'd deliberately break a rooster's legs, utter incantations over them, and the injured person would get better as soon as the rooster walked—and that would be in a few hours or a day at the most, unless the bone had broken into too many pieces—in which case, he'd put it in a bamboo cast—it'd heal in two weeks. What was your mother's sickness?" Mrs. Seton asked Joshua.

"Extreme weakness; couldn't eat or stand on her feet. Very embarrassing for a son! Had my wife not taken her to our home and cared for her, she wouldn't have made it."

"Maybe it was malnutrition. Did you try Island Clinic? They say the Nigerian man running it is very powerful. He can heal people with evil spirits!"

"He told us to find a country doctor for Mother. Well, thank God we're back with good news! She now lives with me. I believe she was suffering from loneliness. I'm her only child."

"My people, let's go to the table and eat," Mrs. Seton said. "Borwulo— Oh, I forgot. Borwulo has new parents. Sarah, bring us wine." A tall plump girl with big breasts brought five large bottles of French wine in a tray to the table.

"Who are Borwulo's new parents?" asked Joshua.

"They're sitting right beside you," Mrs. Seton said. "Korli and Leanya."

Joshua laughed while dishing out a plate of well-cooked, new swamp rice.

"Good food!" he said, inhaling the appetizing fragrance of the rice through his bulbous nose. "My lucky home! Each time I come here, rich food is ready!"

"Eat all you can," said Mrs. Seton. "We have much, much more. Tonight's dinner is pure coincidence, Joshua. We never expected you. Korli often comes home late at night—the same with Leanya. By the time they come home, we've already eaten and gone to sleep. We'll be sending them a dish whenever we cook something good."

"Anything you cook will be good enough for us," Korli said. "We too will now be sending you people a dish whenever we cook. That's the only way we'll eat from each other. My schedule is tight." Then, turning to Joshua he said, "I now work at the Department of Treasury as a cadet, assigned to the office of the Secretary."

"Good for you!" Joshua exclaimed. "You were born lucky! However, you also worked hard for it: swallowing up eight grades in less than four years! Now you have one foot in a great office! Pretty soon you'll put the other one inside!"

"He was lucky to start government service in the highest office of an important department," said Mr. Seton. "Korli is brainy. Boys upcountry have nothing to depend on but their brain. They have no connections or properties to inherit, so when they get an opportunity, they make the best use of it. Korli applied for a messenger job and was employed as a cadet."

"Korli came to town with ambition, so he's bound to succeed," Joshua admitted. "Some country boys get the same opportunity but prefer to enjoy. Look, my friend," he looked Korli squarely in the eyes, "don't let the girls at Treasury trap you. They're all tied up with their bosses. If you step on a Secretary's toe, you'll see yourself outside before you bat your eyes. Now that you've settled properly in a lucky home, keep your mind on your job."

"Mr. Seton has become my father," said Korli. "He guides my every step and I listen to him."

"Thanks be to God!" cried Joshua, raising both arms to heaven. "I made no mistake by bringing you people here! Mr. Seton is rich with experience and he's friendly—like his wife. He served the government more than thirty-five years. It's too bad you don't leave government service in Liberia with a pension, but he did well for himself by building a good home—and he can walk the streets of Monrovia with his head up."

"What's the use of stealing?" said Mr. Seton. "Anything you do in the darkness appears in daylight. When you fall from grace, the first problem you face is the auditor-general. No corrupt former government official has ever left his office scot-free."

"Mrs. Seton is my wife's new mother," said Korli. "Joshua, we are blessed! Thank you for bringing us to them. We'll leave this house only when we build ours."

"They'll live with us for a long time," said Mr. Seton. "Korli, when you build your house, put it under rent and continue living with us."

Korli said, "I don't like moving from place to place. We lived five round years in White Plains before coming here. We moved only because our landlord went to America."

"This one will not go anywhere," said Mrs. Seton. Everybody laughed. "Rolling stones gather no moss. Don't ever move from where you live without trouble—I mean trouble like a bad sickness or a bad landlord. You never know what problem you'll meet elsewhere."

"I'll come over each Saturday evening," said Joshua. "So whatever you people cook on Saturday, put mine aside. Martha will be coming with me. Mother too, perhaps. I told her to be walking around for exercise."

"No problem," Mrs. Seton said. "Bring everybody. It's agreed and binding. If you break this binding agreement, you'll pay for my food plus a heavy fine." She emphasized each word with a whisk of her spoon hand.

"It's agreed," said Joshua.

"And binding," Mrs. Seton added.

"Agreed and binding," Joshua said.

"We too will keep food for you," Korli told Joshua. "Agreed?"

"Agreed. If my stomach can't hold that much food, I'll take some home. Martha too will cook something and bring it along. She cooks well. When she cooks collard greens—"

"Hey!" cried Mrs. Seton. "Only country dishes, my friend! No *mekin* food. We're not Congo people."

"Okay, she'll cook *torborgee*, then."

"Why take us to Lofa County? Either cassava leaves or palm butter. Bong or Sinoe County! Cassava leaves with dry meat, or palm butter with lobsters, crabs, and crawfish."

"The only way we'll see him often is fining him whenever he breaks the agreement," said Korli.

"Should you run into trouble, don't hesitate to come to us," Mr. Seton told Joshua on a serious note. "Your trouble is our trouble, too."

"The sickness was an emergency," Joshua said. "I had to be with Mother round the clock. That's why I couldn't come to let you people know."

"I understand," said Mrs. Seton. "But I believe serious sickness seldom kills a person. I've seen people die of common headache, running stomach, and malaria. I've also seen people recover from sickness that kept them in bed for months." Looking at Leanya's plate, Mrs. Seton noted that it was only half empty. "Leanya," she told her in Kpelle, "don't play shame face before these men. Men don't joke when it comes to eating, and they don't have the sort of responsibility you have. Eat! You're eating for two people!"

"I love eating," Leanya said quietly. "But we ate bread and butter on the beach a while ago."

"Since when Kpelle people became bread eaters? Eat your rice and cassava leaf, my child."

Mr. Seton did not eat much food, but he drank some wine, excused himself, and went to bed. Leanya too excused herself to go give the baby milk.

Mrs. Seton told her as she went to the back door, "Leanya, don't continue depriving Korli of his right. Liimu is not a baby any more. She walks and talks. As of today I'll call her Old Lady."

Leanya stood in her track and said, laughing, "Kpelle people wean a child only when they're old enough to give someone water to drink."

"That girl can give someone water to drink," said Mrs. Seton. "I'm advising you because Monrovia girls are tempting and quick to take a woman's husband from her. They are shameless! The way they rock their butts and fix their hair can send a man crazy! If a man ignores them, they go after him. Should a man make the mistake to have a little fun with them, he becomes responsible for their clothes, their rents, their food, and their hospital bills."

Korli laughed and said, "Leanya is my first and only wife. Only death will part us."

"That's what men usually say until they're hooked. Leanya, have him tell you his salary. You take it. Korli, the day you get in trouble with Leanya, I'll take her side and make your life miserable. Send the girl to night school. Let her learn to speak English and wear skirts and blouses. That's the big thing Monrovia girls brag about—they know book and wear *mekin* clothes."

"I've already bought a book for her. We began the first lesson last night. Ma'am, American clothes don't impress me. I didn't see my mother wearing them."

"Make him stay home at night to teach you, Leanya. No man is made of iron and steel. The man who is so sure of himself is quick to fall when he sees the rocking hips and the bosoms."

Slightly disturbed, Leanya simply smiled and said goodnight to everyone as she got up to leave.

"The night is far spent," Mrs. Seton yawned. "Joshua, you brought an umbrella with you?"

"No, Ma'am," said Joshua. "It wasn't raining when we were coming."

"Well, this is the rainy season, for your information. Never leave home without an umbrella. Monrovia rain is full of surprises and sickness." As if to prove the veracity of her statement, the rain came down heavily then stopped abruptly. "Sarah, bring your Pa's umbrella for Joshua," she called. "You had better go home, Joshua. You have a patient. Old people are hard to recover from sickness. Goodnight." She gave him the umbrella and a lingering hug.

Mrs. Seton's comments had surprised Korli. Liquor seemed not to agree with her. He'd advise Leanya not to worry about her provocative talks.

"I'm walking with Joshua to the market to find a taxi," he told Mrs. Seton. "After seeing him bring so many things here, thieves might attack him in a dark corner."

"Do you have a flashlight?"

"No, Ma'am. It doesn't matter. The houses along the way are well lighted."

"You'll still need a flashlight. Our light isn't reliable. Sarah, bring me your Pa's flashlight for Korli!"

When Joshua opened the front door, he found four uniformed police on the porch, their badges flashing in the porch light. Two of them stood in combat postures on either side of the door with submachine guns held at the ready. The other two, pistols at their sides, sat cross-legged on the low concrete wall round the porch, looking about with detachment. "Halt!" cried one of those at the door, pointing his gun at Joshua.

Taken by utter surprise, Joshua looked bewildered. He halted and peered at the police with frightened eyes and trembling lips—but not for long. The other one quickly hung his gun on his shoulder, knocked Joshua down, and applied handcuffs to his wrists.

"What have I done?" Joshua cried piteously, writhing on the tiled floor in his captor's hands.

Sarah, who was probably sleeping, had not brought the flashlight and Mrs. Seton had gone for it while Korli waited for her. Hearing the accented talks and scuffling, Korli ran after her.

"Ma'am! Ma'am! Joshua and some people are fighting on the porch," he shouted.

"What! They must be thieves thinking he has money on him! Let me go for a gun."

"No, Ma'am," Korli said. "If they see a gun with you, they might shoot. Let me go there."

"Be careful. I'm waking up the old man."

"Let him sleep. If I fail to handle it, you may wake him up."

Opening the door, Korli found his friend in handcuffs, a policeman pointing gun at him.

"Don't you know what you did?" the policeman asked Joshua.

"What? What has this man done?" cried Mrs. Seton who had followed Korli, her thin hands clasped on her head, stamping the floor and crying. Korli looked at the police glumly. Were they unarmed, he'd have taken care of them with no problem.

"That's the other man!" the officer on the porch fence said, pointing at Korli. Then he turned his back to everybody and watched the rain, which had started to fall again.

Joshua stared around with impotent rage as one of the policemen applied handcuffs to Korli's wrists.

"My people, let's go in," Mrs. Seton cried, placing her open palms on her bosom.

"No," said the policeman who now held Korli by the arm. "We don't want people saying we came to rob you at gun point. Let all the talking take place out here."

"John Mark!" cried Korli, giving the tall officer a smile of recognition when he turned around.

"Don't John Mark me!" he cried harshly, walking up to him. "You are a liar," he jabbed Korli with a finger. "I never knew that you and your friend were thieves."

"Who are thieves?" Joshua asked in anger.

"You people are dealing in stolen goods," Captain Mark said, looking very angry.

Joshua's arresting officer slapped him and said, "Don't argue with the Captain."

"Let's take them to Headquarters for investigation," said Captain Mark.

The pandemonium brought Mr. Seton out to the porch, white bedclothes wrapped round him like a toga. He held a fold of the bedclothes at his midriff. His mouth was open with surprise.

"Mark, what's the commotion about—and—and—what is this?" he looked at Joshua and Korli with distress. "Gentlemen, let's go in." The officers looked at each other and nodded consent.

Mrs. Seton put drinks on the center table for them, trying to wear a smile on her face as they took their seats and started gulping the wine from the bottles.

"Remove the cuffs from them," Captain Mark told the arresting officers. "Well, Mr. Seton, we didn't come to stay long. Farouk Salami reported at Headquarters this morning that thieves broke into his store last night and stole many things. We conducted an investigation into the matter and found one of his store boys guilty of theft of property. He says your sons Joshua and Korli are his accomplices. We've been around for some time, but knowing you as a respectable citizen of this country, we couldn't disturb your meeting. Once we retrieve the stolen properties and get something for gas, we'll set your children free."

"What has Korli got to do with it? Did he take part in the break-in?"

"No. He received the stolen properties. Once he returns them to us, they are free."

There was a knock on the door. Mr. Seton cracked it open and saw Leanya standing there, quite upset.

"Bornyonoh, come to your friend," he called to his wife, who came running to the living room. "Go to Leanya on the porch. Go with her to her apartment until we are through with this discussion."

"I paid good money for those things, Mr. Seton," said Joshua. "Boys who work for Lebanese don't get cash for their pay. They're given goods to sell. So I gave Nyinatee money for fifty crates of beer and fifty crates of Coca-Cola. He gave me only twenty of each and said he'd give me the rest as he got them. Through the same arrangement, I got the other things from other boys—"

"Let them have the goods," Korli interrupted. "I don't want my name mentioned in connection with stealing."

"Why should they have everything?" Joshua protested. "As of today I'll get receipts for anything I buy from people. I'm not a thief! Captain Mark knows me very well. Let's give the officers something for their gas so they can go."

"Joshua, I work in an important government office, handling sensitive documents. I have to be beyond reproach."

"Which office?" asked one of the officers.

"The Department of Treasury," Korli admitted.

"Where in that department do you work? The revenue section?"

"The office of the Secretary of Treasury. I handle some of his correspondence."

"Why didn't you tell us this ever since? No policeman in Liberia is supposed to arrest or question you. Look, you people find our gas money so we can go." Mrs. Seton replenished the drinks while Mr. Seton went to get some cash for the officers.

"Gentlemen, let's go," said Captain Mark. Each officer took a bottle of wine. As they walked out, the captain called Korli aside and told him,

"I looked for Joshua all over Monrovia and didn't find him. Someone told me that he had gone to Sinoe. Do you know that I went to Sinoe? The place is big, and the village he went to is small and deep in the forest. Look, what I'll do for you is give you two of my officers to protect you for a few days. A common messenger in the office of the Secretary of Treasury is beyond arrest—unless he kills someone. No Lebanese will ever come here looking for things. Those fellows asked me to go with them on the beat tonight. I never knew we were coming here to you. I had to act like their captain; that's why I made that display. I am sorry."

Korli knew that Captain Mark was lying, but he kept his peace and looked at Mr. Seton.

"Don't post any police round here," said Mr. Seton who had overheard Captain Mark's remark. "I'll get my own officers to live with me for a week or two. Since people have seen goods brought into this house, we'll continue having problems with police and thieves."

When the police left, Korli told Mr. Seton, "Leanya will do her business, and I'll take care of my job. I won't run a shop after all. We'll sell the things from the house and Leanya will use the money from the sale to expand her market."

"Run your shop," Mr. Seton said. "The problem is you didn't confide in me the arrangement you made with Joshua. You wouldn't have run into this trouble had you done so. Business gives you petty cash for daily expenses so that you may use your salary for important things. You talked of building a house. When you have done that, you may leave the shop business and save money from your salary for retirement. I don't see you as a shopkeeper in the future but a government official or senator. For now, do business to get extra cash; in the future when you become prosperous, nobody will accuse you of corruption."

16

THE FLIGHT OF TIME

A WEEK AFTER THE INCIDENT at the Setons, when Mr. Seton had gone on a trip to Sinoe to see about a funeral, the Director of Police came with a group of officers around midnight to arrest Korli "for theft of property." Mrs. Seton and Leanya put together two thousand dollars and implored him to leave Korli alone.

"In addition to this amount," the Director said, "I must carry the goods. This is a serious crime; it has reached the ears of the president. If I get ten thousand dollars, that will satisfy Salami. Then I'll drop the matter and tell the president that it's a lie. He has confidence in me."

Korli knew that it was a lie. The potbellied director wanted the money for himself. "You'll have to just carry the goods," he said in disgust. "We don't have another cent with us."

That night the Director's men packed everything in a pickup and took it away.

The shock of the catastrophic loss made them all speechless and numb. For a week Korli and Leanya made no contact with anyone, not even with the Setons whose warnings, advice, and kindness meant so much to them. Korli sent an excuse to Marie that he was sick and would resume duty in a week. Marie accepted the excuse without question because it was his first time staying away from work on account of illness.

But Korli was really sick. His head split with pain, and he was feverish and nauseous. Leanya too was experiencing the same discomforts. She declined to go to the market, but as a mother, she had to get up and take care of the family. Borwulo sold what she could of her greens, pepper, onions, fish, and other perishables around the community. Late one night their reflections on the loss brought them a little comfort and hope, though the problem remained perplexing.

"We should have built our house with that money," Leanya had said, a belated observation that did not impress Korli. "Or built a zinc shack as General Jackson suggested to avoid rent. Fortunately, the children have not started school yet." Korli paid no attention to that, either. "Joshua is a crook. He connived with the police to share our money with them. A market woman and a close friend of mine told me that such cheating is common in Monrovia. She says a crook once brought a briefcase to her husband and harassed him to buy it for any amount he could afford. The man did not work in an office; he operated a crane at the Freeport. However, seeing how distressed the fellow looked—he said his family was starving to death—the man bought the briefcase for ten dollars. A day later the fellow returned handcuffed in the hands of a police officer. The police charged this respectable man with buying stolen property and wanted to take him to prison. To save his good name, he gave them the briefcase, but as for his money, it was gone. We should never again get into business with anyone in this town."

"Most people are reliable, Leanya," Korli, who was still in bed, said. "I got plenty of warnings and advice from Mr. Seton and other friends, but they came too late. I had already made the deals. The deal with Boimah worked; that's why I got the job. I made the mistake of involving police in my search for Joshua."

"Suppose you write to General Jackson and tell him what has happened to us? He's expecting money from us; perhaps when he learns of our trouble, he might help us with money to cross this bridge."

"It won't be fair. The general gave us all his money before going to America. He is old and infirm, Leanya, so he's not working. His children, who already have a grievance against him, will not see to his medical problems and give him money to send us. The old man doesn't have long to live. To bring his body here will cost the children a fortune. It should be enough to let him know what has happened to us. Let's go on living as usual and try not to repeat the same mistakes."

The expression "time flies" had made no impression on Korli until he settled in his job at Treasury while teaching his wife and going to school himself. They agreed to bury themselves in their work. Work became a means of exploring their sources of strength and clinging to hopes and dreams of a better future. Before going to the market each day, Leanya left the children with Mrs. Seton who was more than happy to babysit them.

Two years slipped through his fingers like a breeze. Having grown in an environment where the deadline for things to be done was tomorrow, he now discovered that each day had its own tasks that couldn't wait for another day. Compelled to budget and use his time effectively, he realized that he didn't have much of it. No matter how hard he exerted himself, the volume of correspondence increased from day to day—his lessons and teaching grew more complicated—but his hard work was rewarded: He received a double promotion in his second year at Central High, a rare achievement for a high school student; Secretary Johnson appointed him research assistant, and Leanya could read and write simple English.

Korli's success on the job was largely due to sensible steps he took to discourage people appealing to the Secretary for letters of recommendation. Those writers converged on his office every working hour. He told them to seek recommendations from their former employers, heads of the institutions that educated or trained them for the jobs they sought, or people in authority who knew them personally.

"If Muna's nursing instructor recommends her for a nursing job," he often gave them the reasonable example, "she'll more likely get the job than if the recommendation came from a government official or legislator who doesn't know her or anything about nursing."

The applicants rejected this illustration because, in their opinion, "even if you know the job well, you won't get it unless a big government official recommends you." They told Korli about friends of theirs who got jobs by recommendations from superintendents, cabinet members, and legislators.

Remembering his own frustration in finding a job and the irregular manner in which employment was done in the society, Korli tried to be understanding and helpful but not at the expense of his conscience. The drafts he prepared for the Secretary's signature were noncommittal. He'd have him know the applicants "for some time" rather than "for ten years" as they preferred he should claim—or have him state that the applicants "impress" him as hardworking and ambitious rather than be "convinced" that they were diligent, resourceful, reliable, and highly disciplined. Recipients of these "evasive letters" (as the job seekers termed them) often declined to employ the applicants for reasons that were just as evasive, such as lack of openings or shortage of funds. The applicants would come to Korli, crying:

"The people are employing, but they refused to give me a job because of nepotism or disregard for the Secretary's letter."

Often some were duly employed but lost their jobs because of pride. Mistakenly assured that with their recommendations their jobs were guaranteed regardless of how they did them, they would tell bosses who questioned their poor performance, tardiness, or unbecoming attitudes on the job, "Do you know how I got this job? You may be the boss, but I have the power to dismiss you." Disappointed employers told the Secretary that they would never again honor his letters of recommendation because the people he had recommended to them were unqualified. Once an applicant whom the Secretary had recommended failed to get a well-paid job because the Hon. Johnson had told the company's manager at a luncheon that he didn't know the applicant.

"How could he say such a thing?" the desperate young man tearfully confronted Korli. "If the Secretary sees me, he'll know me because we're neighbors! Take me to him!"

Korli tried to solve the problem in an article specifying the categories of people the heads of government departments could recommend: those with transcripts from accredited training or educational institutions, individuals a Secretary knew in person, and former employees of the Department who desired jobs in different parts of the country. Secretary Johnson approved the memo, and Korli published it in the *Liberian Age*. Pleased with this bold initiative, which substantially relieved him and his deputies of job seekers' harassment, Hon. Johnson authorized him to sign his letters of recommendation by directive. Korli made many enemies because he was highly selective about people he recommended. Those he refused to recommend often appealed to his wife, to his landlord, to Marie, or to his friends to persuade him to reconsider his decision.

"Give the people their letters of recommendation," Leanya had told him. "If they don't get the jobs, it isn't your business. It costs you nothing to write and sign a letter. The government pays you to serve the people. No need making them your enemies." Mr. Seton and Marie gave him the same advice.

Korli knew that wrong action could cost him his life. He wrote another article reiterating what he had put in the first one, adding that the best recommendation was qualification for a job since employers were always on the hunt for qualified workers. This new article did not stop unwarranted requests for recommendations from job seekers. Some began putting money in their letters of request for recommendation or taking goats to Korli's house "for his soup." Thinking that she might help him determine what to do about the dilemma, Korli appealed to Marie for advice.

"You need something for your sweat," Marie had told him in a highpitched voice. "A reward you get from people you serve is not corruption. It's gratuity! What is the government paying you? If you don't like it, bring it to me." Korli did not give Marie any gratuity. He returned each bribe to its sender. Many of his co-workers called him a fool for "behaving like Jesus Christ." But his honesty increasingly gained the Secretary's confidence. It was one reason why he had appointed him research assistant, a position equivalent in rank to assistant secretary.

Korli's elevation to this enviable post was also due to his excellent performance at Central High. While in the eighth grade, he had bought ninth grade textbooks and employed the services of a private instructor. After doing exceptionally well in the ninth grade national exam and in the first semester of the tenth, the faculty committee recommended him for the eleventh grade. Upon inspecting the academic records of all cadets in his department, Secretary Johnson had given Korli the promotion. Summoning him to his luxurious office, he personally handed him the letter of appointment, much to Korli's delightful surprise, for his messenger usually delivered such routine letters.

"Thank you, sir," he said with a deep bow.

"I gave you this promotion because I appreciate your hard work and good manner," the Secretary told him, his eyes radiating with satisfaction. "Congratulations!" he declared. "The president has instructed us to employ native people with good education. To unify the country, it is important that all segments of the population participate in running the government." Rising, he shook Korli's hand heartily and sat down. "Sit down," he told him. "You're not a police officer or messenger but an official of this department, working directly with me. Don't let anyone intimidate you. I wanted to send you abroad for college, but I need your help to run this office. I have many degree holders here, but most of them are a disappointment. They're more interested in the honor and emoluments of their offices than in serving the people. What annoys me is their oversimplification of problems. Well, we can't import people from other countries to run our government, but when I see hardworking, honest, and intelligent employees, I put them in key positions to keep things on the right track. You have these qualities." Handing a fat envelope to Korli, he said, "Take this to furnish your house and buy clothes. As a member of my official family, you are expected to dress well and live a lifestyle befitting a representative of the Secretary of Treasury.

You should marry a civilized woman before your next promotion. It will come from the president himself. If you don't find a girl you like in this department, look elsewhere. Now, get ready; we are going to the

Mansion for an emergency cabinet meeting."

"Thank you, sir," Korli said. "Thank you very much." Returning to his office, Korli slumped in his black swivel chair, held his head in his hands, and planted his elbows on the desk. Speechless and deeply touched, he pondered the incredible development for which there was no rational explanation. He wouldn't attempt to understand it but only submit to its practical deduction: do his best in all circumstances and leave the results with others to judge.

The emergency cabinet meeting was distinguished more for the sumptuous five-course Western dinner and liquors the officials ate and drank rather than for its agenda: a discussion on whether to celebrate the birthday of the Chief Executive by turns in the counties, or only in the capital city as has been the tradition. The officials agreed by consensus that celebrating in all counties would give people in all parts of the country an opportunity to pay their tributes to a man who had taken them out of the darkness into the light. Further, they agreed, the government should build a local Mansion in each county capital to accommodate the president while celebrating his birthday and conducting executive conferences. Finally, it was agreed that the government earmark one million dollars for festivities during each birthday celebration, and another million for development projects in the county in which it would be celebrated. Korli was astonished that the cabinet could spend such a large sum of money on celebrations. But then again, he thought, these were the same people who had no compunctions about riding expensive cars through the capital city's foulest slums—one of which was right under the eaves of the resplendent Mansion.

Speaking for his colleagues, the Secretary of Foreign Affairs and Doyen of the Cabinet thanked the president—who arrived long after the dinner—for the rich foods and drinks they had enjoyed, and pledged their loyalty and unflinching support for his administration. He said their decision to celebrate his birthday around the country would oblige all citizens to contribute their quota to the development of the country in this age of unification. He proposed to the president a committee to organize and implement all activities connected with his birthday celebrations, which the Chief Executive approved with no debate.

On their return to Treasury, Secretary Johnson told Marie to take Korli home and have the deputy secretary for administration prepare a voucher for a Toyota Crown sedan for his office. He wanted to sign it before noon the next working day.

"My friend, learn how to drive; otherwise, your car will be for the driver," the Secretary told Korli. "If my driver can do it to me and my deputies, yours will certainly do it to you. I'm fortunate to have several cars. The official car sleeps with the driver, and when he doesn't come to work, I do my own driving."

When the Secretary went into his office, Marie hugged Korli fervently, smiling in his face. "Congratulations, Mr. Assistant Secretary!" she declared. "I wish you a happy and successful tenure of office!"

"Thank you, Madam Executive Secretary," Korli told her when they disengaged. "It came as a total surprise to me. I intend to keep it a secret."

Marie laughed. "There are no secrets in this town. People will soon be at your house to wash this promotion. I know the chief put something in your pocket. Give me my share for me to get drunk tonight."

"I haven't opened it yet," Korli said. "I want to take it to my wife before opening it. Otherwise, she might think I spent most of it partying."

"So you are afraid of your wife?" Marie asked, slinging her handbag onto her shoulder. "Make her understand that a government official doesn't belong to one woman. Anyway, let air blow the promotion a bit before celebrating. My driver will teach you how to drive. No. I myself will teach you."

When they went to the ground floor, Korli told Marie, "I could get a taxi so you can go home early, eat something, and rest. You work too hard!"

"My friend, don't turn down the honor that falls in your lap! Don't you know that you're now an important government official? You don't want gangsters to attack you in the street, do you? I've been told to take you home. That I'll do."

"When do I start learning how to drive?"

"Tomorrow after work if you like. You had better make haste and learn. Your car will be here in two weeks. Don't let it sit round too long, or somebody else will take it."

The next day, after work, when they arrived at Marie's blue concrete house located on Congo Town Beach, Korli sat unruffled in the well-furnished air-conditioned sitting room, thoroughly exhausted.

"Drinks on me, Mr. Assistant Secretary," Marie said and gave him her customary sweet smile. "If we don't celebrate a little, bad luck might come." She brought a bottle of gin with tonic, poured two glasses on ice, and proposed a toast to Korli's good health, prosperity, and happiness. They knocked glasses together and drank. Marie leaned towards him and he kissed her cheek lightly, as he had seen people do in such cases. Then she put on the television.

ELTV was reporting that another civil war had broken out in a neighboring African country. UN troops were trying to bring it under control. Marie looked disgusted.

"It's better to make love than war," she said. "Don't you agree?" Korli didn't answer.

Marie poured another drink, drained half the glass, and invited Korli to see the new bed she had bought from Jantzen a week ago.

As if he hadn't heard her, Korli only sipped his drink, cleared his throat, and listlessly crossed his legs, his eyes fixed on the TV screen. Marie repeated her invitation aloud, her voice echoing in the lofty sitting room, and posed to go into the bedroom.

"Fear nothing," she told Korli. "Today is your happy day, my friend! You don't know when you'll die, so whenever you get the opportunity, enjoy yourself. I'll let you tour the house and have dinner with me sometime next week. Tell your wife that you'll be engaged with office business because it will be a whole day affair."

Crawling out of his torpor, Korli said amiably, "I know why Africa is beset with wars."

"Why?" Marie asked, resuming her seat. She laid her arm on his shoulder and said, "Don't worry. My children are spending time with their grandma in Clay-Ashland this month, so I'm alone in this big house. The Secretary told me to take care of you because you handle sensitive documents. It would be dangerous if a girl outside our office gets hold of you. You might leak some secrets to her. Who knows what she'll do with them?"

"Why did we Africans want independence from colonial rule?" Korli asked. "Was it to kill one another? Our leaders told us that independence would bring us prosperity. Now all we're getting from it is calamity. There was peace in Africa when the colonial rulers were in charge."

"So you love politics? When you become political in this country, you get in trouble," Marie said and stood up. "Let's enjoy ourselves and go to sleep."

She opened the yellow panel door of the master bedroom, Korli following. The bedroom was well furnished with a huge redwood bed, matching side tables, and a large dresser. The curtains were imported.

"Our leaders are the cause of the mess we're in," Marie said. "Maybe all of us are the cause, I suppose. We make them little gods, especially those who spearheaded independence. Now they like to stay in office until they die. I'm surprised because many of them have PhDs in politics from

Western universities—and they make noise round the world about democracy!"

"Marie, you're interested in African politics, too," Korli said. "Our politicians are too selfish. A small group grabs power and takes over everything! Everything! The rest of the people become mere spectators— slaves! All they get from their governments is lip service!"

"We're not supposed to say such things, Korli. We are expected to praise our leaders. Flatter them as liberators! Godsends! Men of great wisdom and renown! Infallible! You can be free with me, but don't go round criticizing the government—or any African government, for that matter. You're too good to languish in jail."

"I want to build a house some day, but the confusion over land in this country is disturbing," Korli changed the topic and looked at Marie, enraptured.

"There's nothing we can do about our politics, but we can build decent homes and raise our children," Marie said. "When you buy a lot in this town, build a house on it quickly—at least a foundation. Nobody will take it from you. It's vacant lots that people sell repeatedly. This house belongs to the government. I've already built one for myself in Paynesville and put it under rent. The day the government puts me down, I'll live in it myself—or when I retire. Let me take you home. I'm sure you're itching to carry the good news to your wife. So impatient you can't spend a little moment with me!"

Yawning, and inebriated, Korli dropped on the bed and Marie lay beside him. It was after midnight when he realized that he wasn't making love to Leanya but to a different woman. Putting on her clothes, Marie helped him stand on his feet and get dressed, then she led him out to the car.

Except for Liimu, who was sleeping, the whole family waited for him with anxiety in the sitting room.

"We thought something happened to you!" Leanya told him when she opened the door and he dragged himself in. Marie had put him down at the gate and gone.

"Nothing happened," he said in a dull voice. "Let's go in." The children scrambled to their rooms as they went to theirs.

They sat at the room table. Korli carefully took the envelope out of his side pocket and handed it to Leanya.

Leanya's heart jumped when she saw the thick bundle of banknotes of high denominations. "Your pay?"

"Leanya, you're a lucky woman!" Korli said and hugged her passionately. "I got a promotion today. Don't mention it to anyone. Let them hear the rumors. The Secretary gave me this money to furnish the apartment and buy clothes. I'll now wear coat and tie to work. Government people will be visiting us, and we are supposed to dress well and entertain them."

"Let's bow our heads and pray." Leanya thanked God for his mercy and kindness. She prayed that he strengthen their faith, give them courage and stamina to work hard, and protect them from sickness and harm. Then she told Korli, "Let's use some of this money to build our house—at least to window level."

"In two weeks I'll have a car," Korli said.

Leanya gasped, danced around, and hugged him avidly.

"You'll help me buy produce!" she said excitedly.

"Of course! Some of my friends and I were celebrating today. That's why I didn't come soon. I didn't use a cent of this money. They bought the drinks. I'll put it in a Lebanese bank tomorrow, and use it as we need it. If something happens to it, we'll know who is responsible."

"I trust you, my dear. You've never been away from home after dark, and you've brought good luck your first time staying out late. Thank you very much. Let's celebrate." She smiled and began to take off her clothes.

"What about Liimu?" Korli asked her.

"She will drink bottled milk as of now. She's getting used to it."

"Building a home is a good idea, but we have to buy clothes first," Korli said as he too took off his clothes and lay beside her.

"Don't let anyone put your hand in corruption, my dear," Leanya pleaded. "God is taking care of us. He knows our needs better than we do and provides them at the right time."

Korli was already snoring. It was his first time going to sleep without touching her after she had stripped for him. Leanya grew concerned for a moment but shrugged when she saw the money on the table. She put it in her leather purse, which was already half-filled with money, and shoved it under the mattress. By cockcrow Korli awoke and grabbed her aggressively as if it were his first time having her. Happily, it was Saturday. They stayed in bed until sunrise when Leanya got up to prepare breakfast.

Korli remained in bed reflecting on yesterday's surprise events. The promotion was reassuring though it had increased his responsibilities. The salary increment and the convenience of having his own car fully compensated for the extra time and effort he'd put into the job. Leanya was right; it was time to build a house. That was the best insurance for the family. If they had their own roof, they would finally be settled in the *kwii* world. He felt sorry for Marie because he couldn't marry her despite her passionate love for him. They could be intimate friends and workmates, helpful to each other. That was enough. Fortunately, she had an income, so he wouldn't deprive his family to take care of her. She only needed his love and companionship—that, he had in abundance. He couldn't afford to leave Leanya who was so affectionate, innocent, and devoted to him. She had yielded to him when he was only a hunter. In fulfillment of her promise to be everything to him, she had healed his wounded heart and mind and stood with him in his struggles. Monrovia women, who luxuriated in wealth and pleasure at the expense of working men, appreciated you only when you had already become somebody. Now in a position to grasp any amount of money without problem, he could get any number of them, but if he did, he would have to live in fear and suspicion. He would have to secure himself with a large foreign bank account, and keep a passport, visa, and plane ticket on hand to flee the country when the government's mismanagement led to catastrophe. It would be a violent end. He was surprised that the elite who placed so much emphasis on church attendance and the Bible saw nothing wrong with corruption.

After breakfast Korli went downtown and set up an account at Tradevco Bank, bought clothes and shoes for his boys and himself, and, on returning home, gave Leanya money to buy clothes for Liimu, Borwulo, and herself. Then he paid a year's rent in advance. This time Mr. Seton's only remark was:

"If you are handling such cash, start building your house."

With Marie's help, Korli learned how to drive. He took delivery of his car at the end of the month. He wasted no time assembling a workforce and starting the construction of his house. Building materials being inexpensive those days, he took no more than six months to complete the house.

A month before moving his family to the new home, Korli told his landlord and foster father, "We'll pay your rent until you find someone else to take the apartment. If we don't go into the new house now, thieves won't let it stand. They have already stolen doors, roofing zinc, bathroom and kitchen fixtures, and many other things."

"You have a good case, Korli," Mr. Seton agreed. "That's how thieves behave in this town. They collect materials from building sites to do their own building. We'll miss you people, but you have the right to make life on your own. We are here for you. Don't hesitate to call on us whenever you have a problem. It's good you people are not going far from us. We too will be visiting you."

Shortly after they moved to their new home, Leanya told her husband that she wanted to visit her home because she had had an unpleasant dream about her mother. In the dream, Ma Gbavor was well dressed, plump, happy, and dancing with new initiates at a Sande graduation festival. Kuntaa was crowded with players from all over Deyn Gola. Food was plentiful and drinks were overflowing.

"Something has definitely gone wrong," she said with a dark frown. "Had she been sick or dead in the dream, everything would have been all right with her. Do you remember I once told you about an owl at our window? On my way to the market yesterday, I heard a dodo crying in a coconut tree."

"I'm not skilled at interpreting dreams, but your dream seems portentous," Korli said. "Go check on the family, and take as many things as you can for the people. Don't worry about what they say. If you see someone going to Haindi, give the person something for my mother and sister, and let them come to you for you to bring them here."

Leanya packed a suitcase with clothes, soaps, powders, hair lotions, blankets, T-shirts, flashlights, and other things for the journey. Korli drove her to White Plains one Saturday morning and made sure she traveled with people going upcountry.

Leanya was away for a month, during which period Korli was beside himself with anxiety, wondering what was keeping her so long. He had not expected her to be away from home more than a few days, or one week at the most. Had her mother died? Or her father? Most unlikely. Had anything so serious happened, Zolu or Dieley would have combed Monrovia to find them and give them the news. Perhaps one of his uncles-in-law Bema or NanGwoi had died. Or his mother—but certainly not his sister who was young. Korli wanted to go upcountry to find out, but it was risky to leave the children and his sensitive job and go on a journey that might keep him away for an unspecified length of time. Leanya was resourceful enough to handle any eventuality. Each day he left the children with Mrs. Seton and went to work.

Leanya finally returned one Saturday afternoon to find Korli and the children planting flowers in the yard. His mother—with a small child on her back—and two grown boys accompanied her. Korli and the children cheerfully greeted them. Liimu held Leanya by the legs while Korli took the suitcase off her head. Felenkpeh and the boys looked frail and shabby. The boys carried bags of dry meat on their shoulders. Korli was happy they did not cry on seeing him, a sign of bereavement. He hugged his wife fondly and took the frail child off his mother's back, then hugged her too. Leanya picked Liimu up, and they all went inside.

When they were seated in the sitting room, Korli gave the child back to his mother and put food on the table. Felenkpeh looked round the room as if she were misplaced.

"So, what news?" Korli asked

"Nothing unusual happened on the journey," Leanya began reporting formally. "The people only missed us because I hadn't been there for two years. They couldn't even get news about us. Your uncle-in-law Bema died a week before I got there. That, you should expect; he was very old."

"Yes, he was," Korli said. "He lived his years fully. How did you make contact with my mother? And who are these?" Korli glanced at the boys who looked familiar.

Leanya said that she had sent Felenkpeh and Moima two headties, two cakes of soap, and two tins of powder plus a message urging them to come over to Kuntaa to her. One Kekula Dakpaanah of Haindi took the gifts to Haindi but only his mother was there.

"So only she came to me," Leanya continued. "She'll tell you the rest of her story. My parents sent you their greetings. They thanked you for the things I carried for them and for taking good care of the children and me. They hope to see you as soon as possible. Korli, they are very old now. You had better make haste and go to them if you expect to see them alive."

Although he had many questions for Leanya, Korli was anxious to hear from his mother.

"What news from home, Mama?" he asked her. They sat at the table to eat, and Felenkpeh began to talk:

"I thank God for making it possible for me to see you people and my grandchildren," Felenkpeh said, trying to hold back her tears. "As you know, your brothers deserted us long ago when you were but a toddler. After the death of your father, they did well to come over and bury him. Of course, the Big Thing conducted the funeral, and, as you know, all women and children had to be indoors as it took place. Your brothers paid ten pounds and a white sheep to remove the blood you shed on the Land. Despite all the kindness your father rendered people in that town, not a single person contributed a piece of kola nut, not to speak of money, for his burial." Felenkpeh took a bite at a chicken thigh.

Judging that his tired old mother had spoken long enough, Korli asked Leanya about the two boys again.

"This is Borkpalon," Leanya pointed at the one who had a cluster of kinky hair and a sheepish face. "And this is Darnlaa," she pointed at the other one with a wrinkled neck. "Borkpalon is Zolu's oldest son, while Darnlaa is Dieley's only son. They were living with their mothers in a remote village deep in the forest when you were in Kuntaa. Although they are married and have children, they want to go to school and get jobs to send their children to school. Your determination to go to school at your age has inspired many boys in Kuntaa to do the same. Some of them are right here in Monrovia trying to work their way through school as you are doing."

Late in the evening, Korli met with his mother in the girls' bedroom to talk in private. She told him that after Nuulaa's burial and his departure after his confinement at the Shrine, his brothers had taken her with them to Bhorlia to wipe the tears from her eyes, but their wives did not like her because his brothers had poisoned their minds with the false belief that she was responsible for Nuulaa's death.

"That father of yours," she confessed with tears in her eyes, "wanted to sacrifice you to the river goddess to become a chief. He had to sacrifice his most beloved son. Naturally, it had to be you, our heartstring. Your courage, hard work, and good looks endeared you not only to us but also to everybody in Fuama. A poor mother, what could I have done but yield to his demand? After his death and your disappearance—I believed that they had killed you—I decided never to marry again. However, some women advised me to get a husband because I still had a child or two in my stomach. Otherwise, they said, I might develop a fatal stomach complaint. A widower fell in love with me in Borlia and we had this child. He died of wounds he incurred from fighting a leopard in the forest. As for the rest of the family—a Digei man married your sister, and they moved to Saamai in pursuit of fallow farmland. They've had three children and she is pregnant again. When Keleng died, I decided to move to Haindi. Friends and neighbors took care of me. After losing two husbands by accident, I made up my mind never to marry again. This little girl is determined to live. Put her in school when she grows up. I'll be with you until you put my bones away." Felenkpeh suddenly had a fit of stifled sobs, and tears coursed down her cheeks.

"Weep no more, Mother," Korli told her. "All your troubles are over. I'll take good care of you. God has put our enemies to shame. I now work for the government. I'll take you people to hospital and get you clothes." Korli called Leanya to be with his mother.

He lodged her and his two nephews-in-law in the apartment since they still paid rent for it. The Setons received them gladly and said they were a seal to the ties God had established between them and the Korli family.

17

"DISSIDENT"

KORLI RESOLVED THAT this would be his last time attending a meeting of New Day Party if it accomplished nothing besides holding lively conversations and festivities. The fellowship and hospitalities were quite in place, especially the services of caretakers, but the long expensive trip and the time invested in the meeting deserved better results. Making Sanniquellie the party's headquarters was reasonable enough although it was 200 miles upcountry away from Monrovia, and half the road was unpaved, dusty, and bumpy. The town gave birth to the OAU. Perhaps the ideals that inspired the founding of this all-important organization would motivate founders of New Day Party to unite the underprivileged in their struggle for freedom, justice, and development, and imbue them with hope.

Heeding Mr. Seton's repeated warnings against engaging in Liberian politics because "it is fraught with suspicions, intrigues, and violence", Korli had avoided politics altogether. "A dissenting opinion, however well-meant lands you in prison as an enemy of the state," Mr. Seton had told him. "People who value their lives and live for a purpose don't bother with our brand of politics." Consequently, politics never featured in Korli's conversations except in discussing the political theories of ancient philosophers, which had no relation to practical experience.

But the president and his cabinet, the legislature, and other stalwarts of the ruling party frequently proclaimed Liberia "a bastion of freedom and justice." The proclamation had aroused Korli's interest in politics though not substantially because he saw no evidence to support it.

"Under our law," they often declared, "300 citizens can organize and operate their own party. We're only concerned about the nation's stability and its conformity with Western values." To test the sincerity of this claim, Korli had gone to Bassa Community in Monrovia to vote for the first time during the last presidential election although some of his classmates had told him that the results had already been decided in favor of the Old Man. So, he wasn't surprised when he discovered that all the ballots were marked for the standard bearer of the ruling party. A soldier in khaki uniform, a sub-machine gun lying under the bench on which he sat, handed him a ballot and told him to cast it in a large wooden box. Korli debated with himself whether to cast the ballot or hand it back to the soldier and go home.

"Make haste and vote to eat some of the rich dinner," the soldier told him, smacking his lips. "If you waste time, the people will eat everything."

Scores of people were eating rice and palm butter in the palaver house, while several women were busy filling other voters' plates with rice and stew from large pots. Bassa, Gio, Loma, Vai, and Gola cultural troupes danced around the precinct. The main attraction was a stilt dancer and a snake Zoe who was throwing a malleable six-year-old girl—"the snake baby"—up in the air, grasping her, and swinging her around by the legs. They and their musicians were exquisitely dressed in striking cowrie uniforms.

After a while the soldier spoke up again. "If you're not voting, give me the ballot and sit on that bench," he told Korli, who seemed to have forgotten about voting.

"But I want to vote for a different candidate!" Korli said. "I'm supposed to cast my ballot in secret."

"My friend, where do you come from? America or England?" the soldier said harshly. "We don't have a different candidate! If you're a member of the opposition, let me know so that I may put you where you belong." The soldier looked at Korli with venomous red eyes.

"If there's no other candidate, what's the use of voting?" Korli said bravely.

"We want to know how many registered voters support the Old Man," said the soldier, trying to control his temper. "Over 90% of the voters have already cast their ballots for him. If you don't vote for him, it means you belong to the opposition. Do you support him or not?" The soldier was fetching his weapon.

Not wishing to risk a jail term, Korli recoiled into his shell and said, "I support him! Who wouldn't support the father of the nation?" He dropped his ballot into the box and walked away.

"Don't you want to eat?" the soldier called to him, but he did not look back or reply.

Korli remembered Mr. Seton telling him about a group of citizens numbering in the thousands forming an opposition party ten years ago—how their "ring leaders" were arrested, charged with treason, and incarcerated, never to be heard of again. Since then no individual or organization had ever challenged the ruling party, which had been in power more than a hundred years. Liberia had become essentially a oneparty state. Subjugated Africans struggling for independence often regarded the miscarriage of democracy in the first African republic an embarrassment. It made their quest for self-rule questionable. "You're better off under colonial rule," their colonial masters often told them. "Look at Liberia—how corruption has stifled its growth and development. The ruling class virtually enslaves the people. That country is headed for catastrophe. Is that what you people want?" Hearing this opinion expressed at many international conferences, the president had instituted measures to remove "the garbage" from the nation's political landscape. Those measures focused on integration of all segments of the population, and inclusion of everyone—especially the natives—in running the affairs of the state. To this end, the legislature had passed a bill he had introduced creating four counties out of the three provinces, which were governed by traditional laws, to maintain a uniformed administrative structure in the country. He appointed an indigenous superintendent for each and adjured them to improve the quality of life for their people. "Henceforth, the fate of your people is in your hands," the president had emphasized at their induction. "You'll have nobody else to blame but yourselves if they continue suffering. Organize your people into groups in each political subdivision and as a single group to discuss your common problems and find solutions. The government will be in a better position to help you if you know what you want and try to do something about it. This country belongs to all its citizens without discrimination. Therefore, we will not let one citizen take advantage of another, and the nation's resources will be shared among all its people equally."

Korli's impression of the president changed after that speech. He wasn't the implacable, disgruntled, dictatorial old man his detractors portrayed. He was friendly, kind, understanding, and committed to the people's welfare. His remarks were good, encouraging, and promising. Korli waited to see if they would be supported with action. Judging from the laudatory press reports that followed the executive conferences the president conducted round the country, Korli thought that he was backing his words with concrete deeds. Many government officials had lost their jobs for robbing and cheating the country people, neglecting their duties, stealing government money, undermining one another, and taking false reports to the president. Since these meetings usually followed his birthday celebrations, Korli decided to attend those scheduled for Gbarnga, Bong County, to see for himself.

What impressed him about the occasion was not the convergence of nearly the whole country on the impoverished town, or the surfeit of foods and drinks, or the diverse cultural dances, or the resplendent mansion the county had constructed for the convenience of the president, but the redress of grievances during the conference.

Dressed in a flashy homespun gown and cap like a Kpelle chief, black cow tail in hand, the Chief Executive had opened the conference in the large administration building by stating that his government was committed to justice for all, irrespective of status. He was especially concerned about the poor, voiceless masses who were innocent victims of naked aggression and exploitation by those in power. Anyone with a grievance against anyone—even if it's against a government official—should bring it to his attention for redress, he told them.

"Don't be afraid," he declared. "I'm your president. Long before assuming this office, I was 'the poor man's lawyer.' Give me the name of your offender, whoever that person may be. Speak your native language if you can't speak English. Don't be ashamed of speaking your mother tongue. It is as precious and important as English. We have plenty of interpreters here." The speech built up the confidence of those who couldn't speak English, for hitherto they were considered heathens and barbarians. Their smiling faces and impatience to speak showed that they were happy to count for something.

Many government officials, especially superintendents, district commissioners, and the Secretaries of Internal Affairs and of Treasury, looked uneasy in their seats when the president made the pronouncement. Their faces flitted from side to side under the penetrating gaze of the crowd, many of whom were victims of their exploitation.

Korli was so impressed and so proud of the president that his heart leapt for joy. He was relaxed and happy. He wanted to hug the president and thank him for championing the cause of the common people. Indeed, he was the kind of leader Liberia needed—someone who had feelings for the poor and helpless—someone who stood for justice, honesty, equality, and development. "Chiefs, come forward," Korli cried in his heart "and tell the president that his soldiers threaten, beat, and kill your people and loot their properties! Tell him to build schools and clinics and motor roads in your chiefdoms! Tell him to put your names on the government's payroll so that you may stop depriving the poor people of their foodstuffs for your pay. Tell him to abolish the hut tax because the people play no part in the monetary economy of the country, and the taxes they pay bring them no development! Tell him to let your people elect their superintendents and district commissioners so that they may feel obligated to them. Talk! Talk! Talk for your people! You are their voices! You are their only hope!"

Knowing that the chiefs were the principal exploiters of the people—guilty of taking their food and forcing them to labor on their farms—Korli's enthusiasm sagged a bit as everybody waited to see who would break the tension. Obviously, the people had many complaints but were afraid to report the transgressions of authorities who would retaliate against them after the president left. With all the assurances the president had given them, his royal demeanor, which frightened even the most expert speaker in his presence, did not invite a free airing of grievances.

At length the Paramount Chief of Zorkwelle Chiefdom in Bong County, a huge man dressed in a yellow and white striped homespun gown, rose to speak. A pall of silence descended on the great hall, for the chief enjoyed the love and honor of his people. He waited for a signal from the president before speaking.

"Speak," the president told him. "We are under your authority because we are in your territory." Low laughter followed the remark.

"Thank you, Mr. President," the elderly spoke through an interpreter. "On behalf of my people and myself, I thank you for honoring Bong County by celebrating your natal day here. You are the first leader traveling to all parts of the country to meet your people. Most of the others considered us heathens and nobodies. They had nothing to do with us but collect our foodstuffs and forcibly recruit us as laborers. Mr. President, God will reward you for your kindness. As a token of our thanks and appreciation for conferring this honor upon us, Zorkwelle Chiefdom hereby gives you ten cows and seven virgins in honor of your 70th birthday. We pray that you live as long as a rock and lead us from poverty to prosperity. The cows are grazing in the field. Here come the virgins! They are new Sande initiates!"

There was a rousing applause as the girls, bent double, walked into the hall and started dancing to the tune of a royal band. To everybody's surprise and delight, the president joined the dance. Gradually, all the people got up and joined it too. After a while, the president returned to the dais, stood at the lectern, and said he accepted the hospitality with gratitude but would pay for the cows. He told his butler Johnny Walker— so nicknamed for his love of whisky—to pay the chief a hundred dollars for each one. Then he announced that he would send the seven girls to school.

"The days are gone when human beings were property you could sell or give away as gifts," he declared. "You said you wanted me to live as long as a rock, but you have endangered this wish by giving me seven virgins!" Everybody laughed heartily. "What a seventy-year-old man needs is enough to eat while waiting for his time. I'll take the cows and educate the girls for them to help build the nation. They can do much more than simply bear and raise children." A resounding round of applause and cheers followed.

Korli's heart pounded with joy. Here was a leader who was more concerned about the welfare of his people than his own. Truly, he was a father of the nation. "If we had had ten such presidents," he said under his breath, "this country would have been the most blessed place on earth."

A man wearing a homespun shirt extending to his knees came forward, held onto a rope that was tied to the ceiling to keep steady, and stamped his foot on the concrete floor. "Thank you, Mr. President," he said. "My name is Flomo Kolleh. We learned that you gave the superintendent money to pay all the expenses for these celebrations, but he imposed a birthday tax of ten dollars on each house in this county for the same celebrations. I was hard pressed for money and couldn't find someone to lend me any. The superintendent took by force the only goat I had. I had been raising and selling its offspring to pay my children's school fees."

The president flashed his gold-rimmed spectacles at the superintendent for an explanation. Standing up with trepidation, perspiring profusely, the superintendent said brokenly:

"Your Excellency, although the birthday committee gave us money for the celebrations, out of love, respect, and appreciation for your kindness to us, we the citizens of Bong County decided to make a contribution. At a meeting with all paramount and clan chiefs of the county, we agreed to raise additional cash to renovate two clinics and two schools in and around Gbarnga."

"Mr. Superintendent, we must dismiss you for administrative

reasons," the president said in anger. "Only the Department of Treasury is authorized to tax people in this country. So, you exceeded the mandate of your office. You should have made your plans to fit the funds you were given. We repeat: Only the Department of Treasury is authorized to tax people in this country! Henceforth, any other official of government who assumes this responsibility will be dismissed. The Auditor-General of Liberia is hereby directed to investigate you and submit a report to our office ten working days from today. As of now the assistant superintendent for development will act as superintendent until we appoint your replacement. Johnny Walker, give Mr. Flomo Kolleh two hundred dollars to pay for his goat and his children's school fees. Next!"

Another man dressed in old clothes, which elicited hushed comments from the crowd, came forward shamelessly and said that his father had just died and he had no money to bury him. May the president please help him with money to see about his father's funeral. Johnny Walker was again summoned and ordered to give the man two hundred dollars to bury his father and buy clothes.

A paramount chief from Nimba County, whose domain bordered Bong County, complained that the people of Bong County were using up his people's farmland. The president should please stop them.

"Any land unencumbered," the president explained, "is government land, which any citizen may use for farming. We are one people. Therefore, the people of Bong County are also your people. They have the right to make farms in Nimba County in the same way the people of Nimba County have the right to make farms in Bong County. Next!"

An old woman came forward and said that her husband beat her day and night. He didn't support her, yet when she got a few dollars from doing odd jobs, he used the money to drink and support girlfriends all over Gbarnga. Whenever she makes a protest, he beats her. May the president please protect her from the man.

"Mother," the president said, "whenever your husband beats you again or even threatens to beat you, let the Acting Superintendent know. He will put him where he belongs. Meanwhile, your husband is fined twenty dollars. Mr. Acting Superintendent, see that he pays this money to her before nightfall. Johnny Walker, give her a hundred and fifty dollars to take care of some of her responsibilities. Next!"

Another old woman came forward and said that her eldest brother had taken over their late father's properties: a flock of ten goats and seven kola trees. He refused to share any of them with her because she was a woman. Now that he was old and paralyzed, he would leave the properties with his eldest son. She and her children won't have any share in them.

May the president help her please.

The president said he'd go right away to settle the matter in the woman's village since her brother could not come to Gbarnga. It was the most amazing event ever to happen in the interior. Normally the average government officials rode hammocks carried on men's heads when they patrolled the country, but the president walked to the village in the company of his officials and crowds of people. An old man who wasn't used to walking, he took several breaks on the rutted path to rest. During one of the breaks, he sat on a rock to rest. The press made an issue of the gesture. The next edition of the *Liberian Age* featured the president sitting on the rock! After that trip the Department of Public Works constructed a motor road to the village.

In the village palaver house, the president decided that the woman should get three kola trees and five goats as her share of her father's inheritance. He instructed Johnny Walker to give her two hundred dollars to take care of herself.

After witnessing these and other incredible doings of the president, Korli had no more fear of politics. He believed that the politicking that earned government's reprisal was that which turned the people against the government. Liberia had a leader who cared for the people and wanted to know the truth. Because he had seen it for himself, he agreed to join New Day Party upon the invitation of the native superintendents who organized it to administer justice and carry on development in their domains. They invited many other educated natives to join the party. Mr. Seton saw no problem with the New Day Party as long as it was mainly concerned with development.

At the Party's first meeting in Sanniquellie in an impressive mansion Nimba County had built for the president, the Acting Superintendent of Bong County, Ezekiel Paye, who served as Acting Chairman, opened the meeting with the following remarks:

"Gentlemen, this is our opportunity to take care of our people and ourselves. Since the founding of this nation, we the natives have been excluded from its economic, social, and political activities although we constitute a majority of the population. Now we have a president who is determined to give us our legitimate rights as citizens. The purpose of the New Day Party is not political but to help our people improve their quality of life. With all the resources available to us, we should fight the plagues of illiteracy, disease, and poverty so that our people may live a happy and fulfilled life and participate more meaningfully in running the affairs of this nation. They need enough food, good health, sound education, and all-weather roads. Power belongs to them, but they can't use it if they are not well equipped."

The Superintendents of Lofa, Nimba, and Grand Gedeh Counties spoke lengthily along the same line. They talked of organizing development brigades to build roads, schools, and clinics. They decided to conduct fund-raising rallies and appeal to humanitarian agencies to come to their aid. The acting chairman then invited Korli to speak on behalf of other members of the party.

Korli thanked the superintendents for inviting him and other nonofficials to join the New Day Party. He said the party's name symbolized the need to put aside all mistakes of the past and embark on the mission of developing the homeland. The success of leaders depended on the support they got from their people. Therefore, they were prepared to spare no effort to work with the superintendents to achieve the noble objectives they had set for the party.

"How can you have democracy when the people are hungry, poor, sick, and illiterate?" he asked. "Anyone with food and cash can buy their votes and loyalty. Any dictator can misuse their trust. They won't have time for people who champion their cause. Members of the party should therefore take concrete steps to enable the people to produce their basic needs such as food, shelter, and clothing. Let's identify projects in each county and, with the cooperation of all party members, tackle them until they are fully implemented. We should start with the ones whose implementation naturally leads to the implementation of others. For example, if we build enough roads and provide electricity throughout the counties, business will boom, especially public transportation; people will build private schools and clinics in our towns and villages as it is done in Monrovia. One good university in Bong County can accommodate students not only from Bong but also from Nimba, Grand Gedeh, and Lofa Counties. At our next meeting, let's make a master plan. Most donors give money to people only if they know exactly what they will do with it. We should also draw up a position statement spelling out the goals of this party to avoid the likelihood of some enemy misrepresenting us to the president. Our aim is development, not political power, as Acting Superintendent Paye has said."

A week after that meeting, Acting Superintendent Paye disappeared mysteriously during a hunting expedition in Gbansu Sulonma forest, and search parties failed to find him. When the president was informed about it, he mandated the National Bureau of Investigation (NBI) to leave no stone unturned until he was found. In a preliminary report, the NBI claimed to have combed all the forests of northern Bong County without finding him. He might have wandered into Guinea, or a lion or leopard might have eaten him up, they concluded. The president instructed the Secretary of Foreign Affairs to collaborate with the government of Guinea to find Hon. Paye, but he was never found.

Six months after the disappearance, the president appointed a new superintendent for the county, an Americo-Liberian who claimed to be a bona fide Kpelle and citizen of Bong County. The press said the contribution he had made to the county, which qualified him as its superintendent, was fathering more than a hundred children and owning thousands of acres of farmland. A man of light skin color, he did nothing for the mothers of these children and disowned those whose complexion had no resemblance to his. There was a little protest in Gbarnga when the Secretary of Internal Affairs inducted him into office. The people wanted another indigenous superintendent. The police broke the shuddering wings of the protesters in a hurry. Some members of the New Day Party wondered whether it was safe to maintain the party. A majority of the members warned against connecting Mr. Paye's fate to his membership in the party. The tragedy and the appointment of a descendant of settlers as the new superintendent of Bong County made it urgent for them to write a position statement for the public to know where they stood in the scheme of things. After a week of hard work in Sanniquellie, they came up with the following statement:

We the officers and members of the New Day Party do constitute and declare ourselves by these presents a bona fide party named New Day Party under the constitution and laws of Liberia with the following aims and objectives:

1. We believe that integrating the people of the republic is the beginning of its development and progress. As long as 95% of them are not playing any significant role in the social, economic, and political life of the nation, its peace and security will continue being in jeopardy;

2. Integration should begin with removing divisive elements in the instruments that govern and symbolize the aspirations of the nation. For example, our declaration of independence erroneously

states that only those who immigrated to these shores from the United States are Liberians. It condemns West Africans as barbarians. Our constitution declares that only the purchase of land from repatriates is legitimate although the declaration of independence calls the indigenous people "Lords of the Soil." Our national anthem regards Africans as "a race benighted." Our national motto states, "The love of liberty brought us here," excluding those who were here before the founding of the nation. No wonder the indigenous people are not only regarded as second-class citizens, but are systematically victimized and discriminated against in their own country. We think the national motto should simply state, "Love, Liberty, Justice"—principles with which every citizen can identify. The legislature should muster the courage to remove these stumbling blocks to national unity, which trouble makers can use as a pretext to destabilize the nation;

3. We recommend that all parts of the country be connected with road, radio, and television networks to hasten the integration of the people. As long as we are out of touch with each other, our relationship will always be marked by fear, suspicion, and hatred, which will invariably lead to the collapse and disintegration of the nation. We believe that the failure of the ruling class to develop the country derives from the fear that the natives will remove them from power once their eyes are opened. This fear is baseless because, once the democratic process functions, the likelihood of a military takeover of the government will be remote;

4. As many African countries have done, we should adopt an indigenous language as our national language. It is unfair to measure the intelligence of Liberians by their ability to read, write, and speak English fluently. The people will think and communicate better with a language that originates with them. An indigenous national language will not only help us to become better communicators, it will relate us to one another more easily and give us a unique identity. It should therefore be taught in all our schools. English should still be our official language for business and international cooperation;

5. The government should make a yearly master plan for national development and program its appropriate agencies to implement it fully. Each year's plan should indicate what the people should do

for themselves as well as what the government should do for them;

6. There should be strict accountability for the expenditure of public funds, which are often stolen and misappropriated by those who handle them or spent mostly on administration. The government seems to benefit only those who govern rather than those they govern. This injustice is a potential source of social upheaval. People found guilty of stealing or misappropriating government funds should not only repay such funds, they should serve prison terms as a deterrent to such corruption;

7. All superintendents, district commissioners, and chiefs should be elected for a period of two years so that they may feel obligated and accountable to the people;

8. The presidential term of office should be limited to four years. If the incumbent president performs to the expectations of the people, he or she may be reelected for one additional term of office. Prolonging the presidential term of office beyond four years is an invitation to tyranny;

9. Government should strictly enforce retirement and pension plans for all employees in the country including civil servants so that at the end of their most productive years they may retire with resources to carry them through the rest of their lives with honor; and

10. The provision in our constitution barring white people from becoming citizens of Liberia should be abolished, for we need expertise and capital from all parts of the world to hasten national development. Further, if segregation is bad for black people, it is equally bad for white people—or for all peoples, for that matter.

Done at the City of Sanniquellie this First Day of January
in the Year of our Lord, 1967
Signed: The Superintendents of Bong, Nimba, Lofa,
and Grand Gedeh Counties.
Attested: Sumowor V. Gbamokorli

After they had prepared the position statement, presenting it to the president became a major problem. The Superintendent of Lofa County felt that the two-page document was skeletal and therefore vulnerable to misinterpretation. Enemies could read anything they liked into it and put them in trouble. He wanted it expanded for clarification and sent to the president with a cover letter.

"No," cried the Superintendent of Nimba County. "Official statements are usually brief and to the point. We shouldn't waste time on details; we can always go on radio and television to clarify it. The president already knows our problems. Let's give him the statement as it is. He'll understand."

"No matter how well we write this statement," maintained the Superintendent of Grand Gedeh County, "somebody else will summarize it for the president and likely distort the meaning. So we should include our points in a statement of loyalty and support for him. It is the only way to avoid the danger of someone taking our recommendations out of context."

"Look, to act is to be in danger," said the Superintendent of Bong County. "Therefore, we shouldn't be afraid to take responsibility for our statement. To preempt misinterpretation, let's publish it in a press release, go on radio and television as a group, and explain it to the world as my colleague from Nimba County suggests."

"The press release approach seems most reasonable to me," said Korli. "If we believe in what we have written, we should let it stand on its own feet. Delivering it to the president privately will make it seem suspicious or an agenda for a cabinet meeting. Everybody will believe any conclusion the cabinet might draw from it even if it is mistaken. When the press release is published, we should take a copy to the president for his attention. That, to me, is the safest solution to the problem."

"I recommend that we now put the matter into vote," suggested the acting chairman. "Before then, let's elect our chairman and a general secretary."

The Superintendent of Nimba County was elected chairman, while Korli was elected secretary general, and the press release approach was unanimously endorsed. As the secretary general, Korli was authorized to write the press release.

Trusting the Liberian News Agency, Korli sent them the final statement. But to the party's embarrassment and consternation, an article appeared in *The Standard* under the headline, "New Opposition Party Formed!" The paper quoted Korli extensively, crediting him with crafting what it termed "the party platform."

"The New Day Party condemns all instruments that govern the nation and symbolize its aspirations," stated the article. "These include the declaration of independence, the constitution, the national motto, and the national anthem. New Day Party also condemns the domination of the political, social, and economic life of the nation by descendants of the pioneers. It advocates a takeover of the machinery of government by the native people, which constitutes 95% of the population. It also advocates making white people citizens of the country. The organizers of the new party are the superintendents of Bong, Lofa, Nimba, and Grand Gedeh Counties. The brain behind this new political movement is one Sumowor Vakpeeh Gbamokorli of Bong County who wrote its platform."

That evening Korli went on national radio and television and clarified that New Day Party was a developmental organization, not a political party. He explained that the superintendents of the new counties had organized it in keeping with a mandate of the president to undertake development projects in their counties in collaboration with the government. The statement, he said, was meant to identify obstacles to the unity and speedy development of the nation, which only the government could remove. He apologized to the public for the misleading, inaccurate, and unprofessional manner in which *The Standard* had paraphrased the document. He appealed to his fellow citizens for their kind understanding and cooperation as no part of a nation could be developed in isolation.

They came for him round midnight. Leanya was usually not alarmed by late night knocks on the door because hosting visitors at odd hours of the night had become routine in their home since Korli's last promotion. A key figure at the Department of Treasury, he followed up vouchers for numerous public agencies whose business managers called on him at all times and places. But this late night call was suspect because it came shortly after the government radio and TV stations had released press reports about the New Day Party, crediting her husband with being the brain behind it. Heading a group of four secret agents dressed in black overalls, the notoriously brutal director of the NBI himself, known as The Rooster, effected his arrest. The Rooster had spies posted at the most unlikely places including private homes and outlying farms and villages. Leanya wanted to shout for help or run over to the Setons and inform them of developments, but the arresting officers were not brutal, and Korli looked calm and collected. She had no cause for alarm. Korli's clarification of the issue would suffice.

"Go to bed. Nothing will happen to your husband," The Rooster assured her. "We came to get our friend for a little chat. He'll soon come back."

"Leanya, don't worry," Korli assured her. "Had I broken some law, they would have handcuffed me. Once I give them the information they want, everything will calm down. The reporters misunderstood everything we put in that statement."

When they left, Leanya went into the room and prayed on her knees for Korli's safety.

The Rooster's plush office was well lighted. He was a garrulous man who always wore a brilliant smile, and often assumed a pugnacious character whenever he confronted a suspect. But he had no grounds for grievance against Korli because the Old Man had not yet ordered him arrested. He was only doing his homework in case the Old Man asked him about this new development.

"Is it true that you native people are forming an opposition party?" he asked Korli, who sat stiff across the large desk. "I don't want to believe it. The president put a pioneer descendant among you people, the Superintendent of Bong County. We learned that you people opposed him, eh?"

"No, sir," Korli said calmly. "I'm surprised how *The Standard* phrased our statement. They wanted to put us in trouble. I clarified everything on radio and television. Maybe they did it like that because of the name we gave the organization. In a sense, it is a party but with a new direction. We want Liberian politics to be concerned mainly with development."

"In your clarification you stated that the president authorized the formation of your party—or your organization, to be exact."

"He told us to organize ourselves and see after the development of our counties. We chose the name New Day Party to show the world that under his administration, a new day has dawned in Liberia. Before this administration, who ever heard of a president walking to a village on foot? In fact, the government officials of this country lived only in Monrovia and sent their soldiers upcountry to collect money, foodstuffs, slaves, and the like—"

"You seem to be going out of bounds, Mr. Secretary General. There is no slavery in this country—and no political prisoners. Don't put us in trouble with Amnesty International. May I get an original copy of your statement?"

"By all means!"

Korli pulled out the bulky document out of his pocket and handed it to The Rooster. He skimmed it at length and laid it aside.

"If you people had no political intention, why did you give your organization a political name?"

"That's the only way it will get the people's attention, sir. I'm sorry the press published only comments about it. They should have published the document in its entirety for the people to read it and draw their own conclusions. Nobody in that party intends to take over the government. We believe in the democratic process. However, I'll tell the superintendents that we should change our name since it seems confusing."

"Well, for your information, they have all been dismissed and imprisoned."

"Upon whose orders?"

"Who runs this country? My man, you're sleeping. You've been spared because you're innocent. The politicians wanted to make use of your brilliance. That's the conclusion we drew from our discussion of the case at a security meeting. Because you are brilliant—my man, you flew through the grades and entered college—the president thinks you have a good future if you exercise prudence. Don't let the political war horses mislead you or use you to accomplish their wicked aims. What's wrong with the country man? He misuses every opportunity he gets. I'll let you go, but remember my words: always be careful."

"Can I meet with the president and explain our position to him and give him a copy of the document?"

"The president already knows all he needs to know about the problem. If he wants more clarification from you, he will send for you. Take your hands out of this party business. You are still a child with the milk smelling in your mouth. Go to your job. The president is impressed by your honesty and diligence. Something is in the making for you, but I don't want to be talkative."

"Thank you, Mr. Director. I'm really sorry everything ended this way. I wanted to play a part in that development effort. Our people mire in poverty, disease, and ignorance— I can be frank with you because you're one of the few people in this country I know with a good mind. Director, the writing is already on the wall. When a nation turns against itself, the result is very unpleasant! I'm not a prophet," Korli said, "but anyone with common sense can see that we're tottering on the brink of a precipice! We are sitting on a time bomb! The only way to avoid disaster is to develop the country."

"My brother," said the Rooster, "I don't know book! It seems to me that you read widely. A foreign power is paying people to spoil this country. Think twice before aligning yourself with any political group besides the one running the country. We all want development but not at the expense of the peace and stability of the country."

The Rooster tapped the glossy redwood desk nervously with his fingertips, and stared at the Old Man's gold-framed color picture hanging on the western wall. Elegantly dressed in a top hat, spectacles, a black tie, and a cutaway with decorations and medals in rows across his breast, the Chief Executive looked at once fierce and poised with self-assurance, a trait his admirers regarded as "diplomatic complexion." After gazing at the picture for some moments, The Rooster bowed his head in reverence and trifled with piles of documents on the desk, pretending to read.

Korli viewed the father of the nation with fleeting interest and said to The Rooster, "Chief, we can't afford to continue sweeping our mounting problems under the rug! We must do something about them or we'll perish!"

The Rooster cleared his throat, rolled his eyes, rose and leaned his weight on the desk with his knuckles. He cast a challenging gaze at Korli. "Don't worry about anything, my son," he said. "Nothing will happen to this country with the Old Man in charge." Sitting down, he interlaced his fingers on the back of his head and said, "The Old Man is the only rooster who crows in this country, you know."

Korli said calmly, "The patriot is the person who spots trouble in time and tells their leader. People consider such a person an enemy of the state. They trust liars rather than tellers of truths."

For a while The Rooster walked round the desk with his hands in his pockets, then said, "My friend, our people are not educated. They are easy to fool. We don't want any trouble here! When trouble comes, investors will go home! Then where will we be?"

"Don't worry, Director," Korli answered with a disarming smile. "What we usually fear doesn't happen. Goodnight. I'll remember what you have told me."

"There are people who want to set this country on fire, my friend! We are prepared for them! You have enjoyed the full benefit of my advice. If you refuse to heed it, don't blame me if something happens to you." He turned towards the door. "Sergeant!" A tall man in black overalls appeared instantly. "Take this gentleman home."

All will go well, Korli thought as he walked out with the security. The Rooster is wicked enough to kill me for speaking my mind, but I'm happy I won't die a slave to my conscience—a betrayer of my convictions. Had I been blind and ignorant with no conscience—not knowing that things could be better—I'd be perfectly content. Why should the first African republic—which should be a shining example to the newly independent states—be deplorably poor and desolate?"

Downstairs, Korli was surprised to see Marie waiting. She led him to her car. It was almost daybreak.

"I heard about your trouble," she said as they drove to Sinkor. "Someone called me from the mansion and said that they had jailed you! Let's stop by my place. I want to talk with you."

"I want to see the president and clarify our position," Korli said.

"You have already done that on radio and television with no good result. If I were you, I'd drop the whole issue. Just keep going to school and studying whatever it is you're studying in college."

"I'm studying literature and minoring in management. I want to be a writer some day."

"What will literature do for you or your country? Your people are dying of disease, poverty, and injustice—and here you are majoring in literature instead of medicine, business, or law! Do you know that most writers in this country end up in jail? I'm afraid for you, Korli."

"Literature helps me understand myself and others. We need not be poor and helpless, Marie, for we have the ability and the resources to do for ourselves what people in the most advanced countries have done for themselves. But we have no development plan or commitment to the national interest."

"Literature makes you confused, foolhardy, and unhappy. The aim of education is to be happy and adjusted to the world—and make a comfortable living."

Korli wasn't inclined to argue with Marie because convincing others about the importance of his chosen profession was a problem. Everybody else but he seemed to know exactly what he ought to do with his life, and they considered the accumulation of material things life's principal goal.

"Marie, I have some ideas about how best this country can be developed. I'll put them in a book. The only way you can heal a sickness is to know exactly what it is."

"Our press is not free, Korli. Many of our writers end up in jail for telling the truth! Major in business instead. Think about your children."

"Half the problems derive from our writers," Korli said. "They need more training. See how they distorted the meaning of our statement!

They're more interested in the symptoms of problems and creating crisis." Arriving at the house, they went in and Marie put drinks on the table. "I know you are coming out of hell," she said, smiling. "Very few people escape the claws of The Rooster unscathed. Let's drink to your escape." Marie poured two drinks and they raised their glasses.

"Marie," Korli said, "the white man has made phenomenal progress in the world because he keeps records of everything he does and everything that happens to him. He examines these records from time to time to tackle his problems. But *we* think people in authority or who have gray heads know everything. That's why we see ourselves in a dungeon." Marie made no rejoinder to that. Continuing, Korli said, "The true story of Liberia is yet to be written. The wisdom of our ancestors can help us build a prosperous nation, but we overlook it. In traditional society, everybody goes to work, but in our modern society, we ignore the virtue of honest labor." Korli took another drink.

Marie suspected that he had deserted her and was addressing an imaginary audience, making full use of his accumulated knowledge. She felt sorry for him. He belonged in Britain or America where he'd have a responsive friendly audience for his high ideals, which had no place in Liberian society. The people here were concerned about making a comfortable living, now! The politicians got everything they wanted with no sweat. Those who broke their backs with hard work got little or nothing. She felt sorry for herself too because she was inclined to believe Korli, and he might be sharing his "seditious" thoughts with his instructors and fellow students on the university campus, which was under surveillance for subversion. She had lost a good man, someone she could gain something from besides the pleasures of the flesh. Well, with time he'd learn to be practical.

"I know your wife is dying to see you," Marie told him.

"We should be going," Korli said, rising.

"Korli, I suggest you join a church—preferably the president's church—and the Masons or UBF," Marie told him. "Let the people know that you're on their side. Let them see you at all official functions."

"I feel dismayed to see people dying of preventable diseases—especially our children—and going to bed hungry while our leaders are concerned with only their own interests," Korli said. "I'm still a Christian, Marie, though my work doesn't permit me to be active in the church. Attending church and social programs are a full-time occupation in this country. Independence Day celebrations, for instance, take no less than two weeks and the government spends a minimum of two million dollars on them. Then the birthday! Imagine how many miles of roads and bridges four million dollars could build."

"Those are good ideas, Korli, but the only way you can help solve the country's problems is by being involved with the people," Marie said. "If this were Europe or America, you could put your ideas in a book.

Someone would read it and probably put them into practice. But here, politicians consider critics their natural enemies. Korli, you need the church and a society for fellowship."

"Our churches are more interested in preaching and praying and preparing people for heaven than helping to solve our problems here on earth. The Bible says faith without work is dead. Our people must respect the virtue of honest labor. The missionaries tell us not to worry about development, but their countries are well developed. Marie, poverty is humiliating and embarrassing. It stifles growth and makes people miserable."

"Korli, you're crazy. Stop talking so much and go get some sleep."

"What bothers me is that Christians are responsible for the corruption destroying our country. I tend to lose my faith when I mingle with people who tell you not to steal but are busy shipping our wealth abroad for themselves. We're heading for disaster, Marie. I'm afraid."

"Your worrying will solve the problem? All it does is make you unhappy and put you in trouble. I believe all that you're saying, but this world isn't perfect, Korli. For ages, many good people have worried and died to make it a better place to live in, yet it remains the same. In fact, it gets worse. If you wait for the perfect government, the perfect church, the perfect anything before going on with your life, you'll die of frustration."

"Some of the mainline churches run schools, clinics, hospitals, and so on, but our people don't have money to pay for these services. I'm ashamed too of the churches our own native people establish. They exist mostly to give economic support to the preachers."

"Tell me pointblank you don't want to go to church."

"Our preachers dig up little secrets in the community and broadcast them in the pulpits. People already know they're sinners; what they need to know is how to be saved."

"What about the society? Korli, join the Masons. Be a member of some social group for your own protection. Do it for my sake."

"The Poro is quite sufficient for me, Marie," Korli said. "It isn't perfect, but it punishes criminals. The kwii societies *protect* criminals!"

"Korli, you can't live upcountry and down here at the same time. I'll pray for you. Only God will change you."

Korli's attack on the backbone of the nation the so-called pioneers had built would not be tolerated. Frightened, Marie made no further rejoinder; she could be arrested for consorting with a dissident. She dropped him at his gate, where members of his family were waiting for him with anxiety, and rushed home.

18

LISTENING TO THE ANGEL

AROUND TEN IN THE MORNING on May 25, 1967, a black Mercedes-Benz driven by a uniformed police officer plied the main avenue of Sinkor Old Road. The unusual spectacle drew throngs of curious onlookers from zinc shacks and the sweltering market to the dusty broken street winding from Airport Junction to a sparsely inhabited portion of Old Road. The crowd screamed conflicting opinions about the strange incident in various tongues and temperaments:

"They will now pave our street! This bigshot must be a member of the inner circle."

"I hope he isn't fooling a girl round here as they usually do! They come here for enjoyment only."

"Bigshots don't care about poor people. Instead of paving our streets they wind up the windshields of their expensive cars so they can't see us."

"They develop only where they live or own land. Liberia has to be their personal property before they develop it."

"They own all the land, for native people don't own or sell government land in this country. So, they have no excuse for failing to develop the country."

"This area used to be a forest with animals roving about. Now it's a modern city. Let's be patient. Development will come."

"What is modern about potholes, dust, and stench? Go where the bigshots live to see a modern city."

"It took a hundred years to get deer and monkeys out of here. We'll probably wait another hundred to get paved streets. How many of us will be around then?"

"What do they do with the taxes they collect from business people and concessions?"

"They put our money in their pockets."

"Had America not opened up the country, we'd still be roaming naked in the forests."

"America could have done more for us if our rulers were interested in development. They give them large sums of money but nothing happens. America is tired of us."

"Unless a native man takes over this country, it won't develop."

"Native men act the same way when they're in power. They serve only themselves and their families. Two rich ones live round here. One is a former director of the Freeport. He is rotten rich, but he only built a luxurious house for himself, where he lives enjoying the best of foods and liquors. The other one works with the Secretary of Treasury who handles all the country's money. He too only built a big house for himself. No— the country man in power is our enemy."

"As for the one working at Treasury, he and his wife work for their money. I see the woman in the market everyday selling potato greens and pepper."

"That's just a cover-up. Who can build that kind of mansion by making market?"

"Time will come when they'll run away from their modern bungalows and hide in our zinc shacks."

"My friend, the people have their passports, visas, and air tickets in their pockets, ready to flee the country in case of war. When war comes, we the poor people will suffer the most, not the rich people."

Korli was dressing when jogging crowds trailed the Mercedes-Benz to his yard. Leanya had gone to the market and Junior and Borwulo were selling greens around the community. Suddenly, Famang, who had been playing ball in the yard, furiously pounded his room door, crying:

"Papa! Papa! De police na come for you!"

Korli shouted that he was putting on his clothes to come outside. He knelt down by the bed, prayed the Lord's Prayer, and stepped into the marble hallway to find his frightened son standing at the door, his lips quivering and his wide eyes swimming with tears.

"Who? Who? What?" Korli asked urgently. Leaning against the wall for support, the boy opened and closed his mouth without saying a word.

"Go into your room," Korli told him and rushed to the living room.

Pushing the curtains aside, he saw crowds standing around the strange car, pointing accusing fingers at it and at his house. Since moving to the new suburban neighborhood, they had been victims of robbery many times. Groups of brave boys, acting as vigilantes, often caught some of the thieves, beat them up, paraded them round the community with a booing crowd, and then brought them to face him for punishment. This crowd was different. It wasn't booing a thief, but castigating him and all rich Liberians for their opulence. Opening the door with force, Korli confronted a broad-faced, uniformed police officer standing on the porch apathetically viewing the frantic crowd. Had the officer come to arrest him? Had someone betrayed him to the authorities? No—they wouldn't have sent a plush car for a prisoner. Had his boss sent for him? No—should Secretary Johnson need his service overtime, which was rare and happened mostly at the end of the year when the department's annual report was due, he dispatched a messenger in a small Datsun or Mazda sedan to summon him. In fact, the Secretary knew that he was scheduled to deliver the keynote address for African Liberation Day at the university. Perhaps the police officer would explain the mystery. He invited him to the living room and asked in a friendly tone:

"My friend, what happened?"

"Nothing bad, Chief," the officer said and gave him an awkward salute, looking wistfully at the beautiful furniture. "Sit down," Korli told him. "What are you drinking?" "Coke," said the officer.

Korli brought him a bottle of coke from the new icebox. The officer popped the bottle open with an opener attached to a bunch of keys and drank with relief, a happy escape, albeit brief, from the hot weather outside.

"I came to take you to the university for your speech," said the officer after drinking half the coke. "The dress code for the occasion is coat and tie. I am Captain Moses Blama."

"You frightened me, Captain Blama!" said Korli, sighing with relief. "I thought you came to arrest me! They should have sent an ordinary messenger with an office car instead of an official guest car from the Department of Foreign Affairs! I have my own means of transportation. See the commotion you've caused at my house!"

"I'm sorry, sir," said the officer. "The university asked the Secretary of Foreign Affairs for cars to bring several government officials to the program. They told me to come for you because you will deliver the Keynote Address. A chauffer has to take you according to the protocol."

"I was getting ready to go. As you can see, I only need a coat."

He went to get it and a moment later Leanya and the children came rushing into the house. They ran to Korli in the bedroom.

"What's this I hear? The police have come for you?" Leanya asked Korli breathlessly as he put on his coat. Dressed in a gray suit, red tie, and brown leather shoes, he looked superb like the government official that he was, a real *kwii*. Leanya was proud of her husband who would have been wasting away in the backwoods had they not come to Monrovia. Now he was the person he was meant to be. He may well have been a superintendent, a representative, a senator, or even a member of the cabinet.

"You forgot?" Korli told her. "I'm speaking at the university. Today is African Liberation Day. The students elected me to give the Keynote Address."

"Thank God for that. They should have sent a messenger for you instead of an official car. The crowds don't like us. They are saying bad things about us. After that New Day Party fracas, I hate to see you meddle with politics."

"This is not politics, my dear. You know the people are not used to seeing a car like this in this area. They are just curious to know who came to us."

In a special bulletin, the university president had announced, "With the advice and consent of the Faculty Senate, Student Body, and with the power in me vested by the Board of Trustees, I hereby appoint Sumowor Vakpeeh Gbamokorli, the Keynote Speaker for the 4th anniversary of African Liberation Day at the University of Liberia. It is hereby so ordered!" Both faculty and students read the proclamation with pleasure, expressing relief for a breathing space from the empty rhetoric government officials often unleashed on national holidays.

Korli enjoyed a high rating among the students because he had distinguished himself as a fearless discussant of national issues at student gatherings. Unlike most other speakers whose speeches were notable for their impressiveness rather than substance, he shunned abstraction and patronizing rhetoric. He had an independent mind and did not mince words in putting his points across. His language was down-to-earth and engaging, and his subjects were matters of immediate concern such as abolishing corruption, increasing food production; and building enough roads, schools, and clinics throughout the country. His colleagues feared for his safety, but lauded his courage, honesty, and brilliance. After sustaining countless humiliations, jail terms, and tortures at the hands of the security, they had grown weary of being social critics, especially as their criticism did not improve the condition of the country. Korli had grown further in stature after surviving a brush with The Rooster and after the president submitted the statement he had helped compose for the New Day Party as a bill for the legislature to pass into law. This brave new voice promised a fresh and practical start in analyzing and assessing the nation's problems.

During his weeklong struggle in composing the most important speech of his life, Korli had promised himself that he wouldn't let the speech sound depressive, controversial, or cynical. He'd consider the nation's problems soluble. He had made such a resolution many times but it always crumbled whenever he saw the piteous sight of shabby beggars wheedling coins from well-to-do passersby in the sullied streets, or when he saw half-naked malnourished children scrounging for food in mountains of garbage.

As they drove through the crowds, Korli felt guilty on seeing people who were supposed to be "the Lords of the Soil" walking barefoot in the dust and fighting over dilapidated buses and taxis while he, one of them, rode a luxurious car with an official license plate like a diplomat or business executive. No—he didn't like it at all. Callous indifference to the people's welfare was a seed of destruction, for soon the limit of their endurance would arrive, and this beautiful country would vanish in flames because the anger of a people dispossessed was fiery. In searching for the good life, he had become an enemy of his own people. Some were proud of him, of course, for his success was undeniably their success. Well, they could achieve the same success if they liked, Korli thought. He had not climbed the social ladder by a miracle but by his unwavering devotion to duty and the belief that nothing was beyond anyone's aspiration.

Some people claimed that Korli's remarkable success was due to witchcraft, the same accusation they had slapped on him in White Plains. But those who knew and admired him maintained that he wasn't the type of person to succumb to magical influence or superstition. A self-made man of good education, intelligence, and integrity, he had made his mark through hard work and sheer brainpower. The inner circle had absorbed him because of his productivity and the fear that a native man of sterling qualities who did not fall in line would likely join the opposition to overthrow the government. Other admirers believed that his success was due to luck. Whatever the case might have been, Korli's success defied scrutiny.

Korli wasn't surprised to see the auditorium full beyond capacity, not only with students but also with government officials, marketeers, and hustlers. His reputation as a fearless speaker of the truth accounted for the massive turnout. Traditionally, keynote speakers lauded the government's achievements, while deep down in their hearts they knew that the nation was dying. But people knew that Korli would be different.

Korli climbed the concrete steps at the extreme eastern corner of the long hall, walked firmly—a smile frozen on his face—to the rostrum, and sat with ranking government officials and members of the faculty. He wasn't surprised that the president and vice president of the university were absent. By gracing the occasion with their presence, the NBI would have accused them of turning the nation's highest institution of learning into an opposition party. The university's administration knew too well that such an accusation had only one consequence: summary imprisonment or mysterious disappearance. And they were certain that Korli wouldn't speak about the meaning of freedom, democracy, Plato's republic or philosopher king, or the government's "unprecedented accomplishments" as conventional speakers would do. He'd condemn corruption and incompetence in the civil service. He would denounce and deride ritual killing, incest, profligacy, debauchery, laziness, and roguery in high places. He'd indict the ruling class for its criminal neglect of the nation's development—and before you knew it, the leadership of the institution would be dismissed and imprisoned.

Without much ado the Dean of Liberia College, Dr. Ambulai Fahnbulleh, deputizing for the president, warmly introduced Korli as "a man of principle and resolve, a patriot in the true sense of the word, who was so inspired by love of country and his race that he wanted to see Africa developed in a hurry." The diminutive academic, who was dressed in an ornate Vai shirt and cap with a black tassel, shook his head as he spoke, the tassel slapping his jaw and the nape of his neck. Taking a deep breath and surveying the crowd somberly, he continued: "Korli has studied the problems of the developing world at great length on his own. His honest opinions are not meant to disparage the immense achievements the country has made under the dynamic, farsighted, progressive, and inspired leadership of our God-chosen leader but to remind us that our journey on the long road to progress has just begun. We must play our part in this drama with commitment and diligence before passing the torch to future generations. Ladies and gentlemen, I don't want to steal the show—and our keynote speaker needs no introduction. Let's listen to his words of wisdom with undivided attention. It is for me a great honor and privilege to present to you our keynote speaker for this historic occasion—a distinguished, patriotic, farsighted, and indefatigable self-made man of integrity, courage, and erudition. He is nobody else but our own Honorable Sumowor Vakpeeh Gbamokorli of Bong County! Please give him a big hand!"

There was a standing ovation and a prolonged round of hearty applause. Waving a white handkerchief at the crowd, Korli walked briskly to the lectern, opened the manila folder containing his speech and formally addressed his audience—government and academic dignitaries, the student body, marketeers and wayfarers whom he called "distinguished visitors." Putting on a pair of glasses he pulled out of his coat pocket, he asked everybody to rise and observe a moment of silence in memory of those who had made "the supreme sacrifice" in the cause of African liberation. Protesting murmurs, especially from students, sounded in the hall, but everyone complied.

"I will speak to you on *The Pathway to Progress*," Korli began. There was warm applause. "I salute our leaders who have freed the bulk of Africa, our sacred heritage." More applause. "It's our patriotic duty to develop this continent for the benefit of contemporary and future generations. Ladies and gentlemen, development entails discerning hard work, patience, and sacrifice. Posterity will not forgive us if we continue deferring this responsibility because we have the needed resources to fulfill it. Liberia is especially blessed with immense natural wealth and the example of the United States of America, our mother country, the richest and most powerful nation on earth, to emulate in building a vibrant nation. Liberia should therefore be among the most developed nations not only in Africa but in the entire world community because of its long historic bond with America, but this hasn't happened because we refuse to learn from the examples of the Americans.

"After composing a draft of this speech, I had a dream in which God himself pointed out the root causes and solutions to the problems of black Africa. I observed that this dream was far better than what I had written because it revealed a practical pathway to progress. So I decided to make it my speech for this great occasion.

"In my dream, I saw the people of black Africa gathered at the foot of Mt. Sinai, praying fervently, fasting, making costly sacrifices, and singing sad gospel songs for God to come down to the mountaintop and tell them why he had made them black. The color of their skin had denied them their human rights and progress. Did he not hear their cries for justice? The more they prayed to him for relief from bondage, the worse their condition became! Either God had forgotten them or had refused to come to their aid. Was he not the father of all humanity?

"At sunrise, as they lay prostrate, canting solemn prayers, the mountain shook and a heavy cloud descended on it. No longer concerned with justice but their lives, the people implored God for mercy. A southern wind blew the cloud away, and the mountain shone with a light that was brighter than the light of the sun. Raising their heads, they saw the Angel Gabriel standing on the mountain summit with upraised arms—and peace descended upon them. Introducing himself in a voice that resounded in the far reaches of the desert, the angel wished them joy and said that God was now ready to answer their prayers, but that he no longer visited the earth in person. The angel explained that God had noted that his almighty splendor was too much for human beings to endure and that was why he had sent his only begotten son to earth in human form to teach humanity all they needed to know about salvation, and leave the Holy Spirit with them to strengthen their faith. The angel asked them to appoint a spokesperson to go with him to heaven and lay their complaints before God. Normally, God did not permit any of his earthly children to go to him in heaven with the dust out of which He had made them, but he would make this one exception to show his love and care for black Africans.

"After a lengthy debate that tested the angel's patience, the Africans decided that their spokesperson be a Nigerian since Nigeria is the most populous country in black Africa. But the Nigerians could not agree on which of their five hundred tribes should produce the spokesperson. Should the person be an Igbo, a Hausa, a Fulani, or a Yoruba? Another prolonged debate ensued until the angel lost his patience:

"'The root cause of your problems is disunity!' Angel Gabriel told the Africans. 'By tomorrow at this same time and place, I'll bring God's answers to your prayers. I won't take a spokesperson with me to heaven. God already knows your problems: colonialism, neo-colonialism, tribalism, corruption, abject poverty, civil war, superstition, and laziness.' Then he vanished.

"Suddenly the pilgrim throng found themselves miraculously at heaven's golden gate, all dressed in white clothes. Had God decided that each of them be their own spokesperson? God's love for the Africans must be great indeed, for they couldn't recall his taking any other racial group to heaven's gate.

"Speaking in a loud, resonant voice from his glorious mansion in the center of heaven, God welcomed the black Africans to his gate and sympathized with them for their centuries of grueling oppression at the hands of the white man, but he said they were largely responsible for the problem so they should make the necessary efforts and sacrifices to solve it. Parting their lips in surprise, the Africans cast incredulous stares at each other. They couldn't believe that the words came from the God whom they had been worshiping and adoring all their lives.

"'There is a solution to every problem,' God continued in a mild voice. 'All it takes is courage and sacrifice to find it. My children, I have given you enough wisdom, strength, and material resources to live a free, happy, prosperous, and triumphant life. Stop being overwhelmed by problems and develop your knowledge, skills, and the natural wealth available to you to tackle them—and you too will have the fate of the world in your hands.'

"Don't consider your enslavement and colonial experience an excuse for failing to develop your continent. Everybody has been colonized and enslaved. Now that you have your freedom, forget about jubilation and devote much more time and effort to hard work to develop your continent. You need not continue enduring grinding poverty, disease, and ignorance. You don't have to invent or even manufacture the telephone, the radio, the television, the automobile, the tractor, the airplane, the ship, the caterpillar, clothing, the printing press, the computer, building materials, and other amenities that facilitate vast improvement in the quality of life. You need not invent medicines and medical equipment that can wipe out the hosts of contagious diseases retarding your progress and threatening your survival. These things have already been invented and they are always being improved for better service, but you prefer going round the world begging for handouts because you are afraid of hard work. Remember that whatever others give you free with the right hand they take away from you a thousand-fold with the left.

"Millions of books have been written that can enlighten you to make meaning of your life. Yours is the richest continent on earth; it has plenty of fertile land, rainfall, fresh water, virgin forests, and minerals to facilitate large-scale farming all year round as well as significant timber and mining industries. Yet, you look up to others for food and finished products—those who have only three to four months in the year to do their farming—and most of the products they sell to you at exorbitant prices come from raw materials they have taken out of your own soil.

"Put your drums down for a moment, stop grumbling, and do some work. It isn't that I hate happiness. I admire the black man's courage in affirming life despite the incredible sufferings he has endured for ages and continues to suffer. But there is a time to play and a time to work. Respect and prosperity come from constant devotion to hard work and imagination for the future.

"Your next problem is lack of unity, as Angel Gabriel told you. Pool together the best minds and means available in Africa to build great enterprises. Stop estranging your brilliant men and women from participating meaningfully in your politics and development efforts. Otherwise, atrocious rebels will grasp power in your countries with your full support, use it to oppress you, dissipate your wealth on image-building and profligacy, and put the rest in Western banks to enjoy while you languish in abject poverty and humiliation. They'll confuse you with tawdry revolutionary ideas, but when a real revolution comes, they'll flee to the West, leaving you destitute and subject to the designs of avaricious humanitarians who are more interested in enriching themselves at your expense than in solving your problems.

"By my grace you'll sometimes depose some of these dictators, but you'll replace them with others who are even more terrible because you prefer living the hard way. You'll cut down in a hurry any advocate of your welfare or critic who points out your self-destructive attitudes. If you don't reform your behavior, your continent will always be in turmoil—and you will always live in fear and suspicion.

"Your intellectuals, who should be helping you solve your problems, would rather impress you with borrowed ideas from the East and the West, not knowing that the solutions to your problems will come only by analyzing and assessing your own experience.

"My final advice to you is, look to yourselves for answers to your problems. Time is still on your side, and I have given you without discrimination all the needed resources to prosper and survive with honor in the world. If you take full advantage of them, you too will have the fate of the world in your hands. Farewell.'

"Denied an opportunity to say something in their own defense, the Africans only fell on their knees at heaven's gate and repeated the Lord's Prayer."

When Korli finished delivering his lengthy dream speech, he stood transfixed with his hands holding onto the lectern to keep steady, his eyes closed, and his face teeming with beads of perspiration. There was no applause—only murmurs, grunts, shuffles of feet, and the strident sounds of car horns on Capital Bypass and beyond. Like one roused from a deep sleep or returning from a long mental excursion, Korli opened his eyes slowly, stared at the empty hall and near-vacant platform. Only Dean Fahnbulleh was standing at his side. He smiled blandly. Obviously, he had lost his audience and had been speaking to an imaginary one.

"A good speech, Korli, but the people ran away because of fear. The government's security forces will soon raid the campus. Let's go to my office."

"Your na goin' anywhere!" announced a man who appeared by the platform as if out of thin air. There were three other thugs with him, all dressed in black uniforms. The four jumped onto the platform, grabbed them, twisted their arms and applied handcuffs to their wrists. Hustling them outside, they shoved them in a long black car, which sped away to the Executive Mansion at high speed. The Rooster was driving.

Korli gazed with amazement at the huge Mansion standing resplendent on the Atlantic's breezy shore, towering majestically above its mean surroundings. A small flock of large birds soared over it, cawing loudly as they headed toward the ocean. Korli remembered visiting the presidential office and residence on several occasions, but he had been so involved with his own thoughts that he had not inspected West Africa's most grandiose piece of architecture erected in its poorest country. He had heard that during its construction, the public had feared that the fifty-million-dollar investment was vulnerable to attack by sea, land, and air. At least the risk of sea attack could have been eliminated were it built deep in the forest region of the country—and why should Liberia have the most expensive executive edifice in West Africa and nothing else? The Old Man had retorted that, in modern warfare, no place was secured from attack. As an ordinary citizen he could live in a thatched hut, but as President of Liberia he was entitled to living in the best home the government could provide. Liberia had been denied foreign aid many times on account of this misplaced priority.

The Old Man was sitting behind a magnificent, paneled desk glowing under fluorescent lighting from the vaulted ceiling. He looked offended.

"What's your problem, my friend?" he asked The Rooster with a frown. "We've told you over and over not to arrest teachers or students on the university campus for expressing their opinions. We'll soon look for a different director for the NBI. We believe in academic freedom—in all freedoms! We signed the United Nations' Charter and helped found the OAU, ECOWAS, and the Non-Aligned Movement! Why have you brought these academics to our office?"

"Your Excellency, Mr. President, our Head of State, Leader of Africa's oldest Republic—"

"No beating round the bush, my friend! I need my rest. Come to the main point! You've spoiled our plan."

The humor did not invoke laughter, though it was amusing enough. Trembling, The Rooster spoke brokenly:

"Korli is an enemy of the state, Mr. President. In a speech he delivered today during a well-attended program at the University of Liberia—I have the recording—he accused this administration and all its predecessors of corruption and incompetence."

"Do you dispute that?" the president asked. "Are you not corrupt like the rest of them? How many times have I reshuffled my cabinet for better performance? Each time I replace a Secretary with someone else, the condition of that department worsens because of corruption. What else he said?"

"He said that black Africans are responsible for all the atrocities the white man has perpetrated against them, especially their enslavement. That is unfair, Your Excellency, holding the victims responsible for their oppression."

"But he is telling the truth! Were we not the ones who sold our own people to the white man for tobacco, smoked fish, salt, and gunpowder? Are we not still carrying on slavery in Africa? Now that we have our freedom, what are we doing with it besides killing one another for power? My friend, say something else."

"Mr. President, it is unfair to blame the victims for their suffering rather than their oppressors."

"We are victims of our own aggression, my friend."

"When I tried to arrest Korli, he engaged me in physical combat."

"He should have flogged you. If you hadn't a gun, would you have dared attack a man with solid muscles like him? Look, I've heard plenty of your nonsense. Your lies have sent many innocent and respectable people to their graves. If you say another word, you'll be imprisoned. Remove the cuffs from these gentlemen. I thought you said Korli gave the address. Why is the Dean in handcuffs?"

The Rooster quickly removed the cuffs and said, "We brought the Dean as a witness, Mr. President. He was there when Korli gave the address."

"How will you get the truth out of him while he is handcuffed? Whoever puts a key witness in handcuffs? Gentlemen, please sit down." The Old Man looked at The Rooster and asked, "My friend, do you understand the meaning of the words 'justice and academic freedom'?"

"Yes, Mr. President," said The Rooster.

"I don't think you do. You want to put us in trouble with the whole world! Next thing you know, Amnesty International will be on our backs. We are a poor country, depending on the developed nations of the world for survival. They will stop helping us if our human rights record is stained with atrocities." Turning to Korli and Professor Fahnbulleh, he said, "We're sorry for the inconvenience, my people. It'll never be repeated. Hon. Korli, we hereby appoint you Ambassador Extraordinary and Plenipotentiary of Liberia to the Kingdom of Ethiopia. You need to get away from this nest of jealousy and ignorance. Dr. Fahnbulleh, you are hereby appointed Special Assistant to the President of Liberia for Academic Affairs. These appointments take immediate effect. And it is so ordered!" The president pounded the desk and then pressed a button. A man poked his head through the door. "Tell Johnny Walker to give each of these men a thousand dollars for their trouble," the Old Man told him.

Much to the surprise and relief of the university family, the Department of Information issued the following press release that evening:

"The Chief Executive has been pleased to appoint Hon. Sumowor Vakpeeh Gbamokorli Liberia's Ambassador to the Kingdom of Ethiopia. Hon. Korli's appointment is based on his astute intellect and political acumen. The Chief Executive hopes that the learned diplomat will not only help ensure that freedom comes to all remaining colonized African states, particularly Apartheid South Africa and Namibia, but that he will also play a leading role in making the divisibility of Africa indivisible. The president was also pleased to appoint Dr. Ambulai Fahnbulleh, Dean of Liberia College, as his Special Assistant for Academic Affairs."

At Korli's house, the new development was celebrated with joy, relief, and thanksgiving to God. It was decided that Korli would go first, and Leanya and the rest of the family would follow after he had settled down. Amidst entertaining the steady flow of well-wishers who came daily, Leanya busied herself with preparations for his move. When it was finally time for him to travel, the whole family wanted to accompany him to the airport but he told them security had instructed him to go alone. They bade him farewell at the house, with many neighbors and friends present.

Three days passed before Leanya began to worry about not hearing from Korli since his departure. Then, without any communication with her, the Department of Information issued another press release to the newspapers:

"The Government of Liberia announces with profound regrets the death of His Excellency Ambassador Sumowor Vakpeeh Gbamokorli in a plane crash in the Sahara desert *en route* to Addis Ababa to assume his duties as Liberia's Ambassador to Ethiopia. The Department of Foreign Affairs will conduct a memorial service for the late Ambassador at Centennial Memorial Pavilion this Sunday. The Chief Executive, the Cabinet, the Legislature, members of the Supreme Court, Doyen and members of the Diplomatic Corps will be in full attendance. The National Ensign will be flown at half staff on the day of interment. Meanwhile, a book of condolence is opened at the Department of Foreign Affairs for sympathizers to sign."

Credible rumors began to circulate that The Rooster and his henchmen, overzealous to demonstrate their loyalty to the president, had murdered Hon. Korli in cold blood on South Beach, and that the story of the plane crash was an elaborate lie made up by the Department of Information at the request of the embarrassed president.

19

LISTENING TO THE BIRDS

LEANYA BORE THE TRAGEDY with surprising fortitude. His mere absence from home often threw her mind in disarray, but now that his death had been announced, she conducted herself with an equanimity that amazed the family who were crying their eyes out. As the heavy hours dragged, the family concluded that, having become their backbone and only hope now, she couldn't afford to break down. It would be a disaster, especially for the little ones. She had no choice but to stand strong. Another reason for her courage, some thought, could be her doubt about the death of Korli. Or perhaps Leanya was calm and collected because she was thinking of how to tell the children about their father's death. Their young and innocent minds had never been exposed to such calamity. No matter how she told it, it would confuse and anger them. Liimu did not give her much time to contemplate a solution to the problem. At bedtime she hugged her snugly and said:

"Mama, I want to go to sleep. Where's Papa?" Liimu loved to fall asleep in her father's arms or at his side in bed. Then he'd take her to her room or lay her at the foot of their bed. Without her father she found it almost impossible to go to sleep at night.

Unable to give a ready answer to her question, Leanya grew unnerved with smoldering sorrow and her eyes welled with tears. Fortunately, Liimu was half asleep. Tightening her lips and wiping her face with the back of her hand, Leanya placed her in her lap and rocked her until she closed her eyes. It was fortunate too that the boys were already sleeping or they might have burdened her with many more questions demanding answers far more complex. After sleeping for a moment, Liimu shook awake and repeated her question. Leanya told her in a tender voice that her father had gone to Jesus in heaven, the town in which God lived, waiting for them to join him. She should sleep and not worry. Her father was perfectly safe in heaven.

"So he won't come back tonight?"

"No," Leanya said ruefully. "He won't come back tonight. When you go to heaven you don't come back. You live there forever. Heaven is more beautiful than here. People live there in peace and happiness. Everybody will go there."

"Let's go there now! I want to see Papa."

"Everybody has their own time to go there. It was your father's time to go. When our time comes, we'll go to him."

"Oh!" Liimu cried and slobbered on her mother. Felenkpeh tried to help by taking her away but she refused. "I want to go to Papa now! I want to go to Papa now!" she cried. Leanya laid her in the bed, tumbled to the floor, and shook with sobs.

Meanwhile, the Setons, who had just heard the news, called on Leanya. Mrs. Seton and Borwulo broke down when they saw her lying on the floor crying hoarsely, her loose hair tumbled to her shoulders; she wore only a lappa round her breasts. The only calm person in the room was Mr. Seton. Unable to hush the criers, he picked up Liimu who was whining, placed her against his shoulder, and went to the sitting room. He laid her in his lap and urged her to sleep. When she slept, he took her to the bedroom and went to the criers. Leanya was sitting on the floor now, leaning against the bed with Mrs. Seton and Borwulo sitting on either her side of her. Touching her shoulder, Mr. Seton told her soothingly:

"You're doing well. This cry is an everlasting cry. Don't let it break you down. You have the children to care for; you're now both their father and mother, and your people upcountry are counting on you. So be strong."

"Korli will come," Leanya said meditatively. "He didn't die in a plane crash. He wasn't going anywhere. He was determined to remain in this country and fight for justice. If he could escape death in the dark country, he wouldn't meet his end in such an unexplained way in a civilized country. Korli will come."

"I told him not to meddle with politics," Mr. Seton said, "but the government is the only employer in this country. When you work for it, you have to be a politician. People who don't work for the government don't command any respect or succeed in anything in this country."

"Korli will come," Leanya maintained, the belief lighting her eyes briefly. "They're keeping him in jail somewhere. They put out that false announcement that we may give in; then they'll kill him. Please take me to the president. I want to plead with him to take my husband from the hands of his security."

"It's no use, Leanya," Mr. Seton said quietly. "The president is surrounded by liars and wicked men who fight to gain his favor by destroying other people. Once he is fond of someone, that person becomes a threat to them. That's why you don't see any development. Nearly all the money goes to the security, which pretends to know the enemies of the state. To be frank, *they* are the enemy of the state. I'm sure the president will take care of you."

"Korli will come," Leanya said. "He doesn't expect me alone to take care of his children. Where is the hand I have? What man will agree to bring up another man's children? Korli is hiding somewhere to come home when it is safe for him to do so."

A sudden outburst of weeping on the porch took Mr. Seton there. Marie had arrived. Mr. Seton took her into the room and she fell upon Leanya, both of them weeping inconsolably. Mrs. Seton, who had grown quiet, began consoling them and Mr. Seton went back out to the sitting room.

After the women had cried awhile, Marie gave Leanya a bale of black cloth and said, "You have to wear black while mourning for a year according to the *kwii* custom. Our tears will not bring him back. They'll only cast a dark cloud on his way. So keep quiet and look up to God and the president."

"But Korli is coming back," Leanya said.

"I saw his body at Anderson's Funeral Home, Leanya," Marie said tearfully. "I can't lie to you. He has gone. They got rid of him because they say he closed their eating holes. But don't cry. You have friends— plenty of friends. The president will deal with his killers and take care of you. The Rooster and his bunch of henchmen have disappeared."

"Who is The Rooster?" Leanya grew curious.

"The man who came for Korli one night saying he was taking him for a chat."

For a long moment Leanya was speechless. Then she shook her head and said with a sigh:

"Thank you for the cloth, but I prefer wearing white for mourning, for I know that he is in heaven with Jesus. Black will darken his way."

"I'll find you white, then, and bring it this evening when I come back. You may keep the black in case you need it." With that, Marie returned to her office.

By noon a group of Kpelle people living in the neighborhood came dancing to sympathize with Leanya. A crowd of spectators converged on them in the yard. Leanya dressed and went out to receive their sympathy. There was a rousing cheer when she appeared on the porch. A man dressed in an exotic costume, a *sangba* between his legs, climbed to the porch and told her in a singsong voice that they had come to comfort her. He spoke as he beat the drum: Korli was their father, he said. Korli was their brother. Korli was their uncle. Korli was their friend. His loss was extremely grievous. A part of them had died. The only way they could handle the irreparable loss was by singing and dancing. Leanya broke down, but a group of girls dressed in Sande costumes rushed onto the porch and took hold of her, urging her to dance the tears away or she'd pay a heavy fine.

Leanya was no longer accustomed to dancing, but she made tentative attempts at the dance of the initiates to the rousing cheers of the crowd. A Zoe commanded her to smile to complete the merriment. When she smiled, she seemed transfigured into a different woman, ebullient, sturdy, charged with limitless energy. Soon the porch became too small for her. Going to the yard, she danced so well that some spectators threw money at her nimble feet; there was no measure to the cheering. Only the solemn music suggested that the dance was a funeral dance. When she left the semicircle, a group of young men wiped the sweat from her face with white handkerchiefs. The girls lined up and danced gently, singing lowly, swinging their hips and gyrating their bodies in keeping with the rhythm of the beautiful music. The crowd watched them, mesmerized. Even the birds who had been singing in the trees since daybreak seemed to stop their chattering to watch.

Later that afternoon Auntie Noai came crying with her hands interlaced on her head. Leanya, who had grown hoarse with weeping, only hugged her and shook with stifled sobs, then took her into the bedroom.

"My dear, don't cry again," Auntie Noai told Leanya, wiping her face. "Now they have accomplished their wicked aim! Nothing more can they do to Korli. Let them have their big jobs! Let them have their cars! Let them have everything as long as you live to take care of your children! We heard the news. There are rumors that you intend to retaliate—but what can a poor woman like you do? They're only looking for a pretext to get rid of you, too, so leave the country before it's too late."

"And go where?" Leanya asked.

"Anywhere else besides Liberia. Go to Guinea. You'll find some of our relatives there. There are many more Kpelle people in Guinea than in Liberia. Forget about the house. I'll put it up for rent and send you the money—or bring it to you myself. Your life and the lives of your children are more important than anything else. Go to Guinea and live there until everything cools down before you put your foot back in this country."

"I would prefer going to Sierra Leone, Auntie," Leanya said quietly. "Whenever you run away from our mad security, go where nobody knows you."

"You may be right. Anyhow, the sooner you leave the country the better it'll be for you. I want the children to live and carry Korli's name into the future. His mother could live with me until conditions return to normal."

"I want to see about his burial before leaving, Auntie. I can't abandon him in death. He was very good to me and my people. Many people urged him to leave me and marry a civilized woman but he refused. I'm sure when I meet him in heaven he'll marry me again." Tears rolled down her cheeks.

"Korli should have contented himself with making a comfortable living for his family and not worry about developing this country. Only God will bring improvement to Liberia."

"No educated person will be content with merely making a comfortable living, Auntie. They want to improve the conditions in which they live. They want to see justice. They want peace and friendship in the world. That's their problem. But our country does not want peace or development or friendship. They teach you how to think, but forbid you to say what you think. They want the condition of the country to remain the same for the rulers to rob everything from it. Are they saying then that the only benefit we get from the government is oppression and suppression? One day there'll be change. We'll get our freedom and our rights. Korli lit the torch; it will pass on to all future generations." When Auntie Noai made no rejoinder, Leanya continued: "Korli always told me that war solves no problem. Only education will free the tribes. He came to the *kwii* world to learn something and fight to make life better for his people, not to plunge them into war. They should send their children to school. That's the only way they'll take their rightful place in their own country."

"They've made life impossible for us poor people in this country!" Auntie Noai cried in a loud voice, slapping her thighs and stamping her foot. "We're in slavery, my people! We are slaves! God help us! Let Korli depart in peace! He's far better off where he is."

"No, Auntie, don't put us in trouble," Leanya said. "The Rooster has eyes and ears everywhere in this city even if he has disappeared as they say. Perhaps he has gone under cover to see who might arise to fight or talk for Korli. Pray for me and the children. Help me pack up. Korli refused to play their wicked game according to the rules, so he had to die. He should have left this country long ago as most country people with good education do. Whether you live upcountry or down in Monrovia—they want your blood!"

The following day, to everybody's surprise, the president came to sympathize with Leanya. He looked grim and weighty with sorrow. It was the most memorable event to have ever occurred on Sinkor Old Road. Crowds of people lined the street from Airfield Junction all the way to Korli's house. They did not cheer the motorcade as crowds usually did whenever the head of state drove through a community. They only watched the train of long black cars solemnly. No—this was no time for jubilation, for the flag and the presidential seal did not flutter on the presidential limousine. They were wrapped up. The army detail looked somber in their truck. They held their guns upside down in contrast to holding them at the ready whenever they escorted the president's convoy. They were mourning. Perhaps Korli was a relative of the president, the crowds were thinking. His rank in the government was too low to warrant the president's involvement in his funeral, but things were happening in unexpected ways these days. A new day had dawned, the day of the country people—the day for everybody. If this president had adequate support among his own people, Liberia would have been a paradise long ago.

Dressed in a black suit without decoration, the president emerged slowly from the limousine and climbed to the porch already occupied by uniformed and plainclothes members of the Special Security Service, each one striving to be in the forefront so the president could notice him. Leanya collapsed at the president's feet when he entered the house, appealing to him to find her husband who, she said, was innocent of any crime. He only wanted to help his people lead a better life and support his family. He had no political ambition. The Old Man pulled her to her feet with the help of a security guard and sat by her on a sofa. Speaking slowly and solemnly to her through an interpreter, he said:

"Don't cry, my daughter. You're not the only one to have lost Korli.

He was my son. Had he lived he would have become an important leader for his people. The whole country is bereaved. I learned about Korli long before you people came to Monrovia. He was a hardworking, brilliant, young man, but good people don't live long. The government will give your husband a state funeral to put his enemies to shame. His body will lie in state at this house, at the Departments of Treasury and Foreign Affairs, at the University of Liberia, and at the Centennial Pavilion. We'll give him the country's highest decoration and the flag will fly at half-staff on the day of his burial and for thirty days thereafter.

"As of today the government is responsible for your upkeep as well as the upkeep and education of his children, and the upkeep of your relatives and Korli's mother and relatives. The government will give you food supplies and pocket change each month. Whenever you need more money, ask me. You must leave this area and live near the Mansion for my soldiers to take care of you under my own eyes. My very visit here will make you an enemy of the people around here. When conditions become normal, you may decide what to do."

The president then directed Johnny Walker to give Leanya five thousand dollars to take care of the immediate needs of her children, dependents, and herself.

Leanya looked at him gratefully and was just about to say something when a small bird swooped down and landed at the feet of the Old Man. Several people tried to shoo it away, but the bird showed no fear. It simply hopped between the Old Man's feet, and hers, singing its shrill song so loudly that everyone on the porch—and even the crowd in the yard—fell silent to listen. The bird suddenly stopped its song and gazed up at Leanya. She stared at it for a long moment, then gasped, smiled, and blinked back her tears. Only then did it fly away, singing again its message to the people.

Glossary

Wilton Sankawulo's original manuscript for *Birds Are Singing* included footnotes to explain some of the terms and phrases he used. In the first edition of the novel, the footnotes were taken out for readability, since most terms were defined or discernible in the context of the story.

This glossary contains Sankawulo's footnotes, in his own words. All of them occur in Part One of the novel, when the main character is still in the interior and making his way to Monrovia. For easy reference, the terms and phrases are defined in the order that they appear in each chapter.

Sankawulo's definitions and explanations add a greater depth of knowledge to Kpelle culture in particular, and to Liberian culture as a whole. Who knew that some people in the interior were still calculating their money in British pounds in the 60s? Or that teenage pregnancy was not always frowned upon but encouraged because life expectancy was so short?

Birds Are Singing contains a trove of information and ideas that will enlighten and inspire. We hope the author's notes will further enrich your reading experience.

Chapter 1 – A Distant Road

Old Man – Children usually call their parents Old Man and Old Ma as a mark of respect. The designations, also used by people to refer to their leaders or elders, do not necessarily connote old age.

Kpaan – A meeting place usually on the outskirts or a town or village for members of the Poro society, where important matters are decided. Decisions made in the Kpaan are final.

Gborlorkpilii – Literally, "caterpillar"—name adopted by the water society.

Poro – A mandatory society for all males that teaches men the history and traditional values of the tribe, the importance of courage and industry, how to subdue the jungle to earn a livelihood, and how to be a successful husband, father, and good citizen. Its counterpart for women is called Sande.

Kenamu – A member of the Poro society.

Zoes – Zoes are predominantly herbalists or healers, and they sometimes wield supernatural powers. Some are administrators of secret societies, especially the Poro and the Sande, two compulsory institutions for training boys and girls, respectively, to be responsible parents knowledgeable in the history and traditions of the tribe.

The Land – When capitalized the word "land" doesn't refer only to topography but also to the living, the dead, and the unborn members of the tribe. It also refers to Zoes, Chiefs, and Elders who are custodians of the traditions and laws of the tribe.

Fuama – A distortion of "furanma" meaning "abundance" or "extravagance", a reference to the fertility of the land where food crops grow in abundance and extravagant meals are commonly prepared.

Kaaseng – A double. The Kpelle believe that each person has an animal double, and people manifest the characteristics of their doubles. If their doubles are harmed, they too are affected.

Koyorokpoh – Malaria herb; also used to treat constipation.

The Great One – The leader of the Poro society is variously called The Great One, The Big Thing, The Bush Thing, The Master, The Overload, and so on.

Gaigai – The innards of an animal are usually reserved for members of the Poro society.

Gei – Reiterated shouts in celebration of victory or some significant accomplishment.

Died before and risen again – Initiation into the Poro and Sande Societies and graduation from them are considered the death and resurrection of a boy or girl. After their initiation, they becomes new persons, matured, fearless, and wise in the ways of the tribe. Old bad habits and childishness become things of the past.

The Place of Truth – Heaven, also the abode of the ancestors.

Kono – A musical instrument made of a hallow stick with parallel, cylindrical holes and tapped with sticks, a kind of xylophone.

Kenablaa – The plural of *kenamu*, a member of the Poro society.

Kpolowa – A non-initiate of the Poro or Sande Society.

Kwii – Modern or civilized world. A *kwii* person is one who is educated or lives a modern lifestyle.

CHAPTER 2 - DIVINE DELIVERANCE

Sande – Women's counterpart of the Poro society; it trains girls to be good mothers, wives, and citizens knowledgeable in the history and traditions of the tribe.

Of age – Since life expectancy is short, marriage takes place in the tribe at an early age.

Pounds – The British pound was used briefly in the 19th century as Liberian currency. Although it has been replaced by the American dollar, people of the interior often calculate their money in pounds. The pound in their calculation is equivalent to two American dollars.

Eating Kai – "Eating *kai*" is an idiomatic expression meaning "committing incest."

Kperor – Lie detecting medicine, usually in the form of liquid that is swallowed. It kills a liar.

"Mark the Pregnancy" – Girls could be engaged in their infancy or even before they are born, but upon maturity, they must consent to marriage proposals before they are married. The tradition is common among the Loma, Kpelle, and other tribes in western Liberia.

Kenja – Long backpack carrier plaited with palm or piassava fronds.

Gbolo hunting – When a hunter or group of hunters hunts with a dog, it is *gbolo* hunting.

Sala – An animal offered as a sacrifice to the ancestors to prolong a person's life. It is not supposed to be killed and is replaced at once should it die. Anyone who kills it or eats some of its meat dies mysteriously, according to traditional belief.

"Putting them in the bush" – Metaphor referring to a Zoe or herbalist's search for herbs in the bush. It's believed that a Zoe's client must make a down payment of any amount as an incentive for the Zoe to solve their problem. Otherwise, the medicine won't work.

Kpankpa – *Kpankpa* is medicine of supernatural power used to protect a town, house, or property from thieves and witches. Also used as a verb: She will kpankpa the town.

Porlortor – Forced laborer(s).

Zuu – Crocodile

CHAPTER 3 – A HAPPY SURPRISE

Leanya – Come near me

Zieh – Bamboo splints plaited like a checkerboard; it's used for the construction of a ceiling, fence, or hut.

"On traveling feet" – On a journey or in transit.

"Thrown cutlass" – Done some work, usually with a cutlass.

Trial wife – Sometimes a couple lives together for a number of years to ensure that they are compatible or could have children before marrying. A marriage is legitimate only if blessed with children.

Cold water – Metaphor for a drink to conclude a case and make peace.

Cut the log – pay a nominal fine for having premarital sex with a girl.

Bury the navel cord – The navel cord of a baby is usually planted with a kola nut to show that it is a legitimate citizen of the tribe and the land.

Bombor – Homespun panties.

Gbehgbeh – A bamboo or wattle bench or bedstead.

CHAPTER 4 – PUNISHMENT

The Overlord – A variety of the Master's name.

To "die" in the Poro/Sande society – Initiation symbolizes the death of the old "self" and the assumption of a new one.

Piyong – Accidental death.

Look aside – Go under cover or flee.

"Your head will not remain in this trouble" – You won't be killed as a result of the trouble you caused.

"Hang head" – Think seriously about a problem to find its solution.

Chapter 5 – The Songs of Birds

Cross water before returning – The Kpelle believe that people accompanying travelers partway when they commence a journey must cross some water (creek, stream, or river) before returning home. Otherwise, the travelers would find it impossible to cross the river of death when they die.

Soya – Yellow rice birds.

Gbatulu – A bull's whip used to punish lawbreakers.

Cutting sand – The Kpelle Zoe usually forecasts the future and explains mysteries after reading fingerprints he makes in special sand he spreads on a floor. This activity is known as sand cutting.

Camp Belle Yallah – A maximum security prison for people found guilty of treason and capital offense. It is located in Lofa County.

Calling his name – Confessing that he had had sexual intercourse with her.

Go with – Euphemism for having sex with a girl. Most tribes believe that having sexual intercourse with a girl is following or going along with her.

Niji – Niji is the Bassa equivalent of Gborlorkpilii.

Chapter 6 – The Price of Success

Hold your foot – Ask your pardon.

Chapter 7 – A Trap?

Puwan – Rice without stew or soup; cooked with okra or bitter balls and eaten with palm oil.

Twenty-Sixth season – Liberia's independence day is July 26. Liberia declared her independence on July 26, 1947.

"Don't let the same flooded river make you take your pants off twice" – Don't make the same mistake twice.

AGAINST ANNIHILATION:
A Conversation on Liberian Literature
with Wilton Gbakolo Sengbe Sankawulo

By Annaird Naxela

Annaird Naxela was born in Liberia, educated there and in the United States, and is now writing a doctoral thesis on Liberian fiction at the University of the Witwatersrand in South Africa.

INTRODUCTION

Interviews are complete in and of themselves, in that they contain supplementary information about the interviewer and interviewee—information that lies in what the questions assume and what the answers ignore; this information, together with the actual interview, may illuminate a larger meaning to the exercise. In this sense, interviews, as a body of literature, present themselves for analysis, for careful "reading." Hence qualifications may seem forced, but the following aims only to give a background note about the interview in question.

Professor Sankawulo agreed straightaway, despite his very pressed schedule (writing, conducting writing workshops, and honoring speaking engagements). The interview had been conceived on the basis of three installments. To assure a conversational approach and tenor, the three questions of the first installment were intended as a launching pad (if you would) for the interview; the responses to them, it was thought, would open the way for other interesting questions relevant to a developing theme in mind. Circumstances changed the plan, and, as the publication deadline drew near, an additional seven questions were generated. The ten questions were e-mailed at once to the interviewee. We trust that readers would infer the main theme from reading and thinking about the interview as a whole, its title notwithstanding. Care has been taken to annotate where the interviewer saw fit.

This is the first installment of what is hoped will be a collection of interviews and statements by Liberian artists on their work and its place and future in Liberia. Liberia's emergence as a viable state seems to demand such statements, needless to say, from an important and yet marginalized group. We, therefore, invite Liberian artists of all stripes to add to this collage of personal, critical, and philosophical views. We make this invitation public with the awareness that others could rush a similar book to press, though if that were to happen, Liberia's literary future would still be the better for it. In this spirit, we are willing—and do encourage—collaboration with well-meaning researchers and writers.

Thanks to Professor Sankawulo for his tireless work in an otherwise undervalued calling. Thanks, too, to Stephanie Horton, for courage and confidence in Liberia's literary flowering.

— Annaird Naxela

ANNAIRD NAXELA: How important was literature to Liberia before the civil war began in 1989? How important is literature now in 2006?

WILTON SANKAWULO: Literature is very important for any society, especially developing ones. Through literature people record, analyze, and assess their progress. Such processes enable them to understand and resolve the problems they must contend with, and use the right measures to attain those goals they have fashioned for themselves.

Liberia's development has faltered through the years because very little attention has been given to the creation of a respectable body of national literature. The development of our literature before the civil war of 1989 and up to now has been left to the initiatives of our writers alone. We have no book or magazine publishers in Liberia, no grants or training programs for our artists. Consequently, Liberian writers must do their own publishing, usually abroad, and market their works.

Before the civil war, the Liberian press was not free, except during the Tolbert administration. One result of this situation was that the press became chiefly a medium for glorifying politicians and portraying a national image that had no relation whatsoever to the nation's actual accomplishments. The book *Growth Without Development*, published by Northwestern economists in the sixties, sheds light on this problem.

Had the press been free to tell the truth about the country, I think Liberia would be one of the most developed countries in Africa, and the civil war could have been prevented. When Tolbert introduced press freedom in the seventies, it was widely abused because of technical and professional problems. No writer is perfect, nor can ever be perfect since knowledge grows from day to day, but I sincerely believe that a writer, whether a journalist, essayist, novelist or what have you, should have complete mastery of their medium of expression, which is language. This is especially important for us who write in a second language.

In the eighties, G. Henry Andrews and I took issue with the Liberian press for language problems and logical loopholes. What a writer says is as important as how it is said. Unfortunately, some of our writers overlooked language and ran into needless difficulty with the authorities because of inaccurate reportage. For example, the following headline appeared in one of our papers: "Businessmen Complain Finance Ministry." The editor of the paper defended this grammatical fault by saying that it was permissible in journalism to economize words in a headline. He gave as an example the heading, "The President Departs the Country." But "complain" is intransitive, whereas "depart" is transitive and intransitive. Economy of language is an important guideline for writing, but it should never be achieved at the expense of grammar.

What is more serious was the tendency of the press to make unsubstantiated allegations and capitalize on issues that destabilized the country and put people at loggerheads. What they [the press] did not know was not true; opinions they did not like or agree with were not valid; what they did not like was not good, and anyone who liked it was condemned. I don't want this interview to be a classroom exercise, but having lived through all our wars, I believe that unprofessional reporting constituted a significant part of the causes related to national confusion. Of course, many of our journalists and writers did not have any training in the field; some were only high school graduates. But doing a job for which one lacks the necessary competence is indefensible.

Another consequence of press suppression in Liberia was that Liberian writers did not tackle the problems of the country for fear of offending the authorities. Many of our writers suffered gravely for writing their frank opinions about national issues. In this post-war era, the question of training our writers and providing publishing institutions for their production is imperative. Our universities must establish presses. The purpose of a university is not only to grant degrees but also to make knowledge available by publication.

Only writers can help us understand ourselves, our potential, and the practical means we can adopt to build what President Tolbert called "a wholesome functioning society." If the contributions of our writers continue to be sidelined, we will be building in order to destroy again what we have built. Ninety-nine percent of the textbooks used in our schools are foreign-authored. Consequently, our children get a foreign education, and they do not hesitate to take up arms to destroy their own country. The best writers we have should be recruited to produce materials of good quality that can either replace or supplement the foreign textbooks. Liberian writers are producing books but most of them live in exile. The temptation they face is dwelling exclusively on the symptoms of our problems rather than their underlying causes. It is not enough to simply delineate the incalculable harms we have done to ourselves but to also identify their underlying causes; otherwise, we'll only be postponing the solution of our problems. The time has come for us to do so because no nation can make meaningful progress without a body of national literature.

ANNAIRD NAXELA: In your allegory, The Marriage of Wisdom, a coup d'état—and possibly outright civil war—is diverted by the Princess's quick thinking. How might her reaction relate to Liberia now and in the future?

WILTON SANKAWULO: The main theme of *The Marriage of Wisdom* is that wisdom plays a crucial role in life. This story shows that Africans of the traditional society are not simple-minded as it is widely supposed. They value and celebrate wisdom as the most important tool that makes life work. Of course the drama in the story has a political overtone, but its main point is that wisdom is the most valuable thing in life.

In my collection titled *The Marriage of Wisdom*, there is a tale called *The Marriage of Beauty;* where the marriage of wisdom succeeded, the marriage of beauty failed. *In The Marriage of Wisdom*, the Queen saves the life of her husband, the King, because of her wisdom, whereas in *The Marriage of Beauty*, a girl marries a man for his beauty only to discover to her amazement that she had married a dragon. The story is saying that if wisdom is applied to the problems of everyday living, whether they be political, economic, or religious, these problems can be resolved or brought under control. We in Africa will experience peace, stability, and progress if we put greater emphasis on traditional wisdom in tackling our social and political problems.

ANNAIRD NAXELA: Can you think of other examples of this kind of diversion in Liberian literature?

WILTON SANKAWULO: I venture to say that except for those who write history, our writers are chiefly concerned with our cultural heritage. Beginning with myself, I wrote Liberian folktales because they are not only interesting, they also portray our patterns of culture and traditional values extremely well. Studying them enables us to understand ourselves and chart the best course to our destiny.

I have collected over fifty folk tales which are published in one volume titled *Great Tales of Liberia*; these tales are not only entertaining, they are quite informative as moral stories. Other Liberian writers such as Bai T. Moore, Roland Tombekai Dempster, E. Tuimu Reeves, S. Jangaba M. Johnson, Patricia Jabbeh Wesley, and Robert H. Brown portray the Liberian experience in a lyrical manner.

Many Liberians do not think much of our folklore. There was a time when writing our folk tales or about village life was considered frivolous in Liberia. But folklore is superior to modern literature; in fact, it gave birth to it. It contains the ideas that people live by, their concept of the universe and destiny, and so on. For example, Dempster's *Mystic Reformation of Gondolia* is a powerful satire that uses the Vai folklorist hero, Blama, who materializes when a person engages in corruption and punishes the person. Bai T. Moore's poetry and fiction are based on traditional life. His *Ebony Dust, Murder in the Cassava Patch*, and *The Money Doubler* take us to our roots. There is much pleasure in reading about our traditional societies.

ANNAIRD NAXELA: How do you define "Liberian literature?"

WILTON SANKAWULO: To me literature is but literature. Liberian literature could be defined as a record of the traditional and contemporary life of the Liberian people. Our writers attempt to describe Liberian life, the ideas we live by, and the traditional institutions that govern our society, such as the Poro and the Sande. Presently our writers are attempting to analyze our modern society. I would suggest that they help us descend into ourselves to discover those beliefs and values that originate with us, modernize them, so that they may be reflected in how we live. We can safely maintain our national character and still modernize as people have done in Asia, Israel, Ghana, and Nigeria. I think one major cause of our civil war is our failure to understand and accept ourselves.

ANNAIRD NAXELA: Is a writer of Liberian literature defined by Liberian nationality?

WILTON SANKAWULO: I believe that Liberian literature should be defined as that body of national literature Liberians have produced. If an American writes a novel about Liberia, it is ideally American literature because he or she is looking at issues from the American point of view. You will note that much of British literature is set in other countries. Shakespeare's *Hamlet* is set in Denmark; Graham Greene's *Journey Without Maps* is set in Liberia; his *The Comedian* is about Haiti, and his *The Quiet American* is about Vietnam. All this literature is British. Americans, too, write about foreign countries. Hemingway's *Green Hills of Africa* is an example.

ANNAIRD NAXELA: What, for you, are the thematic concerns of Liberian writers now? And do these concerns differ from those in Liberia's past?

WILTON SANKAWULO: Before the civil war Liberian writers were concerned about the great questions of life: "Where did I come from?" "Why am I here?" "Who am I?" "Where am I going?" We've had metaphysical poets like Edwin Barclay and Roland Dempster, and great thinkers such as Edward Blyden who tried to answer these questions; many of them were influenced by European thinkers of the 19th century.

Bai T. Moore led the literary movement that made the Liberian experience a focus for Liberian literature. Before Bai T. Moore, our writers were preoccupied with modern life as seen in the west, but Bai T. Moore made village life a respectable subject for literature. This tradition was pursued by many African writers including Chinua Achebe, Wole Soyinka, and many other Nigerian writers; Ngugi wa' Thi'ongo of Kenya, and so on. The missionaries made us ashamed of ourselves, but African culture emerged as something to be proud of after independence. Today's Liberian writers are still concerned about the eternal questions of life, but they are now focusing on the great catastrophes the nation has sustained, namely the military coup and the civil war.

ANNAIRD NAXELA: The title of your latest novel, Sundown at Dawn, seems to be a metaphor for the Republic of Liberia. It seems, as with the protagonist, Liberia too held great promise?

WILTON SANKAWULO: Yes, Liberia is a rich country, but it has broken down because of selfishness. I chose the title *Sundown at Dawn* to symbolize the availability of the requisite means for the development of Liberia—this is the dawn—but this means has been neglected or misused—this is the sundown. Unless we put the national interest first, our country is in danger of annihilation. If the national interest isn't served, nobody's interest can be well served. People who consider their personal interests more important than that of the nation will continue to exploit it to the disadvantage of the people.

ANNAIRD NAXELA: It seems to me that Liberian literature presents opportunities for understanding what has happened in Liberia since her inception. If so, what questions do you suggest readers should pose in their reading of Liberian literature?

WILTON SANKAWULO: Since the founding of the nation, no systematic effort has been made to develop its literature.[1] Because the press was suppressed to protect the interests of those that governed, writers did not focus on the problems of the country. It is only recently that Liberian writers are beginning to tell the true story of Liberia, to call a spade a spade. Of course the damage has already been done, but this new breed of writers is raising questions we should all be concerned with: What really brought about the collapse and disintegration of our society? How can we resolve the underlying causes of our country's tragedy? The tendency to shift blame for the Liberian tragedy is great. But if our own children take up arms and kill us, shifting blame will not help.

The Liberian tragedy is symptomatic of the failure of our society to

---

[1] Cursory in critical scope, S. Henry Cordor's and K. Moses Nagbe's bibliographical compilation and textual summaries are exceptions for an otherwise fair assessment. *Towards the Study of Liberian Literature: An Anthology of Critical Essays on the Literature of Liberia*, edited by Cordor, is impressive for compiling critical views of a number of other Liberian writers, across genres and administrative districts in Liberia.

respond to the legitimate needs and aspirations of the people. The only realistic approach to the problem is beginning a new social order that can address this problem; it is a challenge for all Liberians. We need to forge reconciliation among ourselves and tackle the development of our country with determination. Each Liberian should do his or her part to the best of their ability. This is the question readers of Liberian literature want answered at this juncture in our history.

ANNAIRD NAXELA: Given your experience as a veteran Liberian writer, what are some of the themes that concern you most at this point in your writing career?

WILTON SANKAWULO: When I first began writing, my chief concern was to compile the rich folktales of the Liberian people in order to encourage our people to explore and appreciate their cultural heritage, which contains ideas of justice, social relations, government, economy, and the like. These ideas may not be developed, but they provide a basic foundation on which we could build a modern state.

Our departure from our roots is a major contributing factor to the collapse of our society. We need to do what Westerners have done; they dug into their past and developed those concepts and policies that characterized their societies through the ages and developed them, resulting in the evolution of the progressive social orders they have built for themselves. Our blind adoption of alien cultures and ideologies accounts for the social upheavals in Africa today. This is one message I want my writing to convey.

We need to muster the courage to examine our society critically. No society is perfect; humanity is always challenged to find better ways of doing things. It is my observation that Liberians are intolerant of criticism even if it is well meant. Of course our critics have their limitations, but good criticism should always be welcome; otherwise, we will continue repeating the same mistakes over and over.

Posterity will never forgive us if we continue failing to build a solid foundation for the progress of the nation. Improving the quality of our life begins with self-examination. In most cases the answers to our problems are known to us but we refuse to acknowledge them because they require change that may conflict with our personal interests. We should realize—and I repeat—that nobody's interest can be well served if the interest of the nation as a whole is ignored. For example, although we are all members of the same race, we segregate one another in Liberia. Again, we think other nations should be responsible for the development of Liberia. When you become president of Liberia, the people want to know if you have outside connections to bring in money to develop the country. What we fail to know is that nobody will ever give us anything for nothing; unless we take the driver's seat in the development of our country, noting will happen. There must be accountability in government; each Liberian should determine to be somebody in life and work towards a practical goal. We are not very loyal to our country; we'd rather take all its resources to other countries and live there to enjoy them. Discovering ourselves as well as analyzing and assessing our experience are the major thematic concerns I have as a writer.

ANNAIRD NAXELA: What advice would you give to aspiring Liberian writers?

WILTON SANKAWULO: I have been disappointed in the writer's clubs we often organize in Liberia. They usually do everything else but produce books. As a group I think Liberian writers should pool their resources together to perfect the quality of their works and publish. Whenever I make this suggestion, critics blame me for not establishing a publishing industry after being in the writing profession so long. But writing is more than enough challenge for any one person. As James Baldwin said, "if you want to do it you cannot do many other things."

The only practical approach to the problem of publishing in Liberia is team work. Our writers must work together to achieve this goal. If you write a book about New York, it is mostly the people of New York that read that book. Our works as Liberian writers will not find a home unless we build our own publishing industry. If we the writers must individually do our own writing, publishing, and marketing, the quality and quantity of Liberian literature will never improve substantially. Thus, my advice to Liberian writers is, come together as a group and help each other to improve your writing styles. You are in competition with all writers— there is no substitute for the best technique.

To aspiring Liberian writers, I say *write*. Once you get an adequate knowledge of grammar and syntax, *write*. Don't wait to write the perfect sentence to start with. You can always go back to what you have written and correct language problems; experienced writers, editors and English teachers can help you with revisions, but you must first put something on paper. There is no conceivable obstacle to writing; age has nothing to do with it. The best writers are not necessarily those with PhDs. From my experience, the more education you get the more difficulty you tend to experience in being a productive writer.

My next piece of advice is, be true to yourself. If you write what people expect of you, you will sooner or later find yourself in confusion. Writing is not simply putting words on paper, but trying to tell the truth as you understand it. Our country has broken down because people were more interested in what they could get out of it than what they could put into it. To reverse this trend, Liberian writers should muster the courage to tell the truth. They should not fall in the trap of the myopic who only shifts blame. The truth is not pleasant but it alone is the source of human redemption.

This interview first appeared in *Sea Breeze Journal of Contemporary Liberian Writings*, Volume 3, Issue 2, May 2006. Reprinted with permission.

For general inquiries or information regarding special sales or bulk orders of *Birds Are Singing* for educational institutions, charities and organizations, please write to info@ctpbooks.com, or visit our website at www.ctpbooks.com. All titles by Cotton Tree Press can also be found at African Books Collective.

www.ingramcontent.com/pod-product-compliance
Lightning Source LLC
Chambersburg PA
CBHW021412110726
47901CB00008B/2155